CHAMPIONS OF
THE DRAGON

CHAMPIONS OF THE DRAGON

EPIC FALLACY

Book 1

Michael James Ploof

ISBN: 1544268491
ISBN 13: 9781544268491

This trilogy is dedicated to my grandfather, Murland, who often needed to remind me to put my boots on the right feet before setting out on an adventure.

First and foremost, I would like to thank Paul Fiacco, for his excellent advice during the infancy of this series, and for helping me to discover exactly what kind of story I was trying to write (and more importantly, what kind of story Epic Fallacy wanted to be). You can thank him for Gibrig Hogstead's Humanism, Sir Slursalot's reverse nickname, Rootbeard from book 2, and many other nuances that helped to make this story what it is.

Edited by Holly M. Kothe. https://espressoeditor.com/

I would like to thank all my awesome beta readers: Melanie Ploof, Devin Ploof, Destiny Ploof, Haley Mnatzaganian, Marshall Mutch, Karen Marstein, Margo Stewart, Floryie, Ashley (Smashley) Conway, Dee, and my narrator, David (Saethon) Williams. If I have forgotten anyone, I apologize, and offer a sincere thank you.

Other Books
By
Michael James Ploof

<u>Whill of Agora</u>
Whill of Agora
A Quest of Kings
A Song of Swords
A Crown of War
Kingdoms in Chaos
Champions of the Gods
The Mantle of Darkness

<u>The Windwalker Archive</u>
Talon
Sea Queen
Exodus

<u>Blackthorn</u>
Blackthorn Rising

<u>The Orion Rezner Chronicles</u>
Afterworld

<u>Epic Fallacy</u>
Champions of the Dragon
Beyond the Wide Wall
The Legend of Drak'Noir

MAP OF FALLACETINE

CHAPTER 1

THE CHAMPION OF MAGESTRA

Murland Kadabra had always dreamed of becoming a great wizard, but it seemed all he was good for was shoveling dung. There was surely enough of it around for him to prove his prowess with the shovel. Springtime had come to Magestra, and the manure piles around the pens had thawed out, to create a right awful stink.

For Abra Tower, spring was always a busy and bustling time of year. The vegetables and herbs needed for various spells had to be planted and tended to, which meant harrowing the gardens, clearing irrigation trenches, and mixing into the soil Elder Wizard Bumblemoore's rotting manure concoction. On top of all that, the spring babes had to be nursed. For our friend Murland, all this meant endless work. He would be lucky to get in any study at the pace the elder wizards kept him running about.

You see, Murland was an apprentice at Abra Tower—one of the best schools of wizardly learning in all the kingdoms. His father, one Lord Albert Kadabra, had gotten his son into the school with the help of a large donation. Murland had shown *some* proficiency when he took the simple test to determine magical aptitude that all children received, but it alone had not been enough for him to be chosen.

At nineteen, he was quite old for his station. He had failed to grow any wizard leaf to maturity in all his years at the school, but he had a new plant started, and he was determined not to let it die like the others. For without the leaf, he would never be able to open his mind fully to the mysteries of magic.

"I'll show them all this year, eh Ole Bessy?"

Being that she was a cow, Ole Bessy of course did not reply. Murland tossed the rest of the hay in front of her and sighed. She ignored his lamentations and proceeded to chew her cud lazily.

"Must be nice to just be a cow," he said. "You get to sit around all day, have your food brought to you. Nobody on you about hanging their wash, cooking 'em breakfast, taking out their rotting bedpan—but of course… there is always someone tugging at your teats…"

"Murland! Murland!"

The grating voice of High Wizard Waverly shook Murland into action. He took up two buckets and began trudging along toward the hen house, trying to look busy.

"There you are," Waverly called from behind him.

Murland kept walking, hoping that the old man would forget about him—it often worked.

"Well then, you deaf? Stop!"

Reluctantly, Murland did as he was told.

The old wizard shuffled over to him, bunching his robes in front so as not to trail them in the mud and dung. Murland had given up on that a long time ago, and the weight of his soiled robe kept it clinging to his thin frame.

The elder regarded him over thin spectacles, his bushy white eyebrows poking out from behind them like two extremely old caterpillars.

"I've been looking all over for you," said Waverly in a huff.

"I apologize, High Wizard. I've yet to gather the eggs and milk the cow."

"What? Never mind all that, you can get to it later. Everyone has been called to the square. *He* has arrived."

"*He?*"

"The *Most* High Wizard."

"The Great Kazimir?" said Murland, almost in a whisper.

"Do not speak his name, fool boy! You are far from worthy."

"Forgive me, High Wizard, but…well…the Most High Wizard has chosen the warriors already, only a week into spring?"

Waverly scowled down on him and turned with a flourish of robes. "Come!"

Murland left his chores behind and followed the old wizard back to the tower. The day was suddenly turning out to be an exciting one. Kazimir was coming to town—the Most High Wizard himself! He hadn't been seen in these parts in twenty-seven years, not since the last time he'd chosen a champion.

You see, once every generation, Kazimir chose a champion from each of the five kingdoms of Fallacetine. The brave souls then marched west to King's Crossing, beyond the Wide Wall, through the Forest of the Dead, past the Swamp of Doom, over the Horrible Hills, across the Long Sand, all the way to the shadowy peak of Bad Mountain. There they were destined to do battle with the dreaded black dragon, Drak'Noir.

Murland could only imagine who Kazimir would choose this generation. Perhaps the young knight Maclmoore, or the valiant Sir Johnstonburg. Maybe even Lance Lancer, the best of the wizard apprentices.

He followed High Wizard Waverly around the back of the tower and found the wagon already prepared to leave. The entire school was there, consisting of some twenty-seven apprentices ranging from twelve to twenty years old, along with the other six high wizards. Murland found his young friend Gram gathered with the others and joined him behind the elders.

"Holy witch tits, Murland. You hear what's going on?" said Gram.

Murland laughed at his younger friend, hardly able to contain his own excitement. "Waverly said Kazimir is to choose a champion. What else do you know?"

"He knows it isn't going to be you, dung slinger." The boy, Lance Lancer, slapped one of his stoolies on the back and laughed. Nearly everyone followed suit—guys like Lance always got the laughs, whether they were funny or not.

Murland laughed with them, wanting Lance to like him. "Nah, Lance, course not. You have a good chance though."

Lance scowled at him, judging his sincerity. Thankfully his scrutiny was interrupted by the other boys, who expressed their agreement with Murland's claim with much jubilation.

When the attention shifted from Murland, Gram shook his head at him. "Why you always kissing his ass?"

"I'm not kissing anything. It's true—Lance is Abra's best wizard apprentice. He is sure to be Kazimir's choice."

"You're still kissing his ass," said Gram, shaking his head and returning his attention to the podium.

"Quiet down, boys!" one of the elders yelled from the top of the wagon. He leaned back and eyed them all. "Go on then. Neat rows of three, no pushing, that's it."

The boys did as they were told, grouping into rows of three that strung all the way around to the back of the tower. Everyone fell in line before Murland and Gram, who found themselves taking up the rear with the youngest of the school's apprentices.

The trip to the square from the tower took a good fifteen minutes due to the congested streets. Word had gotten around quickly, and everyone with one good leg was making their way to see the legendary wizard of mystery. As the boys and elders got closer, a commotion unlike anything Murland had ever heard came from the center of the city.

The crowd gushed in from each of the seven streets and surrounded the central podium. Thousands of people filed into the square, and soon, the intersections were clogged with those trying to get a closer look. Onlookers took to wagons and rooftops, crowding every window and peeking above every wall.

The wizards of Abra Tower, who enjoyed a bit of celebrity in the city, were allowed to get closer than most, and Murland stood with the other apprentices atop the wagons close to the podium.

"Hey Kadabra, when Kazimir picks me, I might just insist he let me bring you along." Lance grinned at the other boys with a smirk before adding, "I could always use someone who's good at handling shit."

Murland shook his head happily while everyone laughed.

Everyone but Gram.

"That must be 'cause you're so full of it," said Gram.

A collective "ooh" traveled through the group. Lance silenced the boys with a dangerous glare. The worst of it he saved for Gram and Murland. He stalked toward them slowly, hand moving into his robes as if to take up a wand.

Gram did not relent, and squared on the taller boy, reaching for his own wand.

Murland grabbed his arm. "Gram, not here."

"You should listen to your sweetheart," Lance told Gram.

"Quiet down, boys!" one of the high wizards hissed.

"Go on then," said Lance, eyes daring Gram to make a move.

Gram ignored him and turned to Murland. "Never mind them, every one of 'em would shit themselves if they even *saw* Drak'Noir."

Murland laughed weakly, glancing back at a scoffing Lance. "Yeah, I bet they would."

"Shut up!" said one of the boys. He pointed at the distant podium.

The quiet that followed was so complete that Murland might have heard a mouse fart.

All eyes turned to the high podium. The portly king of Magestra had taken the many flights of stairs to the top and now stood, seemingly out of breath, with a heavily adorned scepter in his hand.

He stood before the congregation with his arms wide. After a minute of silence thick with anticipation, he began to speak into the scepter.

Nothing happened.

Murland and the others strained to hear, but the king's voice would not carry far enough. Many in the square began to grumble in kind. The king turned around and seemed to be arguing with someone out of sight on the high podium. Suddenly his voice boomed, "...idiots can't even hear me!"

The king shot upright and turned slowly to face the now gawking crowd. He cleared his throat with an authoritative cough and went on. "The Most High Wizard, Kazimir himself, has called us all to the square this fine morning...for the whispers are true. The sign has been seen at King's Crossing, and word has come from the Wide Wall of a dark, hungry, evil stirring on Bad Mountain."

A panicked exclamation flowed through the crowd, and many voices rose up in protest. King Nimrod unsheathed his sword and slammed it into the wooden rail before him, chopping it in half and breaking it off from the post. Silence fell over the crowd as the board fell, and far below, someone cried out in pain.

The king continued. "Every generation, Drak'Noir attempts to settle Bad Mountain, and every generation, Kazimir and the Champions of the Dragon fight her off. This year will be no different! For prophecy tells of the ones who will come together from all kingdoms, and turn back the evil wyrm! Today, Magestra's champion shall be chosen!"

The crowd began to cheer, but just then, an explosion of light atop the podium silenced them all. A great puff of smoke rose into the sky, and there beside the king stood Kazimir. Surprise turned to shock, shock became wonderment, and the crowd cheered with joy.

Murland and Gram shared looks of enchantment and cheered along with the rest.

Kazimir wore immaculate white robes with many hanging folds. His long, pointed hood covered his face, and a white braided beard hung to his knees and...the beard was on fire! Murland could see the small glow already growing up the front of his robes. One drunk fool in the crowd laughed, and a flustered Kazimir barked a spell word.

The fire puffed out.

The wizard straightened and raised his glowing staff. Finally, in a voice deep, sure and full of power, he spoke.

"Worms and blood and ooze and sweat.

A streaking comet mine eyes have met.

The winds of time and whispered names.

Five kingdoms, heroes, and dragon games.

I come for one of power and might.

Your champion, I shall name this night."

He paused as the crowd's anticipation grew. Murland glanced over at Lance, who wore a big, hopeful smile. He hoped that Lance would be named by Kazimir as well. A wizard of Abra Tower had not been chosen by the Most High Wizard in over a hundred years.

"Your champion is a wizard of Abra..."

Everyone in the square turned to regard the gathered boys and their masters. Lance took a confident step forward.

Kazimir pointed at the group of young apprentices. "Come forth to glory...Murland Kadabra!"

The apprentices and elders all turned, slack-jawed, and stared at Murland. He looked from one to another, not quite comprehending what was happening.

Gram looked utterly delighted. He was patting Murland on the back and saying something. Everyone else was talking as well, but Murland could hear nothing. Suddenly he found himself walking through a parting crowd, being pushed along by a beaming yet flustered elder wizard. The crowd was cheering jubilantly and smiling at him.

Murland finally reached the enormous podium and was led up the stairs inside by High Wizard Waverly and a knight in shimmering armor. His ears were ringing now, and he became dizzy. Strong hands took him by the shoulders when he reached the top of the stairs, and Waverly smiled down at him. The sun blinded him temporarily; he held his hand to the sky and blocked the light enough to see Kazimir and the king standing there. Murland froze, unable to speak, unable to breathe.

A bright flash exploded as Kazimir suddenly snapped his fingers, and the sound of the world came rushing back to Murland. He was led to stand beside Kazimir, who squinted at him from behind large, round spectacles.

"Whatever you say, say it loud," said the ancient wizard. "Now stop looking stupid and face the crowd."

Murland blinked, stupefied. "How...how can this be?" he managed to ask.

Kazimir took him roughly by the arm and turned to wave at the crowd, raising Murland's hand victoriously.

The people cheered his name over and over.

"So it has been said, so shall it be!" said Kazimir. "Murland Kadabra will fight for thee!"

Murland waved, and a wide smile crept across his face. Had he really been chosen? What untold magic must he possess?

"Say something," Kazimir urged out of the corner of his mouth as he handed Murland the scepter.

Murland was petrified, and though he tried desperately to speak, all that came forth was a confounded, "Uhh…" His voice echoed for miles as a piercing, high-pitched noise issued from the scepter.

Kazimir pulled it back from his face a bit, and the noise disappeared.

"I, uh…don't know why he picked me…I'm not really that good at performing mag—"

The ancient wizard quickly yanked the scepter away. "Three cheers for Murland Kadabra the Humble!"

The crowd cheered again, but with slightly less fervor than before. Murland could already see many of them heading for the beer tents.

Kazimir grabbed his arm roughly and tossed something to the floor. A great flash of light was followed by choking white smoke as the wizard pulled Murland back down through the trapdoor.

As they hurried down the stairs, a delighted Murland asked, "Did we just disappear?"

"Sure, kid," said Kazimir with obvious annoyance. "Just try to keep up."

When they reached the base of the enormous podium, the great wizard opened another hidden trapdoor, revealing a narrow stairwell that led down to the dark catacombs below.

With a whispered incantation from Kazimir, the wizard's staff began to shine enough for them to see.

"Whoa," Murland gasped.

"Stick with me, kid, and you can ride my coattails right to the top," said Kazimir.

To Murland's surprise, the tunnel led them to the wine cellar of Abra Tower. He followed the old wizard up into the kitchen and out to the main hall.

"Go on then," said Kazimir, "get your things. I must speak with your superiors."

"Yes, sir! Er, Most High Wizard." Murland tripped over his robes, but he found his feet and hurried up the spiraling stairs to the top of the tower.

Kazimir shook his head as he watched Murland stumble up the stairs. He turned to the headmaster's office and easily disengaged the locking enchantment and pushed the door open with a word.

Headmaster Zorromon the Off-White didn't look surprised in the least, for he was in the middle of pouring wine.

"Yes, thank you, I will take some wine," said Kazimir, closing the door behind him with a wave of his hand.

Zorromon had been about to ask just that, and he glared at the ancient wizard. "Your tricks do not fool me, Kazimir." Regardless, he poured him a glass and set it on the other side of the desk.

The Most High Wizard sat down across from him, downed the glass in one large gulp, and tossed the headmaster a heavy coin purse. "That should be sufficient to replace the fool."

Zorromon nodded and sipped his wine, eyeing the sack nervously.

"So, what's this kid's story?" Kazimir asked. "Is he slow in the head or something?"

"No, goodness no. He's bright enough, and a hard worker. He just can't seem to grow any wizard leaf."

Kazimir raised a brow and snorted arrogantly, sounding rather like a pig in the throes of passion. It was a laugh that he thought he had remedied when he was a teen, back when he was a student of the wizarding school. That hideous snort had gained him much teasing back then, and

Zorromon did not miss the chance to smirk, as though he had won some small battle. "It isn't that hard," said Kazimir with a huff. "I take it someone is sabotaging his plants?"

"Yes, and the poor fool just plants another and tries again." Zorromon sighed. "I had hoped he would have figured it out years ago."

"Sounds like he's slow after all," said Kazimir, raising his glass.

Zorromon shrugged and gave him a refill. "He's a good lad. But we can't graduate him, and as you know, Abra Tower hasn't had a dropout in over a century. Our funding from the crown has been cut in half in the last decade as it is, what with all this peace time. If apprentices start failing… well, it is better this way. At least he will be remembered as a hero."

"I don't know why you all grovel at the feet of that ridiculous king," said Kazimir, glowering at his old peer as though he were a disgusting insect. "It is insulting to the world of wizardry. In our day, wizards were respected for the superiors that we are, not beholden to the whims of the royal treasury."

"You have always had your point of view, Kazimir, and I have always had mine."

"Yes," said Kazimir, downing his drink and setting it on the desk. "And one of us is right."

He got up and turned for the door, having nothing more to say to his old acquaintance.

"See to it that death comes to him swiftly," the headmaster called after him, as though the boy's fate had been weighing heavily on his mind.

Kazimir turned at the door, his long white beard hiding a sneer. "I shall feed him to the dragon *first* then, when she is hungriest."

Zorromon gulped.

Murland ran down the stairs two at a time, his pillowcase full and tied to a stick resting on his shoulder. He came to the bottom of the stairs and found Kazimir waiting for him. The door to the headmaster's office suddenly opened, and Zorromon emerged, holding a wooden box out before him.

His voice seemed to croak with grief. "Dear, dear apprentice Kadabra. It appears that the wide world has more in store for you than the manure pile. Please, take this, from all of us, as a token of our faith in you."

Murland could hardly contain himself. He knew what kind of box the headmaster held before him.

Zorromon lifted the lid, and Murland dreamily reached for the wand inside. His fingers touched the smooth wood…

SNAP!

The lid suddenly closed, and Murland pulled his hand back and gave a delighted squeal of surprise.

The headmaster laughed.

Kazimir rolled his eyes.

"Go on then, take it." Zorromon opened the box wide.

Murland carefully took the wand from its velvet bedding. It was oak, he could tell, and lined with silver runes carved into the sides. At its tip was bound a ruby, and in the middle…

"Headmaster, er, is that tape?"

"Yes, that. It is the broken wand of Allan Kazam, he who threw down the Dark Lord Zuul. It is said that one might rise up who can mend it," said Zorromon.

"It is? I've never heard that before," said Murland.

"The wand of Allan Kazam?" said Kazimir, suddenly beside Murland and glaring at Zorromon dangerously. "Where did you get that?"

Zorromon said nothing. It was his turn to sneer at Kazimir.

"Thank you," said Murland, quite enchanted.

Zorromon pointed a finger to the sky. "Ah! I almost forgot. I've a special invention for you. I just finished the incantation last night." He put two fingers to his lips and gave a shrill whistle.

Out of the office flew a leather backpack with wide white wings. It landed on the floor beside Murland, but having no feet, it simply fell over and tucked in its wings.

"The road is long, and a traveler needs a good bag to carry his burden," said Zorromon proudly.

Murland put the wand and his pillow case inside the pack and tightened the strap. It beat its wings swiftly and flew up to hover beside him.

"Come then," said Kazimir, offering Zorromon one last scowl. "Drak'Noir waits for no man."

Murland was pulled along by the old wizard and waved jubilantly back to his headmaster. "I will do Abra Tower proud!"

"You already have!" Zorromon waved back, silently sniffling.

CHAPTER 2

THE CHAMPION OF VHALOVIA

I N THE HUMAN kingdom of Vhalovia, far to the south of Magestra and east of the Golden Gulf, one Sir Eldrick awoke with a pounding head.

How much had he drank last night?

He tried to clear his muddled mind as he sat up. The back of his head was tender, and when he investigated with his fingers, he found crusted blood around the spot. He rubbed his bleary eyes to get his bearings.

Refuse surrounded him, and two tall brick walls loomed on either side—he was in an alley.

The sun was bright in the street beyond, and the noise of the crowd emanating from it was impossibly loud. He attributed his sensitive hearing to a bad hangover, but then the memory of the night before came back to him—he had gone to a pub, but had gotten in a fight with seven infantry-men before even wetting his whistle.

The rest was a blur, but by the bruises, scrapes, and cuts on his knuckles, he knew that he must have gotten in his share.

He got up, dusted off his brown trousers, and tucked in his ruffled and stained blue shirt. He went to the street and he watched, surprised to find people hurrying by. He hadn't seen the streets so crowded since the king's wedding ten years before. Listening closely to the murmuring voic-es, he discerned one name spoken repeatedly in excited tones, "Kazimir! Kazimir!"

He then understood. The Champion of the Dragon was being chosen today; Drak'Noir had returned to Bad Mountain.

Sir Eldrick followed the masses down Baker Street, past the docks, over the Silver Gate Bridge, and finally to the amphitheater. He had attended many plays and orchestras here over the years, yet he had never seen such a gathering. Judging by the overflowing crowd pushing their way in, Sir Eldrick guessed that everyone and their sister had come to hear the proclamation of Kazimir the Most High Wizard.

As he was shouldering through the crowd, he bumped into a woman and began to apologize, but when she turned around and saw his face, she beamed at him.

"Sir Eldrick…there you are!"

"I…uh, yes, here I am." Sir Eldrick studied her face, but for the life of him he couldn't remember her name. This must have been very apparent to the woman, for her smile slowly died, and she searched his eyes.

"You can't be serious…"

"Sorry, it was a long night. I know that I should know your name…"

"You've been in my bed twice, and you don't know my…" She glanced around, embarrassed.

Sir Eldrick shrugged. "Sorry lass. Not your fault. The old memory ain't what it used to be. Perhaps if you showed me your backside, it would jog my memory."

He had been trying to be funny, but the woman didn't find it amusing in the least, it seemed, for she slapped him across the face.

"What's my name?" she said, cocking back the hand again.

"Uh, Laura?"

Another slap.

"Try again, hero."

"Brittany?"

Her eyes went wide, and this time she kicked him in the crotch.

The crowd nearby gave a laugh as he doubled over with a groan.

"That's my sister's name, you pig!"

Sir Eldrick tried to speak, for he had finally remembered that the woman's name was Catherine, but she had already turned on her heel sharply and was storming off.

The crowd laughed and jeered, and someone helped Sir Eldrick to his feet.

"Still up to your old tricks, eh Queen Defiler?" said the man who had helped him up.

People looked at him with sudden recognition. He gave the man a shove and pushed through the crowd. Taunts and jeers of "the king should have hung you from the gallows" and "shame on you, traitor" followed him into the arena.

When he was finally free of the taunts and had once again become just another face in the crowd, he made his way down to one of the few remaining spots where someone might stand and watch the high podium.

Far below, standing in long rows in front of the raised stage, Sir Eldrick saw his former brethren, the Knights of Vhalovia. His old best friend, Sir Ardthar, was there, along with many others he had known for years. They had been his brothers one and all, but that had been a long time ago, when Sir Eldrick was still the hero of Vhalovia.

Higher up stood the queen and her three grown children. The eldest daughter, Princess Penelope, held her baby brother, bundled in a bright blue blanket. Sir Eldrick had heard of the newest addition to the royal family, Prince Edwin. Indeed, rumors of the child's parentage flowed like chimney smoke through every town and village in Vhalovia.

Queen Elzabethalynn Winterthorn stood tall and proud, as though she hadn't been a part of one of the juiciest royal sex scandals that Vhalovia had ever known. Her long black hair hung in thick curls about her shoulders, and her voluptuous frame was well hidden behind a puffy dress—which Sir Eldrick knew must have been the result of her head advisor's attempt to show her in a less sultry light.

Sir Eldrick stood far away from the queen with the commoners, but even from the distance, he could make out her deep-green eyes—eyes that had so often held him in a loving gaze, but no longer.

Staring at the woman he had loved so deeply and feeling that old ache in his heart, Sir Eldrick wondered why he had returned to the city. He had been pondering the question for days. But still he did not remember what mad idea might have driven him back to the city that had once loved him so. He had woken up in a pub in the city a week ago, with no memory of how he had gotten there. Likely he had been on another days-long bender, which was not an uncommon occurrence, but since leaving a year before, he had never had any inkling to return.

Sir Eldrick had decided that his drunk self had returned to the city to steal away with the queen, as they had often imagined during their hours of pillow talk. But the talk had just been talk, and to the queen, Sir Eldrick had just been a convenient distraction, and a way to get revenge on her unfaithful husband.

The king's personal guards soon took to the stage, and the buzz of the crowd only intensified. When King Henry Winterthorn at last appeared, the noise became unbearable. Sir Eldrick fished in his pockets until he found his flask, his eyes never leaving the king he had betrayed. He hadn't seen the man in over a year, but the wounds bled anew.

He tipped back the flask, but to his dismay, it was empty.

Finally, the king raised his hand, and the racket died down to a low hum.

"The rumors are true," said the king in that deep, authoritative voice that Sir Eldrick remembered so well.

The gathering fell deathly quiet. He scanned the crowd, letting the tension build.

"It has been twenty-seven years since the great wyrm was driven from Bad Mountain, and now...she has returned. The time has come once again for the Champions of the Dragon to march forth and vanquish our foe. Once again, a hero will be chosen from the five kingdoms of men, elves, dwarves, and ogres. Kazimir has come to name the Champion of Vhalovia!"

A flash of blinding light suddenly flared on the podium. Shocked exclamations gave way to joyous cheers. When the smoke cleared, the Most High Wizard himself stood tall beside the king.

Kazimir raised his glowing staff, and the crowd fell silent once more, their voices lost to awe.

"Dragon flame seen in the night.
Fleeting shadows taking flight.

The wyrm has claimed its mountain home.

As was written in the ancient tome…"

The man beside Sir Eldrick nudged him. "Who you think he's gonna name, eh?"

"Who gives a shit," said Sir Eldrick with a shrug. "The beer'll be flowing tonight, that's all I care to know."

"Right you are, ole boy, right you are," said the man with a toothless grin.

Sir Eldrick became annoyed listening to Kazimir ramble on with his ridiculous rhyming and monotonous timing. He wished the long-winded wizard would get to the point. A feast was sure to follow, and not only would the beer flow, but wine and spirits as well. And on top of that, the women would be all kinds of worked up…

"…I name this night, Sir Eldrick van Albright!"

The name echoed through the amphitheater.

Silence followed.

The crowd began to stir. "Slur Sirsalot?" someone said in a confused voice. Others laughed, and much more colorful nicknames were called out. Sir Eldrick found himself sinking lower and lower.

When no one stepped forth, Kazimir repeated his proclamation. "The Champion of Vhalovia shall march forth this night. Step forward to glory, Sir Eldrick van Albright!"

Sir Eldrick pulled down his hood and glanced around nervously.

The crowd all looked around for the named one, but no one nearby had recognized him yet. He glanced behind him. People crowded the entrances. He was a big man, but perhaps he could still quietly push through without raising suspicion. Questioning voices began to grow, and the crowd became restless. The chant for "Slur Sirsalot!" echoed through the amphitheater.

He took advantage of the distraction and began to gently push his way through the crowd and up the few flights of stairs to the gate. When he reached the top, he shouldered past a standing guard, making sure to turn his face away in time. With every step, his confidence grew, and soon he was at the top, heading for the crowded streets beyond.

He kept his head low and fished out a piece of paper from his pocket. Due to his drinking, he often blacked out for days on end, and more times than not, he had no memory of where he was or where he had come from. He had gotten in the habit of writing down such information whenever he stayed at a new place.

The paper read: Garrett's Lodge, Smuggler Street. #27.

Smuggler Street was only a few blocks away, and Sir Eldrick headed in that direction with his head down. He seemed to be one of the only people walking in the direction opposite the arena, but no one paid him any mind. There were no guards about, as they were all working the arena. Soon he made it to Garrett's lodge and disappeared inside.

No one was at the front desk, which was just as well as far as he was concerned. In the pocket with the paper was a key, and when he tried it in door number twenty-seven, it worked.

Inside, he gathered his clothes and stuffed them in the sack that held his armor, then slipped his sword sheath onto his thick leather belt. A glance out the window told him that the arena was beginning to empty, for people were walking east from the center of the city. Sir Eldrick rummaged through his pack, looking for the small oak box holding his assorted jewelry. Most of it was enchanted, gained through a lifetime of heroism and questing. He found the sapphire-studded ring he was looking for, one that was said to hide a person from the seeking spells of witches and wizards, and slipped it on his finger.

"I never should have come back here," Sir Eldrick told the mirror.

He knew the King was furious with him, but Sir Eldrick had never imagined Henry would set him up like this, especially after all he had done for the kingdom.

With one last scan of the room, he headed for the door, but when someone knocked, he stopped dead and held his breath.

Shit!

He waited, thinking that any second Kazimir would blow down the door with magic, but then again, the wizard would not have knocked…

"I know you're in there, Eldrick," came a hushed voice.

It was the queen!

Sir Eldrick dropped his things and rushed to the door. He flung it open and came face to face with his former lover. She was shrouded in a lace veil and hooded brown cloak, but her piercing green eyes remained luminescent beyond the shroud.

"You came alone?" he said, glancing up and down the hall.

She pushed past him wordlessly and he closed the door behind himself. He watched, mesmerized, as she strode across the room with the grace that she was famous for.

"You never should have come back," she said, turning at the center of the room and raising the veil.

Sir Eldrick's heart fluttered when he saw her face. He stepped forward purposefully and meant to take her in his arms, but she held up a hand and took a step back. His own reaching arms slowly fell to his sides.

"What did you hope to accomplish coming back here?" She was all business, and was doing a good job at hiding her feelings for him—if indeed she still had any.

"I came back for you," he said, bravely moving forward and taking her face in his hands. He kissed her deeply, and she did not pull back. For a moment, she melted into him, and his passion grew, but then suddenly she pulled back and slapped him across the face.

He laughed, touching his cheek. "That is twice today I have been slapped by a woman. Seems I'm on a roll."

"Never do that again," she said, composing herself and moving away from him.

"Elza..."

"I am the queen of Vhalovia, you were a knight. What did you think was going to happen? How did you think our little fling was going to end?"

"Fling?" he said, surprised by her cold words.

She raised her chin, staring at him with unwavering emerald eyes.

"You know that it was more than that," he said.

"Listen to me. Henry knows that you are back. Why couldn't you just leave it alone? He could have had you hanged, instead he let you leave unscathed. But now, now he is furious."

"And he's told Kazimir to send me on this fool's quest," he said, spitting the words. "You know as well as I the truth of the Prophecy of the Champions of the Dragon, you know the truth of Drak'Noir. How could you let him do this?"

"You must have known that returning would mean certain death," she said, not unkindly.

"I know only that I love you," he said, hoping to break through her façade. "Being without you *is* certain death."

"Don't say that."

"But it is true. I loved you from the first day I met you."

"Stop."

"Come with me, Elza."

Tears began to pool in her eyes, but she quickly wiped them away and put a staying hand on his shoulder. She leaned in and, avoiding his lips, kissed him on the cheek.

"You must leave and never return," she said into his ear, her breath light on his neck. "Go west, make your way to the Golden Gulf. I've a ship prepared for you in Port Peterson. Look for the Valiant."

"And where will I go. What shall I do?"

"Forget about me, and start a new life somewhere else."

"And the child, should I forget about him as well?"

She backed away from him. Her eyes were diamond-hard. "You need not worry about him. He is not yours. Do you understand?"

"Are you sure about that?"

She held him in a steely gaze and seemed to have more to say, but instead she walked past him.

He grabbed her arm and she stopped, patiently waiting and not looking at him. Slowly, reluctantly, he let her go.

She walked to the door and stopped at the threshold. He held his breath, hoping that she would turn and rush back to him. Instead, she remained rigid.

"Goodbye, Eldrick," she said and opened the door.

"Elza…"

She paused, but then walked out the door and out of his life forever.

CHAPTER 3

---✕---

THE CHAMPION OF
FIRE SWAMP

WEST OF VHALOVIA, in the foggy, bog-filled marshes of Fire Swamp, a very hungry and very large ogre awoke with a smile on her food-crusted face.

Willow Muckmuck stretched out and gave a great yawn. She rubbed her large green belly and glanced around, licking one of her tusks absentmindedly. To her surprise, she found herself in one of the baker's storerooms in the center of the village. All around her were half-eaten loaves of bread, wheels of cheese, moss cakes, fern cookies, and a plethora of other delectables.

With slight embarrassment, she realized that she was also naked. Frosting and chocolate and sugar had been spread all over her body, and upon seeing it, she thought of the baker's son. She smiled to herself at the memories of the night before and found her clothes, not wanting to be caught in such a state. With effort, she dressed in her alligator skirt and vest, tucking in her round green belly and large bosom as best she could, reminding herself to have her mother take the outfit out a few sizes yet again.

Once she was properly dressed, she made her way out of the shed, hoping that she hadn't missed breakfast. Her father had caught a twenty-foot python the day before. It was the biggest Willow had ever seen in this part of the Fire Swamps, and she couldn't wait to try it.

She exited the storage shed, head down and eyes peeking around the door as she went, but there was no one about in the village. Figuring this meant that it was still quite early in the morning, Willow hurried through the village unseen, and went straight to the banks of the swamp to clean up.

From there she rushed home as fast as her seven-hundred-pound frame and bulging belly would allow. Her family's abode, like all ogre homes in Fire Swamp, was made of clay and twigs and swamp grass, built in a circle around a tall willow tree. She reached it, quite out of breath, and rushed inside. In the kitchen, a clean pot sat on the small table beside the fireplace, and no wooden dishes sat in the wash bucket.

"Mah, Pah, you two nannywiggins still sleeping?" she said, moving to her parents' room and knocking on the door.

"Mah? Pah?" She opened the circular door, but found the bed made and no one inside.

"Where'd they run off to?" she wondered aloud and returned to the kitchen.

Her growling stomach reminded her again of the snake, and she went outside to see if it was still hanging. She found it to the right of the door, skin stretched and drying on a board and meat hanging from a tree.

Glancing around the village, she noted that still no one stirred. She looked to the sky to determine where the sun was sitting, but the silver glowing mist hanging over the village hid the exact location.

"Great Turtle's shell, what is going on here?" she wondered.

The day itself was much like any other—thick gray fog hung motionless in the air, the constant frog song sounded in the surrounding swamp, lizard monkeys swung overhead on vines hanging from spider trees—yet there was not another ogre to be found.

The smoke from their chimneys was still curling up into the fog, and guard crocodiles sat chained to spikes outside the pod doors, lazily sleeping away the morning. She regarded her family's croc, asking him what he knew, but of course, he didn't answer.

Her stomach growled again, and she returned to the pod to get something to eat; if she was going to investigate the strange disappearance of the tribe, she wasn't about to do it on an empty stomach. She found nothing to eat inside but yesterday's leftover frog legs and a loaf of pussy willow bread. She ate it all quickly and then ventured back outside. After a final look for anyone else still in the village, she headed over to her grandmother's dwelling. Turtle stew hung simmering in a cauldron over the still-burning fire, and she helped herself to three bowls of it before heading on to the next dwelling. She had to investigate, after all, and to come calling around the village was the best way she could think to do it.

But no one answered their doors.

Willow searched the raptor stables at the center of the village and found that the mounts remained. Growing more curious by the moment, she made her way to the banks of the swamp and searched the boats and barges. Still, she found no one.

Willow worked herself up with worry, imagining what mysterious events might have befallen the village. Perhaps the ghosts of the giant Agnarians had swept across the land from the west while she slept. Everyone knew that those long-dead spirits held a special animosity toward the ogres, who had refused to come to their aid when Drak'Noir had descended upon what is now called the Blight. Or perhaps the villagers had been lured to the murky depths by the bog monster and his scaly sirens.

Willow shook the thoughts from her mind and decided to search the dwellings more thoroughly. It appeared that many of the families had been preparing breakfast before suddenly disappearing. In nearly every cooking hut she found food simmering over fires—and, of course, not wanting the overcooked food to go to waste, she helped herself to much of it.

An hour later, she sat on a stump beside her family's dwelling, rubbing her big green belly and wondering what had happened to everyone. Now that she was full and no longer had the distraction of hunger, she became genuinely concerned about what might have occurred. She cupped her hands around her mouth and hollered, "Dingleberry!" as loud as she could. The little bugger was bound to be around somewhere. She had to call three more times, but eventually the telltale jingle of her approach could be heard.

The tiny little six-inch fairy hovered suddenly before Willow, her wings a blue blur of motion.

"Willow, what-what are you doing here? Have you not heard-heard?" Her high-pitched voice was even more keening than usual.

"Heard what?" said Willow, nearly going cross-eyed as she tried to focus on the sprite hovering right in front of her face.

Dingleberry slapped herself in the head and did a backflip. "Kazimir has come-come! He is going to name-name the Champion of Fire Swamp," she yelled over her shoulder, zipping away as fast as a humming bird. "Come on, follow me!"

"Wait for me!" yelled Willow. She ran quickly to the stables and saddled Tor, her father's raptor, as fast as she could.

Willow was suddenly overcome with excitement, for she knew that a grand feast was sure to follow the naming of the champion. The stories of the previous naming were legend in Fire Swamp. Willow hadn't yet been born at the time, but her parents told her that the celebration had lasted for seven days.

Dingleberry led her through the village to the north, past the Foul Falls and the Mushroom Forest, all the way to the mouth of Skull Cavern. Thousands of ogres from all surrounding villages were gathered in and around the ancient bones, and there, at the center of the hollow skull, stood the many chieftains…and the mighty human wizard, Kazimir.

Willow shouldered past the standing ogres at the back of the gathering and stood atop a rock to get a better view. Dingleberry landed on her shoulder and they shared a grin.

Upon seeing her, however, the surrounding ogres began to burp and slap their bellies in appreciation. Willow glanced around, confused, and quickly realized that everyone was looking at her.

"And here she is now," proclaimed her chieftain. "Willow Muckmuck, the Champion of Fire Swamp!"

The crowd cheered and gave great bellowing burps. The sound of slapped bellies became deafening. She saw her parents standing upon the rock with the chieftains and Kazimir the Most High Wizard.

"Wow-wow, Willow!" said Dingleberry, wide-eyed.

Willow slowly realized what was happening. She had been named Champion of Fire Swamp. For a fleeting moment, she was excited, but then she remembered that the celebrations took place *after* the champion set out. She was going to miss the feast! Willow's head swooned, and she passed out at the feet of the adoring ogres.

CHAPTER 4

THE CHAMPION OF HALALA

Brannon the wood elf hummed to himself as he clipped the dead leaves from his rose bush. He cupped a drooping blossom and whispered a gentle word. The flower glowed brightly and straightened, spreading its velvety petals.

"That's better, now isn't it?" He gave the plant some extra water and a pulse of floral magic before finishing off the others. Content, he walked to the balcony overlooking the garden pond and stared out over the water at the city beyond. It was turning out to be a lovely day.

"Brannon, Brannon!" came the shrieking voice of his sister Annallia, jolting him from his reverie.

"Must you screech so?" he asked, rubbing his right temple.

She rushed into the room and ran to his side. "Have you heard the news?"

He snapped his fingers haughtily, and a servant rushed over and began fanning him with a large peacock feather. "Do tell," he said to her impatiently.

She laughed and twirled, clapping her hands like a young lass, though she was over forty years old. "You don't *know*? Oh, but this is juicy."

He feigned indifference and waited, yawning.

"Guess who has just arrived in Halala?" she blurted.

"The king of the dipshits, coming to take you home?" he offered with a grin.

"Clever, but no. Guess again."

"I grow weary of this game, sister. Out with it."

"Kazimir!" she said finally, and then gave a pip of a laugh before quickly covering her mouth, as though she were a child who had just uttered a swear word.

"The Most High Wizard? He comes so soon? But spring has only just arrived."

"I *know*! Isn't it wonderful? Come, let's get ready. Everyone has been summoned to the temple."

Brannon was suddenly filled with dread. "By the Lord of the Wood... what will I wear?" He grabbed the peacock tail from the servant before slumping down on the cushioned bench beside the balcony and began fanning himself worriedly.

"Oh, brother, who cares about you? What am *I* going to do about this hair?" said Annallia as she turned this way and that before one of Brannon's many mirrors.

Brannon snapped to his feet and slapped his hands together. "Forren! Gather together the entire staff. We must prepare for the ceremony!"

The head servant bowed once for him and again for his sister before running off to do his master's bidding.

Brannon paced, biting his long purple thumbnail. Kazimir had come to choose Halala's Dragon Champion. He instantly thought of Valkimir, worrying that his brave lover might be chosen. Val had been away for six months, fighting beyond the Wide Wall, and had only returned but a week ago. To think that Val might once again be torn from his side filled Brannon with dire trepidation.

His sister must have sensed his mood, for she came to him then and wrapped her arms around his neck. "Fret not, brother. If Val is chosen, he will come home victorious."

"Valkimir is the greatest warrior in all of Halala, of course he'll be chosen." Brannon shrugged away from his sister and stared out over the pond. Tears pooled in his eyes and threatened to ruin his maquillage.

Just then their father and king, Rimon, strode into the room. The ever-regal elven king was dressed in his best golden armor. A red cloak trailed ten feet behind him, each corner held by a scantily clad servant girl. "I assume you have been informed of our visitor," he said in a deep, commanding voice that was always laced with disappointment. "We leave within the hour. See that you look presentable...not so much of that coloring you fancy so."

Brannon waved his father off and snapped his fingers. "Oh, she'll be ready, don't you worry."

The king regarded him with a tired scowl. "I was talking to you. This experimentation...this *phase* of yours has come to an end, my flamboyant son. Everyone has been called to attendance, everything has been prepared. Lady Claristra Fallingleaf will be seated beside you."

"Father, this isn't the time to argue about that. I—"

"*I'm* not finished!" said the king.

The servants' eyes all darted to the floor, and Brannon felt his cheeks flush—his father rarely raised his voice, but when he did, it was like thunder.

"After the champion is chosen," the king continued, "you will ask the lady's hand in marriage."

"I will do no such *thing*!" Brannon found himself saying. Having forgotten his place, he cowered for a moment. But then thoughts of Valkimir brought him courage, and he quickly straightened again.

He knew that his father had sent Val to the front lines to punish Brannon—the king didn't agree with his and Val's way of life—and Brannon had been sick with worry for months. Finally, at long last, Val had returned to Halala victorious. The king had slapped a medal on the brave warrior's chest and then given him lands *far* from the city.

"You will do your duty as my sole heir!" the king said, his nostrils flaring and eyes glaring dangerously. "Or by the gods, the kingdom shall be left in the hands of your *sister*!"

"You *wouldn't*," Brannon gasped, clutching his chest.

The king nodded. "Mark my words," he told his son sternly. As he left the chamber, a small army of servants scuttled in to prepare them for the ceremony.

Brannon fell to his knees, distraught, and was taken up by the many servants who then ferried him to the closest sofa. They began fussing over his hair and coloring, and hastily removed the paint from his nails to begin anew.

Wardrobes were brought before the elf prince, but were nodded off one after another. Brannon couldn't focus with so much commotion, so much pressure.

"Calm down," his sister sang. She snapped her fingers at the servant her brother had just sent away. "He'll take that one."

"It's hideous," pouted Brannon.

"It's beautiful, my dear brother, as are you. Come now, get yourself together. No matter what happens at the temple—no matter if Kazimir chooses Val—your beloved will make his way back to you."

Brannon nodded his thanks to her and kissed her cheek. He allowed himself finally to be dressed in the brilliant white garments Annallia had selected. They did look good on him, the sleek knee-high boots with ten-inch heels and white straps winding up his thighs, the single white glove with diamond claws at the fingertips, the tight leather pants with a wide, pluming shock of blue feathers at the hips, and the white leather jerkin with its large upturned collar.

The servants carefully added matching ivory nipple rings and strapped twin daggers to his thick, low-hanging belt, which was ornamented with the finest of jewels.

He admired himself in the mirror, striking a variety of poses. The servants had added a long white wig of horsehair to match the outfit, and then braided it up into a thick bun. One of the long braids was left out, and it curled around his shoulder, resting on his bare chest. They had laid his crown upon his head, completing the look. Brannon turned this way and that, biting his long thumbnail—something was missing.

He snapped his fingers at one of the handmaidens. "That there, bring it to me."

She presented him with his diamond-studded cup, and he held it in front of his groin, checking himself in the mirror.

"Perfect," he said after a moment.

When they arrived at the tree temple by way of carriage, thousands of woodland elves had already gathered. The temple had been grown near-ly a thousand years ago and consisted of fifty sequoia trees grown into each other to form a giant dome. From the outside, nary a branch could be seen beneath the thick vine covering and its multitude of blooming flowers.

Brannon and his sister followed the king and queen as they led the procession into the gathering place.

The crowd fell to a hush as soon as the royal family stepped through the hanging leaf curtains and took their respective thrones at the northern balcony overlooking the wide temple. No sunlight shone through, but the hollow was brightly lit both by the thousands of overgrown lightning bugs that covered the walls and the large crystal chandelier hanging from hundreds of snaking sequoia branches.

Brannon took his seat, finding that Lady Claristra Fallingleaf was already seated beside him. She smiled at him haltingly, her eyes nervous and unsure.

He ignored her and looked for Valkimir.

The Knights of the Wood were gathered in number on the balcony just below the royal family, and Brannon quickly spotted Val among them. His beloved was facing away from him.

All the while, waiting for the ceremony to commence, Brannon stared, waiting for Val to glance his way. He needed to see the strength that he was sure to find in those fierce green eyes.

"Very exciting, isn't it," said Lady Claristra, using her left hand to tuck her golden locks beneath her extremely long ears. It was a gesture that was supposed to elicit intrigue he knew, for he had used it often.

He scoffed. "Don't make a fool of yourself. You know as well as I that your gestures are wasted on me. Do yourself a favor and find an easier target."

She was speechless, and glanced past him to King Rimon.

Brannon followed her gaze, and his father leveled a steady scowl on him. Beside the king, Brannon's mother smiled sheepishly at him. Her eyes were heavy with lack of sleep and dark with the telltale signs of poppy seed abuse.

"I don't like it any more than you do, you pretentious little bastard," Claristra hissed at him suddenly.

Brannon felt his cheeks burning suddenly, and he glared at the elf with newfound curiosity.

"This marriage will be good for my family," she went on, more pleasantly. "You can polish Valkimir's lance all you want, I don't care. I only ask that you give me children. Give me an heir."

She glanced at him, and he must have looked disgusted, for she let out an indignant huff. "Please do try to hide your thoughts better."

Brannon checked himself and glanced around. Only his sister was paying any attention to them.

"Don't worry," said Claristra. "I need only your seed. And that can be gotten from you by many means." She glanced at Valkimir, following Brannon's eyes.

Brannon shifted uncomfortably, but his sister elbowed him in the arm, sobering him with a forced cough.

"I accept your terms," he said shakily. He took a wine glass from a servant and drank it down in one long pull.

"Excellent," she said with a grin.

Finally, the king stood and addressed the gathering. "Elves of the Woodland Realm of Halala, I have called you all here today so that you may once again witness the naming of the Champion…"

Brannon had heard it all before, twice actually. At sixty-nine years old, he was young for an elf, some of whom were at least six hundred, but he was as familiar as any with the legend of Drak'Noir.

But never before had he cared so about the outcome. His worry for Val soon caused his head to swoon, and his father's words became hopelessly muddled. He needed to see his lover's face, needed to see him smile.

Brannon was fighting to get ahold of himself when suddenly a hand touched his. He turned bleary eyes upon his smiling sister and found some strength.

He cleared his mind, focusing on the living tree they had all gathered in, and caused the wooden floor beneath Val to bulge slightly, nudging him. Val looked down, then to the side.

Look at me! Brannon urged with his mind.

Val finally turned and glanced back. He smiled at Brannon and offered a wink.

Brannon's spirits soared, but then a pang of lovesickness tore again at his heart.

An explosion of light suddenly flared in front of him, causing Brannon to give a high-pitched cry. The smoke cleared momentarily, and Kazimir the Most High Wizard stood facing the cheering gathering. Val turned around once more; his eyes shone with love upon Brannon, and his lips whispered three words. He turned bravely to face the wizard once more, and Brannon was left with a terrible thought—had he been saying goodbye? Did he know that he would be chosen?

Brannon nearly fainted. Only the wizard's riddled words kept him lucid:

"Your champion shall travel to Bad Mountain,

where Drak'Noir he will thwart.

Elves of Halala, I name as your hero,

Brannon Woodheart!"

Brannon shot to his feet, even as Kazimir spoke his name. "No, not Val!"

Annallia let out a shriek.

Brannon blinked and regarded the wizard queerly. "Wait…what did you say?"

The king regally rose to his feet and began a slow clap that was soon taken up by all in attendance. A thunderous applause then rose up in the temple, along with exuberant chants for Brannon, Prince of Halala, Champion of the Dragon.

Val turned to regard his lover, and unbelieving eyes found Brannon's through the commotion, and the elf prince turned to his father, who regarded his son with a satisfied smirk.

CHAPTER 5

THE CHAMPION OF THE IRON MOUNTAINS

I F Gibrig Hogstead knew anything, it was hogs. And there was no way a six-hundred-pound beauty like Snorts was going to be traded for an unshaped gold nugget. He bluntly told the older dwarf just as much, and spit on the ground to show him just how serious he was.

The old dwarf trader scoffed and spat as well. "That nugget be as big as that brain o' yours, Gibrig, and that be sayin' somethin'. Yer pap got his ear to the ground? He put ye up to this?"

"Me pap ain't got nothin' to do with this here transaction," said Gibrig proudly. "I raised this hog meself, I did—off me own scraps, even. Spy how smooth and firm them shanks be. Prime meat, that is. Like I said, Snorts here ain't goin' for no tiny nugget."

Gibrig crossed his long arms and nodded firmly.

The trader, a very stubborn old dwarf by the name of Kegley Quartz, eyed Gibrig suspiciously. "Ye fool dwarf. Ye went and done gave him a name, didn't ye." He threw up his arms and shook his fists at the heavens. "By the stone god's moss-covered beard! You ne'er give 'em a name!"

Gibrig slumped beneath the weight of the glare.

Kegley looked over the hog again, shaking his head. "*Snorts.* What kind o' fool name that be for a hog? It be like namin' a cow Moos."

He frowned, glancing back at Gibrig. His face became kind after a moment, and he patted Snorts's hind end.

"He be a fine specimen, there be no mistakin' that claim. Tell ye what, I been doin' business and such with yer pap some fifty-odd years. 'Side from that, his stock always be treated right—the best meat, year after year, season to season.

"But this here nugget weighs near five stone, lad. Could be melted to ten coins and a pendent to boot! An' though I can see the beast means a lot to ye, a dwarf can't be livin' on love alone…else me wives an' I'd never leave the bedroom."

Gibrig couldn't help a small chuckle and was forced to abandon the pathetic look he was trying to convey. He knew Kegley was right. He should have never named the hog. His father had told him as much since he was old enough to understand the slaughter. Hogs weren't pets, they were fruits of labor, a means to trade for things that one could not make or grow oneself.

"I'll throw in five silver and not a shiny turd more," said Kegley. "Already I'm payin' more than he's worth."

"I just can't," Gibrig said with a shuddering breath.

"Now ye're just bein' ridic'lous! You know ye can't be goin' back to yer pap with no gold."

Gibrig began to whimper, and he angrily wiped his face with the end of his long shirt. Others around the market glanced their way.

"Get ahold of yerself," said Kegley with a darting glance around. His face suddenly went stark white.

Gibrig followed his eyes and froze.

Dranlar Ironfist, king of the Iron Mountains, sat upon a large ram five feet away, looking down on them. Behind him was a procession of twenty dwarven guards. "Excuse me, human," said the king, and all eyes turned to Gibrig. "That is perhaps the best-looking hog I've ever seen. There be a banquet coming up, and I would have yer hog's head be me centerpiece and main course. I'll give ye triple what the merchant offered."

Gibrig could only stare, shock-jawed and blinking.

"He's not a human, er, Sire," said Kegley as he fiddled with his hat and tried to stay in one spot. "He's a dwarf to be sure, but he gots that humanism they speak of."

The king frowned at Gibrig. "Ye don't be sayin'. Humanism, eh?" He leaned closer and eyed the strange dwarf closely, taking note of his long legs, skinny torso, and arms that nearly reached his knees.

Looking like a human was humiliating enough. But having the king eyeballing him was another thing altogether. Worse yet, a large crowd of human, elf, dwarf, and ogre traders and merchants had begun to form around them.

The king laughed and shook his head, tossing a bag of coins at Gibrig's feet. "Ye're invited to me dinner as well. Do ye juggle?"

"Juggle, S-Sire?" said Gibrig.

The king regarded Gibrig and stroked his beard as he leaned in to talk to Kegley. "Is the lad slow in the head too?"

Kegley offered Gibrig a warning glance. "Nah, he's a smart lad. Knows when to recognize a good thing at least."

"Consider my offer, human…d-dwarf," said the king. "Me hall be sure to pay more handsomely than hog farmin'." He pointed at Snorts and told one of his soldiers to take the lead rope. Kegley huffed for his loss, and seeing this, the king threw to him a small sack. "For yer troubles."

"Thank ye, thank ye, Sire," Kegley said with many bows.

The king kicked the sides of his ram, and the procession began off toward the mountains again.

The guard led Snorts past Gibrig, who imagined the poor hog being led to the king's halls deep within the Iron Mountains. He saw the fat nobles dining on ham and bacon and pork chops, hocks and side pork…

"NO!" he yelled suddenly and grabbed ahold of the rope, yanking it out of the armored dwarf's hands.

The guard squared on him. "Ye out yer head, boy?"

"What are ye doin', Gib?" Kegley hissed.

"This h-h-hog…ain't for sale," Gibrig dared to say.

The king had turned his ram around, and the entire market was now watching the exchange. Dranlar offered a slow scowl and dismounted with purpose. A page quickly attached his gold cloak to his shoulders, and another handed him the biggest and shiniest double-headed axe Gibrig had ever seen.

Kegley bowed deeply and pulled down Gibrig, forcing him to take a knee.

"Please, Yer Long Beardedness, he's not for sale...for any price," said Gibrig, wringing the rope with his hands.

Staring at the ground, he watched the king's steel boots settle before him. "You would dare refuse your liege?"

"I'm sorry, Y-Yer A-Awesomeness. I ain't meanin' to offend. It's just... he's...he's me friend. I can't sell me friend to be killed for nothin'."

The hog gave a snort, as if to accentuate the point.

"Hand over the hog, lad," said the king.

Gibrig shuddered. A voice in his head screamed that he was being an imbecile. The king had paid thrice Snorts's worth. A dwarf would have to be a fool to refuse such an offer—*especially* from the king. He turned to regard Snorts once more, who was busy eating a tuft of grass growing in between the stone.

"Boy..." said the king, meaning it as a final warning.

"Run, Snorts!" Gibrig yelled, and he smacked the hog on the rump. One of the guards reached for Snorts, and Gibrig socked him on the helmet with a closed fist before giving him a shove.

"Get that hog!" the king cried.

Gibrig leapt to his feet, backpedaled, and tripped over Kegley as two more guards lunged for him. He went head over heels but landed on his feet. Before the guards could get their hands on him, the odd dwarf turned and ran after the hog as fast as he could.

Many hours later, King Dranlar stormed into his chamber deep within the Iron Mountains and found Kazimir waiting for him.

"Good King," said the wizard with a bow that left his long beard grazing the floor. "I am prepared to announce the dwarven champion. Have you made a final decision?"

Dranlar waved off the guards and moved to the bar to pour himself a drink. "I have," said Dranlar before shooting back three fingers of rum. He wiped his mouth with his black beard. "I had thought to send that bumbling idiot Drexle, but I have changed my mind. You will announce the champion to be one Gibrig Hogstead. The little shyte embarrassed me today in the market. I hope Drak'Noir makes him watch while she feeds that damned hog to her whelps."

"Very well, Good King," said Kazimir with a small bow. "As you wish, so shall it be."

CHAPTER 6

ALL ROADS LEAD TO BAD MOUNTAIN

Murland Kadabra followed the ancient wizard down the road and out of the city. He'd expected a horse, or at least a mule. How was a hero supposed to get all the way to Bad Mountain on foot?

He had asked Kazimir just that, but the wizard never answered any of his questions. Murland struggled to catch up to Kazimir, but the old wizard's apparent age said nothing of his stamina, and he always seemed to be five strides ahead of Murland, saying every now and then, "Hurry along then, no time to dilly-dally."

A few hours into the journey, a rider came upon them from the road out of Magestra. To Murland's delight, the rider proved to be his closest childhood friend, the princess.

"Caressa?" he said happily as she reined in her horse.

The princess dismounted deftly, ran to him, and gave him a big hug. "Murland, I'm so glad I caught you," she said, looking him over after they had parted. "I can't believe it. A Champion of the Dragon?"

"I can't believe it either," said Murland.

Caressa laughed musically.

"No," said Murland, leaning in and glancing back at Kazimir. "I mean, I *really* can't believe it. Me, a champion?"

Caressa put a hand to his cheek and smiled up at him, her bright red hair blowing in the breeze. "I believe in you, Murland. I always have. You've a magic all your own, and some day you will be a great wizard."

"You really mean that?" Murland asked, for she knew exactly how inept he was in the wizardly arts. Since he had always failed to grow wizard leaf, he basically worked as a groundskeeper for Abra Tower.

"Of course I do," said Caressa.

"Best to make hay while the sun is shining," Kazimir called from behind them.

Murland glanced back at him worriedly. "I wish you were coming with me," he said, turning back to Caressa.

"I'll be right here waiting when you get back. You hear me? And you *will* come back." A single tear dripped from one long lash and slowly spilled down her freckled cheek.

Murland wanted to tell her that he loved her, that he had always loved her, but before he could speak, she kissed him. His heart leapt and his stomach fluttered as her soft lips met his, and just as quickly as it had happened, it was over.

"Go now, my champion, and the sooner shall be your return."

Murland could only nod, for he did not trust his voice. He turned from her and followed Kazimir down the road. Soon they crested a hill, and Murland was overcome by the urge to look back one last time. He knew the old saying about never looking back, but he did it anyway. Caressa stood watching him from afar, her long red hair dancing in the wind. His heart sank, and he realized that the old saying was true.

That night, when they made camp, Kazimir suddenly disappeared, saying that he would be on watch. Murland didn't mind so much, but he felt very alone sitting in his small tent in the clearing beside the tree line, wondering what might be out there in the dark.

Murland rummaged through his pack for the box that held the wand of Allan Kazam. He found the box, but also something that he had not noticed before. Beneath his extra clothes and food, wrapped in cheesecloth, he found an old and surprisingly heavy tome.

"What's this?" he asked the winged backpack, but of course it did not answer.

The tome was bound in dark leather, and even before he had opened it up, Murland knew what it was, for he could feel the magical power within. The cover had strange golden text that Murland could not understand. He recognized glyphs and runes that looked to be Old Elvish, but he had never been very good at the old languages, and this was a variation that he had never seen.

He opened the book slowly, its old binding creaking. A great gust of wind blew from the pages and a deep voice echoed words in a foreign language. There was a flash of light, and Murland snapped the book shut.

He sat their panting, both terrified and exhilarated. It was then that he noticed the small piece of paper that had landed on his leg. He set the tome aside and carefully unfolded the note.

Murland, I have bestowed upon you the wand of Allan Kazam, and now you have found his spell book. You will no doubt have trouble reading it, for it is written in the language of magic. But I believe that you will soon discover your magic, and I believe that you can mend the wand that was broken. I see greatness in you, Murland, even though you cannot see it yourself. Go forth into the wilds beyond the Wide Wall with confidence. You are destined for great things.

P.S. It wouldn't hurt to grow some wizard leaf!

P.P.S. DO NOT tell Kazimir about the spell book.

P.P.P.S. This note will self-destruct as soon as you finish reading it.

-Headmaster Zorromon the Off-White

The piece of paper suddenly burst into flames, and Murland cried out and pulled back his singed fingers.

He looked to the tome with newfound curiosity and respect. Why would Zorromon give him such priceless magical artifacts? Had the high wizard lost his mind? Or could Murland actually have powerful magic hidden inside him, waiting to be unleashed? The fact that he had been chosen out of thousands to be Magestra's champion said that at least Kazimir thought so. And now Zorromon had bestowed not one but two powerful magic relics upon him.

But why had Zorromon said not to tell Kazimir about the book? Why the secret?

Murland lay back on his bedroll and studied the broken wand by candlelight. He could feel a soft hum of power radiating from it.

If Zorromon and Kazimir think I'm so special…maybe I am, he thought.

He looked to the wand, wondering if he could cast a spell with it. The shaft was cracked, but it was still in one piece, and the tape seemed strong enough.

Can't hurt to try.

Murland glanced around, looking for something to experiment with. He decided upon another candle, thinking that it would be easy enough to produce a small flame to light it with. He prepared himself the way the high wizards had said to: he closed his eyes, took a deep, steadying breath, and imagined gathering his magical energy in his core. Holding the wand an inch above the wide candle, he focused the imagined power into his arm, down into his hand, and out of the wand.

"Ignis," he said softly, not wanting to overdo it.

BOOM!

Murland was blown straight up into the air—taking the tent with him—and screaming, fell blindly in a tangle of tarp, tent poles, and rope. He hit the ground with a thud and lay there, panting and clutching the wand in his right hand. With a groan, he untangled himself from the smoldering tarp and looked around. The soot-covered backpack was hovering above the scorched bedroll, and the ground was on fire. He checked the wand, worried that he had destroyed it, but the wand was still in one piece. There were scorch marks on the tip and along the crack, and the tape had been completely blown off.

He got up and stomped out the fire before it reached the dry forest, and then shook out his blackened blanket and bedroll. Smelling burnt hair, he realized that he too was covered in soot.

"What a mess," he said. "You alright, backpack?"

The pack came to land at his side and quivered, and Murland apologized for nearly blowing it up. After dusting off the backpack, he carefully put the wand back in its wooden box.

"I think it's best not to use that again until it's fixed," he told the backpack. Then something occurred to him—he had cast a spell. It had been a disaster, and much larger than he intended, but he had caused *something* to happen with magic. Granted, it was probably mostly due to the very powerful wand, but still, it was something.

Feeling quite pleased with himself, he washed up in the creek beside camp and changed his clothes. He hung the bedroll and blanket to air out, and curled up beside the fire and stared up at the starry sky.

The fatigue of the long day's march hit him suddenly then, and sleep found him easily, as did dreams of dragons and magic.

In the morning, Murland found the campfire smoldering and Kazimir standing beside the road, looking west. The weather was mild, and the song birds sang in the forests, greeting the new day with great enthusiasm. Murland took in the crisp air and stretched and yawned before smiling up at the clear blue sky.

"Good morning," he said to Kazimir happily. "You didn't happen to make any breakfast…did you?" Murland asked as he pulled on his trousers.

The Most High Wizard stood rigidly, staring at the path back to the road, unmoving, unspeaking.

Murland decided not to press the issue. He *was* hungry, to be sure, but he wasn't that used to eating regular breakfasts anyway—and besides, there was some bread and cheese in his pack.

He went about tearing down his scorched tent with single-minded determination, hoping to impress the old wizard. When he was done, he loaded his tent, bedroll, and pillowcase full of clothes inside his large, winged back-pack. Once he had secured the cover strap, the backpack beat its wings furiously and took to the sky to soar above.

With the flying pack in tow, Murland moved to stand beside Kazimir. "I'm ready to set out."

Kazimir said nothing. He remained staring at the path to the road with eyes as blank as a dead man's, and for a moment, Murland wondered if indeed the ancient wizard had died standing up. Suddenly, however, Kazimir came alive and headed for the road without so much as a word.

Murland hurried to catch up. "Say, uh…Most High One, we've got a long road and all, and I was wondering if you could give me some pointers on growing wizard leaf."

No response was forthcoming. Kazimir just continued in his swift march.

"Do you, uh…think then, maybe…perhaps, you could show me how to mend this wand?"

Still nothing.

Murland was beginning to very much dislike the old wizard. He was a Champion of the Dragon after all, and surely, he deserved the respect worthy of a simple answer.

Still, he trudged on, knowing that soon they would reach King's Crossing, and there he would meet the other champions.

CHAPTER 7

✕

SLUR SIRSALOT

SIR ELDRICK AWOKE beside a woman he didn't recognize. She wasn't terribly good looking, but a careful raising of the sheets told him that she was at least well endowed, with good round birthing hips and plump breasts. She was his type of woman, to be sure.

His head pounded, and his mouth tasted like the pit of a tobacco pipe. Still, he hadn't yet been found out—he was still a free man. The events of the previous days slowly lumbered through the fog of his muddled mind, and he gave a chuckle that caused his sleeping friend to stir.

The king sold me out to Kazimir, that son of a bitch, thought Eldrick. *Hah! Who's the fool now?*

"To the hells with the king, and to the hells with Drak'Noir," he mumbled as he reached for the flask on the nightstand beside the bed—which was now half full of water. After wetting his whistle, he gathered his things, and he gave one last glance under the sheets and bade the sleeping not-quite-beauty good day before silently slipping out of the room.

The inn was quiet this time of morning, but the barkeep was there at the long oak bar, trying to fish a pickled egg out of a jar. The squat man's mustache leapt when Sir Eldrick approached, and he pushed the jar aside—though his fingers were still stuck inside.

"Welcome, welcome. How was your sleep?" he said cordially whilst trying to discretely wrestle his hand from the jar. "Better than mine, I'll bet. The lass I sent to your room sure knows how to take care of guests, she does. Did you find the room to your liking? How were the pillows? Fluffier than a wood elf I reckon, eh? Was there enough water in the basin? I been meaning to—"

"Please," said Eldrick, rubbing his head. "That is too many questions before breakfast."

"Ah!" The man beamed, slapping his leg with rehearsed affability. "Breakfast it is then. What'll it be?"

"Water, and it better not taste like shit."

The man just stood and smiled, as though waiting for the punch line. "Ah, you're serious. Well of course you are. Water it is. Coming right up. Anything else, good Sir?" he added before finally extracting his hand from the jar and smiling stupidly at Sir Eldrick.

"Eggs, four of 'em, all whipped together and fried till brown. I hate soggy eggs, and I'm warning you now, I won't pay for 'em if they come out that way. A big heaping plate of side pork to go with it. And fresh bread, half a loaf."

Eldrick flicked a silver piece at the round man, who caught it deftly and put it in his pocket with rehearsed grace. "Of course, coming right up."

The excitable man poured the water and set it in front of Sir Eldrick before disappearing into the kitchen and ordering someone around.

A prickle swept across Sir Eldrick's back. He didn't have to turn around—he knew from whom the heavy magical energy came.

"Kazimir…come to steer me back to the herd?" Sir Eldrick wasn't wearing his elaborate armor at the moment, but he was carrying a sword, and his hand was now gripping the hilt tightly.

The ancient wizard sat down beside him at the bar with a groan. "Don't be a fool. Never mind your silly sword."

"I know that the king put you up to this," said Eldrick. "Do not deny it."

"I deny nothing, but you would be wise not to threaten me before I have had my breakfast."

Eldrick relaxed his grip slightly. "It is said that you are wise—you know the tales of my heroism are true. I defeated the Giant of Calamity when it marched on Vhalovia, I slew three hundred trolls in the battle of the Northern Blight, and it was I who laid low the Witch of Agnar. Yet, you are calm, even knowing that I would rather die than go on this fool's quest."

Kazimir regarded him with skepticism as his eyes traveled up and down Eldrick's out-of-shape body. "That was many seasons ago, my queen-bedding friend."

"Indeed," Eldrick shot back quickly. "Still, a charlatan wizard whore for Drak'Noir should be no challenge."

Kazimir remained relaxed. He even grinned. "Yet you do not strike."

"I haven't had *my* breakfast either."

"Then it is decided. Breakfast first. Until then, a truce."

Eldrick took his hand off his hilt and rested his elbows on the bar. "As you wish. A parley until breakfast has been eaten."

Kazimir nodded, stroking his long beard.

Eldrick got the feeling that he was formulating a great lie. He looked to the ring on his finger, the one that was supposed to keep wizards and witches from finding him, and shook his head.

The barkeep rushed through the swinging doors just then and stopped short, eyeing the famous wizard wildly. He nodded, as if answering a command from Kazimir, and then poured a tall tankard of mead before placing it in front of the odd couple at the bar. He then disappeared back into the kitchen, to fetch the wizard's breakfast, no doubt.

Kazimir rubbed his hands together and settled over the glass. As an afterthought, he regarded Eldrick and raised it. "To heroes and fools, and those who know the difference."

Eldrick clanged his glass with Kazimir's, never taking his eyes off him.

The drinks were tossed back, and glasses hit the bar. Kazimir rested his gnarled staff against the worn counter and eyed Eldrick in the long mirror on the wall across from them.

"They say you've defiled the queen."

Eldrick snorted at that. "I wasn't the first, and I won't be the last."

"Indeed. But you are a marked man, nonetheless."

Eldrick waited.

"You are no fool. I can see that," said the wizard. "You know as well as I do that the Champions of the Dragon are no more than food for the beast."

"And…" Eldrick prompted.

"*And*, you needn't be like the others."

Eldrick was suddenly interested. "Go on," he said cautiously.

The barkeep twirled out of the kitchen once again, this time with two steaming plates. "There you are, gentlemen. If I can get you anything else, just ask. I've got a nice apple pie just came out of the oven. Hot as a lass's—"

"That will be quite all, my good man," said Kazimir. "Some privacy please, if you don't mind."

The barkeep nodded his way back through the swinging doors and disappeared, and the ancient wizard regarded Eldrick once more in the mirror.

"I am old, Sir Knight. I may not look it, but I am very old indeed."

"No, you totally look like it."

Kazimir glared from beneath bushy eyebrows. "I have ushered seven generations of bumbling idiots to the mouth of Bad Mountain, and I have fought through the wilds beyond the Wide Wall more times than I care to remember. I am just as much a pawn to the dragon as the rest of you."

"Then you would help to defeat Drak'Noir once and for all?" said Eldrick with cautious optimism.

Kazimir gave a croaking laugh that ended in a long cough.

"No...no, you fool! Drak'Noir cannot be defeated. Listen to one who has seen her grow these last two centuries. She is a thing of legend! From head to tail, she measures no less than two hundred yards. Her breath is born from the depths of hell. Her crashing tail is like a felled sequoia, and her claws can crush stone to dust. No, there is no way to defeat a beast so powerful. She is as impervious to magic as she is to steel."

Sir Eldrick nodded understanding. "So you want me to make sure the others arrive on time, is that it?"

Kazimir arched a brow and nodded. "Not as dumb as they say, are you?"

Eldrick chewed on that for a moment as he shoveled eggs and toast into his mouth.

The wizard ate leisurely.

"That's how you survived, isn't it?" said Eldrick. "You were one of the first to be chosen for the quest when the dragon appeared those centuries ago. You were the only one to return victorious...you made a deal with her."

"Perhaps too smart for your own good," said Kazimir, sitting back and laying a hand on his staff. "Your cleverness leaves me with few options."

Eldrick's hand slowly found his hilt once more as they stared each other down in the mirror.

"Lead the others to Bad Mountain and take my place as the Caller of the Champions. You will return victorious and be declared a hero. Your family name will be honored for generations to come. No longer will they call you Slur Sirsalot, and Defiler of the Queen. Women will flock to you in droves. The power of Drak'Noir will see you through many long years if only once per generation you lead the fools to their death."

"What do you mean, the power of Drak'Noir?" Sir Eldrick asked, turning to look at Kazimir straight on for the first time.

"She has a magic all her own. That is all you need to know for now."

"Then why do you want out?"

"I have grown tired of this world. There are many others that I wish to explore before my time is up. Call it a permanent vacation. But I cannot in good conscience leave Fallacetine to its fate. It is high time that I found a replacement."

Sir Eldrick knew that he had only two options—fight Kazimir here and now and hope for the best, or go along with the scheme. Either way, he figured himself a dead man. He gave a belch and rubbed his stomach as he called for the innkeeper.

The little man came waddling through the doors as if he might have been right there listening. "Yessir!" he said happily.

"Your finest bottle of rum," Eldrick ordered, knowing that if he had any chance of defeating Kazimir, he would have to drink liquor.

Kazimir raised a staying hand. "For this quest, my drunken friend, you must remain sober."

Eldrick scoffed at that. "You there—barkeep. You heard my request."

The scared little man eyed the wizard warily, clearly fearing him more, and Kazimir easily waved him off.

"What's this?" said Sir Eldrick. "If I wanted some miserable twat telling me what to do, I would have gotten married long ago."

"Fool! I know why it is that you want liquor." The old wizard nodded knowingly at Sir Eldrick's surprised expression. "Yes, I know what you are trying to do. But it would not work against me. You can drink yourself silly for the next two hundred years if only you can remain sober for a few weeks. Lead the idiots west to King's Crossing, beyond the Wide Wall, through the Forest of the Dead, past the Swamp of Doom, over the Horrible Hills, across the Long Sand, all the way to the shadowy peak of Bad Mountain."

"And if I don't?"

"If you don't, then I will be forced to kill the queen that you love so much."

Sir Eldrick pulled his dagger in a flash and pressed it up against Kazimir's ribs. But the blade was stopped dead by an invisible energy shield. An electric shock shot up his arm and there was a flash of light.

The next thing Sir Eldrick knew, he was against the wall on the other side of the room, being slapped gently by the barkeep.

"Dammit, man, get off me!" said Eldrick. He staggered to his feet and eyed the Most High Wizard, who still sat, leisurely eating his breakfast at the bar.

Sir Eldrick returned to his stool with a slight limp and a newfound respect for wizards. "I'll tell you what, wizard," he said, sitting with a groan. "I'm in no mood to fight an old man today anyway, and this sounds like my kind of adventure. I'm in."

Kazimir dipped his bread in golden yolk and grinned. "Excellent."

CHAPTER 8

SHADOW FOREST

GIBRIG AND SNORTS seemed to have avoided the search party, and soon they found themselves in the middle of Shadow Forest, walking among tall ancient pines whose thick boughs blocked out the sun completely, leaving the ground barren and rocky amid the bed of gnarled roots.

"N-n-nothing to worry about, Snorts."

Gibrig held himself and shivered. The lack of sunlight made the forest dark and ominous, and it was too quiet. The tall trees seemed to always be watching, and he had not dared stop for a second to rest. Instead he trudged on through the forest to the south, away from the Iron Mountains. The night had been a long and hungry one. Gibrig had left with such haste that he hadn't had the time to gather any supplies. He and Snorts had found water in streams along the way, but neither had eaten since the day before.

Gibrig had been through the forest before, years ago when he was just a young lad. His father had taken him and his brother Gillrog through it on a hunting trip, and they had returned with a good-sized stag. Thoughts of the venison that they had harvested from the beast caused Gibrig's belly to rumble. He thought of his brother then, and a dark melancholy overcame him.

"Boy, I wish Gill was with me now," he said to Snorts. "Me brother weren't afraid o' the dark woods like I be. Ye woulda really liked him. He was the nicest dwarf ye ever done want to meet. Had humanism just like me. We was twins, ye see. I ever tell ye about him?"

Snorts looked up from rutting in the soft earth and wiggled his backside.

Gibrig gave a sigh. "He was a good dwarf. Never hurt no one. But the other dwarf lads picked on him nonstop. We weren't identical in looks, ye see. He was a lot taller than I be. The tallest dwarf that ever lived, they say. Well, the others ignored me for the most part, but they were on poor Gill all the time. Finally, I suppose that he couldn't take it no more…"

Gibrig got too choked up to talk to Snorts anymore, and tried to think of something else.

They continued south through the whispering trees, and Gibrig thought of his father, to whom he hadn't even had a chance to say goodbye.

"I reckon Pap'll be alright though, Snorts, so don't ye be worryin' 'bout him. Probably be better off without me. Ain't nobody needs a tall weed like me around anyhow. We'll make our own way, Snorts, just you and me. This here's a big, wide open land. We'll find our place. Maybe there be a village o' dwarves with humanism around somewhere."

Snorts gave an exuberant honk.

"That's right," said Gibrig, wiping his eyes despite his brave words.

Many hours later, they finally reached the edge of the dark forest, and Gibrig stopped, hesitant to continue. As much as he feared the forest, he feared the unknown lands even more. He looked out over the land and gulped. The wide world was just that, and stretched as far as the eye could see. The great expanse of nothingness somehow seemed to carry far more ire toward the two than the terrible forest of dark pines had.

Gibrig swallowed hard. "Ye know what, Snorts? If I take one more step, it'll be the farthest from the Iron Mountains that I've ever been."

Snorts looked sidelong at him, almost expectantly.

"Here goes," said Gibrig. He gathered his courage, closed his eyes, and took a big step forward.

His foot slipped forward slightly, and he opened his eyes to find that he had stepped in a huge cow pie.

"Son of a—"

"Ah! It's about time you found your way through the forest," came a stern voice suddenly. "Come now, no time to dillydally."

Gibrig stood there blinking, unbelieving of whom he saw. The old man was tall, despite the slight curve to his back. A long white beard fell to his knees in a neat braid. He carried a staff in his right hand, and his pointed hat was adorned with stars and moons. His robes were like a cloud's silver lining, and Gibrig had to squint against the sudden glare.

"W-Who are you?" said Gibrig, taking a step back, right into the cow pie again.

"You know who I am, Master Hogstead."

"Ye're...ye're a wizard, aren't ye?"

The wizard gave a nod. "The Most High Wizard."

"Ka...Kazimir? But why in the hells...holy dragon shyte, y've come to take me back to the mountain to be hanged, haven't ye?"

"No, I am not taking you back to the mountain. Now, if you are quite done with your exposition of expletives, you will kindly follow me," Kazimir said over his shoulder, acting quite sure that Gibrig would follow.

But Gibrig's fear paralyzed him, though Snorts gave a happy snort and started moving immediately.

Kazimir stopped suddenly and slowly turned back to the frightened dwarf. "I *never* repeat myself, lad."

"Why should I follow ye? And how do I know that ye be who ye say ye be, eh? They...they say that Kazimir always speaks in riddles. So... so go on and explain that, ye falsifier!" said Gibrig, quite wanting to seem fierce. He tried to remind himself that trembling was not a part of bravado.

"Idiot! Who in their right mind rhymes all the time? It's an act. I'm Kazimir, and Kazimir means me. If I must prove myself to you, I'll do it by turning your hog into bacon with a snap of my fingers."

"Ye wouldn't!" said Gibrig fearfully.

The wizard cocked his head. "Of course I would...and at any rate, you would be best off to kill the poor beast now, smoke the meat, and hope it lasts you to Bad Mountain."

Gibrig scoffed. "I'd never cook me hog—did ye say Bad Mountain? What's this ye be sayin'?"

"Haven't you heard? You have been named the Champion of the Iron Mountains, Master Hogstead. I have come to escort you to King's Crossing, where you will meet the other heroes."

Gibrig stared at Kazimir, dumbfounded. "*I've* been named the Dragon Champion of the Iron Mountains?"

"Indeed," said Kazimir. "I have read it in the stars, and the stars are never wrong."

Gibrig became suddenly dizzy, and he found that it helped to sit.

Snorts licked Gibrig's cheek and settled his round frame on the ground beside his master.

"Ye've got it all wrong," began Gibrig.

There was a sudden bang and a flash of light that left a cloud of smoke hovering where the wizard had been. Gibrig shut his eyes against the glare, and when he opened them, Kazimir stood right in front of him, glaring down. "You are Gibrig Hogstead, and that is your hog, Snorts. I am Kazimir, be there no doubt about it. I am here to do what I have said. Make me repeat myself, and I will hang you in a crow's nest."

"But, the Champions of the Dragon are brave heroes. I'm—I'm just a hog farmer!"

"Young Gibrig, I have seen seven generations of heroes off to Bad Mountain. Would you recoil to know that the great Vexler of Magestra was a simple baker's son before he set out? Or that Sir John Frail once called the shantytowns of Pearnt his home? How about the fabulous Floren van Perth of Halala? When first I met him, he darkened his pretty pants. But one and all helped to defeat the dragon in their time…and you will do the same."

The wizard straightened and eyed Snorts. "You will need a steed for this quest, young Gibrig." He waggled his fingers and spoke strange words. In a flash of light and a puff of smoke, a saddle suddenly appeared on Snorts's back.

Just then, far to the south, a man's horse was leaping over a fence when the saddle suddenly disappeared. The horse landed, jarring the man's crotch and causing him to give a high-pitched squeal as he fell over.

And there went the young farmer's ability to father children, for he would have sired the greatest knight in the southern lands.

CHAPTER 9

COURAGE, IT COULDN'T HAVE COME AT A WORSE TIME

"THIS IS LUDICROUS. I won't do it!" Brannon screamed, rushing into his quarters and throwing himself on his bed.

"Oh, but you will," said the king, marching after him. "You have been chosen by Kazimir, and you will do your duty."

"That's dragon shit and you know it! I'm no warrior…I'm no hero. If I didn't know any better, I'd think that you put him up to this just to be rid of me!"

The king grabbed Brannon's shoulders firmly and lifted him off the bed with ease. The fire in his eyes burned with unmistakable hatred. "I've tolerated your effeminate sensibilities long enough," he yelled. "You will go on this quest, and you *will* make this family proud."

Brannon couldn't help but break down and cry, which caused his make-up to run down his cheeks like wet paint upon a canvas.

The king growled and backhanded him. "Act like a male for once in your life!"

"You can't make me into something I'm not!" Brannon shot back.

The king slapped his son again before tearing off the wig and shoving it in his face, which of course caused further tears and even more of his coloring to smear.

"And neither can you!" said the king, shoving Brannon hard against the wall. He stood there panting, looking down at his son with a face twisted in anger.

"Stop this!" Annallia screamed.

Brannon lifted his head and regarded his furious sister through blurry eyes.

She took a step toward her father, seeming much bigger than she really was. "He's about to leave. Possibly forever. Can't you show your only son some compassion?"

The king looked from her to Brannon, and then to his own hands, as though he didn't recognize himself. His face was twisted in rage and regret. "You leave within the hour," he said breathlessly, before turning and lurching out of the room with none of the highborn grace that he was known for.

"Are you alright, dear brother?" Annallia asked, running to Brannon's side.

He shoved his face in a pillow and started weeping.

Annallia tried to comfort her brother. "It's alright—"

Brannon shot up and began pacing the room. "No it's not!" His hair was a mess, and his coloring had now run down all over his face. He didn't care anymore. His life was over.

"Champion of the Dragon?" he vehemently spat. "I had feared that Val would be the one chosen. But I never imagined…What is this terrible *curse* that Kazimir has cast upon me?"

Annallia straightened bravely. "Perhaps you are a warrior at heart…"

He leveled her with a grounding glare. "Really? *You* of all people know the fallacy that befalls your tongue."

She faltered, but then redoubled her steely façade. Three determined strides brought them face to face. "You are the bravest elf that I have ever known."

"Stop—" He turned from her, but she caught his arm firmly and forced him to face her.

"You are the bravest elf I have ever known!" she said again. "What is a dragon in the face of the prejudice you have had to endure for your love of Val? I have seen you face a crowd, wearing things that you know will bring you disdain and hatred, yet, you care not, because that is who you are. When you kissed Val at the award ceremony two years ago, in front of everyone, I thought it was the bravest thing I had ever seen. You were scorned, harassed, and teased, yet, you acted as though you didn't care."

"I care. It kills me…" He choked up, unable to find his words.

"Of course it does. That is what courage is all about. Doing what you feel is right, even though it might kill you."

He sniffled, meeting her eyes. In them, he saw only sincerity. "But what does that kind of courage have to do with questing to Bad Mountain? What do I have to offer a group of heroes?"

"First of all, your bravery. Secondly, you are quite skilled in floral magic."

He gave a laugh at that. "Yes, indeed! I'll kill the dragon with flowers."

"Do not underestimate your power," said Annallia. "You know how you impressed the elementals. If you had finished your training—"

"They want people like me for the military. They care nothing about creation."

"True as that may be, you're special, you've always been special." She was tearing up now, and her voice threatened to give out. "And now you've got to be brave, for me, for Val…you've got to come back."

"Annallia…"

"You're *going* to come back. You hear me? If it's a dragon Father wishes you to fight, then you bring back its head. You show them—you show them all!"

Her energy was contagious, and Brannon found himself suddenly believing that maybe she was right. But then he faltered again.

Annallia saw how his resolve came and went, and she squeezed his arm harder.

"You can do this, Brannon. I believe in you—*Val* believes in you."

Val…

As usual, Brannon found courage in the thought of Val, and he stood tall for the first time since the naming.

"That's better," said Annallia, wiping her brother's eyes lovingly. "Songs will be sung about you, dear Brannon, songs of victory and heroism. You just watch."

He wanted to believe her. More than anything he wanted to believe her. But he knew the truth of it—he was no warrior. Her words were pretty, and they did much to stir the heart. But of course, that was *her* gift. And in the end, they were just words. There was no way he could face a dragon, band of heroes at his side or not. It just wasn't possible.

"Stop!" came a voice from the hallway.

Brannon and Annallia glanced at each other, for the voice had come from a guard.

"We have orders from the king," said the guard. "I'm sorry, but no one can see him."

Brannon took in a shocked breath. Could it be?

"I will be quick," came another voice, and Brannon's heart leapt. "Valkimir!"

He shot off the bed, ran to the open doorway, and skidded into the hall. Valkimir was in full armor, his black hair shining like raven's wings and a burgundy cloak trailing behind him, as he marched past the guards, who just stood there, looking at each other helplessly.

"Val! I knew you would come!" said Brannon as he rushed into his lover's arms.

Valkimir took him up and lifted him off his feet, kissing him deeply. "Come, we must speak privately," he said, before letting him down.

They left the guards arguing in the hallway, and Brannon smiled at his sister as she closed the door. Neither he nor Valkimir cared if she were in the room with them, for she had often been around when they were sneaking it in the old days, back when everyone thought that Valkimir was courting *her*.

"I'm so glad you came," said Brannon, falling upon him once more. He kissed Valkimir and held him tight.

"Did you think that I would let you go on a quest without bidding you farewell in person?"

Brannon recoiled, crestfallen. "You don't mean to take me away from this nightmare?"

Valkimir looked confused.

"Surely you do not expect me to travel to Bad Mountain and do battle with Drak'Noir," Brannon insisted.

"You have been chosen by the Most High Wizard. You *must* go," said Valkimir.

"Val, are you out of your damned mind? I'll surely be killed long before I even reach Bad Mountain." He looked to Annallia for support, but she just pursed her lips and turned toward the balcony. "This is a nightmare!" he said, pulling at the sides of his hair.

Valkimir took Brannon's hands in his own and squared on him, blue eyes holding him in a deathly serious gaze. He had that look in his eye that he always came back from battle with. It was stoic and hard, with a hint of melancholy. "You have a serious decision to make. One that will determine your fate. I love you, Brannon, but you have a negative streak in you that holds you back from your full potential. Too often you cling to the perception that you are a victim."

Tears welled in Brannon's eyes, but he determinedly stood straight and proud before his beloved. "I am the prince of Halala. Heir to the throne and—"

"No!" said Valkimir in a voice that he had never used on Brannon. It was a tone saved for scared soldiers quivering in the face of an overwhelming foe. "Not anymore. Now you are the Champion of the Dragon of Halala. I cannot save you this time. Do you understand? You have only Kazimir and the other champions and your own strength."

"But, Val…"

Valkimir caressed Brannon's face and smiled on him lovingly. "You have more strength than you know. Please, please remember that."

Brannon felt sick with fear. He was dizzy and exhausted from all the excitement. All he wanted to do was get into bed with Val and snuggle up to his strong, warm body and sleep forever. He didn't know why Val was being so cruel, but it hurt more than anything ever had.

"I know this isn't what you wanted to hear," said Valkimir. "But it is what you needed to hear."

Brannon pushed Valkimir's hands away. "You sound just like my gods-damned father."

"I'm just trying to help."

"Help? Help? You think you're helping by treating me like some soldier? I'm not a soldier. I'm not a warrior. And I'm not a champion. Father knows that, and so do you. Don't you see? He's trying to be rid of me once and for all. He doesn't want me to make it back."

Valkimir was shaking his head. "Brannon, you were chosen by Kazimir, not King Rimon. The Most High Wizard has never been wrong about the champions, and they always push the dragon back to the Eternal Ice. This time will be no different."

Brannon wasn't listening. He had realized something that he didn't want to admit. Something terrible. And it broke his heart. "You want to be rid of me too..." he said, voice quivering.

Valkimir looked genuinely shocked. "Why would you say that?"

"Don't deny it, you bastard!" said Brannon, lunging forward and beating on Valkimir's armored chest.

Valkimir gained control of Brannon easily and held his wrists firmly, shaking him. "You have to stop this, Brannon. You're being crazy."

"Crazy? Crazy?" Brannon ripped his arms away and reached for the closest vase he could find. "You want to see crazy?" he said, and he threw it at Valkimir.

The knight ducked and the vase crashed against the wall behind him.

Annallia came rushing in from the balcony then, looking distraught. "Brannon, stop this!" she pleaded, her voice cracking.

"Get out of here, both of you. Leave me alone to die. It's what you want anyway!"

Brannon threw another vase. Then he grabbed whatever was in reach and threw it at his lover. Valkimir charged through the onslaught, taking more than one hit. When Brannon threw a chair at him, he caught it and smashed it into a hundred pieces at Brannon's feet.

"Enough!" he bellowed, and slapped Brannon across the face hard enough to rattle him.

Brannon cried out and clutched his cheek. Valkimir had never hit him before. He wanted to lash out, wanted to hurt him back, but a part of his mind had calmed, and the calm was now spreading.

"Your father is not trying to get rid of you, and neither am I," said Valkimir. "Do you understand? I need you, Brannon. I love you. And now I need you to fight for yourself for once. I need you to fight for me. And I need you to fight for us."

Valkimir was right. Brannon always clung to the idea that he was a victim. He acted helpless when it got him attention, or threw fits, or dressed in clothes that he knew would gain him animosity. He liked being a victim, because it was easier than trying and failing. Valkimir had been fighting for him for years. He had been the one to announce their love for each other, and he had been the one to fight with words and fists for the respect that he said they deserved. Valkimir and Brannon's coming out had sparked a revolution in elven society, something that hard-liners like King Rimon openly opposed. And through it all, Brannon had hidden behind his champion's big shoulders, imagining that he had gone through the same thing.

"Can you do that?" Valkimir asked, his own eyes watering.

Brannon fought back his pestilent tears. "I'll try," he managed to say.

Valkimir smiled and kissed him. "I know you will."

And If I never retu—"

"Shh," said Valkimir, grabbing him by the studded cup. "Never say never, my beloved. Ever."

CHAPTER 10

---- ✕ ----

FROG LEG NECKLACE

W ILLOW AWOKE AND soon found herself being carried by a group of young male ogres. Hundreds of Fire Swamp ogres marched along with them as they made their way back to the village. They sang as they ferried their champion home, singing songs of victory, valor, glory, and of course, bountiful rewards.

"What's happening? Have I really been chosen?" she asked her carriers, but they, like all others, sang at the top of their lungs, drowning out her voice.

Glancing over her shoulder from her precarious perch, she spotted the one and only Kazimir walking among the ogres, though he sang not at all, and even looked slightly bored.

She was led into a hut and fussed over by half a dozen matron mothers. All the while she asked them what was happening, but her questions were answered by no one. Instead the females busied themselves with their work. She was adorned in red war paint from head to toe, and dressed in the finest crocodile armor—which was hopelessly tight of course, and caused her bosom and belly to bulge out in all the wrong places. With much ceremony and fanfare, she was led out of the hut and to a raised podium at the center of the village. Kazimir was there, as were her parents and the chief of Fire Swamp.

"Look upon your champion now," said Kazimir in a voice that silenced all whispers. "Look upon your champion and bow. For she has been chosen, to help defeat the wyrm. Beneath her heavy boot, Drak'Noir will squirm."

"Four cheers for Willow!" said the chief, and the crowd complied. When they had finished, Chief Gnarlytooth turned to her and presented her with his very own club, carved from the heart of an ancient ironwood.

"Do me the honor of wielding my club," he said with a slight bow as he handed it to her reverently.

Willow took the smooth wood in her hand, amazed and humbled, and offered her chieftain a slow nod. "It is my honor."

Her mother looked on with tears of pride and joy, and her father puffed out his barrel-like chest. She had never seen her parents so happy. Willow endured the attention of the crowd bravely. She was a fierce ogre of Fire Swamp after all, and fear and doubt had no place in their society. Willow did have one fear though—would there be anything good to eat on the quest?

When she had finally been properly prepared for the quest and stood with Kazimir on the bridge leading out of the village, the other ogres raised their tusks to the sky proudly and offered up a chorus of burps in a glorious sendoff.

A low fog hung so thick about the congregation that nary a cattail or bulrush could be seen among the bald cypress, mangrove, and white oak trees that sparsely dotted the bog.

Her father Tharg led her raptor to her and handed over Tor's reins. He scowled at Dingleberry, who was whizzing and buzzing around her head excitedly; the little sprite was very excited to go on what she was calling a "holiday."

Her father beamed, which accentuated his large bottom tusks. "I am proud of you, Dragon Champion of Fire Swamp." He handed her his long gator-tooth dagger. "Bring your old father back a dragon tooth."

"I'll bring you back two dragon teeth," she said with tear-filled eyes.

He beamed and turned toward her mother.

Her mother Negek leaned in close and touched foreheads and tusks with her daughter. "Willow, my gargantuan daughter…Return victorious, and you will have your pick of mates to plant seed."

Willow blushed and glanced at the chief's son.

Her mother, not missing this, offered Willow a knowing nod, unable to keep herself from grinning. She tied a leather line around her daughter's neck, which sported two dozen dangling frog legs. "A snack," she told her happily.

Willow waved at the enthusiastic crowd behind her parents. "Goodbye, Mother. Goodbye, Father," she said. "I will make Fire Swamp proud."

The crowd gave a collective cheer that ended in a grand chorus of belches. Willow herself belched as well. The sound drowned out all others, echoing throughout the swamp, and many nods of approval followed in its wake.

Kazimir coughed impatiently.

She mounted Tor, whose legs nearly buckled beneath her great weight.

It protested, but she reined the beast in easily and began following the wizard across the bridge toward faraway lands.

"The sprite stays here," said Kazimir.

Dingleberry looked to Willow with concern.

"Can't she come?" Willow asked.

"I believe that I have already made it quite clear that she cannot. In other words, no. And for a third time, should you continue to press me, the answer will be no."

Kazimir turned and headed down the road, and Dingleberry gave him a thumbs-up—the rudest gesture in ogre society.

Willow laughed. "You watch over my parents while I'm gone. They will let you stay in my room."

"But...but..."

"Sorry, little one, you heard the old cruster."

Willow offered the ogres one last wave, patted Dingleberry on the head, and followed the wizard north toward her destiny.

Chieftain Gnarlytooth watched, grinning, as the two left, and slapped his belly along with the other ogres. He leaned in conspiratorially toward his closest advisor, Phlem. The skinny little ogre offered a tusky grin and opened a sack enough for the golden glimmer inside to shine in the chief's eyes.

"We did good, Phlem. The tribe will not starve now that she is gone."

"The dragon won't starve now either," Phlem snickered.

CHAPTER 11

KING'S CROSSING

THE TREK FROM Magestra to King's Crossing was a long one. Indeed, it was farther than Murland had ever been in his life. During the long journey, he made camp where the wizard told him to and set out when instructed. The ancient wizard never seemed to sleep, but rather went on watch as soon as they stopped each night, and promptly set out each morning.

As it turned out, the old wizard was not much of a conversationalist. Murland tried to speak with him on numerous occasions, but every time, he was met with things like, "Make hay while the sun is shining," and, "He who shuts his mouth and puts one foot in front of the other never finds himself late for dinner."

It was all quite frustrating. How was he supposed to defeat a legendary dragon if the greatest wizard in all the land wouldn't even answer simple questions? Still, Murland persisted in asking them, more out of boredom than anything else.

At night, when time afforded him, he tried to decipher the impossible spell book Zorromon the Off-White had given him, but much like the broken wand he'd been carrying around, it seemed rather useless.

By the afternoon of the fourteenth day, Murland had had quite enough of the silent wizard and the never-ending road. His feet hurt, and his legs were sore from the endless days of walking.

He finally stopped with an exasperated huff and summoned his courage, cleared his throat, and prepared to give the ancient one a right smart berating. Before he could get out a word, however, Kazimir stopped, turned to him, and said, "Ah, we have arrived." And just like that, he turned to a wisp of smoke.

Murland blinked. He had been so caught up in his own ponderings that he didn't realize they had finally reached King's Crossing. He blinked again when he saw four other Kazimirs standing on each of the conjoining roads. In a flash, three of the others turned to wisps as well. They all flew together and merged, leaving only one Kazimir.

"Welcome, Champions of the Dragon," said the Kazimir who stood beside a knight in full armor. "Come, come," he said, gathering all around.

Aside from the knight, there was also a very tall—and very fat—female ogre sitting on a raptor, a bearded man who had apparently come riding a hog, and the prettiest male elf that Murland had ever seen.

"Wait a minute," said Murland. "If that is the real you…who did I journey here with?"

Kazimir cocked an angry eye at him. "Why, an apparition, of course. Do you expect me to be in five places at once?"

"Well…I…" Murland began.

"Silence!" ordered Kazimir. "I have much to say and little time to say it. You have all been gathered here today to join forces against an ancient enemy of Fallacetine." He paused momentarily and gestured toward the tall knight. "This is Sir Eldrick of Vhalovia, as fierce a warrior as the southlands have ever produced."

Sir Eldrick straightened at that, and the wizard turned to the man getting off his hog.

"This here, my good champions, is not just a mere man, as he appears to be, but he is in fact the dwarf warrior of the Iron Mountains, Gibrig Hogstead."

"Did you say dwarf?" Sir Eldrick asked quizzically, eyeing the lanky little man.

Gibrig couldn't help but blush. "I've got…humanism," he told them.

Everyone shared confused glances, but Kazimir cut off any would-be inquiries by quickly moving on.

"This is Willow Muckmuck, Champion of Fire Swamp."

Willow stopped gnawing on the large drumstick she'd been enjoying just long enough to offer a nod to each of them. "Got anything to eat?" she asked.

"Brannon Woodheart, prince and Champion of Halala," said the wizard, moving down the line once more.

The lithe elf cocked a brow at the group, as though he were far from impressed. "It is your pleasure, I am sure," he said lazily, and went back to buffing his nails and ignoring them all.

Finally, Kazimir came to Murland. "And this is the most gifted wizard to come from Abra Tower since…well, since me."

Murland laughed at that, but when Kazimir scowled at him, he turned to the group and offered them all a "Good day, nice to meet you."

He shook hands with them all but Brannon. The elf continued to ignore him and didn't so much as bend from his high steed. "Humanism—eh?" said Murland, shaking Gibrig's hand. "I've never heard of that."

"Did you bring that hog to eat on the quest?" Willow piped in, wiping her mouth and tossing the bone to her raptor.

Gibrig was beside himself. He slowly shifted his weight. "Ye gonna butcher yer raptor?"

Willow scratched her head in thought and finally gave a slow shrug. "It's a long road to Bad Mountain…"

Gibrig was horrified. "No! I ain't butcherin' me hog. And if ye touch him, I'll…I'll—"

"He's quite sensitive about his hog," said Kazimir, offering Gibrig a knowing glance.

Willow licked her lips, her eyes still lingering on the hog, and Gibrig in turn eyed her with contempt.

"Well then, out with it," said Sir Eldrick. "What's this about humanism?"

Gibrig sighed and raised his arms out to the side. "I be tall, see? Me pap says I got a condition. I grew too tall for a dwarf, and I can't hardly grow a beard for nothing. He says I got humanism."

"Seems to me like you're just a tall dwarf," said Murland. To which Gibrig was appreciative.

"Maybe you're just a human. Maybe you were found in a basket in the river or something," said Willow.

"Maybe the mailman was a human," said Brannon, and he continued lazily blowing on his nails.

Willow gave a snorting laugh, and Sir Eldrick stifled his own mirth, though Murland wasn't impressed.

"The grand mystery that is Gibrig Hogstead's lineage can wait until the road," said Kazimir. "You've a long one ahead of you, and I suggest you get going."

"What? You're not coming with us?" said Murland.

The olden wizard walked to the edge of the forest and lingered beside a wide tree. "Of course not. A wizard has better things to do than babysit a bunch of heroes. I'll pop in from time to time, likely when you least expect and most need me."

He threw something to the ground, and there was a brilliant flash of light. And just like that, he was gone.

"Wow! That one's got some good magix!" said Willow, utterly enthralled.

Sir Eldrick motioned to them all. "Come on. You heard the wizard. Let us be off."

They set off to the west—the only direction that none of them had come from.

Murland was the only one without a mount, and he was forced to hurry after the group of riders. If he slowed them down some, well, he didn't mind that at all—he was in no hurry to get to Bad Mountain. He still had to mend the wand, and then, of course, there was the whole issue of not yet being able to read Allan Kazam's spell book.

"You're the one they call Slur Sirsalot, aren't you?" said Brannon, doing nothing to hide his disdain.

Sir Eldrick scowled at him sidelong as they traveled down the road. They had been journeying together for a little over an hour, and already he disliked the snide little shit.

"Sir *Whats*alot?" Gibrig asked.

Brannon rolled his eyes. "Slur Sirsalot. Try to keep up, you ignorant farmer."

"Come now," said Sir Eldrick. "Is that any way to treat one of your fellow champions?"

"*Champions*," Brannon scoffed, sitting side-saddle and leaning back leisurely on his white steed. "If we're all champions, then *I'm* the queen of Vhalovia."

"Well, you certainly are a queen," Sir Eldrick retorted with a grin.

"Nah," said Gibrig with all seriousness. "He's a prince."

"Hey, what do you mean we're not champions?" Murland called, hurrying to catch up.

Brannon regarded him over his shoulder impatiently. "You can honestly say that you're a champion? Look more like an overgrown squire to me."

Murland considered that. "But...but we were chosen by Kazimir."

"That fraud?" Brannon spat. "Please."

"That's the *Most High Wizard* ye be talkin' 'bout," said Gibrig.

"Most high indeed, a bunch of crazy leaf smokers, that lot. Well, what about you then, *human*?" said Brannon, turning on him. "Do *you* feel like a champion?"

"Don't call me that, it ain't nice," said Gibrig.

"Leave him alone," said Willow.

Brannon leered at her. "You just worry about getting your next meal."

"Alright, alright," said Sir Eldrick with raised hands. "That's enough. Hells, we're about to face the horrors beyond the Wide Wall. No need fighting amongst ourselves."

Brannon snapped his reins and pulled ahead of the group. Sir Eldrick eyed the others. The elf's words had cast a shadow of doubt over them.

"Never mind him—he's just scared," he told them.

"Ye think he be right?" Gibrig asked. "About us not being heroes and all?"

"That little princess doesn't know what he's talking about," said Sir Eldrick. "Kazimir always chooses who he thinks can defeat the dragon, and he's never wrong."

"But…if he's never wrong, why does the dragon always come back?" Murland asked.

Gibrig furled his brow in thought, and Willow scratched her head.

"Well," said Sir Eldrick, glancing at the others. "No one has ever been able to actually *kill* the beast. We've just got to…scare her off."

"And then we can go home?" said Gibrig.

"Of course," said Sir Eldrick with gusto. "And we *will* return victorious like all the other champions, and, like them, we will enjoy a lifetime of parades and celebration. We will be treated like heroes. You are all too young to remember the celebration tours of the champions, but mark my words, it will be grand."

"You hear that, Snorts?" said Gibrig, grinning. "All we gotta do is scare off the monster and we can return home heroes."

Snorts…well, he gave a snort.

Sir Eldrick was relieved that they didn't ask any more about it. He took some time to formulate answers for any future questions, knowing that the elf in particular was going to be a bit of trouble. Being highly educated, the prince was sure to be the smartest of the lot, and might have already put two and two together.

Sir Eldrick had considered killing him for a moment—or perhaps just cutting out his tongue—but one way or another, he had to keep the little weasel quiet. Or…perhaps he could strike a *deal* with the stuck-up prince.

Of course, if there was one thing Sir Eldrick knew about royals, it was that they thought of only themselves. Queen Elzabethalynn had taught him that much.

He gave the reins a smart snap and rode to catch up with Brannon, who was getting a bit too far ahead.

"Maintain the distance," he yelled over his shoulder to the others. "I'll go talk to him."

"Tell him I'm sorry I said he was mean," Gibrig called back.

"You don't need to apologize to that stuck-up prince," said Murland as he watched Sir Eldrick riding to catch up with Brannon. "He was being a jerk."

"Sure," said Gibrig. "But he only be a jerk 'cause someone done been a jerk to him. Me pap says it be like a sickness, like givin' someone a cold when ye breathe on 'em. Says that if ye let meanness die with ye, rather than passin' it off to someone else like, ye can really make the world a better place. And maybe someday, after ye've swallowed up all the meanness, well, maybe then no one will call ye tall no more."

Willow regarded him with puzzlement. "No one *gives* someone a cold. Everybody knows they're caused by angry spirits."

"Your pap sounds like a really nice man," said Murland.

Gibrig laughed. "He is, but he ain't a man—he be a dwarf." But then his face became slack, and he bit on his lip nervously. "Ye think Brannon's right?"

"I don't know…to tell you the truth, I've never felt like the champion of anything."

"Me neither," said Gibrig with a frown.

"I've been the champion mud pie eater since I was twelve," Willow proudly proclaimed.

Murland offered a small laugh, but he felt all bound up inside.

What if Brannon was right? he couldn't help but wonder.

CHAPTER 12

A SECRET KEPT IS A THORN IN THE PAW

"Brannon!" Sir Eldrick called to the elf, but if Brannon heard him, he gave no indication.

"Are you deaf?" the knight called again as his horse caught up to the elf prince's white steed.

"You will address me as Prince, or Your Highness, or My Liege, or—"

"What's your problem?" said Sir Eldrick.

Brannon looked as though he had been slapped. "Excuse me?"

"You were pretty rude to the other champions back there. I think that you owe them an apology."

Brannon laid his hands on his hips and cocked his head, looking the knight up and down as he spoke. "I don't know how things work where you're from, Sir Knight, but in Halala, a prince does not apologize to commoners."

"This isn't Halala, this is the road. And we aren't commoners, we're companions," said Sir Eldrick.

Brannon rolled his eyes and gave a long, slow sigh. "You bore me, Sir Knight. Let me know when you have found a suitable camp," he said before spurring his white steed to quicken.

Sir Eldrick wanted to slap the stuck-up prince right off his horse, but he buried his anger and let him go for the time being.

The road leading west from King's Crossing cut through a dense forest of pine and birch trees, dotted here and there with majestic oaks. The forest was quiet but for the trickle of a stream that followed it for a few miles before snaking south and away to the lowlands north of Fire Swamp.

"We'll make camp here for the night," said Sir Eldrick when they came to a clearing beside a brook.

Murland dropped to his knees and fell on his face, exhausted.

"You gonna be alright?" Willow asked as she dismounted from her raptor.

Murland could only groan.

"Alright," said Sir Eldrick. "Let's get something straight. While Kazimir's away, I'm the leader of this group. And as such, I—"

"Excuse me?" said Brannon. "If there is to be a leader, then that leader will be me, of course."

"You know nothing of survival in the wild," said Sir Eldrick.

"Ah, but you do?" Brannon retorted. "It is a quite simple matter, even for a human to understand. I am a prince, and therefore, I will lead as I am meant to. But do not fret, Sir Knight," he said, waving him off like a servant. "You will be my second in command."

Sir Eldrick gave a laugh. "*Second*? We are not in Halala, my pampered prince. Here, on the road to Bad Mountain, you are not a prince, but a champion—one of five. I have trained my entire *life* for a moment such as this."

He regarded each in the group one at a time. "Tell me, have any of you ever slain a monster? Do you know how to spot and avoid ambush sites? Do you know how to set watch detail, or assign duties that best utilizes everyone's skill sets?"

The four exchanged empty glances.

"I didn't think so," said Sir Eldrick. "*I* should be the leader of this group. But alas! I am not a tyrant. I would call a vote. Who here would like me to blaze a trail through the wilds beyond the Wide Wall?"

Murland was the first to raise his hand. Willow quickly followed suit, but Gibrig kept his down and stared at the dirt, looking quite flummoxed at having to take sides.

"Uh huh," said Sir Eldrick, raising his own hand as well. "And how many would like Prince Brannon here to lead?"

Brannon raised his hand for himself and eyed the hog farmer dangerously. At length, Gibrig raised his hand halfheartedly.

"Well then," said Sir Eldrick. "It is three to two in favor of me. I accept your votes. I will do my best to see us all to Bad Mountain and home again. First things first. We need the hog farmer to dig us a shit hole."

Gibrig was already grabbing the shovel strapped to Snorts. "I'm on it, sir," he said with much enthusiasm.

Sir Eldrick pointed at Murland. "How much magic do you know?"

"Uh…some?" Murland offered with a boney shrug.

"What does that mean?" Sir Eldrick asked. "Can you do anything that would speed up making camp?"

Murland shook his head. "Truth is…I don't—"

"Of course you do! For now, just set up the tents," Sir Eldrick told him, glancing at the others.

He then turned to Willow. "You—be a good ogre and find us a nice lot of firewood to burn. Good and dry now, none of that stinking mossy stuff your kind fancies."

Finally, he came to Brannon and hooked a summoning finger at him. "You and I shall water the horses."

Sir Eldrick took his black stallion and led it to the riverbank, and, reluctantly, Brannon followed close behind. When the horses found the stream, the two champions squared on each other.

"If you expect me to follow *you*," Brannon began, "well, good sir, you are out of your mind."

"Are you quite as stupid as you sound?" Sir Eldrick asked dryly.

Brannon was taken aback. He clutched his chest and huffed dramatically. "Why…I NEVER!"

"Of course you haven't. You're a spoiled little bitch who's never been told no."

"I…I've been told no," Brannon stammered.

"Listen, twinkle toes, I'm not your enemy. You seem rather smart, truth be told. And that is the only reason I'm talking to you." Sir Eldrick leaned in a little closer and glanced around. "I can see you know that something strange is going on here…You do, don't you?"

Brannon forgot his indignation in a flash but regarded Sir Eldrick cautiously. "Yes…I do."

"Of course," said Sir Eldrick. "Now, because you're smart, and because you're a highborn—and above the rest of that ridiculous lot—Kazimir and I have decided to bring you into the fold."

"Tell me the truth then, Sir Knight."

Sir Eldrick glanced back at the camp. "The truth is…this lot is doomed. And you with it, until I decided to bring you in on the plan, of course.

"You see; this whole champion business is a big lie. We're no prophetic champions of the dragon. We are dragon *food*. But, if you help me get those idiots unwittingly to the mountain, you and I shall both return home victors—and without ever even lifting a blade against the dragon."

Brannon choked up and began fanning himself with his hand. "Oh, thank the gods!"

"Shhh—you rainbow cake," snapped Sir Eldrick. "They'll hear."

Brannon sat on the bank of the river and rocked himself. "I'm sorry, I'm sorry. It's just that…you don't know how scared I was. I thought I was doomed."

Sir Eldrick wanted to push him in.

"Listen, flower petal, I don't know if you've ever heard this before, but you need to start acting like a man. If you're going to just go through life in fear, I can slit your throat here and now and toss your frail body in the river. That's about all your life will be worth anyway. But if you want to prove your father wrong, if you want to show him that not only do you love men, but you *are* a man, then get up off your pretty ass and let's do this."

Brannon took in a shocked breath, and it seemed to Sir Eldrick that the prince might cry. But the elf soon stood tall and threw back his padded shoulders with overdramatic flair. "I am with you, Sir Knight!"

Sir Eldrick studied Brannon's sincerity and finally nodded.

"Good. First things first—quit being such a little prick to the others. We've still got to get them to Bad Mountain, which means actually going beyond the Wide Wall. We need them to be confident. We need to bring out the best in them, else it'll be our necks, and we're not going to do that with you treating them like a bunch of simpletons."

"What about Kazimir?" Brannon asked, looking concerned.

Sir Eldrick waved off the notion. "You can only count on wizards when they can't be counted on. They're a queer lot."

Brannon raised a brow.

"Anyway," Sir Eldrick went on. "We've got to give them some confidence. You think you can do that?"

"I'll try," said Brannon.

When they returned to camp, they found a small fire going and all the tents set up. Murland and the others were sitting around the fire pit on large stones, chatting like old friends.

"Well," said Sir Eldrick cheerily, "I see you've all found seats. But what about dinner?"

The three eyed each other.

"Right then," he continued. "Let's take an inventory of what we've got."

They all went for their packs and spilled the contents on the ground in the firelight. There were a few loaves of bread, some smoked meat, a rolled-up wheel of stinky cheese that Willow swore was delicious—and of course, Brannon's dried nuts and berries—but it would not be enough to see them all the way to Bad Mountain.

"This will need to be remedied," said Sir Eldrick.

Just then, there was a flash of light, and when the smoke cleared, Kazimir was standing in front of them on the other side of the fire.

"Kazimir!" cried Willow.

"Ancient One!" said Gibrig excitedly.

"Ah, so I see you've all made camp for the night," said the wizard jovially. "Now, what's this I hear about food?"

"We're hungry," said Willow.

"Hmm," replied Kazimir, tapping his bearded chin. "I suppose that your first night together calls for celebration...yes, I think I might have just the spell."

He waggled his fingers while reciting strange words, and just like that, a long table set for a king's banquet appeared before them.

A moment before, far to the east, King Nimrod of Magestra was standing at the head of a long table, about to give a toast. Seated before him were dignitaries from the far eastern island of Icebite. The peace negotiations had been going well, and now the king needed only to seal the deal with a dinner—the most respected of Icebithian customs.

The king raised his glass. "To the good people of Icebite. May your sails ever catch the wind, and may our alliance flourish. Let this fine dinner be a token of my respect for your people, and a symbol of our undying—"

Before he could finish, the table suddenly vanished into thin air.

"What is the meaning of this!" cried one of the dignitaries as he shot to his feet, bone necklaces chattering. "You insult us with devilry?"

"No...I...I," the king stammered, staring in wonder at the empty space where the table had been.

"This means WAR!" the islander cried.

The champions ate merrily that night. There were dishes of roasted duck, fish, chicken, beef—and to Gibrig's dismay—pig head cheese. Many bottles of wine had come with the table as well, and before the midnight hour had arrived, the lot of them were right drunk—surprisingly, all but Sir Eldrick.

"Here is to the Champions of Drak'Noir," said Kazimir, raising his goblet.

Everyone joined in, even Brannon, whose demeanor had changed dramatically since his talk with Sir Eldrick.

"Does this mean ye're going to be traveling with us the rest of the way?" Gibrig asked hopefully.

"Don't be a fool," said Kazimir. "I've already made myself quite clear in that regard."

"Well," said Gibrig, scratching his head. "Why can't ye just whoosh us off to Bad Mountain like ye brought this table here?"

The group went silent and eyed the wizard curiously.

"Yeah," said Willow with a mouthful of food. "Jush whoosh us."

"It can't be as easy as *that*," said Brannon, eyeing the wizard. "Can it?"

"Of course it's not that easy, else I would have done it already," said Kazimir, waving them off and sipping his wine.

"But why can't you?" asked Willow, confused.

"Hasn't anyone ever told you not to ask a wizard about his craft?" said an increasingly agitated Kazimir. "It's considered rude."

Willow shrugged.

Kazimir shook his head and emptied his glass before wiping his mouth with the end of his beard. Abruptly, he stood and jerked his robe back from his hand to check the small clock strapped to his wrist. "Yes, it is getting late—I must be off."

"So soon?" said Murland.

"Can't ye at least just stay for a song?" Gibrig asked.

Kazimir looked at him with mild disgust. "A song? What do you take me for—a wizard or a bumbling bard? No, my dear champions, you go on and sing till the pigs come home. I have people to be and places to see." He walked toward the road, waving to the drunken fools halfheartedly over his shoulder.

"Ancient One," called Sir Eldrick, running to catch up with the grumpy wizard. "I would have a word."

When they were out of earshot and walking beneath the boughs of some drooping willows, Kazimir said, "Speak your mind, knight, but make it quick. I have much to do."

"I had to bring the elf in on the secret," said Sir Eldrick conspiratorially. "He knows the true nature of this quest."

"Yes, I know. I could see it in his eyes. He was practically *winking* at me…I am surprised that you didn't just toss him in a river and be done with it. But I must say, this shows good judgment on your part. And you didn't drink a drop of spirits at dinner. This is good as well. You just might get through this alive yet. But the elf will still be fed to the dragon. It is bad enough I will only have four fools for her. You just keep leading him on and let him believe whatever fantasies he needs to get him through the journey."

Kazimir turned from Sir Eldrick and whistled. Around a distant bend in the road came a black unicorn with a horn like an onyx saber. The beast stopped and knelt before the wizard, and Kazimir climbed up onto its back.

"Continue on to the west," he said to Sir Eldrick. "I will see you again before the Wide Wall."

The knight watched him go, wondering as always where it was that he went off to.

Just then Murland came running up, all in a huff.

"Damn! He's gone already? But I needed to speak with him about my wand."

"What is this that you are so worked up about, son?" Sir Eldrick asked. He rested a gentle hand on Murland's shoulder, like a father or a big brother, and started leading him back toward the camp.

"Well for one, I've never cast a single spell. Secondly, I've got to figure out a way to fix this wand."

Sir Eldrick scratched his beard. "Hmm…well…it is a long way to Bad Mountain—I'm sure you'll have time to—"

"But who will teach me?"

"Don't worry, young Murland, we'll be sure to see Kazimir again before we cross the Wide Wall. You can ask him about it all then."

Murland let out a long sigh as he kicked a loose stone.

Sir Eldrick knew the young man's mind; he was doubting himself and the group as well. He stopped the wizard apprentice before they reached camp and took him by the shoulders.

"You must have *some* magic in you if you were chosen for this quest. Why do you fret so?"

"I'm not the wizard for this job," said Murland, shaking his head. "I can't even cast one spell without blowing myself up. The truth is, I never passed my test. Technically…I'm not even a wizard."

Sir Eldrick considered this, or seemed to at least. At the moment he was actually thinking about all the bottles of wine on the table back at camp. "Do you have faith in Kazimir?" he asked.

"Well…yeah," said Murland.

"Good. Then you must have faith in his choices. He *is* the Most High, after all. You will find your power. I believe you will, and so does Kazimir. That should be enough for you. Perhaps you should spend less time worrying about what you can't do, and instead focus on what you can do. I don't know much about magic, but I know that one must believe in their ability to do it, else even the most powerful wizard will be unable to perform."

"I guess you're right," said Murland, his back straightening a bit.

"Of course I am. Now let's get back to camp before that food lures the bears—or worse."

CHAPTER 13

---✕---

ONLY FOOLS TRY TO FLY

THE MORNING CAME to Fallacetine much too quickly for the hungover companions' liking. The song birds were out, singing of the glory of spring, but they made Willow's head pound, and she found herself wishing that she could eat them all. Heavy fog hung in the lowlands visible from the hill, but the sight only reminded Gibrig of the dawn as seen from the saddle point of the Mountain Pass, where he had lived with his father all his short life. There was not a cloud in the sky; however, to Brannon, the slowly rising sun burned his dry and itchy eyes. Murland emerged from his small tent holding his aching head and wishing that he had some of old High Wizard Waverly's magic hangover potion, or as the wizard affectionately called it, "Hair of the Dog."

"Good morning!" said Sir Eldrick, who, unlike the others, looked as bright-eyed and bushy-tailed as a Vhalovian hare in spring.

"Morning," Murland said, stifling a yawn.

"What's good about it?" Brannon asked in a sleepy voice.

Sir Eldrick ignored him and took in the morning air as he looked west, like a conquering king feasting his eyes on newly dominated land.

"Where's the food? Didn't you make any breakfast?" Willow asked before giving a big yawn and scratching her backside.

"The food, my dear ogre, is in our bellies," said Sir Eldrick before turning to the group and spreading his arms wide. "Well then, the road awaits. Break down your tents, clean yourselves up, and be ready in ten minutes."

A chorus of groans answered him, and he turned, undeterred, and mounted his horse.

Murland and the others did as they were told. They had voted him in as their leader after all, and besides, the sooner they got going, the sooner they might come upon something to eat.

In ten minutes' time, the companions were ready. Willow sat high upon her monstrous raptor, Gibrig upon his hog, and Brannon on his white steed. The prince was completely preoccupied with applying his coloring, and quite ignoring the others as he fussed over himself. Murland finished lacing up his boots and mentally prepared himself for a long day of marching, though he did have ideas to ask Gibrig for a ride, or perhaps Sir Eldrick. There was no way he was riding on a raptor, and Brannon, well, Murland knew that asking him was pointless, and likely to gain him more than one pert insult. He tried to stay positive, despite the raging headache and fog of dizziness and melancholy hanging over his head, and reminded himself that it could be worse. He packed the last of his things in his backpack and tossed it into the air as one might a dove. It rose, and then began to drop, when suddenly it spread its wings and flew into the sky.

"Ah then, it looks like everyone is ready. Shall we?" said Sir Eldrick, almost singing.

Murland wondered about his chipper mood, and why the legendary drunk who was more often called Slur Sirsalot hadn't indulged in spirits the night before. Perhaps he had taken a vow of sobriety. Perhaps it was his love for the road and grand adventure. Whatever it was, Murland envied the knight his joy.

At Sir Eldrick's direction, the group headed out down the road leading west. The knight even whistled as he rode, and Murland hoped that he didn't break out into song. Sir Eldrick had sang the night before, in a deep baritone that had lent well to the wine-infused merriment, but now that deeply powerful voice would be like having a ringing gong for a pillow.

Willow grumbled all morning long, saying it wasn't natural to start your day without food and drink. She didn't remember the last time she had missed a breakfast, or any other meal for that matter. In a voice filled with longing, she rattled off all the different kinds of ogre food that she had enjoyed for breakfast back in Fire Swamp: crocodile eggs with fire toad blood, swamp weed and pussy willow biscuits, lightning eel soup, snails on a half shell, turtle brains, pickled tadpoles, lizard bile, and her favorite, slug jelly and crispy crickets spread on mushroom caps—the list went on for nearly ten minutes.

Murland and Gibrig shared a sour glance that grew with every word, and had soon completely lost their appetites.

She gave a sigh when she finished. "Don't you know its bad luck to start the day without a proper meal?" she asked Sir Eldrick, whose horse was eying her raptor warily.

"Believing in bad luck *is* bad luck, my ever-hungry ogre," he said with a chuckle. "No, we've a long way to go, and there will not always be food to fill our bellies. Best you get used to tightening your belt."

Willow let her raptor fall back and offered the knight a thumbs-up behind his back, causing Gibrig to take in a shocked breath.

Gibrig eyed her with a scowl when she settled in to keep pace with him. "That was not nice at all," he said with all seriousness. He lowered his voice and whispered, "I know that a thumbs-up is the rudest of gestures in ogre society."

She turned to him and flipped him not one, but two fat green thumbs.

"Hey, that wasn't nice either," he protested, looking quite hurt.

"Oh, for Great Turtle's sake, lighten up," said Willow, rolling her eyes.

"She's just mad because *she* ate all the food last night," said Brannon, who was suddenly on Gibrig's right, his white steed pacing the hog and raptor. "The sound woke me from a dead sleep. I thought it must be that your hog had gotten into the scraps by the sound of it, but when I looked, there she was, stuffing her fat green face."

"Hey!" said Gibrig.

Brannon ignored him and offered Willow one last leering glare before raising his chin high and spurring his steed into a gallop.

"Don't pay no attention to him," said Gibrig. "He just likes to make people feel bad 'cause someone made him feel bad. I don't think yer face be fat."

Willow snapped her head toward Gibrig and stared at him indignantly. "It's not?" she said with alarm and felt her round cheeks with her large hands. "Oh no, I'm getting skinny."

"What? No...er," Gibrig stammered.

"Won't you let us butcher the hog?" Willow asked Gibrig miserably, all the while eyeing Snorts and the way his plump bottom wiggled. She could just imagine the bacon that could be got from the hog, enough for one, maybe even two breakfasts.

Gibrig's face went from confused to indignant in a flash. He crossed his arms tightly. "I'm sorry, but the answer still be no."

"Fine," Willow spat at him, and she quickly turned her eyes on Brannon's horse.

The champions followed the western road for many miserable hours. The forest gave way to rocky hills dotted with bearberries and patches of witch grass, along with twisted junipers and dragon's tongue, whose long red flowers were just beginning to bloom. The foothills led south to a small range, where distant peaks stood clumped shoulder to shoulder. Their silver caps flirted with a blanket of white clouds that seemed frozen in time. Beams of light, like the arrows of the gods, pierced the cloud cover in spots, gloriously illuminating the lush spring foliage and dark, stony valleys.

The range, called by the dwarves the Silver Mountains, had been the home of the ancestors of the dwarves. The mountains had been abandoned by the dwarves centuries before, when a tribe of giants had finally been run out of Fire Swamp by the ogres and sought shelter in the high peaks. It was said that the giants lived there still, and many a brave human knight and dwarven warrior looking to make a name for themselves had ventured into those dark hills, never to be heard from again.

Gibrig eyed those distant peaks gravely. His father had been one of those brave dwarves to try and take back the mountain long before Gibrig was born. Hagus had set out with the late King Bonesteel and a thousand other dwarves. Only fifty had made it back alive. Hagus Hogstead had lost an eye in that battle and still wore the old army issue patch over his empty left socket. He had told Gibrig that though he lost an eye, he now saw more than he had before. "War be a scourge on us all," Hagus had told Gibrig more than once. "Revenge got no end, and its price be blood, and it be paid for generations, 'til no one remembers what they be fightin' for."

There were many dwarves in the Iron Mountains who swore to avenge not only King Bonesteel, but all their fallen ancestors. But Hagus was not one of those dwarves. He, like many others, had given up on the idea. The Silver Mountain mines were not half as bountiful as their much larger counterparts. "Let the blasted giants keep 'em," some would argue at the pubs, only to be refuted by the usual, "Someday, I tell ye, we be takin' back them mountains, mark me words. And a glorious day it's to be."

Gibrig tended to agree with his father. It was better to just let it go and live in peace.

"You're thinking of the giants, ain't you?" said Willow, looking down at Gibrig with a sympathetic frown that left her bottom lip curled beneath her thick tusks.

"A lot of dwarves died down there," said Gibrig somberly.

Willow nodded, not knowing what to say. Many dwarves still blamed the ogres for what happened, being that it was they who drove the giants north into dwarven territory in the first place.

"The elders say that we'll take it back some day," said Gibrig. "But I hope they don't even try. Too many dwarves and giants will get hurt."

"You're worried about the giants?" said Willow incredulously.

"Well...yeah," said Gibrig with a shrug. "It weren't their fault. They was just looking for a place to live. The ogres weren't too nice to them ye know, neither were the humans or elves. It's like me pap says, meanness be like a disease, it be spread from one person to another, and gets stronger and stronger. The only way to beat it be with love."

Willow shook her head. "I don't understand you sometimes."

Gibrig only smiled. "That's alright, not many people do."

Murland had heard the exchange between the ogre and dwarf. He tore his eyes away from the Silver Mountains with a shiver and went back to his spell book. He was forced to walk and read at the same time, being the only one without a mount, and so far, he found it quite frustrating. The flowing script looked to be a combination of dwarven, elven, ogre, and human writing forms, but knowing only human and some Elvish writing, Murland was at a loss to translate it.

Tired and frustrated with the spell book, he turned to the broken wand and focused on a mending spell that he knew. He had never successfully cast the spell, for he had never successfully cast any spell, but it was a long road to Bad Mountain, and even the frustrating task helped him to pass the long, boring hours and forget about his hangover. He waved his hand over the wand, murmuring the words he had learned from the high wizards, but of course, nothing happened.

"Well then, let's see what you got, wizard," said Brannon, who had been riding behind him the entire time.

"What do you mean?" asked Murland sheepishly.

"I mean *magic*, what else?"

Murland's eyes quickly darted to the ground, his mind racing. He glanced from the wand to the spell book before settling back on Brannon.

"I—"

"Yeah, let's see some magix!" Willow said, jumping in. She slowed her raptor to ride on the other side of Murland.

He noticed then that everyone's attention was on him.

"I…well…you see," Murland stammered, not wanting to tell them that he hadn't any magic at all.

He looked to the sky, wondering what he should do, and spotted the backpack as it glided overhead. An idea suddenly struck him.

"How would you like to see me fly?" he asked them all with newfound confidence.

"Whoa, you *serious*?" Willow asked.

Murland put two fingers in his mouth and whistled, and everyone watched eagerly as the backpack swooped down and landed among them.

"*This* should be good," said Brannon with a smirk as he sat back in the saddle.

Sir Eldrick shot him a warning scowl.

"Alright," said Murland, approaching the backpack slowly, as one trying to catch a chicken might stalk the creature. "You just wait and see." With that, he lunged forward and quickly caught the winged pack, slinging it over his shoulder before he lost his nerve.

Everyone watched with growing anticipation as Murland prepared himself, for indeed, it was the most excitement they'd had all day.

Murland let out a long slow breath and rolled his shoulder. "Here goes nothing," he said to himself and took off at a run. When he reached top speed, he began leaping in the air repeatedly and trying to coax the backpack to spread its wings and fly. "Up, up, up...fly you blasted backpack!" he yelled pleadingly.

The others kicked their steeds to catch up to him and cheer him on.

"You can do it!" cried Gibrig, whose eyes had begun to tear up for some reason.

"Jump higher!" Willow yelled jubilantly.

Murland ran and ran. He leapt and jumped, hopped and skipped, and even pleaded with the backpack, but the stubborn leather sack refused to comply.

Brannon laughed when Murland stopped in his charge and took a knee to catch his breath. "Maybe you should try jumping off a cliff," he said, lazily sitting sidesaddle and filing his nails.

"Perhaps he just needs more encouragement," said Sir Eldrick through gritted teeth masked by a too-big smile.

The elf let out a sigh. "You can do it, Murland," he yelled rather unconvincingly.

The frustrated wizard glanced at a twisted old elm tree sitting off to the left of the road. *Maybe Brannon is right*, he thought. He picked himself up and dusted off his star-patterned robes before marching over to the elm. With nimble grace, he began to climb carefully up, up, up.

"Be careful!" Gibrig yelled, biting his nails as he watched.

Sir Eldrick leaned over to Brannon and spoke so that only the elf could hear. "If he breaks a leg, I'm giving him *your* horse for the rest of the trip," he said pleasantly, even offering the elf a wink.

Brannon offered the knight an indignant glare and then turned to watch Murland, who was already halfway up the fifty-foot tree.

When he was near the top, he scuttled out to the middle of a long thick branch and steadied himself, standing shakily. He glanced down and immediately wished he hadn't. The ground beneath him was rocky, and a fall from this height was sure to end his short-lived career as a hero.

"You better open your damned little wings this time," he said, glancing over his shoulder at the backpack. "Else I'm going to turn you into underpants for Willow."

The enchanted backpack offered no indication that it had heard the warning, and its wings remained tucked against its sides, motionless.

Murland found himself wondering for a lucid moment how he had gone from studying the spell book to leaping from an elm tree.

"Here goes nothing," he said under his breath. And before he could change his mind, he leapt off the tree, spreading his arms out wide and closing his eyes.

He sailed out over the branches, hair billowing in the wind, and began to fall like a stone. Murland opened his eyes and cried out when he saw the road rushing up to meet him. "Fly!" he cried, flapping his arms frantically.

And he landed hard in a puddle before the group with an explosive, "Oof!"

Willow gave a squealing, "Eek!"

"You alright?" Gibrig asked, leaping from Snorts and running over.

Brannon suddenly burst into quick and sudden laughter, though he quickly clipped his mirth after glancing over at Sir Eldrick, who sat watching with growing concern.

"Murland, are you alright?" said the knight.

But before Murland could answer, or Gibrig could reach him, the backpack finally decided to start flying. It opened its wings wide and began flapping them furiously, shooting Murland down the road and dragging him across dirt and mud for a hundred yards before finally taking to the sky. The poor wizard's apprentice cried out in fear and exhilaration, desperately wiping at his eyes to see where he was going.

The backpack took him out over the rocky terrain. It then suddenly dove down and flew low over the road before pulling straight up and thrusting toward the clouds.

"That's high enough!" Murland cried, clutching the straps and kicking his legs.

Murland breathed a little easier when the backpack complied and leveled out. "Good...this is good," he said breathlessly.

No sooner had he said the words than the backpack dove straight down once more.

Murland screamed the whole way down and braced himself for impact as they hurtled toward the road where the other champions stood watching. To Murland's relief though, the pack straightened out again and flew level with the road.

"Look out!" Murland cried as they came hurtling toward Brannon.

The elf gave a high-pitched yelp and fell back off his horse, landing in a puddle as Murland zipped by overhead.

"Put me down!" Murland urged the pack.

To his surprise, the backpack spread its wings wide and came to a sudden stop. Murland hit the ground running and quickly shed the pack, tossing it in the air and letting it fly off on its own. He stood there panting and blinking his eyes in disbelief. He turned to the group, who—aside from Brannon—was staring at him in shock and adoration. Murland burst into a sudden fit of laughter and raised his fists into the air triumphantly.

Gibrig and Willow cheered joyfully and ran to congratulate him. They patted his back and shook his hand, wanting to know all about what it was like to fly.

Brannon just sat there in the muck, shaking and staring down at his dirty clothes with disgust.

Murland broke from the others and walked over to Brannon and Sir Eldrick. "Sorry about the fly-by," he said, reaching out a hand to help the pitiful elf prince up.

Brannon ignored the gesture and lifted himself out of the mire with an indignant scoff, huffing in disgust at the state of his clothing.

As Murland went back to the others, Sir Eldrick made his way over to Brannon and stared down at him wryly from atop his steed.

"Perhaps that will teach you not to be such a wench. I told you that we need to help them find their confidence," he said so the others wouldn't hear.

"You saw how the panic crossed his face when I asked him to show me some magic?" said Brannon, pointing at the celebrating wizard apprentice. "He doesn't know anything. Have you seen his wand? It's held together with tape. He'll never be worth his weight in donkey dung—and *I'm* supposed to help him find confidence?"

"He can fly," said Eldrick matter-of-factly. "Can you? Listen, sweetheart, this is going to be a long road, and I don't have time for your mood swings. Stick to the damned plan and keep your attitude in check."

Brannon mocked Sir Eldrick as he rode away, silently mimicking the knight behind his back. He then mounted his own horse, snapped the reins, and followed sullenly, wishing all the while that Val was there with him. If there was one elf who could put Sir Eldrick in his place, it was Valkimir.

CHAPTER 14

BJORN TIBIWILD

THAT NIGHT, THE group made camp off the road on the well-worn bank of the trickling Brook of Many Sorrows. Once the hole was dug, the horses watered and fed, and the fire stoked, Murland sat back with the others around the fire. Sir Eldrick had snared a hare, and Willow had found and killed a small snake. Both kills hung from sticks above the fire. While they waited for the meager meal, Gibrig took his flute from his pack and began playing "Ode to the Highland Maiden."

Oddly enough, the song was familiar to Willow, who sang along with the haunting melody, surprising everyone with her velvety smooth voice.

Even Brannon had nothing bad to say about the night's entertainment. On the contrary, he was spurred by passion to outdo them, and when they had finished, he took up a golden fiddle from one of his many packs and began playing.

The beautiful song that mournfully issued from his instrument that night left even the stoic Sir Eldrick teary-eyed. The knight had been battling with the urge to drink from the flask going around all night, but every time it was offered to him, he refused, saying that morning would be coming soon.

When the meat was brown and sizzling, he cut it into equal portions and handed it out to the eager companions. Willow stared at her share and glanced around at the others'. "These ain't equal portions," she said angrily.

"You are mistaken, my good ogre. They are all the same size, give or take a nibble or two."

"Yeah, well *we* ain't all the same size. I'm four times bigger than most of you, why should I get the same rations?"

"Because you'd still complain that you were hungry, even if you ate it all," said Brannon.

Sir Eldrick gave him a warning scowl. "We all need to get used to being hungry. Kazimir's banquet will not be a regular occurrence, I promise you that."

Willow was not pleased with the dodgy answer. She popped the rabbit leg and bite of snake into her mouth, crunching the bones and eyeing Brannon's horse hungrily.

"Do you like greens?" Brannon asked her, having followed her eyes and wanting to redirect her attention.

"I could eat just about anything right now."

"Good. I have a variety of seeds in my saddle bags," said the elf. "Tomorrow, when the sun is out, I can grow us something more to eat."

Sir Eldrick offered Brannon an approving nod from across the fire.

"What ya mean, grow us some food?" Willow asked with growing intrigue.

"I am quite skilled at floral magic," said Brannon with evident pride.

"You know magic?" said Murland, nearly leaping from the stump he sat on.

"Indeed, but it is elven magic, and not something that I could ever teach you," said Brannon.

"Couldn't hurt to try," said Sir Eldrick, offering Brannon a look.

Brannon returned the gesture with a curt nod. "Perhaps I could try," he told Murland.

Just then, a sound came from the road to the west. Everyone stopped to listen, for the sound was strange, and nothing like any of them had ever heard.

Glurp glurp, clang clang, bizz buzz, the noises sounded in the quiet night.

Sir Eldrick rose first, reaching for his sword but not unsheathing it. With his other hand he indicated for the others to stay back.

Glurp glurp, clang, clang, bizz buzz.

Eldrick took one, two, three steps toward the road and stood tall, pushing out his formidable chest and waiting.

Glurp glurp, clang, clang, bizz buzz.

The sound grew louder, and Murland couldn't imagine what kind of beast it might be that had found them on the road to the Wide Wall.

Another *glurp glurp* brought the thing into the firelight; it was no creature, but a contraption of some sort.

"Who goes there?" Sir Eldrick asked in a commanding voice.

There was a dark figure on the contraption, and Murland got up to see better. His fear was forgotten in the face of his intrigue.

The figure, which Murland guessed to be a man, albeit a very large man dressed in dark leather, dismounted from the big clunking contraption and flicked a switch.

With a final *glurp glurp, clang, clang, bizz buzz*, and a long hiss, the contraption went silent, and steam issued from a pipe at the rear like smoke from a dragon's snout.

"Who, you ask? Who, I ask," came a deep, jolly voice.

"I say again, good sir, who are you?" said Sir Eldrick, standing his ground.

Murland crept up and eyed the contraption as the two men stared at each other. It had big wheels, taller than himself; one in the front and one in the back. In the front, above the wheel, was a lantern encased in some sort of mirror box, which reflected the dim light within and amplified it, illuminating the forest beyond. There was a long leather saddle housed above a shiny silver conglomeration of pipes, which was connected by a wooden frame to the rear tire.

"You have already guessed my name, for I am indeed called 'Good Sir' by many. Who, may I ask, are you who have decided to camp in my hills?"

"These hills belong to no man," said Sir Eldrick. "This land belongs to the unified kingdoms of Fallacetine."

"Of course, of course," said the man. "But I belong to them. As surely as you belong somewhere else. But alas, as your host, I will forego the riddles and speak plainly, for the lot of you look hungry."

The man stepped forward into the firelight and stuck out a strong-looking hand. "I am Bjorn, Bjorn Tibiwild."

Sir Eldrick nodded and forsook his hilt for Bjorn's hand. "Sir Eldrick van Albright. That is one hell of a contraption that you ride upon."

"That, yes, the making of trinkets and contraptions is a hobby of mine," said Bjorn.

Murland offered the man a nod when those deep green eyes fell upon him. Bjorn stood well over six feet tall and was stocky about the chest, like a dwarf. But his arms were long like a man, and he gave an air of magic and mystery like that of an elf. His face was burly with a winter beard, and his skin was well weathered, but those bright eyes twinkled beyond the proud nose.

"These are my companions," said Eldrick, waving a hand back at the group. "We are traveling west, and looking for no trouble."

"Well," said Bjorn with a merry chuckle, "the west is certainly the place to find trouble, but you know that, don't you? What I know is that you are hungry, and I have food. Do you care to join me?"

Sir Eldrick eyed the strange man, taking a good measure of him. "Where is this food you speak of?"

"Why, just over those hills there yonder," he said, pointing north beyond the camp.

"What kind of foods you got?" Willow asked, coming to stand beside Sir Eldrick and Murland.

"Food fit for an ogre," said Bjorn, looking her up and down with admiration. He glanced over the group, seeming to sense their apprehension.

Suddenly he burst into song and began colorfully dancing among them, his loud, boisterous voice rolling over the hills.

"You got your horses running, you went out on the highway.

Looking for adventure, and you have come my way."

He pointed at Willow and added, *"Yeah damsel gonna get wings flappin'. Take you up out of this place. Fire all my arrows at once. And explode in your face."*

He moved next to Murland and put a hand on the young man's shoulder. He spread his other hand across the horizon with eyes of wonder.

"I conjure rain and lightning. Hard rolling thunder.

Mind is racing like the wind. From the wizard leaf I'm under."

With a laugh he threw a fist into the air and brought it down, pointing right at Brannon.

"Yeah damsel gonna get wings flappin'. Take you up out of this place.
Fire all my arrows at once. And explode in your face."

Then with a great flourish of his leather robes he spun in a circle and stopped before them, pointing at himself.

"I'm a true nature's child. I am Bjorn, Bjorn Tibiwild.
We can get so high, never gonna die!"

The companions stared, at a loss for words. Nevertheless, Bjorn took a bow with a flourish and turned back to his wheeled contraption. "Follow me, friends!" he called back, and he kicked a metal bar, which caused the strange wooden mount to roar to life.

Willow wasted no time running to her raptor and leaping onto its back. Brannon just stood and stared at Sir Eldrick, looking worried. Murland and Gibrig waited for the knight's approval as well. "Come on then, let's see what he's got to offer. Seems like a nice enough fellow, if a little…theatrical," said the knight.

Murland followed close behind Snorts at the rear of the group as they followed Bjorn's loud and steaming contraption off the road and into the hills. The night was mild, with only a whisper of wind, and the stars were out, unhindered by all but the tiniest of clouds. Glow bugs danced at the tops of those rolling hills, giving the night a magical feel.

They traversed a dozen hills, and all the while Bjorn sang his strange song. Murland began to wonder how far into the northern hills they might have to venture. The mounds rolled on for miles, and Murland was beginning to wonder if they weren't making a mistake following the strange man into the unknown.

Finally, as they were coming down another of the earthen lumps, Bjorn stopped his contraption and leapt off. He ran, laughing, toward a bolder half buried by the hill that it seemed moored to.

"Come, come my friends," he said, waving them over happily. "Do tie your mounts off on one of the trees. Don't want them running off. Come, come, I believe I hear my blessed wife Ling Ling cooking now!"

Sir Eldrick glanced over at Murland with a cocked brow, but the wizard could only shrug. Willow, of course, had already tied off her raptor and was hustling to follow.

Bjorn pushed down a tree branch and lifted another, and the boulder swung out with a creak, as though it were on large iron hinges. Light spilled out of the opening in the hill, as well as the foreign song of a maiden, and the big man soon disappeared inside.

"Come on then, let's not be rude," said Sir Eldrick, tying off his horse and following Willow. Murland glanced back at Gibrig and Brannon. The elf sniffed at the air suspiciously. The smell of pie was riding upon it, and it lifted Murland's heart, for it reminded him of the kitchens back at Abra Tower. "Smells like we're in luck," he said to the others.

Gibrig nodded happily, while Brannon remained stone-faced and rigid. "We'll see," said the elf ominously. "We'll see."

Murland gulped and hesitated, but the elf laughed and followed Gibrig into the earth tunnel.

The song grew louder as the tunnel wound this way and that before them. Murland took up the rear, straining to see past the taller elf.

"I've brought company, my beloved!" he heard Bjorn boasting.

The tunnel opened into a room, and Murland scanned it quickly. He took in a quick, shocked breath when he saw the maiden, for her look was most exotic. She had long, straight black hair, a lithe form, a soft, bright face, and large, slanted eyes. Her white dress was sleek and tight fitting, with long sleeves and a high collar. Flower patterns were embroidered down the front.

"Are you an angel?" Murland heard Gibrig ask in a dreamy voice.

"This is my beloved Ling Ling," said Bjorn, and the exotic maiden bent at the waist in a smart bow.

"Ni hao," said Ling Ling with a bright smile.

"She says hello," said Bjorn, beaming.

"Hello, and ni hao to you too," said Sir Eldrick with a bow.

"Ni hao," said Murland, grinning. He liked the sound of that.

As the others returned the greeting, Murland took a quick survey of the large room they found themselves in. At the northern end stood Bjorn and

Ling Ling beside a large cooking pit, and behind them were many ovens stacked one on top of another between the cabinetry and shelves. A wash basin was off to the side, fed by a spigot in the wall from which poured crystal clear water. The area to the left looked to be a sitting room, for a large fireplace adorned the eastern wall, and beside it were many volumes of old-looking books upon shelves reaching all the way to the high ceiling of earth and roots. Many chairs, couches, and sofas were arranged around the fire, accompanied by stands holding candles and books both opened and closed. To the right, along the western wall, there sat a finely crafted wooden table with a dozen chairs and places set for seven. An elaborate silver candelabra hung above the table, and twelve candles burned within it. Behind the table was a tunnel that stretched off into darkness.

"Come, sit. You must be weary from the road," said Bjorn, kicking off his huge boots and taking a seat at the head of the table.

Sir Eldrick nodded to the other companions, his quick eyes moving to their own boots, and he took his off before joining Bjorn. The companions followed suit and sat as well, and Ling Ling, obviously well versed in the virtues of a good host, filled their glasses with wine and placed a loaf of steaming bread on the table along with a heaping bowl of butter.

Willow grabbed the loaf before anyone else had a chance to and stuffed it in her mouth. She chewed and chewed with her eyes closed, groaning with pleasure. When she opened them and saw that everyone, even Ling Ling, was staring at her, she gulped the loaf down and tried to muffle a burp.

"I was hungry," she said self-consciously.

"We're all hungry, you giant oaf," said Brannon with disgust.

Ling Ling burst into laughter then and rattled off with a string of strange words. Bjorn laughed as well, in agreement with whatever it was that his wife had said.

"What?" said Willow, wiping her mouth, her eyes wide with obvious paranoia.

"She says that you are a hungry one. And she is pleased. Ling Ling loves to cook, and she says that perhaps she has found a belly that she cannot fill."

Willow glanced around at the others and sat up straighter. She smiled at Ling Ling. "Challenge accepted," she said with great satisfaction.

Another loaf of bread was set before her, and one each for the others as well. But just as Willow was about to bite into the sweet-smelling bread, Bjorn raised his chalice in a toast.

"Might I have something else?" Sir Eldrick said before the toast could be made. "I'm, er, trying to kick the habit."

"But of course!" said Bjorn before conveying to Ling Ling Sir Eldrick's wish. "She asks if you would like goat's milk, tea, cider, or water?"

"Cider will do just fine," said the knight.

When the drink was poured, Sir Eldrick raised his glass with the others.

"To the great wide open, and infinite possibility," said Bjorn.

"Here here!" said Sir Eldrick, and clanged glasses with them all.

Ling Ling brought the first course, a meat pie with gravy that had Willow drooling with desire. They dined and they supped, and all the while, Bjorn told them of the wider world beyond Fallacetine.

"I knew by your exotic wife that you must be a well-traveled man," said Sir Eldrick as he pushed his empty plate to the side. "But I had no idea just how well traveled you were."

Bjorn laughed merrily and lit up his pipe. "It is true that I have been far and wide, but I did not find Ling Ling during my travels. She was a gift from the great Kazimir, who saved her from a terrible marriage set up by her father. She is, how did he put it, not of this world."

Sir Eldrick took a new measure of the man. "You are a friend of the great wizard? Small world," he said, glancing at Brannon.

"We are friends of the wizard as well," said the elf before sucking the butter from the end of a carrot.

Sir Eldrick sighed under his breath.

"Indeed," said Bjorn. "And if I am any good at guessing, I would say that five companions, so different from one another and traveling west toward the Wide Wall, must be none other than the Champions of the Dragon."

"You sure are a smart one," said Willow between slurps of soup.

"Yes, you sure are," said Sir Eldrick.

Bjorn smiled pleasantly. "Please," he said, indicating the food spread out across the table. "Eat up. For the road is long and full of hardships. A little extra fat on your ribs will be sure to get you a long way beyond the Wall."

"If I eat any more, my backpack won't be able to carry me," said Murland, happily patting his belly.

Gibrig burped and glanced at Ling Ling shyly. "Sorry, me lady, that be a compliment to the cook where I be from."

Sir Eldrick glanced at Brannon, who was smiling at Bjorn like a silly lass beneath the maypole. "I might have room for dessert," said Sir Eldrick, rising from his seat. "But first I must use your latrine."

"Down the hall, first left," said Bjorn.

"Out with the old and in with the new, my father always says," Willow said through her stuffed mouth. She snorted a laugh.

Sir Eldrick discretely nodded to Brannon, and the elf offered a knowing glance before excusing himself as well. Brannon followed him into the hall, which was covered in green moss that began to glow as they approached.

"What in the hell are you doing?" Sir Eldrick asked, pulling the elf into the spacious latrine.

"What? What are you talking about?" said Brannon, yanking his clothes free of the knight's grip.

"Are you even paying attention? Bjorn is working for Kazimir, trying to fatten us up for the dragon. If you weren't busy flirting like a little slut, you might have realized that."

"Slut?" Brannon scoffed. He suddenly slapped Sir Eldrick across the face.

"Is that what you call a slap?" said Sir Eldrick, brushing off his beard.

"How dare you?" Brannon continued. "I'm faithful to Valkimir. Besides, Bjorn is such a burly, wild beast of a man…" he said, eyes trailing off and a dopey smile replacing his indignant scowl.

"Yeah, well take off your beer goggles," said Sir Eldrick. "And start thinking with your *other* head."

"Lighten up. So what if Bjorn is working with Kazimir? So are we."

"Look, daffodil, just keep your mouth shut and your eyes open. No one can be trusted, not Bjorn, and sure as hell not Kazimir."

"But, we've a deal with the wizard."

"Don't you know that you can never trust a wizard? How old are you?"

Sudden doubt crossed Brannon's face, and his eyes wandered in thought. "But, but you said—"

"I said that I made a deal with Kazimir, not that he would keep it. If it is in his best interest, he will go against his word. Just keep your ears perked and your eyes open. Don't let down your guard for a minute."

Brannon bit his thumbnail and began to pace, but Sir Eldrick put a staying hand on his shoulder and stopped him.

"Keep your head straight and watch what you say. We must not give anything away to the others or Bjorn. Do you understand?"

Brannon nodded, trying to put on a brave face.

Sir Eldrick sighed and gave him a small shove. "Now get out of here, I've got to piss."

CHAPTER 15

A RODDINGTON NEVER GIVES ANYONE THE SHAFT

Pᴿɪɴᴄᴇss Cᴀᴿᴇssᴀ sᴛᴏᴏᴅ on the balcony looking west over the city. The beautiful view went beyond the walls and out over the rolling hills of green, spilling into the dark blue horizon. She wondered about Murland, worrying of his safety and trying to guess how far he and the other champions had gotten. Surely not all the way to the Wide Wall already, for it had only been two weeks since she bade her oldest friend farewell.

She had been just as shocked as Murland seemed to be that he had been named by Kazimir. He was not the best wizard that Abra Tower had to offer; everyone knew that. And he was no fighter. That was not to say that Murland was useless. Caressa knew him to be a smart, caring, and happy young man, one who saw beauty in everything and never spoke of anyone with a mean tongue. But those traits would not likely help him on his quest, for the dark land beyond the Wide Wall was full of terrors, and only the strongest and bravest dared venture there.

The question had gnawed at her night and day: Why had Kazimir chosen Murland?

Could it be that she was wrong, that she had failed to see something in him? By his own admittance, he was no wizard, and for one of his age to suddenly magically bloom was unheard of. She had tried to instill some confidence in him, for he had always been a shy boy, never one to be cocky in the slightest. Caressa had tried to help him, had tried to bring out the strong young man she knew him to be.

Hadn't she?

The kiss was her gift to him in that regard, and it had surely put some pep in his step afterward. Caressa laughed at the thought, touching her lips and suddenly sobering at the memory. It had only been intended as a kiss to raise his spirits, but to Caressa, it had been something more.

She drew her finger across her lips as she thought of him.

Caressa shook her head and snapped herself out of it. Such thoughts were impossible. She was a princess, and already betrothed to Beuford Winterthorn, prince of Vhalovia. Though he was a vile young man who had been trying since the age of thirteen to look up her skirt when no one was around, teasing that what was under there was rightfully his. She shuddered at the thought of it. She would much rather marry Murland. But of course, that was impossible.

Unless…

If he returned from Bad Mountain victorious, her father would surely name him the Royal Wizard or some such thing. With such an honored title, he would be given lands and treasure, and would then be suitable to marry a princess.

The thought bloomed and grew, nurtured by her excitement and passion until she could no longer pace the balcony wondering, wondering…

She ran out of her room and rushed to her father's study, where he liked to spend the hours after dinner reading by the fireplace. The door to his study was closed, but light spilled out beneath the crack at the bottom.

"Father!" she called as she knocked. "Father, I would like to speak to you!"

The door opened only a moment after, and her father stood, holding a half-full glass of amber liquor, his reading spectacles sitting loosely on the bridge of his nose. He looked at her with his hound dog eyes and frowned. "What is it, my dear? Has something happened? You look distraught."

"No, no, nothing like that," she said, and she took his glass and shot back the contents like a pirate. She walked past her gawking father and moved to the bar. "I have a question, that is all."

"What is it?"

She refilled his glass and brought it back to him, but he only stood, fingers laced over his large round belly, his face scrunching up the way it did when he was intrigued. "What is this question that you have?"

Caressa knew her father to be a lover of secrets, though he was no good at keeping them himself.

"Father, what happens when the champions return from Bad Mountain?"

"Return?" he said, as though he had never heard the word before.

"Well...yes. The champions are always victorious in scaring off Drak'Noir. What happens when they return?"

This time, Nimrod took the glass and emptied it himself. He gulped it down and moved over to the bar to pour another. "Yes, you are only twenty years old. I forgot that you have never been through a year of the dragon. Well, they never truly return. They go on a victory tour that brings them all over the lands, and then, being that they are such esteemed heroes, well, they go about doing hero things."

"You mean that Murland will never return, even if he is victorious?"

"I suppose not. He will be named one of the greatest wizards in all the lands. He will be quite busy, quite busy indeed." The king raised his glass, as if to toast the young man, and drank it down, rubbing his bald head the way he did when he was uncomfortable.

Caressa did not miss the gesture.

"Father, what is it?"

"Hmm? Sorry, dear. What is what?" he asked, rubbing his head and neck.

She stared at his big hound dog eyes, which quickly looked away and into his glass until he saw the bottom. "Another?" he said to himself. "Don't mind if I do."

"Father, what are you not telling me?" Caressa pressed.

"You mean what are you not telling me? Why are you so interested in the fate of the wizard anyway?"

"We've been friends since we were little. Why wouldn't I be interested?"

"Yes, well, you have many friends. Don't worry yourself. Now, I must get back to my books," he said, moving toward his favorite reading chair.

Caressa blocked his path. "I know that look when I see it," she told her father.

"What look?"

"Father…"

"Now you're just being silly."

"Father…"

"Now stop looking at me like that. I don't know what you are trying to do, but—"

"What are you keeping from me? Is it a secret? I know you love secrets. Tell it to me."

King Nimrod tried to avoid his daughter's stare, but she forced herself into his field of vision and glared at him until he cracked.

"The Champions of the Dragon never return; it is a hoax. Oh, my daughter, forgive me. But your friend Murland is doomed."

"What?" said Caressa, utterly shocked. "What do you mean it is a hoax?"

The king sighed and slumped into his chair. "The champions never scare off Drak'Noir. They are…she feeds them to her whelps."

"What? Why would you agree to such a thing?"

"You are old enough to know. This is the way of things. Once every generation, Kazimir chooses someone from every kingdom who is…how do I put this delicately…useless."

"Murland is not useless!"

"Yes, well, the high wizards seem to think so. They offered up Murland to Kazimir to be Magestra's champion, and it is so."

"He is my dearest friend, Father. How could you do this to me?"

"How was I to know that you felt this way about him?"

Caressa was furious. She slapped the drink out of his hand, sending it crashing into a bookcase. "If you paid attention, you would know that I felt that way. For the sake of the gods, Father, Murland and I have been friends for years. And his parents, what of his parents? Lord Kadabra is a close friend of yours. How could you do this to him?"

"Now just a second, young lady. What Murland is doing is heroic. The champions might not actually scare off the dragon, and they might be doomed to be food for whelps, but their sacrifice saves us all from the wrath of Drak'Noir, as it has for centuries."

"It isn't a sacrifice if they do not agree to it. It is murder."

"Who would agree to such a thing?" her father asked, but Caressa had had enough. She turned and began marching to the door before she said or did something that she would regret.

"Caressa!" her father called behind her. "Where are you going?"

She turned at the door to glare at her father. "If anything happens to Murland, I will never, ever, talk to you again. His blood will be on your hands!"

"Caressa!"

She slammed the door to his pleading calls and stormed back to her room, where her handmaiden was just turning down the sheets.

"Never mind that," said Caressa. "Have my horse prepared for long travel, and gather my armor and sword."

"But, where are you going, my lady?"

"Beyond the Wide Wall," said Caressa.

And her handmaiden fainted.

CHAPTER 16

─────── ✕ ───────

OVER THE HILL AND AROUND THE BENDER

THE DAY'S FIRST rays of light crept over the sill beside Murland's bed and greeted him with blinding enthusiasm. He stretched and yawned, rubbing his belly and suddenly remembering Bjorn's promise of hot cakes as big as a knight's shield at first light.

He had been assigned a room with Gibrig and Willow, and he soon discovered that the ogre was already up and at 'em, although Gibrig still snored away.

"Wake up, Gib," said Murland, shaking his friend's shoulder. "Remember, hotcakes?"

Gibrig stirred and mumbled dreamily. But then suddenly his eyes shot open, and he sat up in bed. "Hotcakes…and bacon! Last night Bjorn said hotcakes and bacon!" He bolted out of bed and rushed into the hall. He slammed into the earthen wall, bounced off, and ran toward the kitchen.

Murland glanced out the window, and saw Gibrig come to a skidding halt next to Snorts with a look of relief. Snorts was safe and still tied to the post with the other mounts, far away from the raptor.

Over breakfast, Bjorn admitted that the hog who was honoring their breakfast had been named Ham. He said it with a chuckle, which Gibrig seemed not to appreciate in the slightest.

When the companions had all finished their meal, Ling Ling loaded them up with brown bags full of little paper boxes stuffed with food from the night before. Gibrig took his with a dopey, starry-eyed grin, at which Ling Ling blushed and nodded repeatedly, saying brightly, "No MSG."

"Well, my friends," said Bjorn at the door. "If you are ever journeying this way again, please, look us up. We would love to have you for dinner again and hear your tales of adventure."

"Oh, we'll be back this way," said Sir Eldrick.

"Of course you will," said Bjorn, waving as they left. "Just follow the hills south for a spell, and you will soon find the road."

"Thank you, Bjorn. Thank you, Ling Ling," called Willow, waving with one hand and already eating her share of leftovers with the other.

They found the road easily and started off again to the west. The weather remained agreeable, though Sir Eldrick kept his eyes on a storm front that seemed always to be just on the eastern horizon.

Murland had braved his winged backpack as soon as they were on the road, and now flew high above the companions, enjoying a unique view of the wider world. He'd had a good night's sleep on a feathered mattress, enjoyed a hearty breakfast, and was now flying like a bird. Indeed, Murland was having a good day.

He thought of Princess Caressa as he flew, and his mind brought him back to their last encounter, when she had kissed him. Flying high above the ground, he imagined the roar of the crowd when he returned from the quest victorious, and he imagined Caressa. She would be dressed in a gown of the purest white, and the king would be so enamored with Murland the hero that he would offer his daughter's hand in marriage. Together Murland and Caressa would retire to the highest room in Abra Tower, and they would have half a dozen children.

An hour later, Murland was jolted from his day dreams when an arrow suddenly came from the trees below and hit his backpack, sending him spiraling down toward the treetops. Murland cried out to the others in warning, but he fell so fast that he hadn't gotten more than three terrified words out before he hit a branch, dropped five feet, and hit another, then another, and another still, before hitting the ground with a thud.

Sir Eldrick saw the arrow, and he saw Murland's sickening descent from on high. "Ambush!" he cried as he went for the bow and arrow tied off beside his saddle. The companions had just come out of the rolling hills and entered a dense forest. Even as they reined in their mounts to get away, nets came down and covered Willow and Gibrig. Brannon spurred his horse beyond the nets and archers and zipped through the woods the way they had come.

A net came at Sir Eldrick from on high, and he leapt from his mount just in time. He landed and rolled, coming up with sword drawn and shield out before him. He ran to Willow to cut her free, knowing that she would be the best in a fight, but before he could get to her, half a dozen archers emerged from the bushes and leveled their arrows on him.

"Stand down!" came a voice from the woods. Another man emerged, this one clearly the leader of the group. He wore a ridiculously large plumed hat with a peacock feather sticking up out of it and sleek leather armor. His face was young and smooth, and his eyes were dark, matching his short-cropped hair.

"I am a knight of Vhalovia," said Sir Eldrick in a warning tone. "Release my friends and be on your way, and I will spare you the wrath of King Winterthorn."

The man smirked as he bravely strode up to Sir Eldrick and stopped ten feet away. With him came two more goons, one carrying a mean-looking axe, the other a longsword.

"Let me out of here, you nannywiggins!" said Willow, who was hopelessly tangled up with her raptor. "If my food gets crushed, I'll kill every last one of you!"

"Please, dear ogre, do shut up. The humans are talking," said the dark-haired man.

A sudden commotion came from behind the bandits, and another bandit walked up to his leader and pushed the lanky wizard down on the ground between Gibrig and Willow. Seeing the arrow, Sir Eldrick was at first alarmed, but then he saw how it protruded from the pack, and not from Murland.

"A knight of Vhalovia," said the dark-haired man, tapping his chin in thought. He looked Sir Eldrick up and down, pausing on his belly, and then smiled. He took a step closer and studied his face.

A laugh suddenly escaped him and he turned to the man to his right. "Do you recognize this man?"

The bandit squinted at Sir Eldrick and shook his head. "Should I?" he asked his boss.

"I dare say that you should, for he is a legend. This, my friends, is the queen-shagger himself, the one and only Sir Slursalot."

"Ain't the name Slur Sirsalot, boss?" said one of the goons.

The dark-haired man furled his brow in thought. "I thought that it was Sir Slursalot. The other name makes no sense."

"Oh, but it does," said his friend, laughing. "You see, he's a drunk, right? So instead of Sir Slursalot, you say it like you're drunk, *Slur Sirsalot*."

"Ahh," said the black-haired man. "Now I get it."

The lot of them laughed with their boss, and Sir Eldrick ground his teeth.

"The name is Sir Eldrick, and if you know me then you know of my accolades. I will offer you this one last chance. Release my companions, and I will let you leave with your lives."

The leader glanced at his men and grinned. "Let me formally introduce myself, Sir Knight. I am known in these parts as Wild Willy, and these are the Road Warriors. I assume that you've heard of us."

"Wild Willy and the Road Warriors?" said Sir Eldrick with a chuckle. "You can't be serious."

Willy's smile disappeared and he drew his sword. "Well, after today, everyone will know my name, for I will be known as the man who slayed the queen-shagger. I imagine your head will fetch me a pretty penny from the king of Vhalovia."

Sir Eldrick glanced at the bowmen, who, after a nod from Willy, lowered their weapons.

The two men circled each other, Sir Eldrick with his shield out in front and his sword held loosely to the side at the ready, and Wild Willy with his twin swords. The other man was twenty years his junior, and Sir Eldrick knew better than to take any man for granted in a fight. He paced the younger man slowly and jabbed out his sword, testing Willy's reach. Around they went, slapping each other's testing strikes away easily, until Sir Eldrick finally charged, shield leading the way.

Willy hit the shield with both blades, jarring Sir Eldrick momentarily and spinning out of reach of the follow-up sword strike. Willy then came on with an assault of his own that left Sir Eldrick on his toes and put more than one dent in his old shield. The Road Warriors cheered their leader all the while, telling him to "skewer that queen-shagger!" Not to be outdone, Willow, Murland, and Gibrig cheered Sir Eldrick from their precarious positions at the end of guarding swords.

The men exchanged blows for a time in what seemed to be a well-balanced match, but then Willy surprised Sir Eldrick with a flurry of strikes that ended with his shield being skillfully twisted out of his grip by the twin swords. Sir Eldrick composed himself, trying not to show just how winded he already was from the short fight, and used his long sword to his advantage. He kept the smaller, faster man away with long sweeping strikes for a time, but soon Willy found an opening and came in behind a blow, kicking Sir Eldrick behind the knee. The knight went down and brought his sword back around frantically. Willy's twin blades were there to catch it, however, and with a twist and a thrust, the sword was sent flying through the air. Sir Eldrick had hardly registered what happened when a boot found his face and laid him on his back.

Wild Willy laughed victoriously and roared like a bear as Sir Eldrick struggled to clear his head. He shuffled back on his hands and feet as Willy circled him. Another boot found the side of his face and left him on his belly, sucking dirt in with precious air. He knew that he was doomed, for the blade would soon be at his neck, and Wild Willy would make good on his promise. With effort, Sir Eldrick fished open the small container on his belt, which held his secret flask.

"So, the great Slur Sirsalot has met his match. Let the minstrels sing of it with fervor." He kicked Sir Eldrick in the ribs and walked behind him.

The cap came off the flask, and Sir Eldrick hurriedly brought it to his lips and guzzled down the extremely potent liquor known as Pirate's Lass. Fire instantly erupted in his belly. His vision and mind cleared, and he felt power and strength again return to him.

Willy grabbed a handful of Sir Eldrick's hair from behind, and the former knight exploded into action. He twisted his body and swung his right leg up, hitting Willy hard in the hip. The highwayman staggered to the side. Sir Eldrick spotted his shield and rolled toward it as his opponent recovered. He grabbed the shield and sprang to his feet, meeting Willy's furious charge with one of his own. The twin blades came down from on high, and Sir Eldrick barreled into them and crashed into Wild Willy, sending the man flying through the air and into the underbrush with a loud "ugh."

The surprised archers stared in shock as Sir Eldrick charged the closest of them and slammed into him with the force of a bull. The knight spun, catching the next archer in the chin with the edge of the shield and laying him out. The others let loose their arrows, but Sir Eldrick was ready, and brought his shield to bear as four arrows twanged off it. He threw the shield at the closest, hitting the man in the gut and taking him clean off his feet. By the time he landed, Sir Eldrick had rolled again, this time coming up with his sword and slashing the net containing Willow.

Murland watched helplessly as Willow came up like a bear roused before spring. The archers drew back and took aim at her, and Murland cried out a warning. It was futile, however, for as the archers let loose, Willow stood her ground. A few arrows stuck in her thick green hide, but the others snapped or twanged off, cracked and useless. Willow grinned, and then charged the men, who dropped their weapons and fled into the woods.

"Get back here, you yellow-bellied toads!" she called tauntingly.

Sir Eldrick had already engaged the last two remaining men, and he stood locked with his sword up high, holding back both men's weapons.

Willy emerged from the woods at Sir Eldrick's back, looking furious. And when he saw his men in trouble, he rushed toward them, sword leading and meant for Sir Eldrick's back. Willow crossed the distance between them with alarming speed and hit Willy with an uppercut that carried so much force that he was taken clean off his feet and landed high in the boughs of an elm tree.

Exhilarated, Murland watched through the ropes as Sir Eldrick overpowered the two men and sent the one's weapon flying. But just as he gained the upper hand, he swayed drunkenly and passed out face first in the road.

"Willow!" Gibrig cried.

The furious ogre snapped her head toward the two men standing over Sir Eldrick, and she let out a growl so furious, so menacing, and so terrible, the men turned tail and ran for their lives.

Willow gave a laugh, hurried to her raptor, and freed him from the netting. "Your dinner just ran into the woods. Go on, get it!"

Tor gave a high-pitched, ear-piercing cry and shot off into the forest on his thick red hind legs.

Once Murland was freed of his bindings, he hurried over to Sir Eldrick and took his head in his lap. "Sir Eldrick…Sir Knight…wake up," he said, slapping him lightly on the cheek.

"What in the world is going on here!" came a booming voice that shook the leaves from the trees.

There was a great flash of blinding light, and when it faded, Murland lowered his arm and saw Kazimir standing there on the road leading west.

"Kazimir! Boy, we be glad to see ye!" said Gibrig, who was all kinds of worked up.

"Most High One," said Murland. "Something has happened to Sir Eldrick. He was fighting the bandits, when suddenly he passed out."

"Bandits, you say?" said Kazimir, glancing around at the bodies, netting, and flustered companions.

"The scum tried to catch us unawares, but Sir Eldrick drank some kind of special potion and took half of them out. He freed me, and I thumped some heads," Willow said proudly.

"And where, might I ask, is the elf prince?" said Kazimir, arching an eyebrow.

Everyone glanced around, having completely forgotten about Brannon.

Kazimir sighed. "Must I do everything?" he said to no one in particular. "Stay put, fools. I will be right back."

Brannon spurred his horse on faster when he saw the opening of the forest leading to the rolling hills. He was almost out of the woods. Not a single thought about the others crossed his mind. His only worry was himself. When the bandits attacked, he took the opportunity to rid himself of the idiots and their fool's quest once and for all. Deal or no deal, Kazimir and Sir Eldrick could not ensure his safety beyond the Wide Wall, and Brannon was in no hurry to die.

No, he would not die today, he would escape. He intended on riding straight into Val's arms, where he would be safe. To hell with his father, to hell with the kingdom, and to hell with the prophecy. Brannon was done.

His horse had nearly reached the edge of the forest, where glorious daylight shone upon the well-worn road, when suddenly darkness filled the path, and the light beyond winked out and was replaced by a giant shadow.

"Brannon Woodheart!" The voice was deafening, and the wind that accompanied it blew Brannon clean off his horse.

He landed on the road hard, and the wind exploded from his lungs. Darkness was replaced by a flash of light, and suddenly Kazimir stood looking down at him, shaking his head like a stern schoolmaster.

"Brannon the Cowardly, is that what they will call you?" said the wizard.

Brannon could only gasp and thrash like a fish out of water. He couldn't breathe, let alone respond.

Kazimir rolled his eyes. He grabbed Brannon by his golden belt buckle and lifted him off the ground. Air rushed into the elf's lungs, and he coughed and spat as he was let down again.

"On your feet then, I haven't all day," said the wizard.

Brannon got to his feet weakly. His hair was a mess, full of dirt and grass and twigs, and his clothes were dusty from the road. He wiped a dirty tear from his cheek and glared at Kazimir.

"You might hate me, but I don't give a frothing mug of crap. You have been chosen as a Champion of the Dragon, and by the gods, you will march your ass to Bad Mountain, or else so help me, I'll change you into a toad and carry you there myself!"

"I'm sorry," said Brannon. "But I was so scared—"

"Save your slobbering for Valkimir's lance," said Kazimir with a dismissive hand and flourish of robes. He started back east down the road, and Brannon had enough good sense to mount his steed and follow.

Two hours had gone by, and still Kazimir had not returned. Being that Sir Eldrick was unconscious, Murland took it upon himself to take charge, and the others seemed not to mind at all. They pulled a still sleeping Sir Eldrick off the road, along with the bandits' weapons and horses, and into the forest to the nearest clearing. Night was getting on, and so Murland asked Gibrig to find stones and wood for a fire pit. He set Willow to watch over the road so that they might not miss Kazimir, and then took it upon himself to go through the bandits' saddle bags for any usable supplies.

He was shocked to discover a wealth of gold and jewels on one of the horses, and guessed it to be the booty from Wild Willy and the Road Warriors' most recent hold-up. Among the bags of food stuffs, weapons, and wine, Murland found an old map that proved to be of the forest in which he stood, with a *big X* marked in the northwestern edge, near the coast.

Murland folded up the map and put it back with the other things. When Sir Eldrick woke up, he could decide what to do with it all.

"Kazimir has returned!" came Willow's voice from the woods.

Gibrig came from the other direction just then and dropped his pile of wood by the stone and joined Murland at the edge of camp. Soon Willow came into view, followed by the Most High Wizard and a sullen-looking Brannon leading his horse.

"Boy, I be glad to see you!" said Gibrig tearfully and rushed over to hug Brannon around the waist.

Brannon looked down on the dwarf with disgust and pushed him away. "What happened to Sir Eldrick?" he asked upon seeing the knight lying on the ground beside the makeshift fire pit.

"The fool drank spirits," said Kazimir. He stood over the knight and waggled his fingers, and suddenly a pail of water appeared in his hands. He then dumped the water on the sleeping knight, who gasped and came up swinging.

Moments before, at the top of a hill behind a village, a lad named Jarrick was pulling a heavy pail of water from the well by rope, when suddenly the pail disappeared. Jarrick gave a cry and was pulled backward by his own momentum. He fell end over end down the side of the hill, yelling all the while, and slammed into a girl from the village.

They both went tumbling into a small wagon, and when Jarrick had righted himself and pushed the hay away from his face, he looked upon the most beautiful girl that he had ever seen. She wore a similar expression, and seven years after that fateful day, they were wed upon that same hill.

From their union would come a son named Jack, who would grow up to become one of the greatest heroes Fallacetine had ever known.

"What the hell is going on!" Sir Eldrick demanded as he came up swinging, but was easily subdued by Willow.

Kazimir tossed the pail to the side and shook his head at the knight. "You were drunk again," he said, squaring on the man.

Sir Eldrick blinked, eyes moving this way and that as he tried to remember. Then his face lit up. "I had to! We were attacked by bandits. I would have been killed had I not dra—"

"You wouldn't have almost died if you hadn't let yourself be ambushed. A knight of Vhalovia my ass," the wizard spat. "Have you forgotten all of your training? Or does something of a knight remain in that wet brain of yours?"

Sir Eldrick reined in his temper and forced himself to relax. "You are right. I should never have let that happen."

"And you," said Kazimir, pointing at Murland. "What is the point in having a flying backpack if you can't even keep a proper watch on the road ahead?"

"I…I'm sorry, I guess I should have—"

"What about you, ogre? If you weren't stuffing your face with takeout, you might have smelled the bandits before you got to them."

"What's takeout?" Willow asked.

Kazimir shook his head and leveled his terrible gaze on Sir Eldrick and Brannon. "Come with me," he said, hooking a boney finger at them.

When they were out of earshot, Kazimir turned on Sir Eldrick and Brannon with a dangerous gaze.

"Listen," Sir Eldrick began, "I know that I scr—"

"You two are on your last leg," he said, pointing a crooked finger at them. "I leave for a few days, and you get caught by bandits and nearly killed. And you," he said to Brannon, "you run off like a scared little girl. Tell me, how does you running away help get those morons to Bad Mountain?"

"I'm sorry," said Brannon, bowing his head in shame.

"Did I choose the wrong men for this job?" Kazimir asked them.

"No, of course not," said Sir Eldrick.

"I wish that I could believe you, but…well, your performance today gives me doubt."

"Look, I did what I had to do. Sure, I didn't see the attack coming. That's why they call it an *ambush*. But we are all alive, and no thanks to you."

"It is not my job to lead you all to Bad Mountain; that is your job. If you two cannot do the job, I will wipe your memories of our deal and feed you to the dragon. Do you understand?"

Sir Eldrick calmed his growing temper, knowing that he was no match for the wizard. "I understand," he said with a deep nod. "You can count on me."

"Me too," said Brannon, sheepishly.

Kazimir studied them with obvious disdain before turning and walking into the woods. "We'll see," he said as he faded into shadow and disappeared. "We'll see."

When Sir Eldrick was sure that Kazimir was gone, he whirled on Brannon and slammed him up against a tree. Brannon issued a cry of pain and alarm, and Sir Eldrick covered his mouth with his hand. "Listen to me, you little son of a bitch, you ever pull something like that, and Kazimir will be the least of your worries. Do you understand me?"

Brannon nodded, and Sir Eldrick released him roughly and stormed back to camp.

CHAPTER 17

TRUTH UNSPOKEN

ANNALLIA RETURNED FROM a hunt and found her handmaiden waiting for her.

"Your mother is sick. She has been asking for you. Come, you must hurry," said the elf maiden with a small bow.

"Where?"

"She is in her quarters in the Oaken Palace."

Annallia wasted no time and snapped the reins, which the stable master had just taken hold of. But he let go when the stallion reared. It kicked at the air and sped off as soon as its hooves touched earth. Annallia rode hard through the streets of Halala, cutting through a market with many apologies, tipping over more than one table, and spreading the crowd like an arrow. At the winding steps to the great tree palace, she leapt off and sprinted upward. At the third giant branch, she got off and ran its length, stopping before her mother's quarters of woven branches.

"Where is Mother?" she demanded.

"Inside. She is resting," said the guard.

"Step aside," said Annallia, pushing past him and rushing into her mother's room. She found the queen in bed, being tended to by a healer, and hurried to her side. "Mother, are you alright?"

"Dear Annallia," said her mother sleepily.

"I have just given her a potion that will help her sleep," said the old healer as he rose and straightened his ruffled robes. "She has no ailment that I can detect. I think that she had a spell is all. She keeps mumbling on about the prince. It is probably just stress. She will be fine with some sleep."

"Thank you." Annallia took the seat beside the bed.

The healer left them, and the queen opened her eyes weakly. She smiled at her daughter.

"Mother, you must rest. They say it is just a spell. That you are worried about Brannon, but he will be f—"

"Brannon!" said her mother, suddenly coming alive and grabbing Annallia's wrist so hard that it hurt. "Brannon is in danger!"

"He is with the other companions, Mother. He will return victorious. You will see."

"No, it is a lie, it is all a lie! Oh, my dear, sweet, Brannon. What has your father done?"

"Mother, what are you talking about?"

The queen swooned, and her eyelids fluttered. She struggled against the effects of the potion and gripped Annallia's wrist tighter. "Lies…all lies…"

"Mother, what do you mean? What is a lie? Mother!"

"The prophecy…the quest…lies. They're sent…to feed…" The queen's grip suddenly loosened, and her hand fell to the bed.

"Sent to feed? What are you saying? Please, Mother, what do you mean?"

The queen's lips moved, and her voice was barely a whisper. Annallia bent down and struggled to make out the word.

"The…whelps," said the queen. Then she passed out.

"Mother?" Annallia shook her gently, but it was no use.

What had her mother been saying? Brannon was food for whelps? She had to know more, but there was no way to wake her mother. There was another way to speak to her, however, but Annallia was reluctant to attempt it. Mind melding was forbidden without consent, and if she was caught, the consequences would be severe. But if Brannon was in mortal danger…

To hell with it, Annallia thought, and she placed her palms on each side of her mother's temples.

Mother, can you hear me?

Nothing.

Mother, I must know about Brannon.

Brannon! the queen's mind suddenly called out, echoing in the vast chambers of her consciousness.

Yes, Mother, tell me about the danger he is in.

You must help him. He is in mortal danger. Kazimir is a liar; there is no prophecy. He made a deal with the dragon. The champions are food for whelps.

Have you told Father?

Your father knows. Oh, gods help him, but he knows. He said Brannon will return a hero, or not at all.

"What are you doing?" came the voice of King Rimon.

Annallia jumped, startled, and released her mother. "Father, I did not see you come in."

"I asked you a question," said the king sternly.

"I was just soothing Mother," said Annallia. She rose from the bedside chair and approached her father bravely, trying to ignore the effects of the sudden separation of minds. "What did you think I was doing?"

Rimon and Annallia stood staring at each other. Both knew the other's mind, but their thoughts went unspoken. Annallia knew that her father would never admit to such a thing.

"She needs her rest now," said Rimon.

"I was just leaving," said Annallia, and she brushed past her father.

"Annallia!" her father called when she was almost out the door.

She froze and turned to face him. "Yes, Father?"

He seemed to be mulling over his words. "Your mother has been babbling nonsense all afternoon. Do not fret. She will be better soon."

"Of course she will. Is there anything else?"

"No, you are dismissed," said Rimon, watching her closely.

"Very well," said Annallia.

The door of branches closed behind her on their own accord, and she determinedly made her way back down to her horse. By the time she reached the beast, tears were streaming down her face. Her sorrow wasn't for her mother's condition, it wasn't because of the peril that her brother was in, it was because her father had once again proven himself to be a cold, unloving bastard. One who would send his only son on a suicide mission just to test his manhood.

Annallia mounted her horse and took the eastern road through the city to Val's tree, praying to the gods the entire time that he was still in the city and hadn't yet left for Fort Vista on the eastern coast of Halala.

When she arrived at the tree, it was dark outside, and light shone through the small cracks in the circular, woven rooms of vine among the oldest branches.

"Valkimir!" she called, rushing up the winding branches fashioned into stairs from the base. She noticed other elves on nearby trees watching her from woven balconies and tried to compose herself.

"Annallia?" Valkimir called from three branches up, looking over the edge of the balcony off his bedroom.

She hurried up to it and rushed inside, where Valkimir was waiting. "It's Brannon," she said, panting. "He is in grave danger. Kazimir is a liar, the entire prophecy is a lie. You've got to—"

"Whoa, whoa, hold on. Catch your breath. Here, sit down."

"I don't need to sit down!" she said, pushing away his guiding hands. "You need to listen."

"Alright," he said, regarding her with concern. "I'm listening."

"My mother told me that Brannon and the other champions are not meant to scare off Drak'Noir, they are meant to be food for her whelps!"

Valkimir stepped back from her slowly and put a hand over his heart. "But surely your mother is mad; why would your father allow such a thing to hap—" His eyes slowly fell to the floor in realization. Then suddenly his head snapped alert. "How sure are you that your mother was speaking the truth?"

"I spoke to her through a mind meld. There was no fallacy in her words, I can assure you of that."

Valkimir paced the room back and forth, wringing his hands all the while. Finally, he seemed to notice Annallia was still there. He indicated a vine chair which, like all other furnishings, grew out of the wall. He sat across from her and took her hands in his large ones, callused from a life of constant swordplay. "Tell me from the beginning how you came across this information."

"If you will allow me, I will show you. For there are things that words cannot rightly express."

"A mind meld?"

"Have you ever experienced one?"

"Only once, when being questioned by the king's inquisitors regarding my relationship to you and Brannon," said Valkimir, eyes haunted by the memory.

"I promise that I will be more gentle."

He nodded and leaned forward, bearing his head to her.

"Not that way. For this mind meld, you will be joining my mind. Please, put your hands upon my temples."

He licked his lips and rubbed his hands together before slowly putting them against her temples. She closed her eyes and slowly guided him into her mind, careful not to let him wander. When he was comfortable in the dark room she had created, she showed him the memories from the time that she returned from the hunt, until she left to find him.

When it was over, she bade him to leave her mind, and he released her with a gasp.

She opened her eyes and found Valkimir shaking. Sweat beaded his smooth forehead, and his fierce green eyes were wild with anger.

"I saw the truth in your father's eyes," he said. "It is as Brannon suspected. And I...I didn't believe him. How could Rimon send his own son on such a fool's quest?"

"I don't know," said Annallia, not having any defense for her father. "But you must stop this if you can."

Val took her hands in his and kissed them. "Annallia, I will return with your brother, or I will not return at all."

CHAPTER 18

A GIFT AND A CURSE

*G*IBRIG AWOKE WITH *sudden panic, as if he had been suffering from a bad dream. A deep sadness darkened his mind, consuming him, and he found that he had been crying in his sleep.*

Outside, a powerful wind blew mournfully through the mountain pass.

"Gillrog?" he called in the dark, wiping his eyes.

His brother didn't answer.

Gibrig threw off his sheets and peered through the darkness, trying to make out the bed on the other side of the room.

"Gill?"

Still nothing.

He got up and lit a candle. Gill's bed was empty, but it was still warm to the touch. Gibrig opened the window to the night and the wind took his breath away for a moment. He scoured the mountain valley and thought he saw a tall figure heading into the western fold leading to Ruger's Ridge—Gillrog's favorite place to be alone.

Gibrig considered giving his brother the privacy that he obviously sought, but he was worried for him. The other dwarven boys had been particularly nasty earlier in the day, and Gill hadn't even spoken at dinner.

Gibrig got dressed and put on his boots. He considered waking his father, but then thought better of it. Hagus Hogstead was seldom aware of the taunting that his sons endured, as they always denied it or played down how bad it was. Gillrog was embarrassed of the things the other dwarf boys said to him and his brother, and had made Gibrig swear not to tell their father.

He made his way quietly down the hall and out the door. He couldn't see his brother anymore, and hurried across the field toward the fold.

"Gill!" he called as he reached the crag.

Again, he heard no reply.

Gibrig hurried up the trail to Ruger's Ridge, his apprehension growing with every step. The trail that he and his brother had climbed a thousand times now seemed foreign and treacherous. He slipped more than once in his panic, but ignored his scraped knees and hurried along up the steep cliff. He was crying now, and he knew that it was Gill's sorrow that he was feeling. The twins often shared dreams and emotions, and though Gill tried to play down how much the taunting hurt him, Gibrig knew the truth of it.

The nicknames—human, freak, tall weed—followed them like a shadow, but what hurt Gillrog the most were the accusations that they had killed their mother when they were born.

Sobbing now, Gibrig crested the ridge. He looked east, and there, standing on the edge of the jutting ridge, stood Gillrog.

"Gill!" Gibrig called against the wind.

His brother turned around slowly. He was smiling.

"I've got to go now, Gib. I'm sorry."

"Gill, wait!"

"Don't come any closer!" Gillrog warned.

"I know ye be hurtin', Gill. But ye can't do this."

Gillrog looked upon his brother with pity, though it was he himself who stood upon the precipice of death. "I can't do it anymore, Gib. Don't you understand? I don't want to be here."

"Then...then we'll just run away. Come on, back up from that ledge. Let's talk."

"I ain't no good for ye, and I ain't no good for Pap," said Gillrog, glancing over the edge. "I shoulda never been born. If it weren't for me, ye'd have a mum."

"Don't talk like that."

"Ye know it be true. Ye been a good brother, Gib. I'll miss ye."

"No!" said Gibrig, mind racing. "If ye do that, ye know ye can't ever get into the Mountain in the Clouds. The gods'll never allow it, and ye won't get to see Momma."

Gillrog offered Gibrig another pitying look. "There ain't no gods, Gib. Even if there were, they'd never let me in anyhow."

"Gill..."

"Goodbye, Gib. I love ye."

To Gibrig's horror, his brother turned and took a step off the ledge.

"Gill!"

Gibrig ran to the edge, but sudden pain shot through every fiber in his body and dropped him to the stone. He felt his strange connection to his brother disappear, replaced by cold, dark silence.

"You can't leave me here alone!" Gibrig screamed, and he clawed his way across the rough stone. He pulled himself to the edge, hoping against all odds that he would find his brother clinging to the ledge.

Instead he found his brother's body, twisted and broken one hundred feet below.

"Gibrig...Gib!"

He shot awake and grabbed the person shaking him.

"Gill!"

"It's me, Murland. You were having a bad dream. Are you alright?"

Gibrig clutched Murland's robes as the face of his brother slowly morphed into that of the young wizard's apprentice. He broke down then, sobbing, and Murland pulled him in to cry on his shoulder.

"It's alright, it was just a bad dream," said Murland.

"No...no it weren't. Oh poor, poor Gill. I shoulda said somethin' different. I shoulda known what he intended to do."

Gibrig cried into Murland's shoulder until he had no tears left and, sniffling, released the confused wizard.

"Are you alright?" Murland asked.

"I be fine, thanks."

Gibrig got up and noticed for the first time that it was nearly dawn. Everyone was awake, and they were staring at him. "Sorry if I woke y'all."

"It's alright," said Sir Eldrick, coming toward him. "Are you sure you're alright?"

"Yeah, was just a bad dream is all," said Gibrig. He glanced at the sky, hoping to change the subject. "Looks like it'll be a nice day today."

"Indeed," said the knight, watching him.

Gibrig smiled and went about preparing his things for a day of travel. To his relief, no one asked him anything more about it that morning.

The companions continued on their way shortly after. The forest became sparser as they went, and it soon opened into a long, stretching valley with a wide river snaking from the north to the south and leading into the Blight, a land that was said to be haunted.

There were many questions for Sir Eldrick concerning his incredible fighting prowess while on the bottle. At first, he ignored such questions, not wanting to divulge information about his condition, for it was both his greatest weakness and greatest strength. Willow was tenacious about it, and would not let the topic rest.

"So, what is it, like a curse or something?" she asked as they rode.

Murland hovered just off to the side of the road, gliding along on the wings of his tireless backpack. Brannon rode to the left of the knight, surely glad to have something to keep their attention away from his cowardly abandonment of them at the first sign of trouble the day before. Gibrig, however, rode behind them all. He was sullen, and spoke little to the others. Sir Eldrick knew that it had something to do with his bad dream, and the violence of the day before had shaken him.

"It isn't a curse that I am aware of," said Sir Eldrick, hoping to placate the ogre.

"Well then, what is it, like a magical power?" Willow pressed.

"And why did you pass out for so long?" Murland put in.

"Does that happen every time you drink spirits?" Brannon added, doing his best to look inquisitive.

Sir Eldrick gave a sigh. "It is a gift and a curse, I suppose, for it has brought me my greatest glory, and my greatest shame."

"How do you mean?" Willow asked.

"Well, take yesterday, for instance. I chugged down that bottle and easily defeated the highwaymen, but then I passed out for hours, which is extremely dangerous. And that is just what happens on liquor."

"What do you mean? You have different reactions to different spirits?" said Murland.

"Exactly. On liquor, I am the greatest fighter that Fallacetine has ever seen, but it only lasts a few minutes, and then I am out for hours, as you saw. On beer, I am a tireless fighter, though not as good as I am on liquor. But rather than pass out on beer, I black out and go on day-long binges, often waking up in strange lands, or deep into enemy territory."

"What about wine?" said Murland.

"Wine," said Sir Eldrick, chuckling. "Wine, my young friend, turns me into the greatest lover Fallacetine has ever seen."

"But what is the downside to that?" said Murland, who was quite curious about the topic of lovemaking.

"Having women's husbands after you, I would imagine," said Brannon.

"Indeed," said Sir Eldrick. "Not only that, but I have so many children spread across these lands that I lost count long ago."

"That's too bad," said Gibrig, surprising everyone. "I never knew me mom 'cause she died when I was born, but I think it would be worse if she was alive and just didn't want to see me."

"I never said I didn't want to see my children," said Sir Eldrick, rather defensively. "But how in the hells do you have a relationship with so many children, spread all over like they are?"

"Sorry, Sir Knight. I didn't mean no offense."

"Aw, never mind all that. And quit saying you're sorry all the time."

"Sorry."

Sir Eldrick sighed.

Soon the conversation turned to Willow and her incredible fighting prowess, which seemed to impress even Brannon. The ogre was more than happy to talk about herself and how she beat the bandits and sent them packing.

"Yup," she said with a tusky grin. "Good thing Sir Eldrick got me free when he did. Or else those bandits would have killed all of us."

"You sure did a number on them," said Murland. "I would have helped, but I couldn't get a clear shot with my wand."

Brannon scoffed at that and rolled his eyes.

"What about you?" Willow asked Brannon. "Where did you go when the bandits attacked?"

"I..." Brannon began, his cheeks suddenly flushing. "I went and got Kazimir."

Willow scowled in thought and scratched her head. "How did you know where to find him?"

"I, um..."

"If ye got scared and ran away, it be alright," said Gibrig. "We all get scared sometimes."

"I didn't run away! I came back with the wizard, didn't I? When I saw the bandits attack, I doubled back, meaning to surprise them, but then I ran into Kazimir on the road."

"This is all in the past," said Sir Eldrick, and Brannon seemed relieved to hear it. "We won the day, but we could have done better. From now on, we have to be more careful. There are far more dangerous things besides bandits awaiting us on the other side of the Wide Wall."

"What are we going to do about the map I found?" Murland asked, having been unable to stop thinking of the treasure that they might find.

"We have no time for such things now," said Sir Eldrick. "But when we return this way after we defeat Drak'Noir, we could swing north and find out what it is all about. I wouldn't get too excited though. Knowing highwaymen, it's just a trap. For now, you should focus on practicing your magic."

"With that broken wand of his? Please," said Brannon, who was in a sour mood.

"Your kind have magic," said Sir Eldrick. "Perhaps you could show young Murland a thing or two."

Brannon glanced at Murland with doubtful eyes. "If the high wizards of Abra Tower couldn't teach him anything, I don't know how I could."

Sir Eldrick said nothing, but his hard eyes spoke volumes.

"Fine," said Brannon, and he turned to Murland, who glided beside him. "I can tell you one thing; magic is all about confidence. If you don't have any, it doesn't matter how much wizard leaf you smoke."

"Truth be told, I don't have either one of those things."

"What?" said Sir Eldrick. "You don't have any wizard leaf?"

Murland shook his head. "Part of being an apprentice is learning how to grow it, but I have never been able to grow a good plant. Mine always die before they flower."

"But that makes no sense," said the knight. "You have told us how you tend the gardens every year. The way you made it sound, you have quite a green thumb."

Murland shrugged.

"Sounds like you've got enemies. Someone is killing your plants to keep you from getting any good at wizardry," said Brannon, and beside him Sir Eldrick nodded agreement.

Murland was dumbstruck. "You think so?"

"Isn't it obvious?" said Brannon, none too kindly.

"Sorry someone was killin' yer plants," said Gibrig, sounding choked up. "That wasn't very nice o' them at all."

Murland wondered who might have done such a thing, and then he thought of Lance Lancer. But rather than be angered by the revelation, he was excited to know that he hadn't failed after all. "Brannon, you are so good with growing things. Do you think you could help me to grow wizard leaf?"

Sir Eldrick glanced at the elf with a raised brow, and Brannon sighed. "I guess I could try. But I will need seeds."

"I've got some in my pack," said Murland excitedly. "You know what they say, 'a wizard should never leave home without it.'"

Brannon looked to the quickly setting sun. "Very well, we will plant the seeds in the morning."

"Thank you, Brannon. Thank you so much!"

CHAPTER 19

ON WINGS OF BLUE-BLUE

DINGLEBERRY ZIPPED THROUGH Fire Swamp Village, making her morning rounds. Her first stop was the baker's hut, where fresh loaves of pussy willow bread were being taken out of one of the large ovens. Dingleberry wasn't interested in the bread, and easily flew past the busy ogre baker, into the supply cellar through the gap in the door. To her delight, she found a new bag of sugar from Magestra among the stacked barrels and crates. She glanced at the door as she pulled out a tiny knife and carefully made a small incision in the top of the bag. After filling her small sack with the sugar, she dined on the sweet crystals until her wings were quivering.

The door suddenly opened, and Dingleberry shot into the air, her little heart beating furiously.

"You little thief!" the baker cried upon seeing the sprite with a face full of sugar.

Dingleberry blew past him as he swatted at her like one might a pesky mosquito. She easily dodged the swipes of the slow ogre and shot out of the cellar, into the foggy morning once again. At a fruit stand, she swiped a grape and gobbled it down as she flew. Another stand boasted nuts and berries, and she stuffed her sack with the rare treats. The human traders from Vhalovia had come to market, and Dingleberry was pleased to see a plethora of exotic food.

She retired to the safety of a rooftop and ate leisurely as she watched the ogres go about their day. It had been nearly three weeks since Willow left, and Dingleberry was beginning to get lonely. She had considered exploring the wider world, but Fallacetine was a dangerous place for a six-inch sprite.

On Faeland Island, the wildlife knew that fairies were off-limits, but here in the untamed swamp, with its crocodiles, bats, snakes, spiders, lizards, frogs, and other dangerous creatures, Dingleberry had to constantly be on guard.

After being exiled from Faeland by the queen for selling fairy dust to foreign merchants in the fairy underground market, Dingleberry had made her way across the ocean to Fire Swamp. She had been attacked by a bullfrog, and would have died had Willow not rescued her. The ogre had helped Dingleberry back to health, feeding her milk and honey for a month straight until her broken wing healed. Ever since that fateful day, they had been best friends. Life without Willow in Fire Swamp had proven difficult.

From her perch on top of the blacksmith's shack, Dingleberry spotted Merrick Bricksburg, one of Willow's favorite merchants. Willow was always the first one to market on the days that the human, dwarf, and elf merchants came to town, and the ogre was loved by them all. Her great appetite seemed to have no limit, and her favorite foods were those that came from the wider world. A great lover of cheese, Willow had taken a quick liking to Merrick, who was recognized by the humans of Magestra as the foremost authority on the subject.

Dingleberry landed on the corner post of his cart and was overcome by the poignant aroma of his wares. "Your cart smells like an ogre's bellybutton," said Dingleberry with a musical chuckle.

Merrick, a squat man with a portly belly, bald head, and white, pointed mustache, glanced around both high and low, his busy gray eyebrows furled and a merry glint found his eyes. "Now I would recognize that sweet little voice anywhere," he said before spotting her sitting there on his cart. He smiled brightly. "Ah, there you are, Dingleberry. Where is your hungry friend? I expected her hours ago."

Dingleberry's smile disappeared and she hung her head low. "Gone, gone, gone. Off to Bad Mountain with the champions."

"What's that?" said Merrick, cupping a hand behind his hairy ear. "You didn't say Bad Mountain, did you?"

"Yup, yup," she said in her high-pitched, sing-song voice. "Dingleberry all alone, all alone."

Merrick's smile slowly morphed into a frown.

"Cheese man, give me a sample of marble cheese," said an ogre female behind him. But the merchant didn't seem to hear. He stared off at nothing, pondering.

"Cheese man!"

"What do you want!" he suddenly snapped. But he quickly regained his composure. "I mean, yes, yes, here, try this."

The ogre scowled at him and ground her teeth, causing her tusks to slide back and forth across her face. She nevertheless took the sample and popped it in her mouth before turning and storming off.

Merrick turned back to Dingleberry with worry-filled eyes. "You cannot mean...Willow was chosen as the Fire Swamp Champion?"

"Yup, yup," said Dingleberry.

Merrick looked to the sky, suddenly exasperated. He kicked a crate and swore, growling with pain and dancing around on one foot. Dingleberry didn't know whether to be amused or confused.

"Those bastards!" said Merrick, kicking the crate again.

"You're funny-funny," said Dingleberry. She lifted a blanket covering a brick of cheese in the back of the wagon and broke off a crumbly chunk.

"Funny? My dear little blue friend, you don't understand."

"What you mean?"

Merrick didn't answer her, but began pacing the length of his wide cheese stand. "Hey, Meggleson!" he called to another human two stands down. "Did you hear about Willow?"

"Aye," said the younger man, a trader of salted meats and fine furs. "Damn shame too. I dare say that a quarter of my profits come from that ogre. I swear she must eat more than half the village."

"That's it," Merrick said to himself as he went back to pacing. "They couldn't afford to feed her anymore."

"Funny, funny cheese man," said Dingleberry, munching on her cheese.

"You don't understand," said Merrick, but then he caught himself and glanced around conspiratorially. He moved closer to her and said out of the corner of his mouth, "Willow was not chosen to defeat the dragon. Has she ever told you about the quest she went on two years ago?"

"Yup, yup," said Dingleberry with much enthusiasm. The story of Willow's great accomplishment always made her excited. "She traveled deep-deep into Fire Swamp, looking for the legendary gator, Snaggletooth. Then she found him sleeping away the day-day in the tall weeds." Dingleberry hovered in the air, crouching like a predator. "She jumped on his back, and he thrash, thrash, thrash about. Deep-deep into murky water he took her, but she hold on tight-tight. She use big strength to choke-choke the gator. He roll, twist, squirm and snap-snap, but Willow hold on till he was dead, dead, dead."

"Yes," said Merrick with a grim nod that Dingleberry did not understand. "And as promised by the chief, she was awarded food for life, as much as she could eat, which, I think, proved too much for the village's coffers."

"Hmm?" said Dingleberry absently, having grown bored with the strange man. She absently broke off another piece of cheese and glanced around at the trader's booths, wondering what she should try next.

"Listen, sprite," said Merrick, suddenly very close to her.

She scrunched up her nose at his strong cheese breath as it wafted over her.

"It is little known, and speaking of it can get a man killed, but the Champions of the Dragon are no champions at all. They are chosen by their people because they are a nuisance in one way or another."

Dingleberry forgot her cheese and listened with growing apprehension and dread.

"Do you understand? Your friend is marching to her death."

"No, no," said Dingleberry with a nervous little laugh. "You are wrong-wrong. Willow is big and strong. She is a champ-champ."

"That may be, but Fire Swamp has greater champions. The truth is that the village can no longer support her eating habit. But they cannot just go against their word now, can they? No, that dastardly weasel, Chief Gnarlytooth, made a deal with Kazimir, the Most High Wizard, or I'm a lizard monkey's cousin."

"Kazimir the wiz-wiz?" said Dingleberry, not liking the cheese man's story one bit. "No-no, you are wrong—"

"Listen to me," said Merrick, eyes wide and voice stinky and scary. "Willow is in grave danger. What I say is true. She eats and eats and eats, and the village pays for it. Don't you see? This was the perfect way to be rid of her."

Dingleberry was overcome with dread. "Oh no-no," she said, eyes tearing.

"I'm sorry, it is true. But alas, you can help. You must."

"What-what? Dingleberry is only little, not strong-strong, like Willow."

"No, but you are fast. If anyone can catch up to Willow before she reaches Bad Mountain, then it is you. Go, Dingleberry, warn Willow of the danger that she is in."

Dingleberry bit the end of her fingers nervously. "You think-think?"

"I do."

Thoughts of the dangers that lurked out there in the wide world made Dingleberry's little heart flutter, but then she thought of her dearest friend, walking to her death. She straightened and put on a determined face. "Then I go-go," she said, putting hands on hips and standing tall.

"Yes, very good. But you will need to prepare, for it is a dangerous world out there," said Merrick before turning to his supplies determinedly. He rummaged through his bags, and Dingleberry watched with interest from over his shoulder.

"Ah-ha," he said, finding what he was looking for. He turned and presented Dingleberry with a thimble and needle. "An adventurer on a quest needs a good sword and a good helmet."

He placed the thimble on her head and handed her the needle. She swung it around with fervor, becoming increasingly excited by the prospect of going on a quest.

"I have no other armor for you, so this will have to do. Now go, little sprite, save your friend."

"Yes-yes. I fly fast-fast, save Willow, save the day-day," she said, hovering beside him and raising her little needle.

"Go now, brave Dingleberry. Take the road to King's Crossing. Go west from there. Stay out of the forests, for they are filled with danger for those big and small."

"I will not let you down-down," said Dingleberry with all seriousness. She beat her tiny wings and flew high above the village, heading north toward King's Crossing.

CHAPTER 20

A HAUNTING OF DARKLINGS

MURLAND AWOKE WITH the dawn, eager to plant his seeds with Brannon. He threw off his bedroll and went straight to his winged backpack to retrieve the precious seeds. The other companions were still sleeping soundly, all but Sir Eldrick, who had taken the last watch. He was likely out there among the oaks and birches surrounding the glen that they had made camp in the night before.

The fire burned low, but had been fed less than an hour before by the looks of it. Murland found some fresh meat that they had taken from the highwaymen's packs and threw it in Willow's iron pan. He wanted to do everything possible to ensure that Brannon awoke in a good mood. While the meat cooked, Murland walked to a nearby brook and filled Brannon's water skins, and even picked him a few dandywood flowers, which he knew to be quite fragrant.

When he returned to the camp, he found Willow hunched over the iron pan on the fire.

"Hey!" he yelled, rushing over to her. "Don't eat that, it's for Brannon."

Willow licked the tips of her fingers and chewed the half-cooked meat. "Since when are you Brannon's cook?"

"Since I want him to help me grow my wizard leaf. Ah, you ate half of it already," said Murland, scooping the remaining food onto a wide leaf.

Their voices had awoken Gibrig, who came to with a smile and rubbed his eyes. "Mornin'," he said and sniffed at the air. "Smells good."

"Well it ain't for you," said Willow haughtily. "But don't you worry about that. I'll cook some more, and *I'll* share."

"Will you all just shut up?" said Brannon, rolling over and pulling his blanket over his head.

"I made you some breakfast." Murland put the leaf with the meat by his side and poured some water into Brannon's mug. "Here, have a drink."

Brannon threw back the blanket and looked at the food and drink suspiciously. "What are you up to?" he asked Murland.

"Me? Nothing. I'm just excited to plant my wizard leaf. Thought I would get breakfast out of the way."

"Ah, that," said Brannon, sitting up and taking a drink of water. "Fine, let me eat in peace and then we will begin. In the meantime, you go find some good dark soil and something to put it in."

"Excellent!" said Murland, leaping to his feet and running off into the woods.

"Whoa!" Sir Eldrick called from the other side of camp where he had just emerged. "Do not go into those woods alone."

"But, I have to find soil for my—"

"No. There is no time. We must leave as quickly as possible."

"Why? What did you see?" said Brannon, glancing at the trees.

"I believe they are darklings. Hurry now, everyone. Pack up and let us get to the open road. The sunlight will protect us from those creatures of shadow."

"Darklings?" said Murland.

"They are the servants of Zuul, hurry now!"

"Oh boy, oh boy," said Gibrig, shaking out his hands and walking a tight circle, seemingly unsure where to start, though he only had his bedroll to worry about.

Brannon shot to his feet and packed his things in less than a minute. He was on his horse and ready before Willow had even moved from the fire pit. Murland quite forgot about the soil at the mention of the strange darklings. He imagined all kinds of horrors befitting such a name, and he was right behind Brannon in packing up. Soon, he was hovering over the ground with his backpack.

"Come on, Willow," said Gibrig as he mounted Snorts.

Sir Eldrick and Brannon turned in their saddles as well, waiting for the ogre.

"Hold your pigs, hog farmer. Ain't no dark whatsits making me abandon my breakfast." She popped a chunk of meat in her mouth and brought the pan with her—straight from the fire, in her bare hand—and climbed up on her raptor's back. "Come on, Tor," she said, kicking his sides.

The group moved hurriedly through the woods, back toward the road, and Murland flew high overhead, searching the forest for any sign of the creatures that Sir Eldrick had mentioned.

The sun had been up for a half hour. Still, the clouds upon the horizon glowed with orange and pink streaks of light, which slowly pushed back the last remaining stars in the dark-blue western sky. The sun did little to illuminate the forest, which was abundant with dark pines and shady, fern-filled fens. The companions had made camp near the high ground, and Murland could still see their smoking fire pit.

Suddenly his eyes caught movement in the glen. It was a dark, fleeting, shapeless thing, like the shadow of a bird flying overhead. But nothing flew in the morning sky with Murland. He looked closely, his heart hammering in his ears, and saw another shape, and then two more. Quick as black wolves they shot across the camp, headed toward the companions below.

"Hurry!" Murland cried, but the companions seemed not to hear him. "Down, down backpack, bring me down," he said, tugging on the straps about his shoulders.

The backpack suddenly complied, and dove down toward the forest directly below them. One of the dark shadows passed through a lighted area and gave a shriek. Murland gasped. The backpack was bringing him down right in the creature's path.

"No, no, up, up!"

But too late. The backpack dropped him in a dark clearing with only a single beam of sunlight peering through the thick pine branches. Again came that terrible shrieking sound, which was answered by three other creatures. Murland ran into that small patch of sunlight, urging his backpack to fly with every shaking step. He spun round and round as the creatures continued to call to each other from every direction.

"Come on backpack, we've got to get out of—"

Murland's voice was lost to terror, as directly in front of him, less than ten feet away, one of the shadows emerged from the woods. The creature had no face that could be seen, just an eternal darkness that seemed to churn beneath a low-drawn hood. A dark cloak, like folded bat's wings, covered the creature, its ragged flaps dancing in the still air like black flames.

"Meeerlaaand," came a terrible screeching voice. "Come to usss."

Murland swooned as a soothing wave of sleepiness came over him. He was suddenly overcome with an urge to be out of the sunlight. The cool darkness of the wood called to him.

"Ssstep out of the sssunlight," said the creature, which was now floating toward him.

"Murland!" a faint voice called to him from far away. "Murland, get out of there!"

He knew that he should heed the voice, but he could not fight the urge to be out of the light. He took a step toward the creature, which rippled and writhed in the faint light seeping into the clearing. The creature reached out, and a black, skeletal hand emerged from beneath the ragged sleeve. Murland stood there, entranced, reaching out his own hand.

Suddenly, something lifted him off the ground and into the sunlight, and below him, the four shadowy creatures shrieked with rage. Murland shook his head, snapping himself out of the strange trance and realizing that his backpack had decided to get going after all.

"What took you so long?" he said breathlessly, shivering with the thought of how close he had come to the terrible creature.

The backpack flew him to the road, where the companions sat waiting for him on their mounts.

"There he is!" Gibrig said delightedly, pointing up from his saddle.

"Go, go, go!" cried Sir Eldrick, and the companions spurred their mounts into action.

Murland flew above his friends as they sped down the road, followed closely by the terrible cries of the darklings.

Sir Eldrick pushed the mounts hard for an hour, until the sun had risen over the tallest of trees and bathed the road in bright sunlight. As they came to a bridge spanning a wide river, Sir Eldrick finally reined in his horse and told the others to do the same.

Everyone was panting with the exertion of riding so hard for so long, and each of them glanced back the way they had come more than once as they brought the mounts down to the water.

"What in the world were those things?" Brannon asked, seemingly quite flustered.

"They are said to be servants of the Dark Lord Zuul," said Sir Eldrick.

"Zuul, but, but that is impossible," said Brannon with a shiver. "Zuul was defeated long ago by Allan Kazam the Mighty."

"Yes, he was defeated, but his spirit endured. There have been stories of strange happenings around the Twisted Tower. It seems that perhaps the tales are true. For if the darklings have returned, then it means that Zuul is gaining in power." He turned to Murland, who stood behind the companions, petrified. "They are said to be wreathed in shadow, with only darkness where their faces should be. Is this what you saw?"

Murland slowly nodded, entranced by the memory. He shook it from his mind and shivered. "They called to me in a terrible voice, and I had no control over my body. I...I nearly touched one."

"It is good that you did not," said Sir Eldrick.

"But what do they want with us?" said Gibrig, biting his nails.

"That is a question better suited for Kazimir, for it is one that I cannot answer."

"Boy, I wish he was here right now."

"Fret not, young Hogstead. The darklings cannot bear the sunlight. They will hunker down in the shadows and wait for nightfall. That is why it is imperative that we put as much distance between us and them as possible during the day."

"And what about when night falls?" asked Brannon, absently stroking his white steed as it drank from the river.

"We will continue on after the sun sets without making camp," said Sir Eldrick. "We can put twenty miles between us today if we're lucky, and though they can travel swiftly in the dark, they will not catch up to us by morning. Hopefully by then, Kazimir will come to us."

Murland thought of facing the shadowy creatures again and inwardly cringed.

"Murland...Murland!" said Sir Eldrick.

"What?" said the young apprentice, snapping out of his dark daydreams.

"I said that you should gather that soil there by the riverbank."

"Oh...right." Murland had forgotten all about his wizard leaf seeds, and he was glad for the distraction.

From his backpack he took a mug and scooped up the rich, wet soil by the bank of the river and carried it over to Brannon, who was combing his steed.

"Will this do?" Murland asked.

Brannon put a finger in the soil and brought it to his lips, tasting it. "That will do fine," he said, and spit out the bits of dirt. He dug a small hole in the ground where the sunlight hit, before pouring the moist dirt into it. "Let me see those seeds of yours."

Murland eagerly retrieved his seeds from his pocket and carefully emptied the contents of the small sack into Brannon's outstretched hand. The elf inspected the three seeds for a moment, and then brought them to his lips and began chanting something softly in Elvish.

"How long is this going to take?" Sir Eldrick asked, glancing back east.

"It will only take a few minutes if I am not bothered," said Brannon. "Murland, using your finger, poke a hole in the soil up to your first knuckle."

Murland did as he was told, and Brannon dropped the seeds into the hole and covered them with dirt.

"Get me a cup of water," said the elf, and Murland hurried to comply.

Brannon poured the water over the dirt, motioning for the others to step back. Willow, Gibrig, and Murland watched in awe as Brannon weaved his hands back and forth over the wet earth and began chanting his Elvish words louder and faster.

Suddenly, a seedling poked out of the soil, followed by two more, which quickly grew to six inches, and then a foot. Branches popped out and grew outward as the base thickened. Brannon continued his spell, chanting musically and waving his hands in the air before him. The plants grew to five feet tall and suddenly sprouted fat green buds that glistened in the sunlight.

Brannon finished his spell work and stood back to inspect the specimen.

"Wow!" said Murland. "That was incredible! Look at all that leaf."

"Thank you. It is quite a beauty, if I do say so myself," said Brannon.

"Mount up, you two," Sir Eldrick told Willow and Gibrig. "Make it quick," he said to the other two.

Brannon picked four long buds from the plants and handed them to Murland.

"They're so sticky," said Murland.

"Indeed. They need to dry out for a few days. So put them in something, and do not disturb them or get them wet. Understand?"

"Yes, thank you, Brannon. I really owe you one."

Brannon seemed to like the sound of that, for he genuinely smiled.

"Alright, let's go," said Sir Eldrick. "We've got a long hard road ahead of us."

CHAPTER 21

THE HOG FARMER AND THE KING

Hagus Hogstead reined in his mountain ram and adjusted his eyepatch as he reached the market at the foot of the Iron Mountains. He had traveled all day and night to find answers to the questions that had been keeping him from sleep.

He hadn't had a chance to say goodbye to his son, and couldn't for the life of him figure out why in the hells Gibrig had been chosen to be a Champion of the Dragon. Hagus was proud of his son, to be sure, but Gibrig was no champion, and something smelled fishy to the old dwarven hog farmer.

"Ye seen Kegley 'round?" Hagus asked a merchant he knew well.

"He be down in the human district tryin' to haggle himself a cow, last I seen him," said the merchant.

"Many thanks," said Hagus and snapped the reins.

He found Kegley leading a fat cow out of the human district, wearing a smug grin on his face. When he saw Hagus, his face dropped, but he quickly put on a jovial smile.

"Hagus Hogstead? How ye been? I heard 'bout yer lad, Gibrig. Ain't that somethin'?"

"It be somethin' alright," said Hagus, stopping and dismounting. He hiked up his trousers and squared on the shorter dwarf. "I came to ask ye a few questions."

"Questions," said Kegley, scratching his head.

Hagus watched him closely. The merchant was obviously nervous.

"What happened the day that me lad was chosen as the Champion o' the Dragon? Folks say that they saw ye with him that afternoon."

"Well," said Kegley, not quite able to meet Hagus's eyes. "He came to sell me a hog, if I remember clearly."

"And…"

"And, well, he got all stubborn like, ye see, and wouldn't sell me the hog. Said it was his friend. Named it Snorts, he did."

"I told him not to name that damn hog," said Hagus, shaking his head. "Well, then what happened?"

Kegley rubbed his bearded chin, looking like he would rather not say. "Hells, Hagus, ain't no one told ye?"

"Told me what?"

Kegley let out a sigh and shook his head. "Ye see, the king came along while Gibrig and I was hagglin' and such, and the king offers Gibrig triple the gold that I did for the blasted hog."

"He wanted to pay three times as much?" said Hagus, proud that his hog had caught the king's attention.

"Sure he did, but yer blasted lad there, he told the king *no!*"

"He what!" said Hagus, gaining the attention of the human merchants nearby. He pulled Kegley closer to his ram and glared at him sternly. "What ye sayin'?"

"Just like I said. He went and told the king no. Well, the king was hot, he was. But he threw Gib the money and went about his way with a guard leadin' that hog away." He stopped and took off his hat, wringing it with his hands. "I tried to stop him, Hagus, I really did. But that lad o' yers be pig-headed. No offense intended, ye be knowin'. He went and snatched that rope up and slapped that hog's arse, tellin' the fat beast to run away, run away."

"No…" Hagus breathed, suddenly very afraid for his son.

"He did, or I be a sucklin' whelp. He knocked over a guard and hurried after that hog. Why, I tell ye, the king was furious. It be a good thing Kazimir picked Gib to be the champion, 'cause I swear the king wanted his head on a pike."

"Thank ye, Kegley. Sorry me boy gave ye such trouble," said Hagus, bowing his head in shame and turning back to his mount.

"Ain't no hard feelin's. We all did stupid things when we was young," said Kegley behind him.

Hagus barely registered the merchant's words, so shocked he was by Gibrig's behavior. He steered his ram back toward the mountain and kicked the sides of the beast, intent on apologizing personally to the king.

He rode his ram up the pass and through the hundred-foot iron gates leading into the mountain. As he rode through the city of Hammerstrike, someone recognized him and called out triumphantly, "Long live the Hogsteads!" Others took up the call as well, and Hagus raised his fist to placate their calls. They cheered behind him as he hurried through the city toward the castle at its center, built into a gargantuan stalagmite.

"I be here to see the king," he told the guards, who bowed repeatedly as they opened the gates.

Hagus snapped the reins, riding his ram right into the castle proper before leaping off and rushing to the king's audience chamber. The two guards standing at the door crossed halberds, blocking the way.

"Speak yer name and yer business," said one.

"I be Hagus Hogstead, son o' Harrod Hogstead, father o' Gibrig Hogstead—Champion o' the Dragon o' the Iron Mountains. I wish to have words with me king."

The guards swiftly pulled back their weapons and offered him a bow. "Good Hogstead, please wait but a moment," said one, and turned and disappeared behind the door. He came back a moment later. "He'll see ye in his private chambers shortly. Please, follow me."

"Very well," said Hagus, and he followed the dwarf along the veranda that wound its way up the stalagmite castle. After ten minutes and many stairs, they came to the tip top of the formation, where Hagus was shown to a bench beside the balcony overlooking the city. The hog farmer instead stood while he waited, enjoying the rare view of Hammerstrike.

"The king be seein' ye now," said the guard.

Hagus followed him through the threshold and into a dome-ceilinged chamber, the walls of which were covered with gold leaf. A large candelabra holding a dozen torches hung from strong chains, its light shimmering and shining off those luminescent walls, giving everything within a golden glow. King Dranlar Ironfist sat waiting for him upon an intricately carved golden throne at the center of the room. A quick look around told Hagus that this room was indeed the king's private quarters, for a library containing dozens of tall bookshelves adorned one entire side, and a screen wall blocked off the other, which Hagus assumed to be the sleeping quarters.

The guard led him down the long red carpet to the throne and stopped. Together he and Hagus bowed before the king. "Sire, I give to ye Hagus Hogstead, son o' Harrod Hogstead, father o' Gibrig Hogstead—Champion o' the Dragon o' the Iron Mountains."

"Welcome, Hagus," said the king, offering him a slow nod.

Hagus had only ever met Dranlar once, ten years ago, when one of Hagus's hogs had been chosen to grace the king's table during a dinner with human dignitaries from Magestra. Hagus himself had made the first cuts, and even plated the meat for the king. But he doubted that Dranlar remembered him.

"That will be all, Barkwar," said the king, and the guard turned on his heel and marched out of the room.

Dranlar sat there leisurely upon the throne, looking down at Hagus with a glint of interest in his icy blue eyes. He stroked his black, braided beard as he stared, and Hagus wondered if he saw anger in that unreadable glare.

"What brings ye to me halls, Master Hogstead?"

"Sire," said Hagus, bowing again, and straightening his eyepatch. "I came to offer me apologies for me son's behavior. I heard what he did in the market, and—"

"Heard it from who?"

"From Kegley Quartz, Sire. Says he was there when me lad disrespected ye like he did."

"And ye believe the words o' this dwarf, do ye?"

Hagus was taken aback. He hadn't assumed or suspected that Kegley had been lying. "Well…I known the dwarf goin' on five decades. I ain't ever known him to be a liar."

Dranlar studied Hagus, making him increasingly uneasy. "Come," he said, rising from his throne. "Let us have a drink."

"Yes, Me King."

Hagus followed him to a sitting area in the library and was offered a seat. He waited as the king moved to a small bar and poured two glasses of amber liquor. The king took off his long, trailing cloak, tossed it onto the back of a chair, rolled his thick shoulders, and returned with the two drinks. Hagus rose to take his, feeling quite queer having the king serve him.

"To Gibrig Hogstead, may his sacrifice keep us safe from the wrath of the dreaded Drak'Noir," said the king, and he tapped his glass against Hagus's before shooting back the drink in one swallow.

"Thank ye, Me King," said Hagus after shooting back his drink in the same manner. He fought the cough growing in his throat from the harsh liquor. He wasn't much of a drinker, and only took wine with a meal when he and Gib had company over. He never drank liquor.

"I be acceptin' yer apology," said the king. "And I be trustin' that ye be speakin' 'bout the incident at the market to no one. I can't be havin' me subjects thinkin' they can insult their king without no consequences."

"Of course, Sire. I understand."

"Yer friend Kegley don't understand, though, does he? That must be remedied."

"Ah, he didn't mean nothin' by it," said Hagus, and then he realized his mistake, for the king's brow rose threateningly, and his hard eyes squared on him.

"Sorry, Me King," said Hagus with multiple bows. "I asked him, is all. Any dwarf would answer a father's questions about his lad."

"Yer son, and Kegley, will have a chance to redeem themselves," said the king evenly.

"Then…then ye won't be punishin' Gib when he returns?"

A small smirk played at the edge of Dranlar's mouth. One that gave Hagus a sinking feeling. "I have accepted yer apology, Master Hogstead, but I did not say that I forgive that disrespectful little shyte o' a son o' yers. Never in me years as king have I been treated with such utter contempt. I thought to take his head and make it a centerpiece at me banquet, but then Kazimir arrived to announce the champion, and I thought of a much better punishment."

Hagus felt his bottom lip quivering and fought hard to bite back the terrible words churning around inside his brain.

Dranlar smiled, showing his gold-plated teeth, seeming to thoroughly enjoy Hagus's shock.

"It is little known. But the champions that Kazimir chooses every generation are no heroes. They be worthless idiots, like that son o' yers. People who no one wants—or people who got to be gotten rid of."

Hagus was shaking now. He held his clenched fists to his sides, utterly appalled by the king's words. This only increased Dranlar's pleasure, and he took a step closer, so that his ring-pierced nose was inches from Hagus's.

"That idiot son o' yers is goin' to be dragon whelp food."

"If ye was any other dwarf, I'd...I'd—"

"Ye would what?" said Dranlar, his eyes suddenly widening with gleeful malice.

Hagus cocked back and punched the king square in the jaw, laying him out cold on the stone floor.

"If ye was any other dwarf, I'd kill ye!" said Hagus, and he spat.

He turned from the king and stormed out of the chamber, having the sense of mind to not slam the door behind him. He offered the guards a nod and headed toward the swirling balcony that would bring him to the bottom.

"Halt, good dwarf," said a guard from behind him.

Hagus stiffened and slowly turned, ready to defend himself or run away.

"Guests o' the king be permitted to take the lift."

"Thank ye," said Hagus with a nod and marched in the direction that the guard had pointed. He quickly found the lift and told the operator to bring him to the bottom.

The door closed and the contraption got going way too slowly for his liking, but move it did. He waited for the call to arms, or a cry of alarm from the upper levels, but none came. The lift reached the bottom and the door was slid aside. An old dwarf with a toothless grin offered him a nod. Hagus rushed past the dwarf and leapt onto his ram, spurring it through the castle gates.

He shot like a cannon from the royal castle and sped down the city streets, sending unsuspecting strollers diving for the gutters and nearly colliding with more than one wagon. Soon a ruckus could be heard in the distance, like the sound of twenty screaming dwarves all saying the same thing in a different way. Then the horn blew deep in the city, and all dwarves looked to the castle. Hagus glanced back and saw a spear of flame suddenly shoot from the top of the castle peak, which meant that the castle was under attack.

Every dwarf stopped what they were doing and froze.

Hagus kept on going. He reached the nearest tunnel that he knew would bring him to the outside and slapped the reins wildly, his heart booming in his chest like the mallet of the Iron God.

The sun was an hour from setting when he emerged from the mountain. His ram navigated the rocky terrain easily as he pushed it at breakneck speeds down the side of the mountain. One last great leap brought them to flat land, and Hagus spurred the ram into the market, hoping that it wasn't too late to warn Kegley.

To his relief, he found the old merchant packing up his wagon and wares for the day.

"Kegley!" yelled Hagus in an angry manner, hoping to draw the attention of those around them.

Kegley turned, squinting, and his face lit up halfheartedly when he saw who it was.

"Well, hallo Hagus. What brings ye—"

"Listen. We don't have much time. I can't explain it right now, but soon ye'll know it was for yer own good. Punch me."

Kegley looked as though he meant to say something, but he only stared curiously at Hagus.

"Ye hear me, ye deaf bat?" Hagus yelled in his face, which gained him the attention of everyone around.

Kegley was obviously embarrassed, but his confusion soon turned to anger. "Look here. I don't know what ye be tryin' to pull, but—"

"Ye dolt, the king be right pissed, bah, do I got to spell it out for ye?"

"The king?"

Urgent voices suddenly issued from the road leading from the mountain. Hagus didn't have time to explain, and so he thought up the worst thing he could think to say.

"Yer...yer wife beds ogres, and yer mother watches!" he spat.

Kegley's eyes widened, and he hauled back and socked Hagus right in the gut.

Hagus had expected a punch to the face, instead the wind burst out of him with an, "UGH." He dropped to one knee. A crowd had begun to gather, and some were even shouting encouragement at the two.

"Now you take that back!" said Kegley.

"Hit me again," said Hagus, gasping. "Tell the king ye tried to stop me."

A commotion of barking dogs and yelling dwarves came from somewhere nearby, and sudden realization sparked in Kegley's face. Kegley grabbed him by the front of his fur jerkin and gave him a shake, playing along. "What ye gotten yerself into?" he whispered in Hagus's ear.

Hagus pushed him back, saying, "Sorry," and punched his friend in the forehead enough to dizzy him. Kegley staggered back, grabbing his cart for balance.

"Stop that dwarf!" came the cry of a guard, and a blood hound bayed long and mournfully.

The dwarves, humans, elves, and ogres who had been watching the fight turned their attention solely on Hagus. He hurried to mount his ram before anyone decided to be a hero. The guards came running as the ram reared, bucked its front legs, and shot off down the muddy road leading south.

CHAPTER 22

A HARD CHOICE ON
A DARK ROAD

MURLAND KNEW THE precise moment that the sun dropped behind the horizon at his back, for when it did, a chill came over him that sent the hairs on his neck standing straight. He waited, knowing that the terrible sound was coming, that cry born from the depths of hell. As he glided above the companions on the wings of his trusty backpack, he fought the urge to turn his head and look back to the east. He knew that the shadowy creatures were out there somewhere. They had just come to life with the death of the sun. Now they would be running, no, flying through the woods in pursuit of the one who got away.

Murland gulped.

He soon found himself wishing that he had a regular mount like everyone else. It was lonely and cold flying up above the ground. He imagined all kinds of fowl and winged creatures lurking in the skies. It was like swimming far out from the coast and staring into the darkness beyond the reef. Mystery, danger, and death lurked there in the darkness.

He looked to the south often, his mind wild with imaginings of the ghosts lurking in the fog. It was well known that the Blight was haunted by the spirits of the humans who once inhabited the rocky land.

His early lessons from High Wizard Vleveus came back to him then. The old toothless wizard had seemed ever on his last leg, but when he spoke of the history and heroes and tragedies of Fallacetine, he came alive and bounded about the classroom like a man a hundred years his junior.

"The Blight...What a terrible, terrible story that is," the high wizard would say. "It was once a prosperous land, with a thriving fishing community along the once rich, southern coast. So great was it that it easily outshone the golden coast to the east. The Agnarians were a tall, strong people. In the south, they were sailors and fishermen, and in the north they were shepherds, known for their wool and rare herbs, which only grew in that region in those days.

"But their end came swiftly and terribly the day that Drak'Noir descended from the peak of Bad Mountain and flew over the Wide Wall. The great wyrm turned night into day. Her flames devoured the forests in one fell breath. Towns and cities burned, and those within them were killed instantly...if they were lucky. The call went out to all kingdoms, and each one sent a single warrior, those who came to be known as the Champions of the Dragon."

Murland meant to forget the eerie tale, and turned his eyes north, where the dark hills rolled on into the deep blue sky dancing with the stars. But then he thought of all the people who had perished, and shame turned his head back south. He stared at the foggy valley leading to the ridges and jutting stone formations haunting the barren land like behemoths frozen in time, and he wept for the dead.

Sir Eldrick glanced back at the others, wondering if they could make the long ride ahead of them. The sun had just set, and the darklings would be back on their trail by now. He measured the distance in his mind, concluding that they had put at least twenty-five miles between them, if not more. The road had been well-kept up to the fork, where it branched off north to the coast and south into the Blight. That haunted land stretched out to their left, fog hanging low to the barren valleys that dipped from the ridge the road followed.

He knew enough of the lay of the land to understand the dilemma that might soon befall them, but he was loath to tell the others about it. Instead he continued with his head held high and his shoulders straight, wanting to impart an air of confidence.

"When we stopping to eat?" Willow asked, spurring her raptor to catch up to the knight.

"We will not be stopping until morning, I am afraid," said Sir Eldrick, scanning the foggy valley beside the road.

"What...what ye lookin' for, eh?" Gibrig put in, never one to miss a gesture.

"The darklings. What else?" said Brannon, hurrying to catch up and not be the last one in line.

Sir Eldrick offered him a scowl, and noticing Gibrig looking at him, he smiled. "Anyone riding into the unknown better be looking out all the time. Wouldn't you say, Gib?"

"Aye," said the dwarf, nervously glancing around.

"But don't always believe your eyes at dusk," said the knight, "for the time between day and night plays tricks on the mind and eye."

"That's not very nice o' it."

"No, good Gibrig, it is not."

"You see anything lurking in the shadows, you let me know," said the fearless ogre. "I'll stab it, skin it, and eat it raw, as hungry as I am. Unless it's a darkling. Imagine they taste like crap."

"Your courage is admirable," said Sir Eldrick. "But do not underestimate the power of Zuul's minions."

"I ain't afraid of a bunch of shrieking skeletons," said Willow. She plugged one nostril and blew snot out the other to accentuate her point.

Sir Eldrick smiled and shook his head. "Then you're the only one."

"Ye be afraid too?" said Gibrig, looking astonished.

"A wise man knows when to be afraid, but also how to turn that fear into strength."

"How ye do that, eh?"

"You'll learn, Gib, trust me."

Morning came like a miracle, and rising from the east like the glowing crown of a god, the sun met the cloudless day gloriously.

But then that terrible noise cut through the dawn. It was so out of place in such a wonderful moment that Murland wondered if he had dreamed it.

He had been falling asleep as he glided along with his winged backpack, and could not be sure if he were sleeping or awake.

He looked to the ground below, searching the sparse copses of wicket willow and thorn bushes on the sides of the road, and thought he saw a shadow melt into a gorge. He blinked, not wanting to see but knowing that he must look, and saw three more shapes join the first. To his horror, the companions were only feet from the spot.

"Flee!" he yelled to them. "The darklings are right beside you!"

Sir Eldrick must have heard him, for he spurred the others down the road and did not let up for a half an hour. Murland landed when he saw them stop. He tripped on a stone, falling face first in the dirt. He shook himself off and rushed to Sir Eldrick's side. The knight was dismounting painfully and groaning like an old man.

"I saw them again!" Murland told him, glancing back at the eastern road with worry.

"Yes, I know. Thank you for the warning. But they cannot travel beneath this glorious sunlight. So rest your mind for now."

Murland tried to rest his mind, but he felt like he was holding on to a lightning bolt. The lack of sleep coupled with all the excitement left him buzzing with energy.

"Good job, all of you," said Sir Eldrick, patting Murland on the back. "Now get what rest you can, for we head out again at midday. Rest easy, the darklings will be sleeping as well."

"I'll sleep when I'm fed, or I'll sleep when I'm dead. Like my father always says," said Willow.

Gibrig seemed to be of like mind, for he helped Willow to get a little fire pit going off the side of the road. Brannon brushed his horse weakly and tied a feed bag to its mouth before plopping down on the ground.

"Hell of a ride, eh?" said Murland, taking a seat on the ground beside him.

Brannon only moaned. His eyes were bloodshot and puffy, and he looked like he might have been crying.

"So you think that these buds will be dried out and ready in a week or so?" said Murland, trying to make small talk.

"That is what I said, isn't it?" Brannon snapped.

Murland glanced at Sir Eldrick, who always seemed to have a scowl on hand for the haughty elf, but the knight was lying beside his horse, head on helmet, cloak covering his eyes. Looking back at Brannon, Murland was surprised to see fat tears quivering on his long lashes. He didn't know what to say, guessing that any indication that he had noticed would be met by a hateful outburst from the elf prince.

"Thanks for helping me with the wizard leaf. I really appreciate it," he said instead.

Brannon glanced at him sheepishly and wiped his teary eyes. "You're welcome."

Murland was so surprised by the reply that he sat staring at the elf.

"What?" said Brannon with annoyance.

"Oh…nothing. Nothing," Murland said, getting up and dusting off. He had decided not to push it. "I'm going to get some sleep. Long road ahead, right?"

"Ugh, don't remind me," said Brannon, laying his head on his hands and closing his eyes.

Murland awoke a few hours later to Willow's loud snoring and sat up, alert. He rubbed his itchy, grainy eyes and surveyed the roadside. He found Gibrig and Willow sleeping to his left, and Brannon over by his horse. Sir Eldrick was up, however, and staring south toward the Blight.

Murland took a swig from his water skin to wash the bad taste out of his mouth and got up quietly to join the knight.

"Good afternoon, Murland," said the knight without looking back.

"You see something out there?"

"No, just weighing options."

"What do you mean?"

Sir Eldrick gave a long sigh and looked to Murland gravely. "We will have a hard choice to make very shortly. But for now, you should get something in your belly. I will be waking the others very soon."

Murland asked no questions, but did as he was told. He was hungry after all, and would rather hear bad news on a full stomach.

A half hour later, Sir Eldrick roused the others and gathered them all together once they had eaten and shaken off the remnants of sleep.

"You see that long stretch of forest?" he said, pointing west down the road. "That goes on for thirty miles. The boughs are thick on those tall trees, and the forest is dark. Much of the road is cast in shadow, even during a bright day like this. We have put many miles between ourselves and the darklings, but we will not get through that forest before morning, and the sun will not stop them there."

"What are our options?" Murland asked.

"Yeah, what's our options?" said Willow as she chewed on a brick of cheese.

Sir Eldrick turned and looked south over the long valley leading to the rocky highlands covered in fog.

"The Blight?" said Brannon. "Oh, hells no."

"That land is open, and we will have the high ground. The darklings might be able to travel through the fog during the day, but they will be much swifter in the western forest."

"Are you mad? That land is haunted," said Brannon, looking to the others for agreement.

"So the rumors say," said the knight. "But I would rather chance that the rumors are wrong than face the darklings in the dark forest. I vote for the Blight."

"Well, I vote for the road," said Brannon, raising his hand and looking to the others desperately.

"I say we stick to the road," said Willow with a shrug. "More chance for food that way."

"What about you two?" Sir Eldrick asked Murland and Gibrig.

"I think that the Blight is the safer choice," said Murland.

Gibrig, realizing that his vote would be the tiebreaker, began shaking his head and pacing. "Oh, no, no. This can't be up to me!"

"This is up to all of us," said Sir Eldrick.

The dwarf glanced at Brannon with apprehension, for the elf was glaring at him dangerously. "But, I don't want no one to be mad at me," he said between heavy, nervous breaths.

"Knock that off!" Sir Eldrick told Brannon, swatting him on the shoulder.

"Don't worry about us," said Willow. "Just make up your own damn mind for once."

Gibrig straightened stubbornly and wiped his nose on his sleeve. "Fine, I...I think that I don't want to be in that dark forest with them dark things either."

"The Blight it is!" said Sir Eldrick, to Brannon's great dismay.

The group packed up their things and headed south off the road. Murland decided to jog along with the mounts for a time. His shoulders hurt from the backpack straps, and his neck was tight due to the hours spent flying with his head bent to the ground.

It was beyond midday when they abandoned the road and entered the Blight, and everyone knew that in only a few short hours, the darklings would awaken and be back on the trail.

CHAPTER 23

SEEKING HAVEN ON PONDER HILL

THE VALLEY SOUTH of the road led into a thick sea of fog before rising into rocky, misty highlands. The day waned, and soon night had fallen on the world. The group stayed close, with Sir Eldrick leading with a torch, whose light was swallowed up quickly by the surrounding mist.

They traveled along the ridges, staying away from the dark ravines. Gibrig talked the entire time, telling them all how this land was a lot like the valley between the mountains where he and his father lived.

"I never ever thought I would leave that place," he said as Snorts followed Sir Eldrick's horse up a particularly steep section. "On spring mornings, ye think ye just might be on the Mountain in the Clouds. The sun shines through the clouds in fat beams, lightin' up the peaks o' mountains and warmin' the air. There be tons o'butterflies up there, and the sweet smell o' clover be everywhere."

"It sounds like a wonderful place," said Murland, who was pacing the hog, not wanting to risk flying above and losing them in the fog.

"Hey, Sir Knight. Ye think…ye think I'll ever see me farm again?"

Sir Eldrick glanced over at Brannon with a heavy gaze. "Sure you will, Gib. Why, we should all go there and have a picnic someday. I for one would love to see it."

"That would be great," said Gibrig, quite choked up.

"Yous ever eat them hogs you raise, or you just ride 'em?" Willow asked behind them. She had no qualms whatsoever with taking up the rear, for it meant that she could stare at Snort's fat behind the entire journey.

"Sure, we eat 'em. But I ain't never liked eatin' ham. They be too nice. It be like eatin' a person."

"What else you eat?"

"Well, we eat potatoes and carrots, and other stuff. And sometimes we even buy exotic fruits at market. But mostly I guess we eat corn and bread. It be the cheapest."

"Ever tried snail?"

"Naw, don't think I would like 'em. They be too cute."

"I love snails," said Willow dreamily. "And toads, and gators, and eels, and snakes, and—"

"Quiet!" said Sir Eldrick with a hiss. He stopped.

They all waited and listened, quiet as the mist.

Murland tried to hear what it might have been that sparked the knight's attention, but his pulse was suddenly pounding in his ears.

After a minute, they continued across the ridge, quieter this time. No one asked Sir Eldrick what he thought he heard, for none of them wanted to know. Murland scanned the ravine to their left, but his eyes quickly became confused staring at the swirling fog below. The ghostly mist had thinned considerably there on the ridge, and Sir Eldrick's light covered much more ground. It was a world of silhouettes bathed in moonlight, and dark shapes loomed all along the hills and ridges. Murland knew that they were just tall rock formations, still he watched them cautiously, waiting for one of them to come to life and snatch him up.

Suddenly, the terrible grating shriek of the darklings rang out far away and echoed across the too-still land. Murland jumped, and Brannon gave a high-pitched squeal of surprise.

"Ride!" said Sir Eldrick, spurring his mount into a gallop.

Murland ran and tugged on the straps of his backpack. "Fly!" he yelled, and to his surprise, the stubborn pack gave him no trouble and climbed high into the sky.

Murland scanned the land, noticing a tower a few miles away upon the highest hill in view. He reported his findings to Sir Eldrick, and the knight told him to lead the way.

"If I am not mistaken," said Sir Eldrick, "That is Ponder Hill. It was once home to contemplative monks for five hundred years. Hasten to it quickly, for it is hallowed ground!"

Murland chose the easiest-looking route that he could find and led the group swiftly across the uneven ground.

The cry of the darklings ripped through the night again, closer this time. The eerie call screamed of malice and rage, and it filled Murland with a dread that he had never known.

Oh, please, Kazimir, if you can hear me somehow, we need your help, he said over and over in his mind.

"Hurry!" Sir Eldrick called to the others as he reached the base of the tower.

Murland guided his backpack by tugging on the straps and steered himself down to land on the top of the decrepit tower.

"What do you see?" Sir Eldrick called up to him as he unsheathed his sword.

Murland scanned the land to the northeast, where he thought the cries were coming from. "Nothing yet," he called back.

"Get up here and quiet down that hog," Sir Eldrick told Gibrig. "Willow, watch the western side of the hill. Brannon, watch the south. They will most likely surround us."

"And then what?" said Brannon nervously.

"Then we hope to the gods that this isn't our day to die."

They took their places and waited. Murland watched the eastern hills closely, but shadows were everywhere, and the swirling mist gave the illusion of movement. He took his wand out of the backpack and held it tight. Though he knew that he could not use it, he felt better with it in his hand.

"Murland, take these," said Sir Eldrick, and tossed him up a lit torch and then a sheathed short sword. He lit and handed the others torches as well. "The fire will deter the creatures. Stand strong, my friends. They feed off your fear. Give them nothing. Dig deep, and find the courage that is within you all. You are champions of the dragon, do not forget. Your name strikes fear in those with evil hearts!"

Murland unsheathed the sword and stared wide-eyed at the fire's reflection on the mirror-like blade. Just then, he caught movement down at the base of the hill.

"They're coming!" he yelled to the others two stories down.

"Prepare yourselves," said Sir Eldrick. "Brannon, unsheathe your damn sword! Gib, ready your shovel. Willow…"

A huge boom sounded from the other side of the tower, and Sir Eldrick rushed over. Murland looked over the side and watched, awed, as Willow picked up another large block of stone and hurled it over the side.

"Come and get me, you dark stains. Hah!"

To Murland's horror, one of the darklings suddenly flew out of the shadows below the base of the tower and landed in front of Willow. The ogre gave a war cry and swung her huge club, taking the robed figure in the gut and sending him screeching and flying off the crumbled battlement and out into darkness.

"Sir Eldrick! To your right!" cried Murland as a shadow in the shape of a hunched man crawled like a spider over the stone.

"Back to the hells with you!" said Sir Eldrick, swinging his torch out toward the creature.

A high-pitched scream jerked Murland's head to the side, and down below he saw Brannon weakly swinging his sword at another darkling. The creature stalked the elf slowly, one long crooked finger reaching out past the tattered sleeve.

"Brannon, watch out!" yelled Murland, and before he could think of what he was doing, he leapt off the tower, sword cocked back with both hands, and descended on the darkling with a terror-filled cry.

Something suddenly scraped his tailbone and tore through the back of his pants, and he cried out. He stopped with an "oof", and found himself hanging upside down from a gargoyle's horn by his underwear, which was giving him a painful wedgie.

He watched helpless as, ten feet below, the darkling cornered a mewling Brannon and grabbed at his neck. Brannon slapped the boney hand away with his sword, and Murland saw a flash of silver in the torchlight. The darkling brought his hand back, hooded head bent as though he were looking at the thing in his boney palm.

A shocked breath escaped from Brannon, and he grabbed at his neck. "No! Not Val's pendant."

The darkling took a swipe at the elf, but Brannon suddenly snapped. His voice boomed with authority as he swung his sword with a roar and chopped at the arm coming for him. His curved elven blade cut right through the arm, and the darkling disappeared.

Murland breathed a sigh of relief and hurriedly tried to extricate himself from the gargoyle horn. He could hear Willow laughing and cursing at the darklings. Even her raptor seemed to be battling the wraiths. The clang of swords came from the other side of the tower, where Murland hoped Sir Eldrick was protecting Gibrig.

Brannon's darkling suddenly appeared on his left, but the nimble elf leapt out of the way of the sudden sword strike that followed. Just then, Murland finally tore his underwear free and fell, screaming, on top of the darkling. The crunch of bones sounded as he landed, and the darkling crumbled beneath him. Brannon grabbed his necklace and stomped on the bones, crying and furious as he crushed them beneath his feet. Murland pulled him back, and they both stood with their swords pointed at the rumpled black cloak.

"We killed one!" Murland yelled to the others, but his victory soon turned to astonishment as the cloak rose from the ground with a hundred wet clicking sounds.

The darkling turned to face them, and there beneath the dark hood, Murland thought he saw a rotten, toothy grin.

"We will make you watch everyone you love, buuurrrnnn," said the darklings in many hissing voices.

A wave of utter depression washed over Murland, and he dropped his sword, wondering what had been the point in fighting. Beside him, Brannon's sword clanged to the ground as well.

"Life is pain. Life is death. There is only darkness at the end. Only night. The king of shadow always wins in the end. There is no escape."

The darkling reached out to Murland, who had resigned himself to his fate.

His backpack, however, had other ideas.

Murland suddenly shot into the sky high above the tower, and the sudden jolt jerked him sober. He looked down, worried for the others. But just then, a great flash of light from the top of the tower blinded him, and a booming voice drowned out those of the slithering darklings.

"Be gone from here, minions of Zuul!"

When Murland looked again, he saw Kazimir standing on top of the tower, his staff held high and crackling with lightning. In his other hand was a long, thin water pipe of glass. He brought it to his lips, and a snaking arc of lightning hit the pipe. The pipe gurgled, and Kazimir's chest expanded. He pulled the pipe from his lips and blew out a sparkling, multicolored cloud of glowing smoke.

The darklings hissed and thrashed when the smoke hit them, and they reeled back over the battlements. Kazimir's lightning chased after them, scorching their ragged robes all the way down the side of the hill.

With a word from Kazimir, the lightning disappeared and the staff went out. He blew on the smoking end of the staff and then stood with his hands on his hips, chuckling at the fleeing darklings.

"And don't come back!" Willow yelled over the side of the battlements.

Murland guided the backpack down to the base of the tower and joined his friends in celebration. Kazimir floated down from the top of the tower and laughed with them.

"You came just in time!" said Brannon, fanning himself and leaning against the tower wall.

"Yeah, I thought we were doomed," said a frazzled-looking Gibrig.

"I was just getting warmed up," Willow put in.

"I've been watching you all since you climbed up to this tower. You all did quite well."

The celebration died like a snuffed candle, and everyone stared at the wizard.

"What?" he said, giving them all the cockeye.

"You have been watching us almost die for ten minutes?" said Brannon, aghast.

Kazimir shrugged, as though he didn't understand the problem.

"Damn it, man. One of us could have been seriously hurt," said Sir Eldrick.

"Ah, could have, you say. Well, many things *could have* happened, many things can, many things do, but many more don't. Now, who has food? Magic makes me hungry."

"Why don't you just whoosh some here?" said Willow, licking her lips hungrily.

Kazimir looked at her with a bushy-eyed scowl. "Why don't you just *whoosh* over there and get me something out of that giant sack of yours? I swear, a wizard gets no respect."

"You heard the man," said Sir Eldrick, giving Kazimir a quick, annoyed glance. "Get a fire going. Put some food on the spit. Least we can do is show our mysterious guide some hospitality."

CHAPTER 24

POOR WENDEL

Princess Caressa approached King's Crossing on foot, leading her mount by the bridle and cautiously watching the crow's nest hanging off to the side between the roads to Magestra and Vhalovia. The sign beneath it read *"Horse thieves not welcome!"* Above it, protruding from a swath of tangled and tattered cloth, was a skeletal arm.

As she approached, Caressa saw that the sun-bleached white bone had been picked clean by the ravens long ago. But as she came around the front, to her surprise, she saw that the eyes of the unfortunate soul remained.

And they seemed to be staring at her.

"Caraaaah!" the fiend suddenly hissed in a wet, hollow voice.

The princess jumped back with a start, her hand instinctively going to the hilt of her sword.

"Careeeess…" the skeleton sang before cackling like a mad crow.

"What is this devilry?" Caressa insisted. "Go back to sleep, you wretch."

The skeleton twitched and reached high on the bars. With a jerk and a tremor of spasms, it rose to its boney feet.

"What devilry? What devilry, she says. What devilry is this, hah! Oh, Caressaaa…"

"I mean it, damn you. Quiet down or I'll, I'll—"

"I'll, I'll," the skeleton mocked.

The thin shock of white hair hanging in clumps from the skull sickened her, and Caressa turned from the creature with disgust.

"Your father's devilry! That's what this is! Wench! Whore! Dirty Roddington bitch!"

Caressa turned, furious at the accusations, and she drew back her sword.

"Oh yesss, do it, do it. Free Wendel from this terrible cage."

His pleading gave her pause, and she got ahold of herself. "Perhaps I will free you," she said, pacing back and forth slowly before him. "Perhaps I'll let you rot."

"What can Wendel do?" said the wretch, pulling at his hair.

"You must see everyone who comes and goes this way. What can you tell me of a tall and lanky wizard's apprentice?"

"What does Wendel know about a lanky wizard?" he said, tapping one boney finger against his chin. "Wendel knows everything of course! Free me and I will tell you all about him."

"No. You tell me first. Then I set you free."

"Oh, no. No, no, no. Wendel will not be tricked! Wendel was tricked once. ONCE!"

"Wendel will not be tricked," said Caressa. "I give you my word."

"Blah!" Wendel spat. "I would shit on the word of a Roddington if I still had an ass!"

"You were once a man. Surely you have heard the adage, 'A Roddington never gives anyone the shaft.' Well, it is true."

"No, no. Not the shaft. They give you a cage, and a witch to put a spell on your corpse. Then they hang you up to rot and scare away horse thieves. That is what the Roddington word is worth."

"Is that true? Did my father do that to you?" she asked.

"What does it look like, Princess?"

"Wendel, I'm so sorry, I had no idea that my father could…"

"Ho there!" came a deep, melodic voice, and Caressa turned to see the most handsome elf she had ever met. He sat atop a tall black stallion, wearing red armor to match the horse's braided leather shaffron, crinet, peytral, and other armor.

"I thought so at first as well," said Wendel with a cackle. "But now we are good, good friends. Now get lost, pretty boy!"

"Hello, good elf," said Caressa. "Glad to make your acquaintance…"

"Valkimir the Valiant of the woodland realm," he said, glancing behind her at the grinning skeleton. "Is that wretch pestering you?"

"No, not at all," said Caressa.

"Am I?" Valkimir asked.

"Not at all."

"Good, then I will take my rest here at the crossing if you do not mind. I have been riding for a day and a night."

"I don't mind at all."

"I don't mind at all," said Wendel in a mocking voice. "Gods give me the strength to go on. Why don't you just jump his bones already and be done with it?"

"Shut your filthy mouth!" said Caressa, slapping the cage with the side of her sword.

"You ask me to talk. You tell me to shut up. Which one is it, woman?"

"You've made a strange friend," said Valkimir as he dismounted.

"He has information that I need. But he drives a hard bargain."

"That's not all I'd like to drive hard," said Wendel, eyes spinning in circles in his head as he gyrated against the cage.

"Gods. You *are* a foul creature, aren't you?"

"Takes one to know one."

"What does he claim to know, that you would waste your time with his nonsense?" asked Valkimir.

"My friend came through here a while back. He was…he was named Dragon Champion of Magestra."

"What did you say?" Valkimir's eyes suddenly lit up.

"Champions of the Dragon. Champions of the Dragon," Wendel sang. "A lanky wizard, a fair elf prince, a fat green ogre, a tall knight, and a dwarf with humanism. What a lot of losers they looked like. Hah! You're all doomed."

Valkimir rushed to the cage and grabbed hold of the bars, shaking them. "When was this? How long ago?"

"Oohh, aahh. The handsome elf wants something from Wendel as well."

"Tell me, you bag of bones. Tell me now!"

"Tisk, tisk. What do you have to offer Wendel, hmm?"

"And this is about where I was with him when you arrived," said Caressa. "Do you mind? I was here first."

Valkimir got himself under control and stepped aside for the princess.

"Now, where were we, Wendel? Ah, right. You were about to tell me more about these champions."

"First Wendel flies free, then Wendel sings," he said, crossing his arms in front of him.

"Sorry. That just won't do," said Caressa. "I suppose there isn't much for you to tell me anyway. You have already admitted that they went this way. And I know that they are heading west." She walked away from him, winking at Valkimir.

He sneered at the skeleton and turned away as well.

"Wait! Wendel has much more to tell! Was it a day ago? A week? You will never know."

Caressa stopped and regarded him over her shoulder as an afterthought. "You've one last chance. Speak now or rot forever."

"They went through here weeks ago, heading west like you said. That stinking Kazimir was with them. But then, a few days ago, something else came through, something dark, something terrible." Wendel hugged himself and his teeth chattered. "Free me now and I tell you what it was."

Caressa pulled Valkimir away and leaned in to whisper. "I have given my word to the wretch that I will free him. And I cannot break my word, for a Roddington never gives anyone the shaft. But we cannot in good conscience have the undead fiend running around the countryside. Once I have let him out of his cage, you should put him back in."

Valkimir scowled. "That sounds a lot like giving him the shaft."

"Technically, I will be keeping my promise. Besides, we have to find out what he knows about this…thing following our friends."

"Why are you interested in catching up to them?"

She studied his eyes, gauging whether to trust him. "Let me just say that my friend Murland has gotten himself in over his head."

"So has my friend as well."

A silent understanding passed between them.

"What's so secret, eh?" Wendel yelled, banging on the bars of the crow's nest.

"I have come to a decision," said Caressa, turning from Valkimir and walking up to the cage. "You tell me what was following the champions, and I let you out."

Wendel glanced at Valkimir with suspicion. "They flew through in the dark of night. It was the witching hour. The moon was high. Like shadows they were. Black as a demon's heart. Rags tattered and torn. Faceless. Soundless. Evil!"

"He speaks of the darklings," said Valkimir, his face suddenly ashen.

"Yes, yessss, darklings they were. Black as—"

"But why would they be after the champions?" Caressa asked Valkimir.

"Only the gods know for sure."

"I sing, now you free me!" said Wendel behind them.

"We're wasting our time," said Caressa. "We have to catch up to them."

"*We?*"

"You are looking for Prince Brannon, Dragon Champion of Halala, are you not?"

"Well, yes. But all due respect, I don't need you slowing me down."

"Oh, really? *I* will slow you down?"

"My stallion is of the Verennian breed."

"And mine has enchanted horseshoes," said Caressa.

"Very well then."

"A deal is a deal," Wendel sang. "Break a deal, and your skin will peel."

"Hold your rotting bones!" Caressa suddenly yelled. She turned back to Valkimir with a soft smile. "Let's get this over with."

Wendel shook with anticipation as Caressa approached, but when she drew her blade, he gave a shriek and flew to the other side of the small cage. She brought back the sword and swung hard, hitting the lock and breaking it. After pulling the chains out of the bars, she opened the door and extended her hand.

The skeleton shot out of the cage with a gleeful laugh and started down the eastern road toward Magestra. Valkimir was ready for him, however, and began swinging a lasso made of elven rope over his head. He let the spinning ring fly, and it soared through the air, coming down around the skeleton's body. Valkimir gave a yank, and Wendel was taken off his feet and pulled backward.

"It burns, it burns!" Wendel cried, writhing and smoking.

Valkimir wrestled the screaming skeleton back into the cage, and all the while Wendel assaulted him with insults and curses. When he finally slammed the cage shut, Valkimir tied the door tightly with the rope.

"This is enchanted rope," he said as he tightened the last knot. "That is why it burns your undead bones. I would suggest not touching it, or you will surely lose your fingers."

"Your mother was a pig!" Wendel screamed. He grabbed ahold of the rope in a rage and cried out in anguish.

"I told you not to touch it," said Valkimir, shaking his head.

"Come, I cannot stand the sound of his voice any longer," Caressa called to him.

"You cannot keep Wendel here like this!" the skeleton pleaded.

Valkimir stopped before mounting his horse and regarded the skeleton. "You are right. When I come back this way I shall bring with me a wizard. One who might give your spirit rest. Until then, sit tight."

Wendel thrashed and kicked and sputtered and spat as Caressa and Valkimir steered their horses west toward the setting sun.

CHAPTER 25

---×---

SHELTER FROM THE STORM

"T*HIS IS THE last time,*" *said the queen as Sir Eldrick slowly pulled her blouse down from her shoulder, exposing the smooth skin and kissing it softly.*

"*You said that last time,*" *he said, trailing kisses up to her neck.* "*And the time before that.*"

"*This time I am serious,*" *said the queen breathlessly.* "*Henry is getting suspicious.*"

Sir Eldrick turned her around, took her up in his arms and, spinning, set her down on the four-poster bed. She took his face in her hands and kissed him deeply.

"*I love you,*" *he whispered.*

She kissed him again, and he knew that it was to silence him.

"*I mean it,*" *he said, pulling away.*

She sighed, and slowly pulled her blouse down, teasingly exposing her large bosom. "*Do you want to talk? Or do you want to…*"

Sir Eldrick was awakened by Willow's deep snoring. Cursing the ogre, he squeezed his eyes shut, desperately trying to return to the dream. After many minutes with no success, he resigned himself to reality and rose to meet the day.

He found that Kazimir had disappeared at some point in the night, and he hadn't even had the decency to stoke the fire. He sat up and took a drink from his water skin before pouring some on his face. The night had been mostly sleepless, due to the strange, moaning noises that haunted the hill all night. Eldrick had gotten a few hours at least, which was more than enough for the seasoned knight.

The dream still haunted him, but he shook off his melancholy and put on a stoic face for the others.

"Wake up, my fearless champions. For the sun is bright, and the night is behind us. Let the spirits return to their unmarked graves, and let us get back to the road."

"I thought the morning would never come," said Brannon, glancing around the tower wearily.

"What's for breakfast?" Willow asked as she snuggled up to her raptor, which she had in a tight headlock.

"Whatever you can eat before we get going," said Sir Eldrick. He hooked a finger at Brannon and walked around to the back of the tower.

The elf came along a few seconds later, looking to have shaken sleep quite quickly. "I hope you have some good news, because I'm just about sick and tired of this quest," he hissed.

Sir Eldrick was taken aback. "Please, you have dragon breath," he said, waving a hand before his face.

"What?" said Brannon. He cupped his hand in front of his mouth and huffed into it before sniffing. "Ugh. Well no wonder. Living out here in the wild like homeless dwarves. I haven't had a proper bath in over a week. My hair is in knots, and—"

"Save it, princess. I was just going to congratulate you on your bravery last night. Kazimir was impressed. You know, he said he was this close to giving up on you. Was going to feed you to the dragon after you fled from the bandits. But he has changed his mind."

"Oh. My. Gods," said Brannon, sliding down the side of the tower with a look of shock.

"What got into you last night anyway? You acted like a man for once. I saw how you fought the darkling."

"The beast snatched Val's necklace," said Brannon, pulling the gold chain from beneath his blouse. "Inside the pendent is his blood, sweat, tears, and—"

"I get it!" said Sir Eldrick, holding up a hand. "Whatever gave you courage, I implore you to summon the same thoughts the next time we run into trouble. We aren't even beyond the Wide Wall yet. Trust me, the fun has only started."

"Great."

"Come on. A warrior deserves his breakfast," said Sir Eldrick, extending a hand.

Brannon put on a determined face that almost made the knight laugh, and took his hand.

Murland finished hemming his underwear and hurriedly wolfed down his breakfast. "Go on, I'll catch up!" he yelled to the others, who were all mounted and waiting for him to get his things together.

He quickly took off his pants when their backs were turned and pulled on his repaired underpants. After tugging on his trousers and putting away his things, he swung the backpack over his shoulder and started off after the other champions at a sprint.

"Fly, backpack. Fly!" he said, leaping into the air.

To his delight, the pack extended its wings and brought him high over the heads of the others. He waved down at them, laughing with glee.

Murland was in good spirits this morning, for his wizard leaf was drying out well, and he would soon be able to try it out. Finally, the veil that had separated him from his magical calling would be lifted. He refused to think of the darklings and how close he and his friends had all come to death. He thought only of the magic that he would soon be able to wield. He knew dozens of small spells by heart. Not being able to perform any of them left him with nothing much to excel at besides memorizing the ancient incantations.

He still couldn't believe that someone, likely Lance Lancer, had been killing his wizard leaf. But he wasn't so mad at Lance as he was at himself. He should have known something was wrong. Growing the plant was hard, there was no doubt about that. But Murland had done everything right and he knew it. His only mistake had been letting it get poisoned in the first place. Surely the elder wizards had realized the reason. Why, then, had they not intervened?

Murland realized that it was likely because they thought that if he couldn't get to the bottom of that small mystery, he wouldn't be much use as a wizard anyway.

"Well, just wait until we return victorious from Bad Mountain," he said over his shoulder to his backpack. "I'll bring back one of Drak'Noir's teeth and shove it right up Lance's butt, that'll show him, eh?"

Murland laughed to himself and thought of Caressa. His dreams of winning over her father with his victory had seemed like a pleasant fantasy up until now. Once his wizard leaf was ready, however, he would finally be on his way to becoming a real wizard.

Around midday, Murland noticed a particularly dreadful-looking storm brewing in the south. He watched it grow for a while until he had determined its direction.

"Bring me down, Packy."

The backpack glided down to the rocky hillside that the companions were traversing, and Murland came to a running stop before the knight. "Bad storm coming this way from the south. Dark black clouds. Looks nasty," he said.

Sir Eldrick glanced south and blocked the sun with a hand to his forehead. He looked west as well. "What's over that way?"

"Some big rock formations and cliffs mostly. Looks pretty barren."

"We're going to have to find a place to wait out this storm if it's as bad as you say it is. Come on," he bade them all.

It took the storm less than a half hour to find them. The angry black clouds blocked out the sun, and a suddenly frigid wind howled over the hills. Thunder growled and barked overhead, and lightning flashed in huge arcing webs. A colossal boom shook the ground and the sky broke. The rain came down hard and fast, and soon reduced visibility to a few feet.

"Over here!" said Murland over the tumult. "I saw a cave over here!"

He led the others, who led their terrified mounts by the reins, to the huge rock formations where he had seen the cave entrance. Lightning cracked the ground less than fifty feet away, and Murland jumped with a cry that was drowned out by the crackling surge.

"Here it is, hurry!" he said, spotting the cave.

The rain turned to hail the size of acorns, one of which hit Murland in the back of the head. He saw a flash of dancing stars and went down as he was pummeled by the frozen projectiles. Strong hands took him up, and soon the onslaught stopped.

He opened his eyes groggily and found himself being cradled like a baby by Willow.

"The mounts!" Brannon screamed, and Gibrig gave an alarmed cry.

"What have you done, you moron!" Brannon continued, and Murland raised his head enough to see Sir Eldrick get between the elf and the dwarf.

"They were so scared, they…they slipped out o' me hands. Oh, no, no, no. Snorts!" he yelled into the flashing storm. To Murland's shock, Gibrig ran out into the storm, screaming to his hog.

"Gibrig, No!" Sir Eldrick cried. The knight started after him, but just then, lightning erupted in the entrance, shaking the cave and loosening the stone around the threshold. Sir Eldrick jumped out of the way as the entrance crumbled and darkness filled the chamber.

"Gibrig!"

The voice calling to him was suddenly devoured by the raging storm. Gibrig called to Snorts, yelling at the top of his lungs. But it was as if a witch had cast a spell on him and taken his words. For he heard not his own voice. The ghostly outlines of the fleeing mounts bloomed fully in a flash of lightning, but then they disappeared, swallowed up by the storm.

"Snorts!" Gibrig called again.

A rock-hard hail stone hit him in the shoulder, causing him to cry out mutely. He continued after the mounts blindly, tripping and falling hard on the slick mounds of ice that littered the ground. Hail pummeled his back and legs, and he covered his head with his hands to protect it, taking more than one stinging blow to the fingers as he drunkenly got to his feet and, crying, turned back for the shelter of the cave.

CHAPTER 26

MARGI & EGBERT

THE DEEP MOAN and muffled pounding of the storm vibrated through the stone, and Murland envisioned an army of giants trying to smash their way through the cave. In the thunderous tumult, he heard nothing else. He felt his way around the stone floor of the cave, reaching blindly for Brannon, whom he thought was right beside him. His hand found flesh in the darkness and he nearly recoiled, for it was leathery, bumpy skin.

"Willow," he said over the racket of the storm. "Willow…is that you?"

Somewhere in the cave, a torch blazed to life, and Murland looked around, trying to get used to the sudden light. Sir Eldrick was raising the torch above his head, and Willow was standing to his right, along with a terrified-looking Brannon.

Murland gulped, not wanting to look at what it was that he was touching. He pulled his hand back quickly and looked up to find a fifteen-foot-tall, blue-skinned cyclops standing over him, grinning.

Sir Eldrick's torch suddenly went out, and the knight gave a cry of alarm. A net fell over Murland, and he felt himself scooped up off the floor. The sounds of battle echoed throughout the cave, and Murland hoped for a fleeting moment that Sir Eldrick and Willow might be able to defeat the cyclops. But soon their battle cries turned to angered protest.

Murland swung in the net and felt himself being carried. Soon a faint light began to illuminate a tunnel, and he found that Sir Eldrick, Willow, and Brannon had also been caught in nets. The knight dangled beside him and, glancing back, Murland saw that Willow and Brannon were being carried by another of the creatures.

"Are you guys alright?" Murland whispered.

"Do we look alright?" said Brannon in a panic.

"Let me out of here, you big ugly toads!" said Willow, fighting to free herself from the net.

The cyclops carrying her and Brannon swatted them with his free hand.

"Quiet, you!" said the cyclops, eyeing them dangerously with the one giant orb set in the middle of its face. "Lively dinner we got, eh Margi," he said to the other cyclops.

Margi turned out to be a twelve-foot tall, red-skinned female cyclops. She wore a loincloth like her husband, but also a swath of ragged cloth over her huge bosom.

"Only need one for dinner, Egbert," she said with annoyance in a deep and even voice.

The companions were brought into a wide circular alcove, where a large iron cauldron sat bubbling at the center. Bones littered the floor, most of which had been ground to dust by the two cyclopes' gargantuan feet.

"Try to stay calm," Sir Eldrick told Murland as he fished a dagger from its sheath.

The cyclopes hung the companions' nets from hooked chains moored to the ceiling before turning and hugging each other and dancing in a circle triumphantly.

"We got foods!" Egbert cheered. "Told you storm would chase something in!"

"We do good," said Margi. "Pretty elf will make good jam."

"Jam? I says we eat her now."

"I'm not a *her*," said Brannon haughtily. "I'm the prince of Halala. Release me and my friends, or you will pay dearly!"

"Hmm?" Margi hummed, bending to eyeball the elf. She poked him with a fat finger. "She's a lively one."

"Stop that!" he yelled, squirming in his net.

"Shut up!" Sir Eldrick warned him.

"Next one to talk gets squished for jam!" Margi told them all.

"You and jam," said Egbert. "I'm hungry *now*. Let's cook 'em all up and suck the marrow from their bones."

"Think, Egbert. Use your horn," she said, tapping her head. "We need food to last. I say we make jam out of the prince, pickle two others, and eat one now."

Murland tried to retrieve his knife from his back pocket beneath his robe, but the way he was caught and twisted in the netting, there was no way he could get to it. He worriedly glanced at Sir Eldrick, who was quietly sawing away at the net with his dagger.

Gibrig finally found the cave, but to his dismay he found that a cave-in had blocked the entrance. He climbed the rubble, slipping on the wet boulders, and began carefully heaving the smaller stones away. Gibrig might have looked like a human, but he had always had the strength of a dwarf. Hail pummeled him as he worked, but he kept at it, fighting through the pain and finally freeing enough stone to see into the dark cave.

He wiggled through the small opening and tumbled inside, bouncing down the rubble on the other side and coming to a stop in the darkness.

"Hello? Where is everyone?" he whispered to the dark.

His eyes adjusted quickly, and the faintest of light came from a tunnel far to the back of the cave.

"Where did you guys g—"

Gibrig stopped, for strange voices echoed suddenly. He crept along, making for the faintly lit tunnel. It went on for a few dozen feet, and the pungent odor of unwashed bodies and wet moss assaulted Gibrig's nose.

"I told you, we're only cooking one. Now hurry up and decide. Margi's hungry."

The voice was just around the next corner, and Gibrig stopped at the last bend in the tunnel, shaking uncontrollably.

"What's that smell?" came another, deeper voice.

"Smells like dwarf!" said the female voice.

Gibrig thought to turn and run away as fast as he could, climb out of the cave and…and what? The storm was too much for him to bear, the mounts were gone, and his friends were in trouble.

The rumbling of heavy footsteps drew near, and Gibrig bravely jumped out into the open.

"Ah!" he yelled, meaning to seem fierce, but upon seeing the two giant cyclopes, his roar turned to a high-pitched scream.

"What's this?" said the female cyclops, stopping and bending to get a better look at Gibrig. "A human who smells like a dwarf?"

"Don't t-t-touch me!" said Gibrig. "I...I be cursed! Transformed by a wizard to look like a human."

The male cyclops positioned himself defensively in front of his mate and studied Gibrig with a scowl. "What you doing here, man-dwarf?"

"Them be me friends," said Gibrig, pointing at the others hanging in the nets. "And we all be friends o' the great and powerful Kazimir. Ye best be lettin' us all go, less ye be wantin' to incur his wrath!"

"Kazimir, you say?" said the male. "I never heard of no Kazimir."

"You never heard of nothing," said Margi, slapping him and pushing past to stand before Gibrig. "You are all friends of Kazimir, so you say. But how do we know?"

"Just look at me," said Gibrig, arms wide. "How else does a dwarf get turned into a human?"

"Let the wizard come. We'll eat him too," said Egbert with a toothy grin on his big, round face.

"Shut up!" Margi told him with a slap.

"Best ye let us go now, and no harm'll come to ye. I give ye me word," said Gibrig, glancing at the others.

"We don't want no trouble from that Kazimir," Margi told her mate. "I heard tell tales of that one. An evil one he is."

Egbert scratched his head by his small curved horn and glanced at the hanging companions. "Well bat turds, Margi. We can't let them all go. Even a wizard knows you don't walk into a cyclops den and come out without a scratch. What would the others think if they heard?"

"He's right," Margi told Gibrig. "We can't let you all go. We will keep one. That one!" she said, pointing at Willow.

"No, no, you don't want that one. Look at her, all green and bloated. She is sure to be foul tasting. Besides, she's got that...that swamp fever."

"She does?" said Egbert, looking closely at the very angry, and very upside down ogre.

"Then we'll take the fair elf," said Margi.

Again, Gibrig shook his head. "Oh, no, no. He is just skin and bones. Hardly any meat on him."

"What about that one?" said Egbert, pointing at Murland.

"He's a wizard's apprentice. And everyone knows that eating magical people will give you an upset stomach for weeks. Why not eat the knight? Very valiant. Very tasty."

Sir Eldrick's eyes went wide, but Gibrig just offered him a small shrug.

The two ogres looked Sir Eldrick over like he was meat hanging at market, and finally nodded to each other.

"Fine, you've got a deal," said Margi. "But first he goes in the pot. And you will all watch. See what happens to trespassers who walk in our den unannounced."

Egbert took down the net holding Sir Eldrick and dragged him over to the cauldron. He was about to pick up the knight and toss him in the boiling water when Gibrig suddenly blurted out, "Wait!"

"What now? I'm hungry," said Egbert.

"The knight is strong, and very tough. If I may, I would suggest softening him up with some beer. Me pap and I always soften up our livestock before we eat 'em. Makes the meat nice and soft and juicy."

"I'll eat him tough, I don't care," said Egbert, but his mate shook her head and raised a staying hand.

"Makes the meat more tender, you say?"

"Juicy and tender," said Gibrig, rubbing his tummy. "Mmmm."

"Can't hurt. Egbert, gimme a bottle from the back."

"Awe, come on. I'm hungry now!" Egbert protested.

"Move your lazy no-good-for-nothing blue butt!" Margi yelled.

Sulking, Egbert did as he was told, and returned from the back of the cave with a pint bottle of beer. He uncorked it, helped Sir Eldrick to sit up, and slid the bottle through the net so that the knight could drink it. Sir Eldrick greedily gulped down the entire bottle, winking at Gibrig.

"Best ye give him a few more," said Gibrig, stepping back a pace.

Egbert grumbled, but after a scowl from his mate, he retrieved two more and fed them to Sir Eldrick.

"Now he goes into the pot!" Egbert told them all, even eyeing his wife angrily.

She nodded.

Gibrig watched nervously as the cyclops grabbed the net with a yank. But Sir Eldrick slipped out somehow, and the cyclops staggered back with the momentum. Baffled, he looked to the frayed net and then to Sir Eldrick. The knight stood grinning, holding a dagger in his hand. He tossed the dagger into the air and caught it by the blade, and suddenly flung it at Egbert.

The dagger hit him square in the middle of his big blue eye and stuck. Egbert gave a howl and staggered back into the wall as his mate screamed in horror and rage.

"Watch out!" said Gibrig, but Sir Eldrick saw Margi's big red hand coming for him. He flipped into the air as she grabbed for him, leaping over the reaching hand and landing on the wrist. Sir Eldrick unsheathed his sword and ran up her arm even as she reeled back. He took three quick strides and jumped, avoiding her other hand and slashing her one big eye with his long sword before sailing over her shoulder.

Margi howled and grabbed her wounded eyeball as Sir Eldrick landed and rolled into a crouch. The cyclops staggered back, screaming, and tripped over the knight.

Gibrig leapt out of the way just in time as the big red cyclops fell flat on her back. He ran to the others, who were still stuck in their nets, and began hurriedly cutting Murland's rope with his own dagger.

"Do mine first!" said Willow beside them.

Gibrig sawed frantically, glancing over his shoulder at the fight. Egbert had gotten to his feet and was blindly thrashing about the cave. He punched at the air and kicked, knocking over the boiling cauldron and dousing his mate, and oh how Margi howled.

Gibrig finally cut through the net enough for Murland to scramble out, and he hurriedly began working on Willow's.

"What about me!" Brannon shrieked when the stomping Egbert's foot crashed down two feet away.

Murland finally fished his own small knife out of his pocket and began sawing Brannon's rope.

"Hurry, hurry!" the elf prince cried.

Sir Eldrick was now riding Egbert's back, having wrapped the netting around the cyclops's neck. He yanked on the two ends of the netting as hard as he could, and Egbert grabbed at his throat, desperately trying to get a finger under the ropes.

Murland finally freed Brannon just as Willow ripped her way out of her net.

"Watch out!" Brannon suddenly screamed at Murland and pushed him out of the way as a giant foot came down and smashed the stone right where he had been standing. Brannon tripped and fell on his back as Egbert spun wildly and came down again right on top of the elf.

"No!" cried Murland, but just as the foot came down, Brannon unsheathed his sword and wedged the hilt in the crook of his arm, pointy end up.

Egbert's foot came down hard on the sword, and he suddenly hopped, moments before he would have crushed a shocked-looking Brannon.

Willow tackled the cyclops behind the knees, buckling them, and forced the choking behemoth to the ground, right on top of Margi.

Sir Eldrick did a backflip off Egbert's back and landed neatly beside the groaning cyclopes, drawing back his blade for a great blow.

"Don't kill them!" Gibrig cried out, and Sir Eldrick paused in his strike, giving Margi just enough time to bat him away with her meaty fist.

Sir Eldrick hit the wall behind the companions but sprang to his feet.

"They're beat, see?" said Gibrig, blocking the way. "They're runnin'."

The two cyclopes were scrambling to their feet all in a rush, and they hurriedly headed for the tunnel blindly. They ran into the wall, bounced off, and tried again, this time finding the tunnel.

"Get out of my way!" said Sir Eldrick, pushing the dwarf aside and running down the tunnel after them.

"What you guys waiting for?" said Willow, looking to be having the time of her life. She turned and raced after the knight.

"Come on!" said Murland, running after them.

They rushed down the tunnel, where Sir Eldrick's taunts and challenges echoed off the walls. There was a terrible crashing sound that shook the cave, and as Gibrig came around the corner, he saw that the two cyclopes had smashed through the blocked-up entrance. Willow was just ambling over the debris, and Sir Eldrick was nowhere to be seen.

Hurrying to the entrance, Gibrig and the others found that the storm had passed, though it was dark and wet outside, and the wind moaned, as though it were the voice of the wounded world.

"Willow, wait!" Gibrig cried, hurrying to catch up to her as she disappeared into the gathering mist.

Together with Brannon and Murland, Gibrig raced after Willow. Soon, however, she stopped, and when they caught up to her, panting, she hissed at them to be quiet and raised a staying hand.

Everyone listened, but the night was quiet.

"Sir Eldrick's goin' to get lost," said Gibrig through chattering teeth.

"We're all lost," said Brannon.

"Quiet!" Willow told them both.

Again, they listened. A minute passed, and then two, and finally Willow lowered her hand.

"Oh, what do we do?" Gibrig asked miserably.

"We find the mounts and get the hells out of here," said Brannon. "Sir Eldrick can fend for himself."

"I can't smell Sir Eldrick or the cyclopes anymore," Willow told them, her shoulders dropping.

Murland glanced from one to the other, but they all just stared at him, waiting for him to say something.

"I think...I agree with Brannon. We need to find the mounts. Sir Eldrick is drunk. And what did he say about beer? He goes off on adventures for days? We can't depend on him right now, and it appears that we can't depend on Kazimir either. Come on, let's try and find the mounts."

He seemed surprised when everyone nodded agreement and waited for him to lead the way.

Murland nodded and pulled up his trousers. "Alright then," he said, and began heading north but then stopped, regarding Brannon. "You saved my life back there. Thank you, that sure was some fast thinking."

Brannon straightened and gave him a nod. "You are welcome."

"And you," Murland said to Gibrig, "you saved all of us."

Gibrig blushed and kicked at a stone. "Aww, I didn't do nothin' really. Was Sir Eldrick and Willow done beat the cyclopes."

"Are you kidding?" said Brannon dubiously. "That was brilliant what you did, tricking the two big dummies like that."

"Thanks," said Gibrig, beaming.

CHAPTER 27

※

TALES FROM THE CROW'S NEST

Hagus Hogstead came to King's Crossing and reined in his mountain ram. "Whoa there, Billy," he said before dismounting.

He led the ram cautiously to the crossing, watching the tall grass on the Fire Swamp and Vhalovia side with suspicion. The jingling of chains made him stop, and he brought his shovel to bear, scanning the crossing of the five roads.

"Pssst! You there! Got any rum?"

The voice came from the crow's nest hanging above the point between Vhalovia and Magestra.

"Who's that?" said Hagus.

"Wendel, Wendel, just poor Wendel. Wendel is food for crows. But Wendel, Wendel, oh poor Wendel, secrets Wendel knows." The raspy, wet voice gave Hagus the chills, but like a dwarf, he marched forth bravely and faced the strange riddler.

Upon seeing that "Wendel" was nothing more than a skeleton in rags, he rubbed his eyes in disbelief and looked around for a prankster.

"Boo!" Wendel yelled and suddenly came to life, leaping up and banging on the bars.

Hagus jumped straight up in the air two feet and slapped the cage instinctively with his shovel. "Why ye blasted devil!" he cried, and hit the cage again. Upon realizing what he was looking at, his eyes widened, and he took a step back.

"Hahaha!" Wendel cackled and fell on the floor, skeletal legs dancing in the air. "The dwarf nearly shat his pants he did!"

"Shut yer cursed mouth, ye beast," said Hagus, and turned from the wretch to study the road to the west.

"Wait, wait! The dwarf never answered Wendel's question."

"I don't talk to spirits," said Hagus, and glancing at the sign below the crow's nest, he added, "and I don't talk to no horse thieves either."

As far as Hagus was concerned, that was that, and he turned once again from the skeleton.

"Wendel has hung here for a year and a day. Wendel sees everyone who comes and goes this way. Wendel can tell the dwarf who he has seen, but first Wendel is thirsty."

"I ain't got any blasted rum! Even if I did, there ain't nothin' ye can tell me that I can't find out on me own."

"Piss off then, dwarf! I hope Drak'Noir eats you too, just like that other ugly dwarf headed west."

Hagus turned slowly. "What you riddlin' 'bout, eh! What other dwarf?"

"Ohh, ahh," said Wendel, slinking over to the front of the crow's nest, but avoiding the elven rope tied there. "Dwarf wants to talk with Wendel now. But Wendel is still so thirsty."

"Dammit, ye cursed skeleton. If ye make me ask again, I'll rip off yer skull and use it for a bedpan!"

Wendel's big eyes jiggled in the sockets and he shuddered. "But Wendel is sooo thirsty."

"Well by the king's braided arse hair!" Hagus said to himself and glanced around. "Fine, fine," he told Wendel, handing the skeleton his water flask.

Wendel's boney arm shot out from between the bars like a striking snake and he snatched up the canteen, popped the lid, and poured it into his mouth. The water hit his spine and splashed all through his ribs and hip bones before pooling on the floor. But Wendel went right on as though his thirst were being quenched.

"Ahh, ohh, yessss, Wendel is happy now. Wendel is happy now."

"Great, then Wendel can tell Hagus about the ugly dwarf."

"Looked like a man to me," said Wendel, lying on the bottom of the crow's nest and running his fingers across his ribs, creating a hollow but not unpleasant musical sound.

Hagus grabbed the bars, leaning his face in close. "What did ye say? Looked like a man?"

Wendel leisurely picked his teeth with a sun-bleached finger. "Hmm, now Wendel is getting hungry. Can't think strai—"

Hagus reached through the cage and grabbed Wendel by the spiny throat and pulled his skull hard into the bars. "Yer words best come fast, else I'll snap yer neck and make good on me promise. Ye'll spend yer days in a sack, waiting fer the only sight ye'll ever see, me own fat hairy arse! Now speak!"

"A Champion of the Dragon he was," said Wendel, as though his windpipe were being crushed. "Traveled with an elf prince, an ogre, a wizard apprentice, and a knight of Vhalovia. Kazimir himself was with him for a time!"

Hagus released him, and Wendel fell into a fit of coughing and gagging. But the dwarf barely noticed, for he was contemplating the information. It was good, he thought, that Gibrig was with the other companions, for he had worried that his mild-mannered son hadn't even made it out of Shadow Forest.

"Did he look...happy?" Hagus asked.

"Yes...yes, happy as a pig in shit."

Hagus turned and scowled at the skeleton.

"I swear," said Wendel, raising defensive hands and coughing. "I swear he was. I swear."

"Alright, shut up." Hagus studied the sign hanging from the crow's nest, considering the strange skeleton. "What be yer tale, eh? Ye really a horse thief? And how the hells ye still talkin'?"

Wendel looked to Hagus with wonderment, and his floating orbs even teared up. "No one has ever asked Wendel—"

"Bloody unbreakable stone, man, just answer the damned question."

"Wendel worked for the king for twenty years. Raised the best horses in Magestra. Raised racing horses for the king. One broke its leg in a race.

Beauty, Beauty was her name. King ordered Beauty killed. But Wendel loved that horse. Wendel really did. So Wendel take the horse in the back of a wagon out of the city, try to get away, try to save the horse. King's men find Wendel and Beauty. Kill horse. Have a witch put a curse on Wendel. Wendel wake up in bird cage, already dead, but awake. Maggots and birds and flies and worms eat Wendel, all but the eyes. Wendel felt it all. But Wendel can never, ever, ever die."

Hagus felt sick, and a pang of sorrow and sympathy for the cursed horse trainer made his heart ache.

"Ye tellin' me the truth...Wendel?"

Wendel pressed his boney cheeks right up to the bars and stared at Hagus. "All Wendel has left of humanity is his eyes. Only truth Wendel has left."

Hagus saw sincerity in those large, bloodshot, watery blue eyes.

Without thinking, he drew his skinning knife and began sawing away at the elven rope holding the door closed in a tight knot. The knife had no effect. Hagus looked at it and shook his head. "Damned elves." He put the knife away and grabbed two of the bars. Wendel leapt to the back of the cage fearfully.

Hagus grunted and pulled hard in opposite directions. Chorded muscles and veins bulged in his thick forearms, and the bars began to bend. Hagus gave a grunt and a groan and replanted his feet, and PULLED.

The bars bent with a grating, whining protest.

Hagus stepped back, smiling at the awestruck skeleton.

"Ye told me the truth, or so I believe. Ye be free, Wendel."

"Free?" said Wendel, more to himself than the dwarf. "Wendel is free?"

He crawled to the widened bars and stuck his head out, grinning. But then fear and uncertainty haunted his eyes, and he slunk back into the security of his cage.

"What ye doin'? I said ye be free," Hagus told him.

Wendel shook his head violently. "But...but where will Wendel go? Wendel will be hunted. Wendel will be caught..."

Hagus considered that and looked to the west. "I be headed to the Wide Wall," he said, pointing. "Beyond that lies the Forest o' the Dead. Sounds like a good place for a cursed horse trainer skeleton to retire."

Wendel gave a sudden, boisterous laugh in a voice that Hagus thought must have been his as a living man, and the dwarf couldn't help but laugh as well.

"Hells, ye could probably become the king!" said Hagus with a chuckle.

"HAH!" Wendel fell back in a fit of laughter.

They shared a good laugh, and when they settled down, Hagus looked seriously to Wendel. "So, what'll it be?"

The skeleton looked to the bars, teeth chattering and eyes bulging, and put his head out once again. He looked around, and then maneuvered a shoulder bone through. He waited expectantly, then moved the other shoulder past the bent bars. His skull jerked from side to side, ready for a trap, and with a push he fell out of the crow's nest and landed on the ground with a sound like wooden chimes. Wendel came to all fours and glanced from Hagus to the cage, from the cage to Hagus, and then all around as he backed into the center of the crossing.

"Ye be free, Wendel," said Hagus. "Ain't nobody here to hurt ye."

"Free? Free?" said Wendel, looking at his boney hands and spinning a circle. "Wendel is freeee!" he cheered, pumping his fists to the heavens.

Just then a blue streak zipped through the air and stopped between Hagus and Wendel.

"Either of you two weirdos seen a fat green ogre go this way?" asked a blue sprite.

"Who be askin'?" said Hagus.

"Dingleberry, that's who!"

CHAPTER 28

---✕---

MYSTIC MAGIX

MURLAND GAVE A sigh of relief when the first rays of sunlight shot across the eastern sky, and his joy was two-fold, for not only had the night finally ended, but the rising sun proved that indeed, he had been leading them north.

"Soon we will be back on the road," he told the others happily.

Willow grunted, upset as she was that the food had been strapped to the mounts. Gibrig trudged on, lead-footed and head down, sniffling every now and again. Brannon too seemed not to have heard Murland at all. He just continued in his shuffle, eyes down, head drooping.

The mists glowed in the morning light, and though he felt bad for the loss of the mounts, he was happy to be getting back to the road. Soon enough they would be out of the Blight. And good riddance. The night had been filled with dread and the strange, eerie singing that always seemed faraway but also right beside you. He trudged on through the long dead brush that broke like candy brittle beneath his feet and kept his eyes on the northern hillside. The rocky land rose here, which convinced Murland further that they were on the right track. "Ye thinkin' we'll ever be seein' 'em again?" Gibrig asked sullenly.

"I don't know, Gib," said Murland. "Maybe they headed north back to the road like we are. Sometimes animals are smart like that."

"Yeah," said Gibrig with sudden hope. "Snorts sure be a smart one."

"Nah, if that storm didn't get that hog of yours, then my raptor did," said Willow, and Brannon offered her a big-eyed glare.

Gibrig stared up at her, wide-eyed. "Why would ye say that?"

"Because it is true."

Gibrig stopped, and the others followed suit. "Ye take that back," he told Willow, staring up at her angrily.

"What's gotten into you?"

"Take it back!"

"Fine, fine, I take it back. Whatever good that'll do."

Murland waved Willow and Brannon on and waited back with Gibrig. "You alright?" he asked the red-faced dwarf.

"Why's everybody gotta be so mean to everybody all the time?"

"Ah, she didn't mean nothing by it. Willow's just got a loose tongue is all."

"I know," said Gibrig, suddenly breaking down.

Murland put his arm around Gibrig's shoulder and gave him a friendly squeeze. "Sorry about Snorts. But you know there is a chance that they all survived."

"I be sorry. Tell Willow I be sorry. That wasn't nice o' me yellin' at her like that."

"You know," said Murland, trying to think of how to word it. "Sometimes it is alright, er, well...*justified* to be mean. Sometimes that is the only option. Look at Drak'Noir. We've got to be mean to scare her away."

Gibrig was shaking his head before Murland had even finished. "Meanness never be the way."

"I know that your father says that, but he must have told you that there are exceptions."

"It ain't all about me father. I, I had a..."

"Had a what?" Murland asked, hanging on Gibrig's every word.

But the dwarf just shook his head and trudged on. Murland called to him, but Gibrig kept on going.

For six hours, Murland led them up the stony incline, avoiding the ravines as Sir Eldrick had, and sticking to the long ridges that ran like fingers from the highlands, down through the valley, and up again into greener pastures.

"Look!' he yelled jubilantly.

The others raised their heads, and one after another they smiled, for the road was there, on the other side of a field of clover.

"The road!" Brannon cried and shrugged out of his furs to run to it.

Murland picked up his friend's cloak and ran after him with Gibrig and Willow following closely behind.

Brannon reached the road and fell to his knees, kissing the hard-packed dirt and saying, "Thank you, thank you," repeatedly.

"We did it," said Murland, stopping to catch his breath. "I think we've had enough travel for one day. Let's find a good place to make camp."

The others had no objections, and fifteen minutes down the western road, they found a suitable grassy area where they might take their rest.

Murland, Brannon, Gibrig, and Willow all plopped down on the soft grass and lay there, staring at the light-blue sky. The weather north beyond the Blight was warm and full of spring. Birds chirruped happily in the trees near the glen, and a warm breeze slowly lulled them all to sleep.

Murland awoke sometime later, and with a hand to his forehead and through squinting eyes, he glimpsed the sun sitting in the western sky. It was perhaps two hours until sunset. He sat up and saw Gibrig coming out of the woods with a pile of dead branches.

"Good morning, er, evening, Gib," said Murland.

"Evenin'," Gibrig said with a quick nod as he dropped the wood on a pile that already reached to his hips. He turned around as if to venture back into the woods.

"Hey, wait, Gib." Murland got up with a stretch and walked over to the dwarf, whose eyes were red and puffy, and whose dirty cheeks held streaks from long-dried tears. "What's wrong?"

Gibrig kicked a stone, and his bottom lip quivered. "I can't help but keep on thinkin' 'bout Snorts all alone out there in that storm…and with that hungry raptor."

"Awe, Gib, I'm sorry. He's a smart hog though, and fierce. Besides, I think that he and Tor were getting along pretty good there toward the end."

Gibrig broke down then and, shuddering, buried his head in Murland's shoulder.

"There, there," said Murland, patting Gibrig on the back and not quite knowing what else to say. But Murland soon discovered that he need not say anything. Gibrig cried and cried into his shoulder, clinging to him as a child might to a parent or an older sibling.

Brannon woke then, simply opening his eyes and watching the two, and his half-hearted smile showed his sympathy. Willow's eyes were open as well, and she too was watching them.

"I be sorry," said Gibrig.

"What are friends for?" Murland asked with a smile.

"I ain't never had any friends but me brother."

Murland waited, sensing that Gibrig had more to say about his mysterious brother.

"His name was Gillrog. We was twins. Not the identical kind. He was a head taller than I was."

"He had humanism too?"

Gibrig nodded, and Murland guided him to sit beside the fire. A long sigh escaped the dwarf when he sat, and his eyes found the fire, but they seemed to see a day long ago.

"Gillrog got the worst of the teasing from the other dwarf boys. They was so mean. They dug at him day after day. I knew that it bothered me brother, just like it bothered me. But our pap, he didn't raise us to be no softies. Ye know? So we got through it together. Until…well, finally poor Gill finally had enough. He jumped off Ruger's Ridge…"

Murland felt a lump forming in his throat, but he tried to be strong for his friend. "I'm sorry, Gibrig."

"I be sorry too. I shoulda done somethin'. I shoulda said somethin' different."

"You can't blame yourself for it."

"Me pap says the same thing. But I ain't for knowin' how to let it go. The sorrow just sits in me stomach, day after day. I try to help make the world a better place. I try not to treat no one badly like me brother was treated. But there be so much meanness in the world. Sometimes…sometimes I wish I woulda jumped off that ledge too."

"You don't mean that," said Murland.

"Ye don't know what it be like."

"I have known my share of teasing. Hells, I'm a wizard apprentice who can't do magic. Trust me, I understand."

"I know what it's like too, Gib," said Brannon, rising from his bedroll and coming to sit with them. "All my life I've felt different. And when Val and I came out...well, it was terrible. My subjects call me princess behind my back. They laugh and scoff, whispering to themselves when I walk by. My own father hates me."

"I'm sorry, Brannon," said Gibrig, sniffling.

"Thanks. But listen, you can't go through life getting pushed around just because you're afraid to be mean. Sometimes you have to stand up and push back."

Willow sat up with a yawn and a stretch and a long, drawn out fart that left Gibrig laughing and crying at the same time. Brannon's steely façade shattered then, and he burst out with laughter that Murland had never heard. Murland soon found himself chuckling so giddily that he was leaning on Gibrig for support.

"Bout time the lot of you lightened up," said Willow. She scrunched up her face and let out another musical toot that brought Gibrig and Murland to the ground in a fit of laughter.

With a great stretch and a thorough itching of her backside, Willow rose to meet the world. She moved her tongue around her mouth with a grimace and looked to the forest, scratching one long tusk. "I'm going into the woods and I ain't coming out until I get us some dinner. Give a holler if there is trouble, or if Kazimir shows up." And with that she disappeared into the thick forest.

"See now, I wish I were strong like Willow. Nothin' bothers her," said Gibrig.

An hour later, Murland and Gibrig returned with full water skins. They were delighted to find Brannon and Willow sitting by the fire in the waning daylight with two rabbits on the spit along with nearly a dozen ears of corn roasting on coals. Brannon was carefully turning the stick, and Willow was staring trance-like at the juicy meat. There was also a large bushel of corn lying beside the elf, which Murland guessed Brannon had grown while he and Gibrig were away.

"Ah, just in time!" said Willow, pushing Brannon aside and pulling the two hares off the steaming stick.

She tore one in half and popped it into her mouth, crunching the bones. Brannon took his share and handed the other hare to Murland and Gibrig. They were still pulling off the too-hot meat and shoving it in their mouths when Willow swallowed the last wad of chewed up bone and began eating the stick that they had cooked the food on.

"Those corns done yet?" she asked Brannon, licking her lips.

"Everyone gets two each," he said warily.

She nodded happily, grabbed two of the steaming ears, and bit one in half, husk and all.

Night fell and the companions sat around the fire, enjoying the peace. Murland took the rolled-up bundle of wizard leaf from his backpack and carefully unrolled it, eager to see if the buds had dried out yet.

"Is this good enough, you think?" he asked Brannon, showing it to him.

Brannon selected one. He rolled it between his palms and smelled it. "I believe so," he said, handing it back.

Murland could hardly contain his excitement, and he began carving out a hole in one of the ears of corn, hoping to fashion a makeshift pipe.

"Here," said Gibrig, handing Murland a small bundle wrapped in cloth. "I started working on it after you harvested your leaf."

"What's this?" Murland unwrapped the cloth and was delighted to find a small pipe carved out of wood. "Wow, Gib. You made this for me? Thank you."

"Ye be welcome, Murland."

"Go on and try it out," said Willow enthusiastically.

Murland rubbed his hands together nervously and took a deep breath. "Okay," he said before breaking off a small piece and packing it in the pipe. Brannon handed him a twig burning at the end and nodded.

"Here goes nothing," said Murland, and he put the pipe to his lips and lit the leaf. He sucked in a lungful of the sweet-smelling smoke and meant to hold it, but suddenly the smoke seemed to expand in his lungs and he went into a coughing fit that left him lying on the ground with teary eyes and snot running from his nose.

He sat up, still coughing now and again, and accepted a drink of water from Brannon.

"So?" said Willow, watching him closely. "Ye feel any magix yet?"

"I-I feel..." Murland began, but then suddenly he floated one, two, three feet off the ground. His head became light, and the tips of his fingers and toes tingled. He felt something like a surge of unbridled energy course through his body, making his heart skip a beat and his spirits soar. He saw in his mind's eye the coalescing power of magic all around him, flowing through the trees and grass and pouring into him from all around.

"Whoa!" said Willow. "Look how high he is!"

Murland opened his eyes and dreamily noticed that he was now floating high above the camp, at least fifteen feet.

"You should come down from there before you float away," said Gibrig, sounding terribly concerned.

"I don't know how," said Murland. In truth, he didn't want to. He never wanted to come down, never wanted to let go of this feeling.

Eventually, however, he began to slowly float back down to earth. The tingling left his fingers and toes, and the marvelous feeling of oneness with the world went away. He touched down on the grass and was met by the cheers of the companions.

"That was incredible," he said, panting. "Where's Packy?"

"Packy?" said Brannon.

"Yeah, that's the name I gave my backpack."

"Here it is," said Gibrig, handing it to him.

"Alright," said Murland, fishing out the broken wand and spell book. "Now for the real test."

He opened the spell book carefully, and to his delight, he could read the title page.

The Collected Works of High Wizard Allan Kazam
Foreword by High Wizard Erasmus Farsky

"Well," said Murland, "this spell book was written by the one and only Allan Kazam. And now, I think I can read it!"

"Who's that?" Willow asked.

"Who's that? Just the most famous wizard to ever live."

"I never heard of him," she said with a shrug. "Say, can you whoosh us a dinner table like Kazimir did, now that you're a high wizard and all?"

"High Wizard Allan Kazam is the one who defeated the Dark Lord Zuul a thousand years ago," said Murland, ignoring her. "He disappeared after he cast the spell that sent Zuul into another dimension. Some think that he might still be alive, but trapped in that faraway place in space and time."

"That sounds pretty scary," said Gibrig.

"Wait," said Brannon, looking confused. "You're telling me that the high wizards gave you the spell book of the most powerful wizard that ever lived?"

"Yup, and his wand as well."

Brannon looked dubious. "But, why would they give you such obviously powerful and valuable magical items?"

"Well, I *am* a Champion of the Dragon. Who better to have these things?"

"Oh," said Brannon with a nervous laugh. "Right."

Murland looked to him, wondering what was on his mind, but chalked it up to Brannon's opinion of him.

"So, you gonna do any magix or what?" Willow asked.

"I don't think I should try any of these spells until I make a new wand."

"New wand? What about that one there?"

"Well, I tried using it once, and it didn't go so great. I don't want to damage it."

Willow let out a disappointed sigh and went back to sucking on the others' spent corn cobs.

Long after the others had fallen asleep, Murland stayed up in his tent, reading the thick tome by candlelight. He couldn't believe the wealth of magical knowledge at his fingertips. When he found a spell that was said to mend wands, he became utterly giddy. It was an intricate spell, and one that Murland would need another wand for. Luckily, he knew enough about the making of wands to attempt to create one, something that was only allowed once a wizard apprentice had successfully grown their own leaf. The wand didn't have to be too intricate, just a carved oak branch hardened by fire would likely do.

He wished that Sir Eldrick had been there to see his levitation. He was getting more worried about the knight with every passing minute. Where could he have run off to? Had he been killed by the cyclopes after all? There were a million possibilities, and few of them were good.

Late that night he fell asleep with his face pressed against the pages of the spell book. He dreamt of the first day that he met Caressa, and later, thinking back on it, he wouldn't be sure if the spell book had something to do with it, for the memories were so vivid, so real, that he felt like he had traveled back in time.

Murland sat with his legs dangling off the finely crafted chair in the antechamber of Castle Roddington. It was Monday. The weekend had been nice—a visit to Aunty Kathrine's on the coast and sailing with Uncle Charles. But now the week had begun, and his father had been sent for by the king.

To Murland's delight, Albert Kadabra had decided to bring his only son along. He couldn't wait to explore the halls, chambers, secret passageways, and gardens that Castle Roddington had to offer. But Murland's father had expressed absolute seriousness when he told Murland that he must be on his best behavior during the meeting.

Murland was forbidden from speaking to the king unless spoken to, and he hadn't been spoken to. Instead, his father told him to wait on the chair in the hall outside the king's chambers until the men were done talking business. Even at the age of seven, Murland had enough sense to know that his father was quite nervous to meet with the king, though the tall, lanky, and proud man would have never admitted such a thing.

He was a lord after all.

Murland waited, as he was told, eyeing the two guards who stood at the end of the hall like statues in full armor. He wondered what it was they thought about all day. It seemed like such a boring job.

Many paintings adorned the walls, and Murland passed some time imagining that he was inside the scenes, fighting off sea monsters or jousting in the grand arena. In another, a couple was locked in the throes of a passionate kiss, he a knight, and she a fair maiden on a steed of white. It looked like a goodbye scene, and Murland wondered why they seemed so serious. The knight was about to go off on an adventure, after all, and that was much more exciting than a maiden, no matter how fair she might be.

After growing tired with the paintings, he shifted in his seat to spy the room opposite his chair. The doorway was a few feet to his right, and he could see only the side wall, but that meager view was enough to perk his interest, for he thought that he saw the tip of a dragon horn mounted there.

He glanced back at the guards, thinking that they must be watching him, for what else was there to look at in the hallway?

Sudden movement caught his eye in the doorway. It was fleeting, and had only been seen peripherally. He leaned further, trying to get a better look into the room. A smiling girl suddenly popped into view. She wore pants like a boy, and her shock of curly red hair jutted out from beneath a sailor's hat. Strangest of all, strapped to her hip was a toy wooden sword.

"Do you want to go on an adventure?" she asked in a voice soft and sweet and laced with daring.

"Who, me?" said Murland, glancing around.

"No, those two stiff suits of armor guarding my father. Yeah, you."

"Your father? You mean…you're a princess?"

"Not today. Today I'm a pirate. Name's Captain Blacky Nofearson. And I'm looking for a brave pirate to explore this island with me."

"What island?"

The princess pointed deeper into the room, where Murland could not see.

"Is that a dragon horn on that wall?" he asked.

She glanced back and nodded at him devilishly. "There are all kinds of beasts and dangers lurking in this jungle. Are you brave enough to dare seek out the buried treasure?"

Murland glanced at the guards. "I'm not supposed to…"

She furled her freckled brow. "Pirates don't give a damn about rules!"

Murland laughed; he had never heard a girl swear before. Especially one with such a sweet voice. "Alright, alright, hold on." He crept off the chair as slowly as possible, thinking that if he went slowly enough, the guards wouldn't even see him leaving.

Two minutes into his stealthy retreat, and he had taken only one step toward the door.

"Hurry up already, turtle boy!"

Startled, Murland jumped, glanced at the guards at the end of the hall, and realized that he had just blown his cover. He leapt across the hall and into the room. The princess grabbed him, and together they fell to the floor. She covered his mouth as she lay on top of him, and then put a finger to her lips. Slowly, she shuffled over to the door on her elbows and knees and peeked out.

Murland's heart hammered in his chest.

She came back from the door slowly, nodding. "They don't suspect a thing. You have escaped the clutches of the metal men for now." She held out her hand in greeting. "What's your name, pirate?"

"Uh, my name's Murland."

"Not your real name," she said, standing. "What's your pirate name?"

"Well," he said, getting up as well and dusting off his leather jerkin, "can I be a wizard?"

"Hmm," she said, scrunching her small nose and furling her auburn brow. At length, she nodded. "A pirate captain can always use a wizard, I suppose. Yes, but what is your wizard name?"

"Uh…Murland the Great?"

"How about Murland the Mighty? Much more intimidating for a pirate wizard."

"Alright," he said, liking that.

"But you are going to need a wand," she said, glancing around at the dark room.

The mounted heads of a variety of beast hung on the walls, and other creatures had been stuffed whole. Murland looked to the wall and found that indeed, what he *had seen from the hall had been only the tip of a long horn. So large was it that it spanned the entire twenty-foot wall.*

Murland turned and stared, taking in the "island." The room was deep, at least twice as long as it was wide. Its far outer wall was made of glass, as was the pitched ceiling, and the hundreds of plants told Murland that it was a conservatory.

"Ah, this will do," said the princess. She broke the gnarled branch from a small corkscrew willow.

Murland took the twisted wand, feeling very much the wizard just then.

"Alright," she said, unsheathing her wooden sword, "let us see what treasure this island holds!"

Murland and the princess explored the conservatory for the better part of an hour. They fought their way through the island jungle, battling with trolls and goblins and even a giant white bear. Murland froze the bear with a freezing spell, and the princess made quick work of the goblins. The trolls had them cornered at one point in the battle, but were defeated when the sun shone through the trees and suddenly turned them to stone. The plants came alive in their imaginings, but between Murland's magic wand and the princess's sword, they managed to fight their way through it all.

Finally, they came to an ancient temple that was said to hold the treasure. Murland was about to rush into it when the princess warned him of booby traps and held him back with a staying hand to his pounding chest. Carefully, they made their way through the halls and tunnels of the temple, finally coming out into the antechamber, where sat a wooden chest.

"That's it," said the princess as she took Murland by the hand.

His stomach fluttered, and the excitement of it all left him exhilarated. They were standing before the chest, about to open it together, when suddenly the king called from behind them.

"Ah, there you are!"

Murland released the princess's hand as if he had been doing something wrong and turned with a jerk to face his father and the king.

"I thought that I told you to wait in the hallway," said Murland's father with an arched brow and a waggle of his curled mustache.

"Sorry, but it was awfully boring sitting there, and the princess needed me for a quest."

The two men grinned at each other.

"Well," said the portly king. "Have you completed your quest?"

"Oh yes, Father. It was wonderful. We traveled through the jungle, and we were attacked by wild cats, bears, goblins, trolls, even giants. But Murland is a mighty wizard; he saved me more than once."

"Very good," said the king, chuckling.

Murland's father was laughing as well. "Come now, Murland. We have taken up enough of the king's time."

"Aw, do we have to?"

"I am afraid so."

"Yes, Father."

Murland and Caressa followed the men out of the trophy room and through the conservatory, and once again Caressa took his hand.

"Thanks for exploring with me today. I had a lot of fun."

"Me too," said Murland. He handed her the gnarled piece of wood. "I should give this back."

"No," said Caressa, pushing it away. "It's yours. Besides, I'm not a wizard like you."

"I'm going to be a real wizard, you know. When I grow up I'm going to study at Abra Tower."

"I believe it! I bet you will be the best wizard in the world," she said, smiling.

Murland reluctantly released the princess's hand and clambered into the carriage as the men said their farewells and made plans to meet again soon. As the carriage pulled away, Murland waved at the princess with a sudden sinking feeling.

"So, you had fun with the princess, eh?" his father remarked, watching him from the opposite bench.

"Yeah, she's great," said Murland with a dreamy sigh.

"I imagine that you will see a lot more of her, if you want. For the king has hired me as an advisor," Albert Kadabra said proudly.

"Wow, really?"

Murland couldn't contain his smile. He waved jubilantly at the princess as their carriage pulled around the cul-de-sac. She unsheathed her wooden sword and raised it to the heavens triumphantly.

Murland shot his fist out of the carriage window. It was the best day of his life.

CHAPTER 29

A WIZARD'S WARNING

THE FOOTPRINTS WERE old, at least a week, but Valkimir thought these must be the prints of the Champions of the Dragon. There were two horses' prints, as well as those of a large hog, and the largest ones, which belonged to a raptor. Strangely, they were accompanied by a set of boot prints of medium size for a man. By the indentation and gait of the tracks, he put the person at around nineteen years old, one-hundred and fifty pounds, and slightly over six feet tall. The strange part about the man's tracks was that they suddenly disappeared at one point down the road.

"Perhaps this is the lanky wizard's apprentice," said Valkimir.

"What did you say?" Caressa asked from her saddle.

"They made camp here; I'm sure of it."

"Obviously." Caressa pointed to the large dining set in the middle of the clearing. "What do you make of that?"

"Kazimir," said Valkimir, as though the name soured his tongue. "He leaves no tracks, but I am sure that he was here."

"We should continue," Caressa told him. "We can make another twenty miles before morning."

"The sun has yet to set," he said with a laugh. "You ride like an elven warrior."

"A princess does enough lying about and resting to quench a weary army. I have had enough of rest. Besides, a lady does not bed down with a stranger the very day that she meets him."

"Don't worry about that," said Valkimir. "You're not my type."

"What, because I am human?"

"Because you are female," he said with a wink.

"Oh," said Caressa, sounding a bit surprised.

They were about to leave, when a loud galloping from the east caught their attention. They looked to find a dwarf riding a mountain ram and a blue fairy coming their way.

"Is that…is that Wendel the skeleton?" Valkimir asked Caressa in disbelief as he moved to stand beside her.

"Whoa, Billy!" said the dwarf, pulling hard on the reins, causing the ram to lock up its legs and skid for ten feet before coming to a stop just in front of the shocked pair.

Valkimir waved his hand through the rising dust as the fairy flew three quick circles around them all and came to a stop on Wendel's shoulder.

"You!" said Wendel, pointing a shaking finger at the two from behind the dwarf.

"I said that I would do the talking!" said the dwarf, offering the skeleton a scowl.

"Hoy there! Have ye seen—"

"Those two are dirty tricksters!" said Wendel. "Don't believe a word they say."

"Shut yer yapper!"

"Good dwarf," said Valkimir. "You ride with strange company. I must warn you about this character, he—"

"I be knowin' Wendel's story. Many thanks. But listen, ye seen or heard o' any strange folk riding this way, headed west?"

"What kind of strange folk?" Valkimir asked.

"A mismatched group. There be an elf like yerself, a human knight—"

"A wizard apprentice, a dwarf, and an ogre?" Caressa finished for him.

"Aye, the Champions o' the Dragon," said the dwarf. "Sorry, sorry. I forget me manners. I be Hagus Hogstead o' the Iron Mountains. Me lad be one o' the champions. This be Dingleberry," he said, hooking a thumb over his shoulder.

"Dingleberry the fairy-fairy!" she said, looking proud.

"I am Valkimir of the woodland realm," he said with a small bow. "Why are you looking for your son? Everyone knows that the champions are venturing to Bad Mountain."

"I wish to catch them before the Wide Wall."

"To what end?"

"That be me own damned business, elf," said Hagus, and he pulled the reins to leave.

"Wait," said Caressa. "We mean no disrespect. For we too are searching out the champions."

"Aye?" said Hagus, intrigued.

"Indeed. I am Caressa Roddington, Princess of Magestra."

"Princess Caressa?" said Hagus, taking off his leather cap and straightening his eyepatch. "Forgive me, me lady, for I knew not that I been in the presence o' royalty."

"It is no matter. Please, share your tale with us. There is a camp here that we believe was used by the champions. We have food and drink that has not yet been hardened by the long road."

"I. Will. Not. Eat with the likes of those two!" said Wendel, leaping off the back of the ram and stomping off down the road. He stopped after only ten feet and turned, hands on hips. "You two coming?" he asked Dingleberry and Hagus.

"We want to hear what they have to say-say," said the fairy, and Hagus nodded.

"Well that's just PERFECT," Wendel yelled.

Hagus shrugged. "Lead the way," he told Valkimir.

They got a fire going and sat at the long dining table, sharing their stories as the moon relieved the sun of its heavenly patrol.

"And that is how Dingleberry learned of the lie-lie," said the sprite, suddenly shooting up into the air and unsheathing her needle. "I set out post-haste. Dingleberry to the rescue!"

"Careful where ye be spreadin' that fairy dust o' yers," said Hagus, scooting back away from her and waving at the sparkling dust in the air.

"Stuff'll make ye act queerer than a damned wood…" he trailed off, quickly glancing at Valkimir. "Stuff makes ye loopy."

"My dust is the purest around," said the fairy. "Make big-big loot selling it to pirates."

"You sold your fairy dust to pirates?" said Caressa, amused by the little sprite.

"Sure did, got me the boot-boot from Faeland. Out-out, said the queen."

"So how does a fairy dust dealer end up befriending an ogre?" Valkimir asked.

Dingleberry very animatedly told them how she had broken a wing, and how Willow had nursed her back to health.

"Ye be a good friend," Hagus told her when the tale was through.

"And you are a good father," Valkimir told him. "Not as much can be said for the king of Halala. I still cannot believe the bastard would send his own son on such a fool's quest."

"What gets me," said Hagus, leaning in and eyeing them all with his one good eye, "is how in the hells did Kazimir keep it a secret all this time?"

"Keep what a secret?" came a voice out of the woods.

They all jerked their heads toward the trees to the left as Kazimir walked out into the firelight.

"Most High Wizard," said Valkimir breathlessly. He stood but did not bow. Instead, he waited.

"What a strange group this is," said Kazimir, throwing back his hood to reveal two disapproving eyes. "So far from your homes. What, do tell, are you after?"

"You know damned well what we're after," said Caressa. She got right up in the High Wizard's face. "The great lie is known. This…this epic fallacy of yours has come to an end."

"Surely I do not know what you are talking about, Princess Caressa."

"I should flog yer arse right here and now!" said Hagus, taking up his shovel in two tight fists.

"Yeah!" said Dingleberry, unsheathing her needle and leaping off the long table to hover beside the dwarf.

"ENOUGH!"

A great shockwave of energy blasted out from Kazimir and pushed them all staggering backwards.

"I have not yet had my dinner. Do not test me when I have not had my dinner," Kazimir warned.

"You still deny that the Prophecy of the Dragon Champions is a lie?" said Valkimir, refusing to back down.

"Valiant knight. Say, for a moment, that what you believe is true. Say that I am some evil charlatan who sends fools to their deaths once every generation to save the entirety of the continent of Fallacetine. Say that your friends are simply food to keep the great Drak'Noir pacified. Say all of this is true. What do you intend to do about it? Warn them? Save them? And say that you do, and no one feeds the dragon this generation. What, pray tell, do you think she will do?"

"The world will burn," came the terrified, chattering voice of Wendel from the shadows.

Valkimir, Hagus, Caressa, and Dingleberry all exchanged thoughtful glances.

"Whether you agree with it or not, the Champions of the Dragon are heroes one and all, and will be remembered as such, whether they make it back alive or not. But I can tell you this, I have held back the black dragon every generation by choosing able champions to challenge her. This batch will be no different."

"You expect us to believe you?" said Valkimir. "Brannon is no champion, and from what I have heard from the others, none of them are champions, save perhaps Sir Eldrick, the drunken fool."

"Perhaps you should all reconsider your opinion of your *friends*. Would you all be that surprised to know that they have already defeated bandits, survived the darklings, and escaped a cyclops den together, and all without much help from me?"

"Why should we believe ye?" Hagus asked, though he wanted to believe that his son was the champion that Kazimir spoke of.

"Believe me or nay. I do not so much care, as long as you stay away from them all. They are finally gaining some confidence as a group, and I don't need you four—"

"Five!" yelled Wendel from the shadows.

Kazimir scowled at him and looked back to the others. "I don't need you all bringing them down. Do we understand each other?"

Valkimir nodded grimly. Caressa stood, staring defiantly. Dingleberry mocked the princess's pose. And Hagus spit on the ground at the wizard's feet.

"Good," said Kazimir turning with a flourish of robes toward the road. As if on second thought, he stopped and turned back. "I will leave you with my well wishes, and a gift for you all. Please, enjoy my humble offering, and know that if I see you anywhere west of here, I will turn you all into pigs."

He waggled his fingers, and there was a boom and flash of light.

Far away, one Lord Hegglesberth circled the bed, upon which there lay six prostitutes. He was excited about this batch, for it contained two men, one elven and one human, an exotic human woman, a dwarf female with a beard and a leather whip, and a male pixie less than a foot tall.

"Who would like to rub honey oil on my back and lick it off?" Lord Hegglesberth asked, fingering his deep belly button.

Just then a voice shrieked with delight, and there came a banging on the door to the bed chamber.

"I'm home!" came the voice of his wife.

Lord Hegglesberth turned with a jerk and looked, terrified, toward the door. "Is that you, my b-b-beloved?"

"Yes, yes. I have returned early from my trip. Open the door. I have so much to tell you."

The lord paced back and forth, biting his nails and glancing nervously at the prostitutes, who all looked quite bored.

"Oh no..." he said, clawing at his hair. "Oh, no, no, no..."

"Dearest...Herbert! Open the door."

"Ah...hold on, you woke me. I'm trying to light a lamp."

"Herbert Henry Hegglesberth..." the voice was even and dangerous. "Do you have someone in there with you?"

"What?" he said, laughing nervously. "Of course not."

He heard her heavy feet marching away and knew that she was going to get a set of keys from one of the guards.

"Hide!" he hissed at the prostitutes.

"Where do you expect us to do that?" said the pixie in his high-pitched squeak.

The pounding feet returned up the hall, and Lord Hegglesberth bit his knuckle, spinning in circles. He grabbed the bottle of wine, looking for a place to hide it, and considered jumping out the window.

Suddenly there was a boom and a flash of light, and the bed, along with all six of the prostitutes, disappeared.

The door opened, and a stupefied Hegglesberth stood, holding the bottle and smiling dopily at his wife.

"Welcome home, dear. You caught me redecorating!"

"Why, you sweet, sweet man," said Lady Hegglesberth, kissing her husband on top of his bald head.

Lord Hegglesberth happily accepted a hug from his wife, and he glanced over at the dusty spot on the floor where the bed had been, wondering of his luck.

A bed full of leather- and lace-clad prostitutes appeared beside the fire, and Kazimir turned and disappeared into the night with a *WHOOSH.*

Valkimir glanced at Caressa. "Is he serious?"

Caressa did not answer, however, enamored as she was with the incredibly well-endowed elf on the bed. She just stared, cocking her head to the left to get a better angle.

"I'll tell ye this," said Hagus gruffly, nevertheless admiring the leather-clad dwarf woman and her neatly braided beard. "Anyone who tries to buy ye off like this got somethin' to hide. Now, if ye'll excuse me. The lass there looks rather confused."

Valkimir gave a laugh as the dwarven hog farmer walked over to the bed and introduced himself to the bearded lass. "He's got a point."

"Indeed," said Caressa, shaking herself out of her little trance. "What should we do? Kazimir had a point about Drak'Noir. If she is not fed...Well, you know what will happen."

"Big-big fire-fire. Big-big death," said Dingleberry.

"Then we'll just have to help the champions kill that blasted dragon once and for all," said Hagus, returning with the lass under his arm. He smiled at them all. "Now if ye don't mind, we be retirin' to me tent."

Valkimir and Caressa watched him go, mulling over what he had said.

"I call dibs on the sprite!" said Wendel, rubbing his boney hands together.

CHAPTER 30

A TRIAL BY FLESH

SIR ELDRICK STARED out the window at the waning moon. Queen Elzabethalynn lay against his chest, her warm hand resting on his cheek. The warm summer breeze blew in softly, cool against their wet skin. The glow of lovemaking still flushed their cheeks, and they held each other in silence, savoring the rare moment.

He kissed her forehead and held her tight, pressing himself against her.

"Already?" she said with a musical laugh.

"With a woman such as you in my arms, how can I help it?" he said, kissing her again.

She moved on top of him and kissed him deeply.

"Elza, I Love you—"

Suddenly the door burst open. The queen leapt off and pulled the silk sheet up to her chin. Sir Eldrick's instincts screamed, and dread filled his heart.

King Henry Winterthorn pushed past the guard and stopped dead when he saw the two. His wide eyes moved over Sir Eldrick, and then found the queen.

"Leave us," he told the guard in an even voice.

The door closed.

King Henry stared at Sir Eldrick, and to the knight's surprise, there was not anger, but sorrow.

"Henry—" the queen began.

"No," he said, calmly. "Do not speak, for I neither wish to hear your lies, nor your apologies."

Sir Eldrick stood, and the king walked to stand in front of him. "Henry, my King. It was not her fault—"

"Liar!" King Henry backhanded Sir Eldrick, his jagged ring leaving a cut across his cheek. The blood slowly pooled in the corner of his mouth. "I should kill you here and now," said the king as he unsheathed his sword.

Sir Eldrick bowed his head to the king. "If you wish for me to die, my King, then I shall die."

King Henry pointed the sword at Sir Eldrick's chest, his arm trembling, eyes pooling with tears.

"You have broken my heart," said the king. "Both of you. But I will not kill you. For if indeed you love me, then you shall live with your guilt, and you shall feel the pain of it forever."

He lowered the sword and put a hand to the side of Sir Eldrick's face. "My old friend. Go now. Leave this kingdom and never return. If I see you after this day, know that you will die."

Sir Eldrick awoke from the dream with a terrible headache pounding in his temples. There was bright light everywhere, and the smell of flowers permeated the air, making his head swoon even more. Had he passed out in a perfume shop? he wondered.

"Drink this, you will feel better," an angelic voice told him.

He felt a cold rim touch his lips and drank what was offered, not having the strength to object. In a flash his headache, dizziness, and exhaustion disappeared, and he found himself looking at a pointy-eared and winged female fairy no more than three feet tall.

She gave a cherubic giggle and flew away on quick green wings, and Sir Eldrick gasped when he realized where he was. The chamber walls were made of pure glowing white ivory, arched and smooth like the inside of an eggshell. All the way up the walls were ascending rows of balconies, from which thousands of fairies large and small stared down at him, their wings buzzing.

Sir Eldrick rose from the chair he had been apparently sleeping in, and noticed that the floor of the arena-like chamber was covered in fairy dust rather than sand. Had he been on a fairy dust bender again?

"Sir Knight!" a voice, pure and smooth and laced with seduction, echoed through the dome.

Sir Eldrick turned reluctantly, and there, sitting in the most lavish of balconies, was the queen of the fae, Tittianya.

"Good Queen," he said with a bow, though he was unable to take his eyes off her golden skin and those deep, green, heavily-lashed eyes. "I am honored to be in your presence. But I must ask, how did I get here?"

A fairy bent and whispered in the queen's ear, and she yawned and waved the servant away. "You have trespassed on fairy soil without leave. The punishment is death. How do you plead?"

Sir Eldrick scoffed, then laughed, then glanced around at the unimpressed crowd and gulped. "Well, Your Highness, I can assure you that if I have trespassed on your soil, I have not done so out of malice or ill intent."

"Your intent is not in question, only the fact that you are here, which is proof of your crime. Do you have any last words?"

"Last words? Look, I am—"

"We do not care who you are or who you know. Faeland does not care about the mortals of the mainland."

Sir Eldrick straightened, trying to think of a way out of yet another alcohol-induced catastrophe.

"If you have no last words, your sentence shall be carried out immediately."

"I demand a trial by flesh!" said Sir Eldrick, seeing the wine glass in her hand.

The queen gave a musical laugh, and the gathered fairies joined in. "You, a human? You cannot be serious," she said, though her actions gave away her intrigue as she leaned to look him over more closely from her high perch.

"Bring me closer," she said to no one in particular, and the balcony that she sat upon began to float toward him. It stopped a few feet from him, and the queen stepped off.

Sir Eldrick was paralyzed by her beauty, and tried but failed to keep his eyes above her shoulders. Tittianya, queen of the fae, stood five feet tall, with an ample bosom and a backside that Sir Eldrick thought he could set a drink on while she was standing. All of this was contained by a pink silk robe that did nothing from stopping the glowing light of the chamber from poking through.

He gulped. "I demand a trial by flesh," he managed to croak out.

She looked him up and down, and walked three circles around him. "What do you think?" she asked the gathered fairies.

The place went wild with cheering, and fairy dust rained down on them. Sir Eldrick held his breath, knowing better than to breathe in the exotic stimulant at a time such as this.

"Very well," said the queen, grabbing his face so that his cheeks smooshed together. "Bring the bed."

Sir Eldrick had hoped to put on a private performance, and he glanced warily at the crowd of fairies. "Might I have something to wet my whistle?" he asked, bowing before the queen. "I am parched."

"Bring the defendant wine!" Queen Tittianya demanded, and a cask of wine was promptly brought before him.

The bed, which was ten feet long by ten feet wide and covered with a plethora of white furs and pillows, was carried to the center of the arena. Sir Eldrick drank down the entirety of the cask and cockily climbed up onto the bed and stripped out of his armor. He stood before the queen, who was regarding him with an arched brow, though her eyes were not on his.

"Prepare to fall in love," he said, spreading his arms wide and offering her his most charming smile.

Three hours later, Sir Eldrick dressed himself to the crashing applause of the roaring crowd and took a bow. The queen, who was being fanned by two scantily clad fairies, lay back against the pillows, panting and glistening with sweat.

"You have proven yourself innocent, as is dictated by the trial by flesh," she said breathlessly.

Sir Eldrick raised his fist to the crowd and downed another glass of wine.

The queen rose with the help of two hovering fairies and flew on golden wings to land before him. "Good Knight," she said, and then leaned in so that only he might hear. "I would ask that you stay with us for a time. I could use someone with your firmness of...sword."

Sir Eldrick considered her offer. He would much rather be the fae queen's plaything than travel to Bad Mountain. Perhaps he could just disappear here, and never be found by Kazimir. No, he realized, the wizard would probably find him one way or another. Of course, Tittianya might be able to protect him...

He was about to take her up on the offer when he thought of the other champions. Gibrig had saved his life, he remembered. His mixed feelings swirled in his mind, and he gave a sigh.

"Ah, my fairest of queens, would that I could. But you see, I am one of the five Champions of the Dragon. I must march to Bad Mountain and fight the dreaded Drak'Noir."

She clutched her chest and paced before him, acting suddenly distraught.

"Oh, my dear, brave, brave Sir Eldrick," she said, touching his cheek with her soft, golden palm. She put her hands out before her, and suddenly a long, glowing blade that looked to be made of glass appeared, resting upon her palms. "Please, take this as my token. It is the blade Cryst. Forged from the crystalline wings of the god of fairies, it is said to be unbreakable, and will penetrate anything that you thrust it into."

Sir Eldrick raised a brow and took the offered weapon. "I do not know how to thank you, Tittianya."

She leaned forward and kissed him long on the lips, then whispered in his ear, "You can thank me when you return from Bad Mountain."

"Very well," he said, sheathing the blade and turning for the door without looking back. The cheers of the gathered fairies followed him out of the arena, and he couldn't help but smile.

"There you are!" came the voice of Kazimir as Sir Eldrick walked out of the arena and into the starless night.

"High Wizard, funny meeting you here," said Sir Eldrick.

"What in the worlds am I going to do with you?" the wizard asked, shaking his head.

"Don't even start. I didn't drink on purpose. I was forced to by the cyclopes due to that clever dwarf Gibrig."

"Yes, yes, well, I have come to bring you back before you have thoughts of staying here."

"What happened to the others?"

"Surprisingly, they are doing just fine. Murland has led them north back to the road. They are waiting as we speak."

"Well, I'll be damned."

"Yes," said Kazimir. "Yes, you will, if you keep on like you have been. Dammit, man, caught by bandits? Captured by cyclopes. And whatever the hells else you've been doing these last few days. I had thought you a worthy leader. Perhaps I have been wrong."

"No, of course not. You were right to believe in me. I *will* lead the others to Bad Mountain. Drak'Noir will be quenched."

Kazimir studied the knight's sincerity and finally nodded.

"Very well, come with me then."

Sir Eldrick took the wizard's gnarled hand, and everything went black.

CHAPTER 31

A DRUNKEN KNIGHT'S TALE

M URLAND AND THE others were just settling in to a meager dinner of corn and grubs when there came a brilliant flash of light and a *whoosh*.

When their eyes adjusted to the campfire light once again, they were surprised to see Kazimir and Sir Eldrick standing before them.

"Holy witch tits!" Murland blurted, spilling his plate as he stood erect.

"See, I don't get why he can't just whoosh us to Bad Mountain," said Willow, scratching her head.

"Sir Eldrick!" Gibrig cried and flung himself at the knight.

"Ha ha, fear not, my brave champions, for I have returned to you whole and ready to continue," said Sir Eldrick.

Beside him, Kazimir rolled his eyes.

"Where did you run off to?" Brannon asked.

"That, my fair elven friend, is a long story, a long story indeed."

"And one that he surely does not remember," said Kazimir, shaking his head at the knight and raising a brow to Brannon.

"I awoke to find myself seated before the one and only Queen Tittianya of Faeland…"

When his story commenced, the companions sat there, enthralled. All but Willow.

"Alright, see, now that just don't make any sense. If you can whoosh Sir Eldrick from there to here, then surely you can whoosh us to Bad Mountain."

"If it were that easy to *whoosh* you to Bad Mountain," said Kazimir, standing slowly and seemingly towering over the eight-foot-tall ogre some-how. "Don't you think I would have done so by now!"

His voice boomed and left her on her backside.

"Why must you bother the High Wizard so?" Gibrig asked. "He has only ever helped us."

Sir Eldrick noticed how Brannon's eyes fell then, and he tried to change the subject. "Murland," he said with much enthusiasm. "What is this I hear of you performing magic? I wish I could have seen it."

Kazimir cocked a brow to that, and Murland gulped.

"Ah...yeah, I grew my own wizard leaf, finally. With the help of Brannon. I can read the spell book now."

"Spell book?" said Kazimir. "What spell book?"

"Uh, just one that Zorromon gave me."

"And who, might I ask, was the spell book's author?"

Murland remembered Zorromon's warning about keeping the book a secret from Kazimir, but the old wizard's glare was so intimidating that he was helpless but to tell the truth.

"Allan Kazam."

"Allan Kazam?" said the wizard, seemingly dumbstruck. He shook his head, his white beard flapping, and quickly composed himself. "But of course, no less for the best wizard to come out of Abra Tower in two centuries."

Sir Eldrick glanced at Brannon and found that the elf seemed to be purposefully avoiding looking at him, for the knight stared for a full minute with no effect.

Kazimir seemed not to miss the unspoken sentiment. "Well then," he said, extending his arms at them all. "You are all together again, and not far from the Wide Wall. But I must warn you. The real journey has just begun. Where now you have traveled only a few hundred miles, the road beyond the Wall to Bad Mountain stretches more than a thousand. You must travel through the Forest of the Dead, beyond—"

"Yeah, we know the route," said Willow, picking her teeth with a twig and then eating it. "Ain't there a boat or something that could just bring us around the western lands right to the base of Bad Mountain? I seen the maps before. The mountain sits right smack dab on the northwestern coast."

"Most of the land beyond the Wide Wall is inaccessible by boat," said Kazimir with a fed-up glance at the ogre. "Why don't you think of how you can help the group, rather than wondering about saving yourself some walking?"

"Hey," said Sir Eldrick. "She is trying to help."

The knight was surprised at his own anger toward the wizard, and Kazimir, always alert, did not miss the true sentiment of the statement.

"Come, walk with me," Kazimir told him, and he began walking toward the pines.

"I'll be right back," Sir Eldrick told the group.

Sir Eldrick followed Kazimir into the woods, but the wizard did not stop, even when they were well out of earshot. He continued on down an embankment, across a small stream, up a steep slope leading to a glen, and down again to where the stream snaked this way once more, emptying into a small pond, eddying in the shadows of the tall oaks.

"Behold. The price of your failure," said Kazimir. He pointed toward the pond.

Sir Eldrick stood on the high bank and watched, mystified and fearful, as the swirling pond shimmered, and an aerial view of a dragon in flight shone there in the pristine waters. It was Drak'Noir, and she was marvelous, and beautiful, and just as terrible as he had always imagined. Her wings spread for miles, and her fire spared neither the women nor the children. Her liquid breath of death consumed whole cities. Fire Swamp was reduced to clay, Magestra became a burning beacon on the eastern shores of Fallacetine, Vhalovia was swallowed up by a pit of churning lava, and Halala and the Iron Mountains burned and crumbled, and nothing was safe from the wrath of the great dragon goddess.

"Stop! No more!" cried Sir Eldrick, flinging himself away from the swirling pool and falling into the ferns.

"Now you understand the severity of this quest. Now you understand your role. Your heart might sing for these fools, but fools they are, and heroes in a way as well. For their sacrifice shall ensure that this vision does not come to pass."

"I understand," said Sir Eldrick. "I understand."

When they returned, Murland was sitting with his spell book opened, debating with Brannon on the true meaning of a particularly strange-sounding spell that he had just read.

Kazimir marched up to him and slapped the book shut. To his surprise, a spark issued from the tome and zapped his finger, only making him angrier.

"Don't you know that spell books are sacred, and not to be read aloud like some fruity elf's diary entries?" said Kazimir all in a huff.

"I'm sorry, Most High Wizard," said Murland, wide eyed. "I just...I...I."

"Get your words in a row and meet me in my yurt," said the wizard. He turned and waggled his fingers, and a circular tent covered in snow appeared on a raised platform beside the fire.

Moments before, the Magestrian team of climbers had just popped the top on a fifty-year-old bottle of wine, a bottle that their order's founding member, one Felix Hillman, had once promised he would pop at the summit of Mount Cold Finger, the highest and most treacherous of all mountains on the frozen continent known as the Eternal Ice. Standing just an hour's hike from the summit, the team had decided to drink to their founder, who had died in this very spot, having frozen to death before reaching the top.

They all raised their glasses in a cheer, and suddenly, inexplicably, their yurt, the only shelter from the bitter, deathly cold, disappeared.

Murland followed the wizard into the yurt, pausing only momentarily to regard the map of the Eternal Ice.

"I'm sorry if I—"

"You say that you can read the tome. What else came to you when you smoked your wizard leaf for the first time?" said Kazimir, moving to the small stove burning at the center of the mysterious yurt.

"Well…I don't know," said Murland, rubbing his hands together nervously. "I got all tingly, and I floated into the air."

"You floated?"

"Yeah, but not too high. I came down eventually. Obviously," he said with a nervous laugh.

Kazimir regarded him over his thin spectacles, and Murland had the sudden understanding of what a beetle must feel like, being observed through a learned monk's thick lens.

"What did the tome say?"

"Well, it says a lot, really. It is the collected works of Allan Kazam, with a foreword by—"

"Erasmus Farsky?" said Kazimir, suddenly glowering at Murland with a look like regret.

"Yes. Erasmus Farsky."

Kazimir visibly diminished, and Murland wondered if it were a trick of the light.

"High Wizard?"

"What? What?" said Kazimir, as if being awakened from a deep sleep, or perhaps a trance.

"High Wizard, what did you bring me here to ask me? I have asked you to help me with the wand and the wizard leaf, but you offered none. And now that I have figured it out for myself…well, now you take an interest?"

"Well, of course," said Kazimir, annoyed. "Why do you think that the other high wizards never stopped Lance Lancer from poisoning your plants, and never even told you about it? The job of a wizard is a serious one. We delve in the shadows of mystery on a daily basis. The unknown IS our business. No one could tell you why your plants were dying, just like I couldn't tell you how to fix the wand or grow wizard leaf."

"I understand," said Murland. "Thank you for letting me learn on my own."

"Sure, kid," said Kazimir with a sigh. "Just be careful. Take it slow. No need to dive right into a spell book such as that."

"But...I have only just begun to learn. Surely haste is in order. We will reach Bad Mountain in what...a month, two?"

"Damn it, man, just do as I say!"

Murland bowed his head, chastising himself for doubting Kazimir's wisdom. "I'm sorry, High Wiz—"

"Get out," said Kazimir with a finger pointing to the door. "Just leave."

"Yes, sir," said Murland. Bowing, he backed out of the yurt, not quite sure why he had incurred the High Wizard's anger.

CHAPTER 32

HUNTERS AND THE HUNTED

"Y E JUST FOLLOW the road east until ye get to King's Crossin', then ye take the northern road back to the Iron Mountains," Hagus told the dwarf lass who had so suddenly appeared along with the other prostitutes.

"But won't ye come with me?" she asked, looking fearful.

Hagus glanced over at the others, who were waiting by the road. "Nah, me road be leadin' west. There be a dragon to kill. Go on then, the others be headin' as far as King's Crossin' anyway. Ye won't be alone. Farewell."

He mounted his ram and joined the others, and together they set out toward the Wide Wall.

"This is crazy, you all know that, right?" Caressa told them all. "There is no turning back from this quest."

"I didn't sign up for this," said Wendel, walking behind them. "Once we get to the Forest of the Dead, I'm gone!"

"Shut up, Wendel," they all said in unison.

"I for one ain't afraid o' no dragon," said Hagus.

"Not even a dragon with a mile-long wingspan?" said Caressa.

"Bah, mile long. Ye been listinin' to too many bedtime stories, lass. There ain't no dragon that big. Besides, why would a dragon that big need food brought to her for her whelps, eh? Don't make no sense. Why would a dragon need food brought to them at all?"

"You have a point," said Valkimir. "It makes no more sense than a group of champions 'scaring her away' every generation."

"There is definitely something going on with this Drak'Noir," Caressa agreed. "And I intend to get to the bottom of it."

"What about the Blight-Blight?" said Dingleberry, flying beside them. "If Drak-Drak can do that, she must be big-BIG!"

"We be findin' out soon enough," said Hagus. "Big or small, everythin' that breathes can be killed. Everythin'."

They traveled hard through the day, intent on catching up to the champions before they could make it to the Wide Wall. A few hours after sundown, they came to a spot where Valkimir said he could make out old tracks leading into the hills, and he was sure that they belonged to the champions.

"See here," he said, pointing to a spot a dozen feet from where the tracks went in. "They came out about ten hours later, and they were heavier." He scoured the hills beyond the copses of birch. "They must have met up with someone who gave them a large amount of supplies. Food perhaps."

"Ye can make all that out o' them faint tracks, can ye?" said Hagus, sounding dubious.

"Indeed, good dwarf."

"How old the tracks be?"

"Five, six days."

"Then we best be gettin' a bit o' rest and head out again afore dawn."

They put in beside the road on a piece of flat land ringed by birches whose bark was peeling off in curled strands. The night was warm. It had proven to be a dry spring so far, which boded well for travelers, but not so well for the farmers.

Hagus was surprised by the climate south of the mountains, for on his farm in the green valley nestled between the mountains, there was always a mist in the air. The mountain dew and low-hanging clouds kept the crops always quenched, which led to an excellent yield year after year.

He lay there beneath the stars, unable to sleep, and thought of his farm. He knew that he could never return, not after what he had done. Gibrig would never be welcome there again either.

Unless...

If they faced Drak'Noir together and killed the beast, they would become heroes, renowned throughout all the lands. The king would have no choice but to pardon their indiscretions, and they could then return to the farm and be done with all this questing business.

Hagus had had enough adventure for one lifetime already. He had lost an eye to adventure and warring, and had vowed never again to fight. He had never intended for his son to ever become a soldier. The lad didn't have the stones for violence.

Just like his brother, Hagus thought, *not a mean bone in his body, bless him.*

Sniffling, he rolled over, trying to get comfortable on the lumpy ground.

"Hagus!" Wendel suddenly croaked.

The dwarf shot straight up with a start and Wendel scuttled over to him, his two floating eyes quivering. "Something is out there, something rotten, something evil, something…dead."

"What is he yammering about?" Valkimir asked sleepily from his spot a few feet away.

"Speak plainly," said Hagus.

Wendel's jaw chattered. "Plainly? Plainly! What is more plain? Something is out there. This way, a great evil comes."

Valkimir and Hagus got up and scoured the nearby land, which was bright with the moon's silver glow.

Caressa entered camp from the east, looking ashen. "Something is out there."

"So says Wendel," said Valkimir. "Did you see what it was?"

"No, just a feeling. Terror like I have not felt since I was a child. We must leave. Now."

"Very we—" Valkimir's voice suddenly caught in his throat, for a dread had suddenly crept over them all like a blanket of frigid air. Terror pure and cold took over their minds, consuming them and telling them to flee.

"They be here," said Hagus, taking up his shovel in two strong hands and moving slowly in a circle, eyeing the dark.

"Ride! All of you. Ride!" Valkimir suddenly yelled, and a hellish shriek answered him.

Caressa, Hagus, and Wendel leapt on their mounts and sped down the road as though an army of demons followed. Valkimir's mount caught up and passed them easily as more shrieks now issued from all directions.

Hagus felt as though something was attacking his mind, trying to dig in and devour his soul. He fought to put up a kind of mental wall as waves of depression and despair crashed against his mind. The wall held firm for a time. The mounts, however, had no such protection. They flew wildly down the road, spurred by primal terror.

"What in the hells that be?" Hagus demanded.

"Darklings!" said Valkimir as Dingleberry flew to catch up and landed on his shoulder.

Caressa screamed, and to Hagus's horror, she and her mount were lifted from the ground by a great winged beast that carried her high into the sky.

He looked to Valkimir and Dingleberry riding beside him, and out of the corner of his eye, he saw darkness descend upon them. Dingleberry, Valkimir, and the horse were taken up in black talons and shot into the air.

Hagus swung his shovel upward as the shadow of a beast blocked out the moonlight and scooped up the mountain ram.

CHAPTER 33

BAD TIDINGS FROM
WORSE COMPANY

URLAND AWOKE IN a cold sweat, as though he had been caught in the throes of a terrible nightmare. His eyes shot open and he gasped for air. Heart thumping in his chest, he stared up at the sky. It was dawn, and the deep blues and purples were being replaced by oranges and pinks. He stared at the morning sky, wanting nothing more than to see the sun, for in the corner of his eyes he could see the dark figures standing at the edge of camp, watching. A deep, haunting cold swept over him, and a dark, hateful song like chanting filled his mind.

Darklings...

He dared not look at them, for to do so would make them real. Instead he squeezed his eyes shut and tried desperately to fall back asleep, or wake up, anything to make them go away.

Muuurlaaand.

The voices were whispers in his mind, cold against his soul. He shivered, fighting the urge to look, just look and be done with it. He felt so alone. Where were the others? Had he been carried off by the foul beasts in the night?

He didn't want to know.

Murland remembered his wand and carefully reached for it beneath his blanket. When his fingers wrapped around the smooth hard wood, he felt a sense of calm wash over him, and courage found its way into his spine once more.

He opened his eyes...

And a darkling was standing over him, body crooked and bent beneath the black shroud. The faceless creature was staring at him. Though it had no eyes, he could feel that penetrating gaze boring into his core, down to his very soul.

Murland screamed. The darklings shrieked.

The camp came alive then with that chorus of terrible cries and the alarmed exclamations of his companions.

"Back to the hells with you, foul beasts!" Sir Eldrick demanded, leaping over Murland and swinging his translucent fae blade.

Murland scrambled to his feet as Willow, Brannon, and Gibrig did the same.

Just when Murland remembered Kazimir and looked desperately toward the yurt, the leather door flaps were blasted outward by an explosion of light. The darklings shrieked and hissed, and the light became brighter and brighter still, forcing them back to the shadows at the edge of the forest.

The light disappeared, and Kazimir strode out of the yurt, looking angrily determined. Murland rushed to Gibrig's side, glancing at his friend. Gibrig was ashen, and dark circles hung like half-moons beneath his eyes.

They waited for the darklings to retaliate, but no such attack came; they simply stood there, watching with those dark, eyeless faces as the wizard slowly stalked them.

"You have meddled in my affairs one too many times, my old friends," said the wizard, and he raised his staff as if to cleave the earth.

"Zuul has a message for the championsss," hissed one of the darklings.

Murland and Gibrig exchanged glances.

"He has the ones named Hagus, Caressa, Valkimir, and…Dingleberry."

Kazimir looked back at the companions, who shared surprised glances.

"Enough of your lies, denizens of the d—"

"Zuul will kill them all unless you travel to the Twisted Tower. You have until the new moon."

With that, the darklings all leapt into the air as four hideous winged beasts glided over the clearing and snatched them up. As they flew beyond the tree line and west toward the fading stars, the group all began asking Kazimir questions at the same time.

"What did he mean, he's got Val?" Brannon demanded.

"Not poor little Dingleberry!" Willow was saying over and over.

"Pap? Why would he have me pap?" Gibrig asked.

"Silence!" said Kazimir, and his voice sent birds flying from trees.

"Kazimir, what does Zuul want with me pap?" Gibrig demanded with uncharacteristic anger.

"It seems that Zuul is once again trying to stop the champions from reaching Bad Mountain."

"But why would he want to do that?" Sir Eldrick asked.

"Zuul wants to see the world burn. He wishes for us to fail so that Drak'Noir will ravage the world," said Kazimir gravely.

"Do you think that he really has them?" Murland asked, concerned for Caressa.

"It cannot be known for sure," said Kazimir, stroking his long white beard thoughtfully. "But rest assured, I will investigate this matter, and if indeed he has taken them, I will free them and return them home. You must all continue to the Wide Wall. Do not let this distraction slow you down."

"We lost the mounts to a bad storm," said Sir Eldrick. "The going is going to be slower until we get some new ones."

"Lost your mounts?" said Kazimir, glancing around. "Hmm, well that will have to be remedied."

"Can ye bring 'em back?" Gibrig begged.

"Yeah, whoosh 'em here," said Willow with a grin.

"Silence!" said Kazimir. He pulled out his wand and closed his eyes.

They all waited anxiously as he spoke the spell words.

There was a loud pop, a puff of smoke, and a *whoosh*.

When the smoke cleared, the lost mounts were all standing together. Upon Sir Eldrick's mount sat a small troll, who gave a shriek and leapt off, scurrying into the woods.

"Snorts!" said Gibrig as he rushed to give the hog a hug.

"Precious!" said Brannon, hurrying over as well.

"You didn't eat the hog?" Willow said to Tor. "What, you sick or something?"

Sir Eldrick patted his horse's back and nodded at the wizard. "Thank you, Kazimir."

"May I have a private word with you?" Brannon asked, eyeing the wizard like few ever dared.

Kazimir grudgingly nodded, and Brannon followed him to his yurt.

"Break down camp," Sir Eldrick told the others as he followed the two. "We ride in ten minutes."

Murland and the others did as they were told, and he wondered what it was that Brannon and Sir Eldrick had to say to the wizard in private.

Sir Eldrick followed Brannon into the yurt, and Kazimir waved a hand, casting a spell on the tented building. "That will keep out prying ears. Now speak swiftly, for I have little time for silly questions."

"You never said anything about our friends and family getting mixed up in this," said Brannon, pacing the small room and biting his thumbnail. "And Zuul! The Dark Lord himself? How will you ever free them from the likes of him?"

"Do not underestimate my power, elf," said Kazimir.

"If they all came after us, they must have learned of the deception somehow," Sir Eldrick reasoned.

"Yes, they all learned of the lie in their own way. They set out after you all to stop you from going to Bad Mountain. I intercepted them and told them to turn back, but it appears that they did not heed my warning."

"Why didn't you tell us this before?" Brannon insisted.

The wizard gave him a contemptuous scowl. "I am not your errand boy! Enough of your silly questions. I have said that I will free them from Zuul, and that should be enough for you. Now go, continue west as you were, for the Wall is not far off."

With that he marched out of the yurt and whistled. Soon his black unicorn came dashing out of the woods. The wizard floated up and landed in the saddle and looked to the companions. "Continue on, brave champions. Do not fret about your loved ones, for Kazimir is on his way."

Kazimir snapped the reins, and the unicorn suddenly sprouted long black wings. It galloped toward the road and lifted off gracefully, veering north and disappearing beyond the trees.

When the companions set out, a blanket of gray clouds swept across the sky from the south, and a light rain began to fall, lending to the miserable mood. Worry was etched across every brow save Sir Eldrick's, who led them solemnly. His thoughts were not consumed with worry for his loved one, but rather the fact that no one had come after him at all.

"What did you two talk to Kazimir about in private?" Murland asked, and Sir Eldrick glanced over at Brannon.

"I...warned him that if anything happened to Valkimir, he would have my father's wrath to deal with," said the elf.

"But why would they be coming after us?" Gibrig asked. "It just doesn't make any sense."

"Perhaps the darklings were lying, trying to shake us up," said Sir Eldrick.

"I can't believe me pap would set out to stop me," said Gibrig. "Maybe he was just comin' to lend a helpin' hand. He's always helping me with stuff, even when I don't need it."

"Dingleberry is a little rascal," said Willow with a laugh. "Probably thought she was missing out. She was pretty upset when she wasn't allowed to come."

"Poor Valkimir," said Brannon, looking wet and miserable upon his white steed. He hadn't even bothered to comb his hair or do his makeup. "I should have known that he would come after me."

"I can't believe that Princess Caressa came after me," said Murland. "We're friends, sure, but...well, she's a princess. I think the darklings were lying."

"But why didn't the darklings mention anyone coming for you, Sir Knight?" Gibrig asked.

Murland looked to him with big eyes that suggested it was a bad question, and the dwarf's mouth made a big O shape as he cringed with the realization of his tactless comment.

Sir Eldrick glanced back at them all stoically. "We should not waste worry on it. For Kazimir is the greatest wizard in all the land. Whether these things are true or not, he will get to the bottom of it. Your friends are in good hands. Look there, do you see that dark shadow upon the horizon to the west? That is the Wide Wall, my friends. Only a few days' march from here. You have done well."

The companions followed him through the drizzle and fog, feeling very much alone and quite miserable. The bleak feeling of helplessness caused by the darklings haunted them as they rode in silence, ever westward, ever westward.

CHAPTER 34

THE TWISTED TOWER

Kazimir flew with the unicorn upon the winds of time and space. The journey would have taken anyone else days, for the Twisted Tower lay far to the north, two hundred miles off the mainland on Dark Island. He spoke the words that would bring him back to the physical realm before he got too close, knowing full well that if Zuul had regained enough power, the Twisted Tower would be protected by wards that made such travel too close to the island impossible.

As the streaking blur of stars gave way to a dreary sky and clouds pregnant with rain, he saw that indeed, the Twisted Tower glowed with power once more. Like a unicorn horn it spiraled out from the broken earth and rose a mile into the air above Dark Island.

He steered the unicorn down and landed on the bank before dismissing the creature and staring grimly at that hated tower. Kazimir had not known fear in a long, long time. But now, looking up at the remnant of a time of such darkness that had nearly consumed the world, he was reminded of its meaning.

Overhead, the four darklings flew out of a swirling portal like the one he had just ventured through; Zuul was getting powerful indeed.

Kazzzimirrr.

The wizard jerked his head to the lone window high at the top of the Twisted Tower, frozen by the icy voice of Zuul echoing in his head.

You owe me a sssoul!

"Et egressus est ab animo animal foedum!" said Kazimir, releasing his power with the warding spell and slamming his staff into the stone at his feet.

The hissing, shrieking voice screamed in his mind one last time and was gone.

Zuul had gained in power, it was true, but so too had Kazimir. He grinned up at the window and thought he saw a dark figure standing there, staring down at him.

Valkimir slowly opened his eyes and found himself bound in chains against a cold, jagged wall, wearing nothing but his boots. His warrior instincts took over, and rather than feel alarm, fear, and terror, his mind began to scan the round room and try to formulate a plan of escape. To his left, Caressa hung from similar chains, and to her left hung Wendel. To Valkimir's right, he found Hagus. All of them were still out cold. Dingleberry too hung from the wall on the other side of the dwarf; it looked as though her little wings had been bound, along with her arms and legs. She had done so much thrashing that a two-inch pile of fairy dust had gathered on the floor beneath her and trailed down the jagged wall, gathering in places and sparkling faintly in the dim light.

There was only one window in the circular chamber, but at its center was a large, humming globe covered in clouds. Valkimir looked closer and thought that he saw the outline of Fallacetine.

"I see that you are admiring my ball," came a deep, wet, mechanical voice.

He looked again to the window, catching faint movement in the corner of his eye. Valkimir was surprised to see a hunchbacked and hooded figure standing in the window, looking away.

"Zuul," said Valkimir, refusing to be intimidated by the Dark Lord, but again not forgetting Zuul's true power.

The figure turned, and Valkimir saw that it was not Zuul, but a hag. She had the look of a witch, with a long hooked nose covered in warts and sagging breasts hanging over her big round belly. And on that belly, resting in the crook of her crooked, boney arms, was a baby. It was wrapped in a dark material, like bat wings, and in its mouth was a metallic breathing apparatus connected to a tube.

Valkimir realized with sudden, sick awareness that it had been the baby, not the hag, who had spoken. For the hag stared blankly at the floor near Valkimir's feet, while the baby, with its demonic red eyes, mischievous baby sneer, and shock of red hair, stared expectantly at Valkimir.

"I don't know if I want to throw you from this tower, or squeeze your little cheeks," Valkimir told the baby.

"I am ZUUUUL!" the baby cried in a voice both cherubic and terrifying at the same time, which was amplified by the metal mask.

Caressa awoke with a start. She thrashed briefly against her chains, screaming, but then went limp with horror and disgust when her eyes fell upon the Dark Lord reborn. Dingleberry gave a high-pitched chittering like a squirrel, and Wendel came to, screaming like a man on fire.

Hagus had been roused by the horrible cry as well and shook the drowsiness from his face violently. His eyes soon found Zuul's, and he stared not in horror, but as one might a strange insect. "What in the five hells is ye supposed to be?" he asked, disgusted.

Zuul pointed a tiny, shaking finger at them all, silencing them immediately, and took the metal breathing contraption out of his mouth. His little head darted behind a thin veil covering the hag's weeping breast, and a suckling sound soon filled the chamber.

"Oh, gods," said Valkimir, having the sudden urge to brush his teeth.

"She has a right to breastfeed in public," said Caressa, wisely trying to get on the witch's good side, Valkimir realized.

"I think that milk spoiled a few decades ago, laddie," said Hagus with a chuckle.

"IT'S NOT FUNNY," Zuul shot back in a voice much more baby-like without the mask. "Forward," he told the hag, slapping her with a tiny little wand. The witch carried him closer, until he was only two feet from Valkimir. "I have not died, spent a thousand years in limbo, and clawed my way back into this world through the cobwebbed womb of a witch to be laughed at by the likes of you! Do you know who I am? I am

ZUUUL! The world once trembled at the mere mention of my name, and it will once more. When the Champions of the Dragon come to rescue you, I will kill them all, and there will be no one to stop Drak'Noir from setting the world aflame. I, Zuul, will rise above those ashes and rein for eternity!"

"You will never get away with this!" Caressa told him defiantly.

"Yeah!" Dingleberry squeaked.

Zuul snapped his fingers, and the witch walked him over to stand before Caressa. He looked her over with the hungry eyes of an infant and licked his thin lips. "The milk of a princess is said to be the sweetest of all," he told her, grinning.

"I'll tell you anything you want to know, anything!" cried Wendel. "Hells, I'll milk her for you."

"Leave the lass alone, ye half-pint terror," Hagus growled.

Zuul lashed out with his wand and spoke a spell that crackled out of the wooden tip and hit Hagus square in the chest.

"PAIN!" Zuul screamed. "Doloribusss!"

Hagus thrashed and jittered, grinding his jaw and growling as Zuul's face twisted with sadistic delight.

"Fulgur!" Zuul commanded, and snaking lightning leapt from his clawed little hand and enveloped the dwarf, whose bones glowed beneath the skin and whose beard and hair stuck straight out in all directions. By the time Zuul let up, the dwarf's head looked like a smoldering porcupine.

"Leave him alone!" Caressa cried, thrashing against her bonds.

Zuul rolled his eyes. "Sorry, Princess, but you are a long way away from Magestra. So, shut up and be a good little wench, and Zuul will not bite when he nurses."

A sudden explosion silenced Zuul, and the door blew inward, knocking the hag against the wall and causing her to drop Zuul's infant body. Kazimir appeared in the smoking doorway, looking cross. He followed the bundle as it rolled across the floor, watching it with an arched brow.

Zuul suddenly leapt to his feet, wearing his black baby blanket like a robe, and shot his little wand out at Kazimir, screaming, "Temptat mortim!"

The seasoned wizard was quick on the draw, and he released a spell of his own from a long, crooked wand and bellowed, "Revertere ad mittentis!"

The spells collided with a bang, and Zuul's spell shot back in his direction, forcing him to leap to the side with incredible agility.

"Volo, et fortitudinem," said Zuul, tapping the wand on top of his own head. He suddenly shot out of the blanket and across the room like an arrow, leaping up and landing on Kazimir's face. He pulled the wizard's hair and tried to stab his wand in Kazimir's eyes. Kazimir spun in circles, cursing and trying to dislodge the tiny Dark Lord from his face.

Finally, Kazimir got a grip on Zuul and threw him across the room. He hit the wall with a thud and dropped to the floor. Zuul blinked, looking shocked, and then his large eyes welled up with tears and he began to wail. The cry was no ordinary infant scream, but like that of a banshee, high-pitched and piercing.

Valkimir and the others thrashed in their chains, trying desperately to cover their ears. However, Kazimir weathered the torturous sound with a small grimace.

"Darklings!" the baby cried.

Up through the door, four black shadows swooped and surrounded Kazimir. He turned a circle, pointing his wand dangerously at them, before pointing it at the ground and bellowing, "Vocat lux stella endlune!"

Sudden brilliant white light erupted in the small chamber, washing over the companions like a lover's lingering lips and filling their spirits with joy. To the darklings and Zuul, the lightshow seemed to have a much different effect, for they howled and screamed, cursed and shrieked.

When the light subsided, the darklings were gone, and only Zuul and the dazed-looking witch remained.

"I will peel your fetid skin from your rotting bones," Zuul began, slowly rising to his little bare feet.

"NO!" said Kazimir, as one might to a naughty child.

Zuul looked as though his rosy cheeks had been slapped. "How dare you tell me n—"

"NO!" said Kazimir, with all the authority of a king.

"I'll, I'll…"

"No, you will not. You will be good, or by the gods, I will destroy it."

Zuul looked confused, and perhaps a little scared. He rubbed his little hands together, glaring at Kazimir with utter malice.

"For I know your secret, once great Zuul, pillager of souls." He held out before him a green, glowing water pipe, rough cut and luminescent and beautiful in its sheer power.

"Give it to me!" Zuul screamed, rushing the wizard with two clutching fists out before him.

"Manibus!" said Kazimir, shooting out a choking hand.

Zuul was picked up off his feet and slammed into the wall, where he cried and squirmed like a slug.

"You *will* teach me how to use your former master's pipe, or I will vanquish you to the realm of light, where you will burn, and beg, and plead, and die, forever!"

"Never!" Zuul cried, and Kazimir choked him with the invisible hand until his face was purple.

"Say the words, or be gone forever! Swear fealty to me!"

"I…I swear. I—"

"In the language of magic!"

"Et fidelitatem ad vos," said Zuul, and he promptly dropped to the floor. A faint light swirled out of him and snaked its way over to Kazimir's hand to be absorbed into his palm.

"Now you are mine," he said with a grin. He looked to Valkimir and the others as if they were an afterthought and waggled his fingers, murmuring spell words. Their chains broke, and they all fell to the floor.

"I do not care what tortures you threaten," said Valkimir, straightening despite the pain in his numb legs. "I will follow my beloved to the ends of the earth if I have to. Lock me up, and I shall break free. Kill me, and I shall return as a ghost. You will never stop me."

Kazimir looked to him tiredly and waved a hand wide before them. The chamber melted away like an oil painting beneath the rain and was replaced by the crashing waves of the northern sea and dull gray light of the overcast day.

Valkimir glanced around and found that by Kazimir's magic, Caressa, Hagus, and Dingleberry were there as well, along with Wendel, who stood hunched among them, jaw chattering with terror.

"What do I do with you four?" Kazimir asked, pacing the long stones along the jagged shore.

"F-f-five," said Wendel.

Kazimir sighed. "I have tried to be fair. And I have been more than patient. Your kings have all agreed to this, the Champions of the Dragon have been chosen. No matter what strange conspiracies you might imagine, one fact remains: Drak'Noir must be dealt with!"

Valkimir rushed forward, his face pleading rather than stern. "Together, we might all have a chance to defeat her. Please, Kazimir, we know that you have made some sort of deal with the wyrm, we know that you are somehow beholden to her. Let us help you."

"Help me?" said the wizard, laughing mirthlessly. "You have just seen me defeat Zuul the Terrible, and you think that *I* need help from *you*?"

"If you will not help defeat Drak'Noir, then we will do it ourselves," said Caressa. "Every one of us is prepared to die trying."

"I really didn't sign up for that," said Wendel, raising his hand.

"Shut up, Wendel," said Dingleberry.

"It is good that you are prepared to die, for die you shall," said Kazimir, studying them all. "But not by my hand...oh, no. Venture beyond the Wide Wall, and you will know horrors that you have never dreamed. Otherworldly creatures that children's fairytales cannot even begin to hint at. I beseech you now, go back to your palaces and your farms. Your own kings have given the champions their blessing in this, their greatest sacrifice. Leave it alone, for you know what will happen if Drak'Noir is not...taken care of."

"I have already spoken my intentions," said Valkimir with a raised chin.

"Aye," said Hagus before spitting on the stone.

"Yeah!" Dingleberry put in, shadowboxing and flipping in the air.

Kazimir shook his head. "Then I will lament your loss," he said.

He snapped his fingers, and their clothes, armor, and weapons landed in a pile at their feet. With that he spun on his toes, bringing his cloak up and around him, and in a puff of smoke he was gone.

"What about our mounts?" Hagus yelled at the sky.

"What do we do now?" Wendel asked the group.

"'I'll even milk her'?" said Caressa, stalking over and taking a swipe at the skeleton, smacking his jaw and sending the skull spinning on the neck bone.

Wendel caught his head and straightened it and threw up his arms. "I was scared!"

Caressa scoffed and began to get dressed.

When they were all decent once again, Caressa began to search the rocky shore. "There has to be a boat or something—ah, look here!"

Valkimir rushed over with the others and saw the small rowboat that had apparently gone aground against the island's jutting rocks. They inspected it and found no holes, but no oars either.

"No matter," said Valkimir. "We all have hands."

Together they put the boat in the water and hopped in, pushing off from the rocks and paddling the best they could with their hands. Dingleberry did her part as well, pushing against Hagus's back and beating her little wings furiously.

"We must head southwest," said Valkimir. "That will bring us to the northern border, which will bring us to the Wide Wall."

"How far we talkin'?" Hagus asked.

At first Valkimir did not answer.

"Well?"

"Only a few hundred miles, my good dwarf."

"A few hundred miles!"

CHAPTER 35

HORSE MEAT AND RAPTOR BLOOD

T HE CHAMPIONS OF the Dragon continued down the western road for three days. The land northwest of the Blight was marshy and wet, with crooked moss-covered trees that looked half dead and grew no leaves. The mood remained solemn, for Kazimir had not yet appeared to them with word of their loved ones. Everyone save Sir Eldrick was wracked with worry.

Murland spent his time whittling a wand out of a good sturdy piece of oak he had chiseled out of a block of firewood left behind at one of the camps they found in their travels. It wasn't as dry as he would have liked, but it wasn't green either, which would have been much worse. In other circumstances, the creation of a wand would be an arduous chore spanning weeks, if not months. The perfect piece of wood had to be procured, preferably from a very old hickory, hard maple, white oak, or beech tree. The wand would then be chiseled out and shaped, and often imbued with ancient runes, depending on what kind of magic the practitioner wanted it to enhance. The virgin wand would then be fire hardened using a very slow and time-consuming process. It would then be left to sit for a few days, at which time a hardening salve and other ointments would be applied.

Murland didn't have time for all that, however. He needed the wand to perform only one spell, that of mending the broken wand of Allan Kazam. He dared not attempt any more spells with the taped wand. The simple fire spell he had attempted had nearly killed him.

After the fourth day of travel since the startling encounter with the darklings, Kazimir had still not arrived. They made camp off the road in a clearing that looked to be used often by travelers, likely soldiers from the five kingdoms headed to and from the Wide Wall.

"Two more days I reckon," said Sir Eldrick as he sat by the fire with his arms hooked behind his head and boots up on the fireplace stones.

"Tell us again about the Wide Wall," said Gibrig, who was absolutely distraught with worry for his father. He had been asking a lot of questions about almost everything the last few days, and Murland knew that it was to keep his mind off things.

"Well, what else can I tell you that I haven't before?"

"Just tell it all again. That be fine."

"Alright, well, the Wide Wall was built over a thousand years ago by the now all-but-extinct Agnarian giants with the help of us humans, elves, dwarves, ogres, hells, even trolls were part of the alliance in those days. When Zuul first rose up, he took the lands west of the Wall, which at one time were populated with all the races, as eastern Fallacetine is today. Mind you, the rising of a dark lord is not always an overnight affair. Zuul's attempt at dominion spanned the course of a century. Bad Mountain, once home to the Darwellian dwarves, now extinct, was the first place to be conquered. From there the darkness spread. In ten years, what is now known as the Northern Barrens was taken. Its people, humans of fair skin and red hair, were enslaved and used in his growing army. Another twenty years saw the fall of the Zerellian elves, who were plainspeople, and known for their horses and buffalo furs. Then the human kingdom of Brigmere fell, which, at that time, was the most powerful kingdom in the west. It is now known as the Southern Barrens. The strange and mystic men of the Long Sand joined forces with Zuul after the fall of Brigmere. The ogres of Mossmire tried to hold back the dark tide, but they were overrun by Zuul, who turned all their creatures against them, turning the once beautiful Mossmire into the Swamp of Doom.

"Now, about this time, the many races of Eastern Fallacetine began construction of the Wide Wall. Never in the history of the known lands have the races come together for such a project, and the finished result…well, you shall see. At first the dwarves proposed to make the Wall seven hundred feet tall, but most people thought the idea ludicrous, and of course, as dwarves will do, they set out to prove the naysayers wrong. When the work was finally completed, the Wall stood not seven hundred, but one thousand feet high, and two hundred feet thick, spanning a length from the northern sea to the southern sea—over a thousand miles of land. They say it can be seen from the moon," Sir Eldrick said with a chuckle. "But only wizards and dragons would know that."

"Did the Wall work?" Gibrig asked, although he knew the answer.

"It did, for a time, and the navies kept any attack from sea at bay as well. There were a great number of wizards in those days, too many if you ask most people. They helped greatly in keeping back Zuul and his armies, but everyone knew that sooner or later, one side would have to defeat the other."

"And so began the Great War of Fallacetine," said Brannon, staring at the fire hypnotically. "My great-great-great grandfather died in that war. But it is said that he killed over a hundred Zuulians while protecting Allan Kazam and giving him the time he needed to defeat Zuul."

"Yes, your ancestor Merimus was said to have been a great elf, as is his descendent," said Sir Eldrick, offering Brannon a friendly smile.

But the elf didn't smile back. He didn't scoff or roll his eyes either. He simply went back to staring at the fire, seeming dead inside.

Murland sighed, staring into the fire as well. Just then he wished he had the old Brannon back—snooty, rude, disrespectful, and all, anything but this sulking husk of a prince. Indeed, he wished he had all his old friends back.

"You must be excited to visit the wizardly college at the Wide Wall," Sir Eldrick said to Murland.

"Huh? Er, yeah. I never imagined that I would see that place."

"Wizard college?" said Willow, intrigued.

"The College of Kazam," said Murland dreamily. "It is known as the greatest school of higher wizardly learning in all the land. There are no less than one hundred wizards there at any given time, what with the maintenance of the protective spells and whatnot, they are a busy lot."

"Sounds great," said Willow.

"It is a grand place indeed," said Sir Eldrick. "On a good day, when the sun hits it just right, you can see the layers of wards covering the Wall. It is beautiful."

"Maybe one o' them other wizards will help ye out with yer magic," Gibrig suggested.

"That would sure be nice."

A shriek of horror ripped through the clearing, and Murland awoke with a jolt.

"Precious! Precious!" Brannon was wailing.

Murland grabbed Allan Kazam's limply hanging wand and leapt to his feet. Sir Eldrick had risen with his sword, and Gibrig his shovel. One and all were ready for trouble. But rather than bandits, darklings, trolls, or goblins, they found Willow sitting by the dying fire with blood all over her face, eating a half-cooked horse's leg.

"Oh, my, gods," said Gibrig.

"You ate Precious! You sick, twisted, fat, useless ogre!" Brannon screamed. His hair was all in snarls, his makeup streaking down his cheeks.

Willow was still chewing, but she looked to the companions with raised green brows and a shrug. "I get really, really hungry when I'm worried. And I'm so worried about little Dingleberry that I just had to have someth—"

"You bitch!" Brannon screamed, and he threw a handful of seeds at the ogre. He reached out with clawing hands and chanted a string of cryptic-sounding words so fast that Murland thought smoke might come out of his ears.

Willow regarded the seeds with mild mystery, but continued on chewing.

"Brannon..." said Sir Eldrick, approaching him slowly.

"Elzick mrathmon dorgo un dar briglytho!" Brannon shrieked, and the plants suddenly exploded with life. They sprouted, rooted, and grew five feet tall in the course of five seconds, and Willow gave a shriek.

"Brannon, no!" Sir Eldrick said as he lunged for the elf.

But Brannon surprised them all when he ducked under the lurching arm of the knight and heaved a shoulder into his side, sending Sir Eldrick tumbling on his backside.

The seeds had been pumpkin, gourd, bean, and cucumber, and with Brannon's psychic manipulation, they grew to an astounding size. The curling vines of the plants wound their way around Willow's thick arms and legs in a heartbeat and lifted her off the ground, turning her upside down.

Willow's raptor gave a grating shriek and snapped free of its reins, which had been lazily wrapped around a tree branch.

"Look out!" Murland warned as the raptor took seven quick strides with its meaty legs and leapt, teeth-first, at Brannon.

Brannon didn't look afraid in the least, but furious. He raised a hand toward the raptor, and the vines followed his command, wrapping up the leaping beast and forcing it to stop three feet from Brannon, mouth agape and drooling.

The elf unsheathed his sword and stabbed it through the heart of the raptor. He was crying now, and his eyes shimmered and twinkled as he watched the life bleed out of the raptor, staring it in the eyes until they went blank.

"Tor!" cried Willow, and she yanked herself free of the squeezing vines.

Brannon turned on her with murder in his eyes, and Murland found that indeed, he was suddenly terrified of the elf. "Now let's eat your mount and see how you like it!" Brannon licked the blood off his sword and spread it on his face.

"Brannon, stop this!" said Sir Eldrick, grabbing him by the shoulders and shaking him.

The elf turned to Sir Eldrick, noticed Murland and Gibrig staring blankly at him, and fell to his knees, sobbing. The vines fell with him.

"I'm sorry," said Willow, sniffling and looking at her dead raptor. "I was just so hungry."

Brannon suddenly erupted. "Why not just eat the hog, or Sir Eldrick's horse? Why did you have to eat Precious?"

Willow swallowed hard, glancing around at the others and then back again to Brannon. "I…"

"It's because you hate me!" said Brannon, rising to his feet and pushing Sir Eldrick away. "You all hate me! You think I don't know that? Well, guess what? I hate all of you! I wish I had never been chosen for this fool's mission."

"Watch it," said Sir Eldrick evenly.

"You know why none of you feel like champions? Because you're not!"

"Brannon…"

Brannon pointed at Willow. "A fat, useless ogre who was eating her clan out of house and home. A wizard who took ten years to grow a single measly plant! A dwarf who is obviously a bastard half-breed—"

"Brannon!"

He turned to Sir Eldrick with a shaking, pointing finger, face twisted with sorrow and malice and rage. "And a drunk, over-the-hill queen fucker!"

"That's enough!" Sir Eldrick warned, eyes on fire and veins bulging from his temples.

"Is it? Is it? Or should I tell them—"

Sir Eldrick hit him with a right cross that knocked him out cold.

"King's bloody beard! Why'd ye do that for?" Gibrig yelled, rushing to Brannon's side.

"Leave him alone and break down camp!" Sir Eldrick ordered, sounding very much a military man to them just then.

Gibrig backed away slowly, bottom lip quivering. He looked around to Murland and Willow, eyes pooling. "I don't know what's gotten into ye all!" he said and turned on his heel to run to Snorts.

Sir Eldrick sighed and looked to Willow. "That was incredibly stupid, not to mention insensitive. I mean really? Eating his horse?"

"Leave her alone," said Murland. "You don't know what it's like to be so worried over someone. No one got kidnapped coming for you."

Murland felt bad as soon as the words left his mouth. But they had been said, and they could never be taken back.

But they were true, and Sir Eldrick's aging, tired eyes showed as much, for he hung his head and nodded, looking back at Murland with watery eyes. He said nothing, only smiled like a father might.

Sir Eldrick reached down, grabbed Brannon by the collar, and lumbered off into the woods.

"Do you want to live, or do you want to die?"

Brannon opened his eyes and found himself hanging from his arms, feet dangling inches over the ground. The marsh around them echoed with the early-morning song of frogs, and the air smelled of moss and mud.

"What in the hells—"

"Do you want to live or die?" Sir Eldrick asked again, holding the thick rope keeping Brannon aloft with one muscle-corded arm.

"Help!" Brannon screamed.

"I'll slit your godsdamned throat right now!" Sir Eldrick said with a growl, pressing his sword against Brannon's neck. Instead of killing him, he slowly lowered the elf to the ground.

Brannon was relieved at first, but then his feet hit and sank into the earth.

"That is quicksand," said Sir Eldrick, glancing down. "If I let go, you will get swallowed up, and no one will be the wiser. Perhaps you will be burped up by a tortoise in fifty years, perhaps not."

Brannon looked to Sir Eldrick with a feral snarl. "Do it then! I am sick of this charade!"

Sir Eldrick released a foot of rope, and Brannon sank to his shins.

"You almost cost us everything back there," said Sir Eldrick.

"You're right. You should just let me go."

Sir Eldrick released another foot of rope, and Brannon sank to his knees.

"I'll do it, you know I will!"

"I know you will," said Brannon. "Because you are a bastard."

Sir Eldrick released more rope, and Brannon sank to his hips.

"Go on then, kill me!" Brannon screamed. "What does it matter? Valkimir is dead. Precious is dead. My father wants me dead! Do it, you coward!"

Sir Eldrick released the rope, and Brannon closed his eyes. The quicksand was just that, quick, and it swallowed up the elf like an ogre might a bite of horse meat.

Sir Eldrick paced, glancing at the sand now and again. Half a minute went by, and then a full minute. And still Sir Eldrick paced. He was glad to finally be rid of the elf, but he also knew deep down that he needed Brannon. For some ungodly reason, he needed the pompous bastard.

He tied another rope to his leg, fastened it to a thick tree, and meant to leap into the quicksand, when suddenly vines from the surrounding trees lashed out and shot into the pit.

Sir Eldrick fell back and watched.

The vines went taut, flexed, and pulled the elf prince out of the pit with one great heave. He landed five feet away from Sir Eldrick and knelt, shaking on hands and knees, puking sand.

Sir Eldrick regarded the elf warily. "Now that you know what it is like to die, would you like to live?"

Brannon panted and regarded the knight through golden strands of sandy hair. "You tried to kill me."

Sir Eldrick raised and shook the rope in his hand. "I was just about to go in and get you."

Brannon stalked forward, seething.

Sir Eldrick unsheathed his sword and stood erect. "Stop!" he said, throwing out a defensive hand.

Brannon raised hands of his own, and vines came to life, bearing down on Sir Eldrick like vipers.

The knight regarded them warily and looked back to Brannon. "I knew there was a warrior in there somewhere," he said calmly.

Brannon faltered, and regarded him with a cocked brow.

"Look what you have done," said Sir Eldrick, indicating the vines. "Even back there, you subdued an ogre and killed a raptor."

"And I just might kill you," said Brannon.

"Indeed, you would try," said Sir Eldrick. "Which is more than I can say for that pompous little bitch that I met a few weeks ago."

Brannon relaxed a little, and the vines backed off and waited, swaying like hypnotized cobras. "Where do we go from here?"

"To the Wide Wall and beyond," said Sir Eldrick, spreading his arms. "We lead the others to Bad Mountain and—"

"And we watch them die? Eldrick, I don't know if I can do that."

Sir Eldrick let out a long pensive sigh. "It's us or them, Brannon."

"Is it?" They stared at each other, neither wanting to speak more of the terrible deed.

"Come on," said Sir Eldrick. "They are going to be wondering where we went."

They returned to camp to find that indeed, the others had heeded Sir Eldrick's orders. The only remaining mounts, Sir Eldrick's horse and Snorts the hog, were laden with Willow and Brannon's many bags. Murland, Gibrig, and Willow waited beneath a moss-covered husk of a tree near the road, looking sullen.

Brannon strode up to Willow and regarded her with a contemptuous glare. She waited, they all waited, tense and straight, and not wanting any more yelling.

"I do not forgive you, but we are even," he said, extending his hand.

Willow glanced over at what was left of her harvested raptor. "A tusk for a tusk, like they say," said Willow.

They shook hands, and suddenly what was left of the smoldering fire roared to life, and Kazimir's big head turned to regard them with a cock-eyed look. "Can you fools hear me?"

"Kazimir, is that you?" said Murland, rushing to the fire with the others in tow.

"No, it's your uncle. Listen, nitwit. Caressa, Valkimir, Hagus, and that sprite are all safe."

"Did you say that Valkimir is safe?" asked Brannon.

Kazimir nodded. "You have heard me correctly. It took some doing, but they are all on their way home. Fret not, my champions, for Zuul could not endure the wrath of your good ole friend, Kazimir."

Something shattered in the background, and Kazimir disappeared from the fire for a moment. There was a small scuffle, and what sounded like a baby wailing.

"Look," said Kazimir, coming back into the fire. "Continue on to the Wall and know that all is well. You're all doing great!"

Another crash issued from behind the wizard, and what looked to be a bowl of soup landed on his head. "Dammit, you little dark stain!" said Kazimir. "Look, I've got to go. It appears that I am now a babysitter. I'll be with you again on the other side of the Wall. Peace!"

And the fire winked out.

The companions exchanged glances, shrugged, and headed west down the road toward the shadow of the Wide Wall.

CHAPTER 36

THE IRON FIST

THE ENDLESS SCORCHING sun beat down on Valkimir's shoulders, which had once been fair, but were now raw, blistered, and oozing. He had given up rowing long ago. Dingleberry was passed out on Hagus's shoulder. The burly dwarf had rowed for hours under the effects of fairy dust, but had proven to row them in a circle. Caressa lay draped over the side of the small boat, fingertips still dragging the water. She had passed out early in the morning. Wendel lay there with his jaw half opened, bloodshot eyes staring lifelessly at the sky.

Valkimir shakily raised his hand to the scorching sun, trying to blot it out and get his bearings. They had done well for a time, slowly but steadily paddling south toward Fallacetine, but three days of baking sun and no water had proven too much. They were listlessly floating now somewhere in the northern ocean.

With much effort, Valkimir sat up against the side of the boat and glanced around, fighting the urge to lick his cracked and peeling lips. To his surprise, he saw a large ship heading their way. With a hand to the sun he focused in on the vessel, trying to make out the flag flying high upon the main mast. To his dismay, he realized that it was the Jolly Roger, and it was pink. He noticed as well that the figurehead sticking out from the bow was a long metal fist.

"Pirates," he croaked, shaking Hagus's boot. "Wake up!"

The others slowly roused as the ship drew closer. Soon commands could be heard being barked at the crewmen onboard. An anchor was dropped, and shortly after, a small rowboat was dispatched.

"What do we do?" Caressa asked miserably.

"There is little we can do. We're trapped. Just follow my lead, and don't give them any information about who we are," said Valkimir.

"What the hells do we say instead?" Hagus asked.

"Tell them…tell them that we are merchants. Our ship was attacked by pirates in the night, and we barely survived."

"Prepare to be boarded!" came the voice of a female pirate standing upon the prow of the approaching boat.

The pirates, all women, roughly transported Valkimir and the others to their rowboat and tied their hands behind their backs before confiscating their bags and weapons. When they were brought to the pirate ship, a pulley was used to hoist them all up onto the deck.

The five weary travelers were arranged in a row at sword point as their bags were rummaged through. The pirates kept what they fancied and tossed the rest in a pile on deck. None of the companions had the energy to object.

"We need water," said Wendel in a dry, cracked voice.

"And sugar," said Dingleberry, who had not the strength to fly, but sat on Hagus's shoulder.

The door to the captain's quarters banged open, and in the threshold stood a large woman whose silhouette filled the doorway. She wore baggy brown trousers tied off in a knot about the waist, and big dragon scale boots that must have cost a dwarf king's hoard. A leather jerkin covered a purple shirt, and a pluming peacock feather stuck high out of her long, curved captain's hat. Aside from the nose ring and a large tongue ring, she wore no jewelry. Her only weapons appeared to be a curved sword sheathed on her left hip and a leather whip curled and hanging from her right.

A very curious-looking parrot sat on her shoulder, its wings green, purple, red, and yellow.

"What do we have here?" she asked in a voice deep and husky and sure.

"Thank the gods you found us when you did," said Valkimir. "We—"

"Liar," said the big woman, and she slapped him across the face.

In his exhausted state, Valkimir dropped to one knee.

"What about you, eh dwarf?"

"We be merchants who come in to some bad luck, ye see—"

"Liar!" said the captain, slapping him as well. She walked down the line, puzzling over Wendel. "And what, by the cursed gods, are you?"

"Just an unfortunate horse trainer, Captain..."

"Captain Grimace McArgh," she said, tipping her hat to them all and slapping the backside of another pirate as she walked by.

The entire crew seemed to be made up of women.

"Well then, you going to tell me the truth?" said Captain McArgh, looking Caressa up and down.

"It is as my friend..." she glanced at Valkimir, realizing that they hadn't made up fake names.

"Brawk!" squawked the parrot. "A Roddington never gives anyone the shaft, brawk!"

Captain McArgh squinted at Caressa, leaned in, frowned, and then suddenly her eyebrows shot straight up. "Say it ain't so," she said to the parrot.

"Aye," said one of the crewwomen. "That be the Princess of Magestra, I recognize her from a paintin' I seen."

"But ye...ye," Hagus stammered, "ye be a dwarf!"

"Aye," said the pirate, who was indeed a dwarf.

Captain McArgh winked at the princess and spread her arms out wide to the crew behind her. "This is the crew of the Iron Fist. Women one and all. We are the scorned, the beaten, the malcontents."

Valkimir looked closer, and indeed, all of the crew were women. And not even all humans or dwarves. There were elves, ogres, fairies, small trolls, and even a centaur.

"And who, might I ask, are you?" said the captain, raising a finger before anyone could speak. "If you lie this time, I will slit your throats and feed you to my dragon."

The companions glanced at each other, and it seemed that they all agreed the talking should be done by the princess.

"I am indeed Princess Caressa of Magestra, and I am on the utmost important quest. I demand—"

"There it is!" the captain sang, pointing a finger into the air and spinning to grin at her sisters. "She *demands*."

Valkimir glanced over at Caressa, meaning to shake his head at her, but she did not look his way.

"You do not demand anything here," said McArgh, pointing a finger at her. The captain drew closer, slowly. Her finger traced the rim of Caressa's left breast, then the right. Suddenly she took one in hand and gave a firm squeeze, putting her face so close to Caressa's that they could have kissed.

"I have never tasted a princess," she whispered, her large head leaving Caressa's petite face and frame in shadow.

"I have never tasted a pirate," said Caressa, jerking forward suddenly and biting the captain's bottom lip.

McArgh reeled back and stood, wiping at her lip. When she saw blood on the back of her hand, she grinned and looked to Caressa, licking the blood off her hand slowly.

"Now that is more like it!" she announced gleefully, and the crew cheered. "Take them below. Pull up the anchor! Set a course for eastern Magestra! We've a ransom to collect!"

CHAPTER 37

HAIL! THE CHAMPIONS OF THE DRAGON

URLAND FLEW HIGH over the hillside, trying to get an angle on what was to come and spare the others any ugly surprises. When his backpack crested the hill, and the land beyond was laid out before him in golden light and springtime splendor, Murland took in a breath. What shocked him and put a smile on his face was not only the wide expanse of green grass that seemed to go on for miles, but rather it was the sight of the Wide Wall that gave him pause. It rose silver and gray and colossal above the green earth, and spread off into the northern and southern horizons, curving with the earth and disappearing into haze.

Upon looking at the Wall, Murland felt an overwhelming sense of safety, security, and power. And renewed faith in the power of the combined races.

Then his eyes moved up above the Wall, beyond the green, green grass, into the shadow that dwelled like evil whispers in a mad man's heart. A dark forest lay beyond the Wide Wall. But it was not just the ominous dark that those tall, shadowy trees provided, it was an awareness. There was a feeling of being watched. It was a feeling so naked, so raw, and so terrifying, that Murland had to force his eyes away, lest he be pulled, mind, body, and spirit into that dark forest, to be lost forever.

He shifted his weight and pulled the left strap, telling Packy that he wished to turn back. The backpack complied, circling around and gliding down to where the others were waiting just below the top of the hill.

"How's it looking?" Sir Eldrick asked.

"It all looks clear. Just a long field of grass. Perhaps twenty miles to the Wide Wall."

"You saw it?" Gibrig asked, and Snorts seemed just as interested.

"Yeah, come on, you can too. Just over this hill."

Murland led them, Sir Eldrick on his horse, Gibrig on Snorts, and Brannon and Willow following up the rear on foot.

They crested the hill with many oohs and ahhs, and the companions stood side by side, grinning at their accomplishment.

"Look there," said Sir Eldrick, pointing straight out at the road.

"Looks like soldiers," said Brannon with some interest.

"Indeed," said Sir Eldrick, glancing at the sun. "And they will be making camp soon, very close to where we must put up for the night. Come, let us meet them and see what they know."

He took a few steps forward and stopped when no one followed.

"This is it," said Gibrig. "No more messin' 'round. Once we go beyond the Wide Wall…"

"There is no turning back," said Murland, glancing at the scared-looking dwarf and mirroring his mood.

"Come, come," said Sir Eldrick. "We are the bloody Champions of the Dragon. We are basically celebrities now. Let's use it to our advantage. Willow, you hungry?"

"When have you ever known me to not be hungry?"

"Exactly. Well believe me, heroes are fed, and fed well. Come on."

They followed Sir Eldrick up and over the hill and marched down to meet the soldiers. Murland didn't bother flying above for them, for the view was all encompassing here on the highland ridge leading down like a bowl to the field of green grass and the Wall beyond.

"Ho!" said Sir Eldrick sometime later, after the sun had set and the stars had taken their place in the clear spring sky.

The soldiers had already made camp off the road in a clearing of cut grass that looked to be a common spot for the troops. There were even a few small buildings scattered about.

"Ho, declare yourself!" came the reply.

"We are the Champions of the Dragon!" said Sir Eldrick happily. He dismounted, handing the reins off to Murland. He strode forward with a bowlegged swagger and met the captain with a firm handshake.

"The Champions…" said the captain, shaking Eldrick's hand dreamily and looking them all over with an unbelieving stare. "Did you hear that, boys? We are in the presence of the Champions of the Dragon." He looked back at Sir Eldrick and rattled his mind for a name. "You're…why, you're the one they call Slur…Sir Eldrick! Yes, that is it. And this must be Murland, and Brannon the prince of elves, and Willow, and Gibrig. Yes, yes, we've heard of you all. Who hasn't? Marching west to save us all from Drak'Noir!"

"Oorah!" the soldiers cheered, raising their swords into the air.

"Thank you, thank you for your warm welcome," said Sir Eldrick. "The road has been good to us, but everyone knows that food cooked by someone else is sweeter."

"Of course, of course," said the captain. "Let me introduce myself. I am Captain Markus Verus of Magestra."

He took Sir Eldrick by the shoulder and led him farther into camp. "We have just come from the Wall after six months on duty. We're returning home for a month and then back again."

"How are things on the other side?"

"Nothing too crazy. A rabid troll stormed the gates a few weeks back. But he became target practice for the archers." Markus snorted a bit when he laughed, reminding Sir Eldrick of Snorts. Looking closer, he realized that the man did have a mild resemblance to a pig. He was pudgy, for one, and not the type of man who rose to captain during war times, Sir Eldrick could tell. Things had been quiet up on the Wall and beyond for decades. Now the armies were reduced to soft, lazy boys who had no other options but to go into the military to make something of themselves. It was a blessing that they hadn't been attacked recently and there hadn't been strife between the kingdoms of eastern Fallacetine in a century, but it was also a curse.

"Peaceful men become soft men," Sir Eldrick heard himself saying. "Peaceful nations become easy targets," he said, finishing the adage.

"What's that?" said Markus.

"Oh, nothing. Where's the mess hall?" Sir Eldrick said with gusto.

The champions were received like heroes, and Sir Eldrick's promise of a heroic meal was no lie. The soldiers knew how to eat, and they had come prepared. The road back to Magestra was nearly three weeks' march for a battalion of one hundred, as these men were, and such an army required enough goods to get them home. Therefore, two wagons full of grains, vegetables, smoked and salted meat and fish, barley, cereals, rice, water, mead, and liquor had been awarded them on their journey.

A long table was erected and the companions sat, eagerly eating all that was put before them and sharing their stories of their adventures thus far. They embellished a bit, one and all, but the soldiers seemed not to notice, cheering their tales as they were spun.

Murland had been one of the best wizards of Abra Tower in his tale, and had been singled out among the other apprentices early on. His being named by Kazimir had been no surprise.

"Show us some magic, then," the soldiers had cheered, and Murland looked around sheepishly, glancing at his not yet finished wand.

"Please," said Sir Eldrick, laughing merrily and winking at Murland. "He is not a traveling magician. What fool asks a wizard to cast a spell? One who will likely end up with his pecker where his nose should be, that's who!"

The soldiers erupted with laughter, and Murland gave Sir Eldrick a thankful nod.

Brannon told them all that of course the prince of elves would be chosen as a Dragon Champion. He was, after all, the heir to the throne of Halala, and was well known for his proficiency in floral magic.

Gibrig explained that the king had singlehandedly chosen him from a list of hundreds. But when asked why by the soldiers, he could only blush. "Did I mention I got that humanism?" he had said sheepishly.

"Young Gib here has outsmarted a pair of vicious cyclopes, braved the Blight, survived bandits, prevailed over darklings, and has done so riding a hog and carrying only a shovel," said Sir Eldrick. "Here is to Kazimir's good wisdom!"

"Here, here!" the soldiers cheered.

Willow had explained that she had once defeated a king crocodile and had won a lifetime supply of food, and was the three-time winner of the mud pie eating contest.

When the soldiers glanced at each other questioningly, Sir Eldrick stood and raised a glass of cider to everyone else's mead. "To the Champions of the Dragon, my companions, my friends, my family."

Brannon glanced uneasily at him, but still, he drank.

"But what of *your* accolades?" said one of the soldiers, though Markus raised a calming hand.

"Come now, we all know of Sir Eldrick's deeds."

"Story, story, story," someone began to chant, and the others were all too eager to take it up as well.

"Alright, alright," said Sir Eldrick, waving them down and quite enjoying himself. "What shall it be? My battle with the Troll of Calamity when it marched on Vhalovia? The time I slayed three hundred in a single battle? Or the time I laid low the Witch of Agnar?"

"Tell us about fargin the queen!" someone shouted, and Markus turned a dangerous eye on the crowd of soldiers.

"I am sorry, Sir Eldrick—"

Sir Eldrick nodded understanding and then stood. "Let the man who spoke walk forth and stand before me. If indeed he is a man!"

Murland glanced at Brannon, wondering if perhaps they should do something. The elf only shrugged.

No one in the crowd stirred, and Sir Eldrick climbed up onto the table and glowered at the gathered soldiers, most holding tin plates in their hands. Though none ate.

"Let he who spoke come before me now and ask the question again!" Sir Eldrick demanded.

Finally, someone stirred, and the crowd parted like water before a stone.

Sir Eldrick gazed at the young man as he sulkily strode forth, his brothers parting from him like he had the plague as he went. Soon he stood before Sir Eldrick. He was a pale, freckled young man with skin too smooth to have seen battle, and a mouth too ready to laugh and make jokes, for he had never seen death by his own hand.

Sir Eldrick leapt down from the table with the agility of a much younger man. "What is your name, soldier?" He asked with all the authority of a commander of the eastern legion.

"Sir! Simon Shucker, sir!"

"Shucker, a corn man, eh?"

Simon nodded. "Sir, yes sir!"

"Please, repeat your question, for decades of battle have dampened my ears," he said, cocking his head.

"Sir. I...I asked, what was it like to bed...the queen. Sir!"

"Ah!" said Sir Eldrick, thrusting a finger into the sky so abruptly that poor Simon Shucker jerked back, as if expecting a blow, or worse.

"Well, good Simon, I am glad to not know, for good King Henry could tell you that. But I can tell you that I have plucked her handmaiden's flower, and oh how the Vhalovian coast grows their fruit."

Murland grinned, marveling at the way the bearded knight turned the crowd. Poor Simon Shucker smiled as well.

"They say a noble knight does not kiss and tell, but I have never presumed to be noble, my friends," Sir Eldrick went on, resting a hand on Simon's shoulder. "What shall be said of the handmaiden of the queen of Vhalovia? Hmm, well, for one, her name was Autumn, but her breasts were like a twin summer sunrise, smooth as fire and curved like the moon. She had hips that you wanted to fall asleep on, and an ass that you wanted to jiggle. I swear that I once rested a full glass of brandy on it!"

"Oorah!" the soldiers cheered, raising, clanging, and spilling drinks, and surely scaring away any unfavorables who might have been just then lurking in the tall grass.

"And her golden forest, trimmed like a castle ground and just as sweet smelling as the gardens. I lost myself in those velvety folds, and have never been the same since. But I tell you, all of that was nothing compared to those eyes. Green eyes shimmering like polished emerald, staring at you, taking you in. You lose yourself to those eyes. They are frightened but hungry, unsure yet full of themselves. They are eyes that know everything about you. They see through you. They are home, they are peace. In those eyes you know who you are, gentlemen, and you are humbled…"

Silence swept through camp, and the wind too seemed to be hushed by the weight and truth of his words.

Murland found himself spellbound, for he had felt the way that Sir Eldrick explained, though he had of course never experienced half of what was mentioned. He had experienced that gaze though, and the smile that came with it.

Murland had known that feeling with Caressa, though he did not know if she felt the same.

"I cannot speak for what only the king knows, for I have never bedded the queen. My transgression was with the head maiden, and that is all I wish to say about that. For that is all you need to know."

"Sir Eldrick, I…" Simon began.

"Understood, lad. Understood." Sir Eldrick patted Simon so hard on the back that he nearly stumbled as he staggered back to his pals.

The night was filled with merriment and cheer, and soon Murland and the others forgot about the long road ahead of them beyond the Wide Wall. They forgot about the Forest of the Dead, the Swamp of Doom, the Horrible Hills, the Long Sand. They forgot about the Northern and Southern Barrens, and the Petrified Plains.

For tonight was a night of celebration.

CHAPTER 38

ZUUL'S CONFESSION

KAZIMIR SPOKE THE words that Zuul had told him would activate the pipe. He said it exactly, making sure to use all the rolling syllables in the right place. As the last *r* rolled off his tongue, the emerald water pipe blazed with green light. Kazimir lit his wand and toked deeply of his wizard leaf.

Zuul watched with eager eyes, lips curled around the witch's areola.

Kazimir blew out multicolored smoke, and his eyes went wide, and then droopy. He saw spells laid out before him in a spiraling dance, and voices played at the back of his mind. New understandings of old ideas blossomed in his brain, and he wished just then that he had a quill and paper, and the use of his extremities.

"I am compelled by my servitude to tell you, Master Kazimir," said Zuul, glowering at him from beside the hag's teat. "I had a plan B."

"Hmm," Kazimir grunted as he sunk slowly into his chair.

"I thought that you might try to stop me," said Zuul with a mischievous grin. "So I awoke the harpies."

"What are you saying?"

"They have been sent after the champions. Soon they will reach them…"

"To arms!"

The call went out through camp and was taken up by others. Murland snapped awake and looked around, confused by the rushing soldiers.

"What's happening?" he asked Sir Eldrick, who was already on his feet, scouring the dark sky.

"Quiet!" said the knight. "Listen."

Willow, Brannon, and Gibrig awoke as well. They listened beyond the barked orders and clang of swords and shields being taken up all around them.

A muffled sound like a thousand fluttering crow's wings came to them then, followed by the screams of men and the otherworldly cries of some strange bird.

"Harpies," said Sir Eldrick. He turned to the group. "To arms!"

Murland gathered his new wand and his spell book and strapped his backpack over his shoulders. Overhead, a multitude of wings rustled, and that terrible cry echoed mournfully. The harpies descended on the camp in droves, landing among the tents and groups of soldiers and tearing into them with wicked, talon-clawed hands.

The beasts stood well over seven feet tall, with a woman's head and body, but the legs of a bird, and pluming multicolored wings. The red eyes of the harpies came alight with bloodlust as they ripped and tore at the soldiers.

The men of Magestra hacked and slashed, but the harpies proved elusive indeed, taking to the sky when the humans got too close and bringing with them the unfortunate ones who had gotten too near. Bodies began to fall from the sky, landing with a broken thud on top of their comrades and crashing into tents or bonfires.

A harpy landed before Murland and reached for him with wicked, curved claws. Her eyes were blood-red and aglow, glaring at him hatefully. A sword came down, and Sir Eldrick was there, leaping in front of Murland. Sir Eldrick's glowing fairy sword cut through the harpy's arms with ease, and as it turned to fly away, he severed a wing and let Willow finish the beast off with her massive club.

"Fight, you fools!" Sir Eldrick cried as he leapt into the fray with a war cry.

Murland looked to his newly carved wand and the terrible battle all around him. He heard Gibrig praying to a dwarven god, and Brannon murmuring his elven spell words. A harpy landed in front of Gibrig, and the dwarf cried out, swinging his spade wildly.

"Leave us alone!" the dwarf pleaded.

Murland took aim, summoned his magical energy at his core, and spoke the word as he released the power through his arm and into the wand.

"Ignis!" he bellowed.

A long, snaking streak of fire leapt out of his wand and hit the harpy in the chest, engulfing her and setting her feathered wings ablaze. Another came at them, and Willow sent the beast flying with a great swipe of her club.

Murland stared, dumbfounded at his smoking wand.

A harpy landed on Willow's back and Gibrig leapt, spade cocked back, screaming, "Leave my friend alone!" He came down hard on the back of the harpy's head. It fell to the grass in a pile of ruffled feathers.

Murland was electrified. The magic flowed through him, lighting his core like a newborn sun and buzzing through his veins.

"Ignis!" he said, shooting fireballs at the surrounding harpies, who seemed to be quickly overtaking the soldiers.

"To the Wall!" Captain Markus cried out. "Retreat, retreat!"

Sir Eldrick came charging through the harpies, magical sword severing limbs and heads and wings. "You cannot!" he said to the captain. "They will pick us off one by one. We must stand and fight together."

Captain Markus looked unsure. A soldier fell from the sky just then and landed in a heap beside him. The dead eyes of Simon Shucker stared back at him.

"Captain!" said Sir Eldrick, shaking the man.

"You…you're in charge," said the pudgy man and, dropping his sword, he ran off toward the horses.

"Captain!" Sir Eldrick called after him, but the scared man was quickly taken into the dark of night by one of the winged beasts.

His blood bathed the ground below.

Sir Eldrick reached for his secret flask, but found that it was missing. The soldiers all looked to him, having heard the declaration of their fleeing captain.

"What do we do?" Brannon cried just before he cut down another harpy.

Gibrig was crying as he hacked into the body of one of the dead harpies.

Murland looked to the knight as well and lost his concentration. His next spell had no effect.

Sir Eldrick straightened with grim determination. "Everyone to me!"

The soldiers complied and began to form around the champions.

"Shield bearers to the outside of the circle. Spears behind, swords at the back. Archers in the middle!" Sir Eldrick bellowed, and at that moment, to Murland, the knight seemed the most powerful man in the world.

Arrows twanged, swords hacked, spears lunged, and the shield wall held.

"Give 'em hell, boys!" Sir Eldrick cried, luminescent sword held high. "Show these rotten harpies the wrath of the soldiers of Magestra!"

"Oorah!" the soldiers cried, and with a stomp of their feet, they expanded the circle.

Sir Eldrick turned, his eyes alight with danger and excitement and full of life. He was about to say something to Murland, but suddenly a harpy swooped down, took the knight by the shoulders with digging talons, and whisked him up into the air.

"No!" Murland cried, and before he knew what he was doing, he was running and leaping into the air. The backpack spread its wings and chased after Sir Eldrick.

The knight was taken up high above the camp, but he freed one arm, and with an overhead swipe, he severed the harpy's legs at the ankles and fell through the air with the talons still clutching his shoulders.

"Intercept him!" Murland cried, and Packy arched into a dive.

Sir Eldrick fell through the air facing the sky, his arm reaching for Murland's as the backpack closed in. The ground came rushing up to crush him, and they clasped hands in the last moments before Packy was forced to pull up.

Murland grunted as his right arm screamed with pain. Sir Eldrick was heavy, but his grip was like iron, and Murland couldn't have let him go if he wanted to. The backpack compensated for the new weight, flapping its wings vigorously.

"Put us down!" Murland cried, sure that his arm would break. "Bring us to the center of the circle!"

Harpies attacked them from all sides, but the backpack outmaneuvered them, even with its great burden. Sir Eldrick sang a battle song at the top of his lungs, laughing like a madman and mortally wounding any harpy who got too close to the enchanted blade.

Finally, Murland's feet touched down and he fell on top of Sir Eldrick.

Willow, Brannon, and Gibrig rushed to their aid as the soldiers of Magestra circled all around them. The archers did as they were commanded, and a twanging chorus of arrows ripped through the night. Harpies dropped all around them, and the swordsmen were there to cut them down.

Suddenly the sound of rustling wings grew farther away, and everyone looked to the sky, waiting.

"Steady, men," said Sir Eldrick, ignoring the claws still digging into his shoulder plates.

The sound of the retreating harpies was met by another, louder sound, that of a hundred wings.

"Murland," said Brannon, helping him up. "Do you have a light spell for my seeds?"

"I…uh," said Murland, rifling through the spell book. He knew what Brannon had in mind, but the simple spell to light the end of his wand wouldn't do.

The harpies attacked again, this time with greater force and greater numbers. Men were plucked into the air one after another, and all the while Sir Eldrick commanded the soldiers to stand strong, and to strike true.

Murland crouched down between the companions, who fought to keep the diving harpies back with club and spade and glowing crystalline sword.

"Hurry!" said Brannon, and Murland finally found the spell that he had seen earlier.

He recited it in his mind a few times, nervous that he would get it wrong. But there was no time. The harpies numbered in the hundreds now as they circled the ring of soldiers, their wings creating a wind so great that Brannon's long hair blew about wildly. The inexperienced soldiers were quickly being slaughtered, and soon the circle would fail.

Murland raised his newly crafted wand, took a deep breath, gathered his magic at his core, and bellowed, "Lux solis pater vitam vocat te!"

Nothing happened.

"Murland..." said Brannon pensively.

Murland wiped his sweaty brow, tried with effort to ignore the cries of the dying men, and reread the spell words as he raised his wand again. "Lux solis pater vitam vocat te!"

Glorious light suddenly erupted from the end of his wand, and Brannon spread the seeds on the ground before dumping a bucket of water on them. Brannon bellowed his elven words, and the vines exploded to life at the center of the group. With the help of Murland's light, the vines grew long and twisted in the blink of an eye.

"To me!" Brannon commanded all who might hear, and the companions and soldiers alike smartly complied.

Brannon sent his vines shooting out in all directions, snagging harpies from the air and bearing them down to the ground, where they were laid upon by the bloody swords of the soldiers.

Murland fell to the ground, head swooning. His wand winked out, and dark smoke curled up from the tip. Darkness came over him—soft, pure, beautiful darkness.

CHAPTER 39

THE HEADMASTER OF KAZAM COLLEGE

H<small>IGH</small> W<small>IZARD</small> A<small>LDOUS</small> Hinckley watched from Kazam's highest tower as the Champions of the Dragon were brought into the depths of the Wide Wall. He pulled away from the enchanted telescope and gave a sigh, stroking his long gray beard. Hunched as always, he ambled over to his desk and sipped the last of his tea before settling into his old comfortable chair. He considered more tea, but on second thought, he pulled out the top drawer of the hickory desk and retrieved the twenty-year-old bottle of dwarven rum.

The moment called for it, after all.

He uncorked the spirit with a spell word and barely noticed the bottle pouring itself into a crystal glass.

He smelled the fine dwarven wares, swirled the glass and eyed the amber liquid, listened to it for three heartbeats, and shot it back.

Oakey, hints of leather and quartz, a strong first impression, but a smooth finish and a dry tail. Pleasantly hot in the belly. It was a warm and wet summer when the sugarcane was grown... He noted all of this absently, eyeing the firelight crookedly and murmuring to himself despondently.

"Pipe," he said, and his old trusty ivory pipe floated to his lips. He packed it with fine Vhalovian tobacco and sprinkled a bit of fairy dust on top before lighting it with a flame from the end of his thumb.

He sucked in the smooth smoke softly, contemplatively, and his eyes wandered to the note on his desk as he puffed. Opened a week ago, read thrice, and still curled at the edges, the note on his desk stared back blankly.

And though he received two dozen or more letters a week, this one vexed him more than any before it. Indeed, it had him giddy and horrified at the same time.

He picked it up and called to his spectacles, which floated to the crook of his nose and rested.

He cleared his throat, though he did not read aloud.

High Wizard Hinckley,

It is with delight and dread that I write to you this fine spring evening. I am looking out over the gardens of Abra Tower, listening to the lovebirds sing their songs of adoration, yet my heart does not leap, for it is weighed down by the burden of apprehension.

I have written you previously of one Murland Kadabra, son of Lord Albert Kadabra. To many he is of no consequence. Indeed, to many he might seem a bumbling fool, the worst wizard to grace Abra Tower's many halls. But I see more in the unassuming lad.

If you recall, you taught the divination class one hundred and some-odd years ago at Abra Tower. I was just a first-year then, but you took an interest in me. You said then that I had, "the gift of sight." I never amounted to much in that regard, and I must admit, I believe it was because the gift scared me, for I saw my own death those many years ago. But that is of no consequence in this conversation.

Since becoming headmaster two decades ago, I have begun to dabble in the art of divination once more, and I now relay a prophecy to you, my most revered of teachers.

I know that this will come as a shock, as all good prophecies shall, but I believe wholeheartedly the visions I have seen. During a thirty-day fast, throughout which I only ingested wizard leaf and fairy dust and water, and slept on a bed of nails, I heard the voices of the gods. I saw the sacred geometry. And this is what I have learned.

I believe that this Murland Kadabra, this fool in wizard's robes, is destined to defeat the Dark Lord Zuul after the second coming.

Now, I must warn you. As all good prophecies do, this one has two possible meanings.

One—Murland will defeat Zuul outright, using the wand and spell book of Kazam, as I have given them to him.

Or...

Two—Murland's actions will cause Drak'Noir to descend upon the land, killing Zuul, and indeed everyone in Fallacetine. Thus bringing about the defeat of Zuul.

These things are tricky...

I do not assume to possess the wisdom to know which one is true, and I implore you to choose for me. Meet with the young wizard, and judge for yourself. Is he the one spoken of in the Prophecy of Kazam? I do not know. For your reference, and though I assume that you know it by heart, I have added the Most High Wizard's last words.

"9 Shalls"—the Prophecy of Allan Kazam—the second age of men—A.M. 1984.

For though I shall be victorious against Zuul, I shall surely fall.
There shall be a thousand years of peace.
But then the Dark Lord shall rise again.
One shall rise to challenge him, one who has not been seen before.

He shall be born from the far east.
His eyes shall shine with innocence and kindness.
He shall not know his true power.
And none shall believe in him. None but one.

I know that there have been false saviors before, but a thousand years have passed, and power emanates from the Twisted Tower once more. We have arrived in the dreaded future. The day of reckoning draws near.

Look into young Murland's eyes, and if you do not see what I see, strip him of the wand and tome, and send him to his death. For you know what awaits him on Bad Mountain.

But if you see as I have seen, if you believe as I believe, then nurture the young man as I have tried to. Surely Kazimir the Most High (and most selfish) cares not about such things, and has taught him nothing. But I believe that young Murland needs only a small amount of guidance, and he will become a great wizard. Indeed, he will be a wizard of legend.

I beseech you, my master, my greatest of teachers and most revered of wizards. Give him a chance.

Yours in Magic,
Headmaster Zola Zorromon the Off-White
Abra Tower

High Wizard Aldous read the note again, and then again. Finally, he put it down and poured himself another drink. Tossing it back, he considered Zorromon's words. He lit his pipe and blew out multicolored smoke, pondering the meaning in the swirling patterns.

At length, he rang a bell. His chamber doors opened, and his apprentice walked in and bowed.

"You rang, Headmaster?"

"Yes, Jonathan. I wish for you to summon one Murland Kadabra to my quarters. He and the other Champions of the Dragon have just arrived."

"Yes, Headmaster."

Aldous turned and peered out the window, looking west toward Bad Mountain.

CHAPTER 40

✗

THE WIDE WALL

MURLAND AWOKE TO someone lightly slapping his cheek.
"You'll want to see this," said Sir Eldrick, smiling down at him.

With the knight's help, Murland sat up. He was in the back of a wagon with a half-dozen injured soldiers. Behind them, more followed, some limping, others helping their brothers along. Brannon, Willow, and Gibrig followed as well, and like Sir Eldrick, they too sported numerous bandages.

"Behold, the Wide Wall," said Sir Eldrick stoically.

Murland turned and sucked in a surprised breath, for the Wide Wall loomed overhead, silver and gray and shimmering with the colors of magic. The enchanted Wall hummed with steady power, and Murland felt it in every quivering hair on his body.

"We did it," he said in a whisper of disbelief. "We did it!" he shouted and leapt off the wagon, landing on legs that were suddenly energized and strong.

The wagon train stopped before a pair of twenty-foot doors of wrought iron set on giant hinges.

Sir Eldrick stepped forth and raised his fairy blade, Cryst. "Open the gates. For it is I, Sir Eldrick van Albright of Vhalovia, Champion of the Dragon."

The companions shared eager glances as the door creaked, rumbled, and slowly began to open.

They were led through the threshold, beneath the watchful eyes of the soldiers peering out through two dozen murder holes set in the stone on either side of the passage. They came to another door, and yet another after that, and finally into a large stone antechamber with three tunnels leading deeper into the keep, and a lift situated against the northern wall.

A well-decorated man in shining metal armor and a blue cloak stopped before them and glanced at Sir Eldrick and the companions. One Captain Whillhelm, next in line after the late Captain Markus, stepped forth. "Lord General, we were attacked by a flock of harpies a day's march east of the Wall."

"Harpies?"

"Yes, my lord."

"Where is Captain Markus?"

Whillhelm glanced around. "Taken in battle by the harpies. He died singing the Magestrian anthem. I have assumed command."

"And the Champions of the Dragon?" he said, glancing over the captain's shoulder.

Sir Eldrick strode forth and extended his right hand. "Sir Eldrick van Albright, at your service," he said.

"Carthage, Lord General of the Guardians of the Wide Wall. It would seem, good Sir Eldrick, that it is I who is at your service." He turned to his soldiers and raised an arm. "All hail the Champions of the Dragon!"

"Hail!" cheered the soldiers, fists pumping into the air.

Sir Eldrick gave an appreciative bow, and Murland and the others copied him.

Brannon strode forth and shouldered past Sir Eldrick. "I am Brannon Woodheart, Prince of Halala, and I require a long, hot bath."

The guardians of the Wall laughed, and the general nodded.

"Yes, of course. Though I assume you will be setting out shortly?" he said, glancing at Sir Eldrick.

"A few days' reprieve can't hurt. Wild land it is out there beyond the Wall. We will not be staying here long enough to get soft, though, I promise you that."

"Excellent. Please, my friends, follow me."

The champions were brought to the lift, which groaned and creaked when Willow added her great weight to its burden. Nevertheless, it crawled upward when the wheelmen began to turn the large gears. The lift rose slowly for one hundred floors before suddenly emerging into the morning sunlight.

"Come, you will want to see this," said the general as he walked toward the battlements along the western wall.

The companions followed, intrigued. The wind was brisk up so high, and a slight chill rode upon it. Murland found himself feeling bad for anyone who had to be stationed up here in the dead of winter, especially those farther north at the other outposts.

"This, my champions, is a sight that few people ever get to see," said the general, spreading his arms over the wide world west of the Wall.

Murland gazed west and was amazed at how far he could see. The Forest of the Dead stretched out for a hundred miles before him, and it did not look damned at all, but lush and green and beautiful.

"Well, that don't look so bad," said Gibrig, glancing at Murland.

"No, it doesn't, does it?"

"Don't let it fool you," said the general. "Plenty of guardians have thought the same thing upon looking west from the Wall, and many of them were swallowed up by the horrors lurking in those forests. Sir Eldrick has been beyond the Wall. Surely he has told you what manner of nightmares await you there."

"Yes, of course I have," said Sir Eldrick, looking slightly annoyed.

"Right then, I'll have my squire show you to your lodgings. Stay as long as you need to before you set out on your heroic quest. I will see you before then, I imagine."

Just then, a young man in apprentice robes strode over to them and offered a small bow. "Greetings, Champions of the Dragon. I am Jonathan Tibbets." He looked to Murland. "I have been sent to guide you to Headmaster Hinckley's quarters. He is very eager to meet with you."

Murland glanced at the others, and Sir Eldrick offered him a nod.

"I'll be right back...I think," said Murland, and he followed the older apprentice north along the Wall.

Jonathan said not a word, but brought Murland briskly to the tall white tower set at the center of the Wall. Murland stared up at Kazam College, awed not only by its size, for it was seven stories high, but also by the raw power humming within those stone walls. The base of the tower was wide, and the ascending levels were stacked one upon the other, each one smaller than the one beneath it.

Murland had seen the enchanted tower once before, when it had set down in Magestra five years ago. It was often moored to the Wide Wall, but with the tower's ability to fly, the high wizards could bring it anywhere in Fallacetine, and perhaps beyond.

They walked through the large double doors, which opened on their own accord and closed behind them just the same. The drawing that Murland had seen of the inside of the tower did nothing to relay its true beauty. The inside of the tower was wide open all the way to the glowing capstone. There were six balconies overhead, one for each level, and branching off from them were dozens upon dozens of walkways spanning the wide expanse. Staircases connecting every level stretched across the center as well.

Those wizards young and old on the bottom floor all stopped when the doors boomed shut, and Murland tried to stand tall beneath their inquisitive gazes. He felt naked, as though the wizards could all see the truth of him just by looking. They leaned in to whisper to one another. Their harsh whispers surely expressing disgust at Kazimir's choice.

"This way," said Jonathan, and he led Murland to a staircase.

They climbed the many zigzagging stairways up to the top-floor balcony, and all the while the wizards stared.

"This is the room. Please, he is waiting for you," said Jonathan, stopping before a door and opening it.

"Thanks," said Murland, and he walked through the threshold, rather unsurely.

The room was dark, illuminated by only a handful of candles and the low burning fire in the hearth directly opposite from him. A map of Fallacetine was stretched out over the fireplace, and looking it over, Murland realized just how far from home he really was. To the left of Murland was a window facing west. A gray-haired man in burgundy robes, presumably Headmaster Hinckley, sat staring out of it. The stone walls held dozens of framed portraits, with the names of one headmaster or another embossed in gold at the bottom. A wall of bookshelves dominated the right side of the room, and lower on those shelves were a variety of jars with many strange things floating inside. One held what was obviously a brain, and another a heart. In some jars, eyes floated in murky liquid, and in another a disembodied hand sleepily grasped at nothing, the fingers moving like the tentacles of an octopus. The room smelled of wizard leaf and incense, the smoke of which hung in the air stagnantly.

"Well then, come in," said Hinckley as he stared out the window.

Murland moved on weak legs to stand before the large wooden desk, which had clawed feet like an eagle. He thought of Packy then, and wondered if the desk could walk.

Headmaster Hinckley finally turned around, and Murland shrunk under his steely gaze.

The wizard looked to be over a hundred years old, with large, droopy eyes cradled by puffy bags. He had a long, unbraided beard, thin and straight like his frame, and a shock of curly gray hair spilling out from beneath his tall wizard hat.

"Murland Kadabra. I have heard much about you," he said, extending a hand from across the table.

Murland shook the old man's weathered hand, and though the skin was paper thin and the fingers boney, the grip was strong.

"Hello, Headmaster."

"Please, have a seat."

Murland sat in the tall, straight-backed chair, feeling very much like he had as a child, waiting to be interviewed by Headmaster Zorromon. His hands were sweaty, and he found himself wondering if Hinckley had noticed.

The headmaster said nothing for many uncomfortable moments. He regarded Murland intensely, his brown eyes looking him over slowly. Murland wondered what it was that the headmaster saw. His aura? His magical energy? Nothing?

"I am gladdened to see that you have all made it to the Wall," said Hinckley.

"Thank you."

"Headmaster Zorromon has many good things to say about you."

"He does?"

Hinckley nodded. "Does that surprise you?"

"I, well…" Murland let out a sigh. "Truth is, I'm not the best wizard apprentice."

"Humble," Hinckley noted. "That is a good trait in a wizard."

"I suppose that I got good grades though. I memorized all the basic spells, did well in potions, but I could never get my wizard leaf to grow to maturity."

"I saw magic in the sky during the harpy fight. Was that you?"

"Yes, I have recently managed to grow some leaf, with the elf prince Brannon's help. And I have made my own wand, though I think I broke it."

"Zorromon said that he bestowed upon you the wand that was broken. The wand of Kazam."

Murland nodded.

"May I see it?"

"Of course," said Murland. He fished it out of his pocket, careful to not put any undue stress on the fracture.

The headmaster received the relic as one might a newborn baby. He held it in two hands, staring at it with an unreadable gaze. He turned it in his hands, eyes widening slightly and taking on a dreamlike glaze.

Hinckley jerked his head as though Murland had said something. To Murland's surprise, the high wizard handed it back to him.

"You intend to try and mend it, I presume."

"Yes, but, well, I was wondering. Haven't the elders already tried to mend the wand?"

Hinckley took a pipe out of his drawer. He took his time to pack it with wizard leaf, as though considering his words carefully, or perhaps guardingly. "It is thought that there is only one who might be able to mend it."

"He who is destined to defeat Zuul? Zorromon said something about that."

"And what do you think about that? If you are going to attempt to mend the wand, then you must think yourself worthy."

Murland gulped. "Well, I have been trying to focus on one impossible quest at a time."

"Hah!" Hinckley suddenly laughed, for he had been puffing on his pipe, and now multicolored smoke issued from his nose and mouth as he began to hack.

Murland gave a nervous laugh and wondered if he should do something. Hinckley was getting red in the face.

The high wizard recovered and took a drink from a mug on the desk. "Please, continue," he said in a hoarse voice.

"I don't know about Zuul," said Murland, choosing his words carefully. "All I know is that I must help to defeat Drak'Noir. For if she is not defeated, Zuul will no longer matter."

"Indeed," said Hinckley. "That is a good way to look at it."

"Headmaster…What will happen if I cannot mend the wand. What if I am not meant to have it? What if…"

"Go on."

"What if Kazimir made a mistake," said Murland, as though he were uttering sacrilege.

Hinckley took another puff and blew it out slowly. "One thing I know about the ever elusive Kazimir is that he rarely makes mistakes."

Murland considered that.

"I will tell you this. A wizard's ability to perform magic depends greatly on his confidence. You may want to work on yours. Try to believe in yourself."

"Yes, Headmaster."

"You are dismissed," said Hinckley suddenly, and though he had more he would like to ask, Murland knew better than to disobey a high wizard.

"Thank you for seeing me, Headmaster."

"We shall speak again if you like. I imagine that you will be here for a few days at least. And I should like to see that backpack of yours in action."

CHAPTER 41

LOOKING WESTWARD AND BEYOND

MURLAND REJOINED THE other champions in their quarters, which proved to be a barracks bunkhouse situated beneath the battlements that ran north to south for hundreds of miles. There was a common room with a fire and spit, along with a window looking west, and more than enough cots to keep even Willow comfortable.

"There he is," said Sir Eldrick cheerfully.

He sat with Brannon and Willow at a table in the center of the room, enjoying a meal of stew and bread. Gibrig, however, seemed not to have an appetite, and lay facing the wall on one of the cots.

Murland joined them and nodded over toward Gibrig. "He still being quiet?" he asked in a whisper.

"Aye," said Sir Eldrick between bites of bread. "The violence of last night seems to have really gotten to him. But no matter. He will be fine."

"Eat up," said Willow happily as she ladled a heaping helping of stew into a bowl and slid it to Murland.

"Thanks."

"So, what did the headmaster want?" Brannon asked.

"He wanted to see Kazam's wand. He said that he was glad to see that we had all made it to the Wall."

"Did he say anything else?"

Murland thought of the Prophecy of Zuul, but decided against telling them. He still wasn't sure what it all meant.

"Nothing important."

Sir Eldrick and Brannon shared a glance, and Murland watched them, wondering what it was that they were always silently communicating.

"How long you thinking we should rest up?" Willow asked through a mouthful of stew. "A few weeks?"

"Hah, you wish," said Sir Eldrick with a laugh. "No, just a few days. It is better to get right back into it. Too much comfort will make setting out again that much harder."

Willow scoffed at that and resumed stuffing her face with stew and bread.

"Well," said Murland. "I'm going to use the down time to start on a new wand."

"That is a good idea," said Sir Eldrick.

Gibrig rolled over, and he looked to have been crying.

"You alright, Gib?" Sir Eldrick asked.

"I…it's just. How do ye stop from seein' the faces o' the poor harpies? I been tryin' to think o' somethin' else, but I keep seein' the ones I killed."

Sir Eldrick gave a slow sigh. "I am sorry. But that is a burden that all warriors must carry with them all of their days. Take heart in knowing that what you did was right. Sometimes there is no other way but that of the sword."

Gibrig nodded understanding, though the knight's words did nothing to alter his bleak mood, which seemed to have leeched all joy out of the room.

"Are we going to make it?" Gibrig asked suddenly, and all eyes turned to Sir Eldrick.

"I believe that we will," said the knight.

"We'll show that dragon who's boss," said Willow. "You just wait and see."

Murland took heart in Willow's confidence and looked to Brannon. But the elf just gave a halfhearted smile and, glancing at Sir Eldrick sheepishly, returned to listlessly stirring his stew around with his wooden spoon.

Sir Eldrick pushed his bowl away and moved to the window. To Murland, the knight seemed tired and weighed down by the burden of the quest.

"I'm very proud of all of you," said Sir Eldrick as he stared west out the window. "I just wanted you to know that. No matter what happens on Bad Mountain, I am proud of you all."

Headmaster Zorromon,

You will be heartened to know that young Murland and the other champions have made it to the Wide Wall. As requested, I have met with the lad, and I have considered your words. Murland has finally managed to grow wizard leaf, and he has also constructed a functioning wand, which he used with success against a flock of harpies.

I have given much thought to your theory that Murland is the one mentioned in the Prophecy of Kazam, but I must admit, I am very much undecided in this matter. Of course, the fact that I do not believe in him only reiterates the details of the prophecy. His eyes are indeed kind, he comes from the far east, and he does not believe in himself. Of course, this could be said about a great many apprentices.

As you said, these things are tricky.

I have not stripped him of the wand or the tome; I have chosen to let fate decide. If indeed he is the one named in the prophecy, then he shall be successful in mending the wand that was broken. I will watch this unfold closely, and if he fails, then I will retrieve Kazam's relics. However, if he is successful, he cannot be allowed to continue to Bad Mountain. Another fool must be found to feed Drak'Noir and her whelps.

For now, we shall wait and see how things unfold.

Yours in Magic,
Headmaster Aldous Hinckley
Kazam College

To be continued in Book 2
Beyond the Wide Wall...

LETTER TO THE READER

Dear Reader,

Thank you for reading Champions of the Dragon, I hope that you enjoyed it.

I began this book back in 2014, somewhere between Whill of Agora 5 and Sea Queen. I was daydreaming, as I often do, and was thinking about heroes and prophecies and how much the fantasy genre depends on these tropes. I began to envision a story in which the heroes were no heroes at all, but fools, and the prophecy spoken of so reverently was a flat out lie. Soon, Murland Kadabra popped into my head. He was a lanky nineteen-year-old wizard apprentice with no talent to speak of and too much heart, and I liked him from the beginning. Next came Brannon, the gay elf prince. I was instantly intrigued by Brannon's character, for he leapt off the page with his diamond studded cup and a haughty air, and demanded to be noticed. Then my group of non-heroes expanded. After nearly thirteen years of writing about bad ass dwarf warriors, I thought that a sensitive, pacifist dwarf would be interesting, and so Gibrig Hogstead was born. Willow was an easy addition to the group, and brought with her one of my favorites, Dingleberry Fairy-Fairy. Lastly, I envisioned the archetypical knight in shining armor, but he had to be rough, gritty, and a total screw-up. That was the moment when I was introduced to Sir Aldrick van Albright, fallen hero of Vhalovia, and legendary drunk. Non-heroes in place, all the story needed was a lead wizard. Kazimir *whooshed* himself onto the page, and the story began to take form.

As I write this in early March 2017, I have just finished book 2, and will soon begin book 3. All three books will be released back to back, so you needn't worry about a long wait. The trilogy will be completely self-contained, but I have a hunch that there are many more stories to tell about Fallacetine.

I would love to hear what you thought of the story, so please, leave a review, good or bad. I read them all, and while a few have left me feeling like a fraud who never should have quit his day job, most leave me with a deep sense of accomplishment and gratitude, knowing that I have done my job, which is to entertain you, the reader.

Yours in Magic,
Michael James Ploof

Printed in Great Britain
by Amazon